CITY OF MASKS

BOOK I

THE BONE MASK CYCLE

ASHLEY CAPES

For Brooke

CHAPTER 1

The chill of prison bars against his temple did little to ease Notch's headache. Decades of dank didn't help either, nor snoring from another cell, where someone was impersonating a bear. Or dying. In the poor light it was hard to tell.

Notch squinted. Noon sun barely crept through the small, grated windows on his side of the building. Even cells across the way were shadowed. Sunlight, in addition to a piece of bread and some water, were high points, while the straw 'bed' and stale body odour of criminals were typically unpleasant. Worse places than Anaskar City prison existed. At least he hadn't been beaten yet – a twinge in his shoulder reminded him how much some guards enjoyed their work.

His cellmate raised his voice and Notch turned. The man had probably been speaking for some time; his drawn face was expectant. Years of imprisonment had washed out his Anaskari tan.

Notch leaned against the bars. "What is it, Bren?"

"Did you kill her, truly?"

"No."

Bren nodded. "Innocent then." He knelt in the corner, his fine coat of blue long since gone to grime, his face pressed against the stone wall. "Listen to this one." He scratched at an armpit with some vigour. "It's hard to see but I think it says 'death to the Shields of Anaskar' and it's got a signature, but I can't make it out."

Notch grunted. Nothing special for a convicted man to write; since waking on a pile of old blankets that morning and meeting his cellmate, he'd heard a dozen similar sentiments. Through Bren's meandering introduction, Notch had winced, probing his body. Both arms and chest were heavily bruised and his head so fragile he wouldn't be surprised to learn a wagon rolled over it last night. Possibly twice. He wasn't drunk, though the smell of ale was on his breath. One damn drink, that was all.

And there was blood.

His leathers and tunic were splattered a dark red. Not his own blood, the City Vigil told him as much when they hauled him off the street, as if he couldn't figure that much out. But whose? His own memory was unreliable, which made no sense. He hadn't been drunk, truly drunk, since right after the war. When he bore another name. A name he left on some tavern floor, after making a convincing go of drinking the memories away. A good bath did for the sand on his body, but the blood-soaked sand in his mind? No amount of ale had washed that away.

And now the Vigil were telling him he'd been so intoxicated he had to be dragged to the prison?

Unlikely.

"The Shields probably caught him doing something

bad, that's why he wrote this," Bren continued, tapping on the wall. His too-bright eyes looked up at Notch.

"I'd say so."

"Like us, Notch. We've done bad things, we have."

"So you keep saying."

Bren laughed, its shrillness cutting through Notch's skull. If it hadn't been unsettling, Notch would have thumped him, but there was something wrong with Bren. Any fool could see that.

"The guards say you've got a few days. That they can't hang you sooner, because there's too many in the queue. Waiting to hang."

"Thanks, Bren."

A moment of quiet fell between them. Distant voices drifted from beyond the prison walls. Notch clenched his jaw. He should have been out there. On his way to another job. The Blue Lady, a fat merchant ship, would have sailed with most of his possessions on board.

His father's sword.

No chance of seeing it again. He wrapped his hands around cold bars and squeezed.

"The guards say it too, the guards say you killed her," Bren said, unperturbed.

"I know."

He crept forward. "So?"

"So I don't remember." He frowned. "But I wouldn't harm a child."

Bren grinned, as if he thought it all a joke, and went back to the wall. A scraping sound followed. "This one says 'down with the Shields' and has no name. I wonder how many people have been here before us, eh Notch?"

"Maybe just you, Bren," he muttered, rubbing at his temples.

Bren prattled on. "I could deal with the Mascare too, you know. They aren't so powerful. It's just their precious bone masks. And their robes. All that crimson. They scare people, the faces. And the eyes too. Did you ever meet any, Notch, before you murdered that girl?"

He ignored the last bit. "I've seen the Mascare plenty of times."

"And were they protecting 'the city, the people and its history' as they love to claim?"

"Each time?"

Bren laughed. "Ever ask them why they won't show their faces?"

"They aren't very talkative, Bren."

Bren stopped scratching and moved to a spot beneath the window, running a set of cracked fingernails over the stone. "This is my favourite. I think it's the oldest one."

The clank of a key in a lock did not deter Bren from his examination, but Notch took hold of the bars again, letting the man's voice recede into the background. At the far end of their row, the guard, a scruffy man who'd made some effort to straighten his blue and silver uniform, led three figures toward the cell.

"Quiet now, Bren," he said as the group approached, their footfalls echoing. A slender woman – a Lady no doubt – stopped before Notch's cell. She was accompanied by a girl and a stony-faced man with broad shoulders, the orange tunic and gleaming breastplate of a Palace Shield in stark contrast with the prison keeper's appearance. The woman's hair was pulled back from her face, fanning down around her shoulders and covering the collar of an impeccably clean white dress. Bone earrings swung when she turned her head. A sneer that must have been permanent marred her otherwise smooth face.

Notch adjusted his grip on the bars. To come to Anaskar Prison in such clothing – she was either mighty vain or mighty important. Most likely both. Which meant trouble.

The girl stood in similar attire and shared the sneer but had trouble meeting his gaze.

"Here's the mercenary, my lady." The prison guard pointed with his key, making a low bow before scurrying off.

The woman took a single step forward, glaring at him. Her footfall clapped. "Your name?"

He blinked. Her distaste was like a battering ram. "Notch."

The palace guard bristled and she waved a clean hand at him. "Bring the torch, Holindo."

"Yes, my lady." His voice was a rasp.

Behind him, Bren shrunk back into the corner. He did not resume his scraping.

The woman levelled a finger at Notch. "You will address me as 'Lady Cera,' or not at all. Now, do not move."

"Can I ask why, Lady Cera?"

"Because if you do I will have the Captain here gut you."

Notch did as he was told. The impulse to wipe her face clean of its expression was strong enough that he had to school his features. Palace folk. Even before he'd taken to the life of a hired sword, they'd looked down their noses at him. 'Mountain Family', they'd say to each other and snigger.

When Captain Holindo returned, the soldier thrust the torch forward, catching Notch's shoulder with his free hand. He narrowed his eyes but said nothing, only adding a crease to his brow. Did Holindo recognise him? Notch couldn't place the man.

"Be still now," the soldier said.

The flames singed a little of Notch's hair and he started to sweat. No-one moved or spoke, though the girl he took for Lady Cera's daughter stared wide-eyed at the blood on his clothing.

"Well?" The Lady snapped. "Look. Is it him? Is that the man?"

"I… I think so, mother," said the girl.

Lady Cera and her captain shared a glance before she addressed her daughter again, her tones becoming honeyed. "Dear, are you sure? This is the man they caught by her body, in the street on our way from the harbour –"

"It's hard to tell. I didn't see him that well." She met his gaze. "I suppose it could be this man."

Captain Holindo withdrew the torch. "We have other witnesses, my lady. You've done far more than enough by coming here; it will satisfy the Justice. Furthermore, your own daughter identified the prisoner, that's enough for any man of law." Such a long string of words strained the man's voice, and for the first time Notch noticed a long, faded scar crossing his throat.

She gave a short nod. "Truly. I've had more than enough of this stench in any event. Take my daughter back to the palace."

"Of course, Lady Cera."

He ushered the girl toward the exit. Lady Cera did not follow. "I don't know the whole truth of what happened. But you are a criminal, of that I have no doubt."

"Mercenary, Lady Cera."

"Do you think there's a difference?"

"There can be."

"Well, Notch the Mercenary, I will ensure you hang for this. The girl might have only been a pale-skinned, half-blood brat, but I can ill-afford to replace her."

Notch sneered. "That all she was to you? Something to be replaced?"

She raised her arm but he stepped back.

"Fool." Lady Cera spun and stormed off.

Notch spat. He was already going to hang, what did it matter if some bone-headed noblewoman wanted him dead? Bren shuffled forward and placed a hand on his shoulder. Notch had forgotten him. "She knows what you are. What we are."

"You might be right," Notch said, sitting on the floor and scratching at a new, disturbingly persistent itch in his hair. "But I didn't kill that girl."

CHAPTER 2

"Listen. Footsteps." Bren mimed a soldier's march, managing only a few steps before having to turn. "Coming to hang you. Early too."

Notch straightened on the straw. Three days of Bren's prattle disappeared between one breath and another. He could have raged at the injustice of it, that his final days had been pointless. That stepping into the Iron Pig, the inn near the harbour, got him killed. And just a haze of useless images to take with him to the grave. The inn's floorboards. An ale mug. Black water sloshing on stone. Ship masts. A fat beggar? None of it made sense, so what did it matter?

And worse. Otonos's betrayal would go unanswered.

"Doesn't matter now."

Bren continued to march. "Matter?"

The footsteps paused at another cell and Notch stood. His pulse quickened but he didn't flinch or make a sound. No true soldier would. The dull jangle of the jailor's heavy key neared and he made a fist. If only he'd been able to remember what really happened. It wouldn't matter to the poor girl, but it mattered to Notch. He'd never killed a child.

"I'll miss you, Notch. You're a good one."

Notch didn't reply.

He'd witnessed a hanging as a boy. There was no black cloth for the criminal's head and the man's face soon turned purple. Eyes strained from their sockets and the kicking went on a long time. Someone stole the man's boots afterwards, bare feet hanging over the grim-cart's tailgate.

Whoever got Notch's boots would have to make do with scuff marks and a thinning left sole.

A scraping sound rose from below his feet. He listened and it came again.

"Bren, did you hear –"

The floor gave way, dumping him several feet below. Stone crashed around him, straw and dust swirling as he scrambled to his feet, blinking when he found himself eye to eye with the edge of the floor. Bren gaped down at him.

"Come on," a voice hissed.

Shouts filtered down from the guards, but Notch was already being pulled into a crouch, then dragged along a pitch tunnel. The grip on his hand was strong, almost enough to break his fingers, and he coughed in the dust, unable to ask a question or even call to Bren. His knees smacked on damp stone and his free hand scrambled to keep pace.

Several turns later, lost, blind and trembling with adrenaline, Notch stopped, dragging back whoever held him. "Flir? Is that you?"

A small hand patted his cheek and a woman's voice whispered. "Of course. Now keep moving. I've got something for the guards."

She led him round a corner and pushed him up against a wall. "Stay a moment."

"Wait, I can't see." His chest still heaved but his heart rate slowed.

"Then don't move," she called as her footsteps slipped away.

"Good advice," he said to the dark. Soon after, a crack echoed and the crashing of stone rumbled the tunnels.

Flir returned, sounding satisfied. "That should stop them."

She led him on a steady descent, the floor uneven. He at least had control of both hands, using the damp brickwork as a guide. The scraping of their feet filled the quiet until he spoke. "Where are we going?"

"Out of here." Her voice echoed. "You should be able to stand now."

He did so slowly, squinting when light bloomed. Flir stood, a grin on her round face, pale skin and slight frame yellowed by the lantern she held.

Barely as tall as his chest, and dressed as she was in the rags of a pickpocket, he might have mistaken her for a child. It happened often enough in Anaskar, something she just as often turned to her advantage. And he had made that very mistake upon meeting her across a battlefield years past, staying his blow long enough for her to put him on his backside with a kick.

Renovar folk all had her pale complexion, though he assumed she was considered short even there. He rubbed his hand. Small as she was, she was still the strongest person he knew. He smiled. "It's good to see you, Flir. I appreciate the rescue too, but you didn't have to crush my hand."

She laughed. "I was gentle."

Notch snorted.

"Come on, we have a ways to go yet." She stepped out of the tunnel and into a much wider passage with a narrow path at its edge. The brickwork was more elaborate here, with larger slabs resting beneath patterned walls, where the king's leaping swordfish also sat. The crest, along with the rest of the walls, had a distinct green tint in the lamp light.

"We're in the aqueducts."

"You're a clever man, Notch."

Water flowed, dark and slithering over the stones, separating them from the path opposite, which was barely visible. He couldn't see the roof but it was up there, not too far above, judging from the echo of their footsteps. Access points appeared as gaping maws as they passed, most grated by rusting steel. "How did you find me? I thought you were still at the iron mines with Silenna?"

"She brought us back early. You should have seen it, Notch. The rebels weren't organised. They were just a bunch of thieves – and mostly Mountain-men at that. That first strike of theirs was a lucky one."

He stepped over the corpse of a rat. "And me?"

"Asked around. Even Braonn half-bloods get attention when they're murdered." A sneer crept into her voice. "The benefits of being part Anaskari are endless, aren't they? The whole First Tier has heard of Notch the Mercenary now. Probably a good deal of the Second and Lower too."

He swore.

"I paid a kid to show me a way in to the aqueducts," she said, slowing. She lowered her lamp. "Quiet now."

He reached for his blade... and muttered another curse.

Gone with the Blue Lady. Even his cloak and purse were back at the jail. Flir had stopped.

"What is it?"

She touched his arm. "I thought I heard something."

"I didn't hear anything."

"I must have imagined it."

Flir resumed walking, and Notch kept on, straining his ears. Not a thing out of place. The tiny ripples of water, the scrape of their boots or the faint squeak of the lamp's handle was all. He stepped over another rat, this one bloated. Two more steps and he found three more. Then a whole pile, which he had to nudge aside with his boot. Flir had leapt over them without a hitch, casting wild shadows, but Notch wasn't feeling so nimble.

When one of the rats rolled aside, it left a trail of fresh blood.

"Flir, have you noticed all the –"

The light died.

Notch fell into a crouch, the stench of wet rat filling his nose. He searched for a weapon, fingers passing over furry, sticky bodies before closing over a shard of brick. It was heavy enough to do some damage, but he was blind. A big splash broke the hush, followed by a low sound, as if a man were humming half a bar of a song. It came from up ahead, from where Flir had stood.

His fingers tightened. The hum came again, closer now. It didn't sound entirely natural. It could have been a man making a sound of curiosity. A 'hmmm' sound. But it was lazier. Wetter, as if a tongue got in the way.

Notch suppressed a shiver, raising the brick.

The sound came again, this time from the water before him. He shifted so his back was against the wall. Where was Flir? And was that a trickle of water from something slipping from the flow? A dank breath stirring the hairs on his wrist? Notch swung the brick but met only air.

The hum came from above.

Something wet and hard slapped over his face. A weight pressed on him and a fetid and slimy substance was forced between his lips. The hum swelled as he gagged, slamming the brick into his attacker. A wet slap rang out. He struck out again and broke free long enough to stagger forward, only to lose his footing.

He crashed into chill water.

Notch thrashed up to his knees in the waist-deep flow, breathing hard. There. Another sound. He swung even as something crashed into him. His attacker caught his head and tried to force his face into the water. His nails tore at what had to be scales and his chest strained as he struggled for air. He tore most of the gunk away and sucked in a breath before he was pressed into the water. Driving an elbow back, he struck out repeatedly, chest expanding as he fought. Nothing changed.

Notch heaved his entire body, roaring as he broke the surface, flinging the creature from his back. The hum came again, closer now, and Notch swung the brick.

A crack echoed in the aqueduct, cutting the hum short. Something heavy splashed and was still. Notch heaved in air, kneeling in the channel. He kept the brick raised, but the creature did not move. He would not touch it. Instead, he cupped his hand to the flow and washed his mouth out, spitting with some vehemence. The slime made his teeth tingle and his lips were... thicker. Numb. He tried to frown but couldn't. Was the slime poison? He dunked his head and washed out his mouth again before moving back to the path.

"Flir?"

Nothing.

He scrambled forward and ran his hands across the path, but found neither Flir nor lamp. He'd gone too far. She should have been no more than a few steps away when the light disappeared. He moved into the water, taking slow steps and searching with his arms, bent like an old man. The channel was wide enough that it was slow going. If she'd been cast into the water, she wouldn't be able to breathe and here he was floundering in the dark.

Notch slammed a fist into his thigh. "Flir, answer me."

His voice echoed. Only the sloshing of his legs replied. His hands grew numb, from the cold or the poison he didn't know. When his foot brushed up against something he spun.

"Flir." He scooped her up, waterlogged body heavy.

Laying her on the path, he searched her body for wounds. She was breathing at least. He flinched when his hand brushed against slime. It covered her ears and face, blocking her nose and mouth. Notch tore at it, scraping the gunk from inside her cheeks with his fingers before moving back to the water and attempting to wash the slime away. He snarled. It wasn't very effective. She could choke if he wasn't careful, but he didn't know what the slime was doing to her.

Still she wasn't responding – despite her chest rising and falling.

She lived, and yet he could not wake her.

CHAPTER 3

Blood blossomed on Sofia's finger and she cursed, chisel clattering to the bench beside an unfinished mask. Bone dust stirred and a row of heads popped up in bright lamplight as young women in the Carver's chamber turned to her.

"What's wrong?" Pietta spun on her stool. Both her grey carver's robe and face were smudged with fine white dust.

"It's nothing." Sofia wiped her finger on the rough fabric of her own robe. "Just a tiny cut."

Pietta pointed. "It's on your mask too."

Sofia groaned. A pink smear marred the otherwise pristine surface of the mask. She had completed one eye. The groove for the mouth and ridges for nose and cheeks were already carved, but she'd have to start again if she couldn't clean it. The Mascare would not accept a mask dishonoured by any stain. Not that it really mattered – the masks were just symbols of office, costume for tradition. A way to honour the past and intimidate the populace.

It wasn't as though she was carving a Greatmask.

She wound a strip of fabric over her cut and reached for a small vial with a clear solution. A few drops and a dry cloth were enough to remove most of the stain. "That's better." She kept rubbing.

"Aren't you annoyed?"

"Of course. But it's not so bad." Sofia grinned. "I'm still one mask ahead."

Pietta glared at her, but her own smile was not far behind. She kept her voice low. "You know, I heard the Mascare might open the order to common folk. To bolster numbers."

"That's just a rumour. Father said it's only being discussed."

Conversations hushed and chisels slowed. Two figures approached. Lady Alda escorted a Shield across the chamber. He stared directly ahead, as if unaware of the sets of eyes trained upon him. Captain Emilio. Youngest member of the Honour Guard.

Pietta stared up at him but Sofia saw only the grave expression on Lady Alda's plump face. "Sofia dear, that will be all for today. The Lord Protector has returned. He wishes to speak with you. Captain Emilio will escort you."

"Has something happened?"

"Not here." The two ushered Sofia toward the exit. The scrape of chisels resumed. Alda pulled open the large doors, their beaten-steel surface showing a looming mask and chisel. Sofia glanced back. Pietta's expression was caught between worry and envy, as the doors swung shut.

"Thank you, Captain."

Lady Alda patted Sofia's hand and went back inside.

Emilio's expression was difficult to read. "Your father wishes for you to meet him in his rooms at once." His deep voice filled the hall. "Regarding your brother."

Sofia froze. Tantos was on his way home. Had something happened? Pirates? A storm? Or was it something simple like a delay? But if so, why send for her? "What's wrong?"

"Lord Danillo only sent word that he wished to see you."

Sofia hurried down a dim passage, Emilio trailing, turning into a well-lit corridor where she nearly bumped into one of the Mascare. The man stepped aside, red robes twirling. His mask seemed to glare at her and she apologised, moving on.

She came to a halt beside a floor-to-ceiling statue of Ana – the Goddess carried a seahorse in one arm and a storm cloud in the other.

"My lady?" Captain Emilio paused beside her.

"This way is quicker." She ran her hand along the wall beside the Goddess, flicking a switch. The statue slid aside and she slipped into darkness, Emilio close behind. No-one but the Mascare were permitted in the hidden ways but Tantos had shown her dozens of shortcuts over the years. "How else can I make hide and seek fair?" He would laugh each time.

"Isn't this forbidden?" Emilio asked.

"Only if we're caught." Sofia hit the switch to slide Ana back into place. "Follow me."

Counting steps, she took a turn, then at twenty paces, a second.

"How do you navigate?"

"Practice."

Several more turns and she stopped. Lady Alda's face had not been encouraging; what was going on?

"Are we lost, my lady?"

"No. I just... you didn't have to escort me, you know. It's kind, but father didn't need to send you."

"I volunteered."

"Oh." Sofia flushed, glad of the dark. She flicked another switch to slide open yet another doorway. The glittering thread of a tapestry soaked up torchlight. She took a breath before slipping out from behind it, waving for Emilio to follow.

An empty hall. The corridor connected her to a servant's passage. She strode along it, stopping outside the Protector's chambers.

Two Palace Shields flanked the doors, their orange tunics and silver breastplates shining in the lamplight. Only four keys opened the locked doors. One each for Sofia's family, and one for the king, whose life her father was sworn to protect, just as her brother, as Successor, was to protect the Prince. Such duties ensured their hours were not her hours.

Emilio stopped, meeting her eyes. "I hope everything is well, Sofia."

"Thank you, Captain."

He bowed and strode off, armour catching torchlight. Sofia turned to the guards.

"Is my father in?"

"We haven't seen Lord Danillo, my lady."

She nodded, fitting her key to the lock and stepping inside. That didn't mean he hadn't returned. Father used the secret passages within the palace as a matter of habit. Her soft shoes slid on the marble floors of the entryway as she hurried to the bright study, its walls lined with shelves. "Father, what's –"

Empty.

Warm light fell on a large writing desk and chairs

arranged before crackling flames in the fireplace. Above the mantle, set in a specially crafted setting, rested her father's Greatmask. Argeon's ancient face of bone stared down at her and she shivered. Impossible not to think of the mask as watching her. He was not a typical mask by any stretch. A presence, a life, lurked within Argeon's dark sockets.

Sofia walked into her father's bedchambers. Its small fireplace glowed red in the quiet.

"Here, Petal."

He wore his travel mask, vermilion robe open to reveal belts strapped over plain black clothing. He was removing each one, placing the attached knives and pouches on a small table by the bed, his large hands moving with a deftness that spoke of long years performing the routine.

She rushed forward and he enfolded her in strong arms. "Father, what's happening?"

His voice was tight. "The King's Cutter was lost in a storm."

She pulled back. "Is Tantos..."

"A longboat was found, driven ashore."

Hope flared. "Then he's safe?"

He turned to the fire, holding out his hands. "No. I rode days along the coast myself, the moment I heard. I saw what remained. He is gone."

"No." Tantos. No warning, no goodbye. Nothing. Sofia wiped tears from her face. When had her hands become so clumsy? Her voice wavered. "How can you be so calm, father?"

"Because I must."

She swallowed a sob. The deep dark of the ocean had her brother. First Mother's illness and now Tantos. Why? Had the Gods seen fit to punish her family? What was the last thing she said to him? Hurry home. She exhaled a shuddering breath.

Her father strode to a cabinet and produced two glasses and a dark bottle. Fire-lemon. He poured a small amount and handed it to her. "Take sips."

She did as instructed. She coughed at first, but welcomed the burning liqueur.

Tantos sent word, barely a week ago. He would leave the Far Islands early, to beat the winter storms. On assignment for father, the trip was to be the final part of Tantos' training. She hadn't seen him for months and missed the chance to send him off, so hasty was his departure. "He was coming home."

Her father had removed his travel-mask, though he still wore his under-mask; an article of office she knew as well as his face, made of white cloth with subtle openings for breathing and holes for his eyes. How quickly did the cruel marks of grief come? Now that Tantos was gone, there would be more lines beneath his eyes. She could imagine more grey at his temples and in his beard too.

He moved to the bed, drink in hand. Sofia sat beside him. She took another sip, and another until it was done.

His arms surrounded her and she wept.

*

She woke on her father's bed to a dim room. How much time had passed? Her throat was dry and her eyes puffy. Tantos.

She rose, muscles stiff. "Father?"

An adjoining door opened. He came to sit beside her, taking her hand. "Sofia, we must talk."

"Can it be Face to Face?"

"Very well." He stepped into the hall a moment, then

returned with a lamp, which he lit before closing the door. He so rarely lowered his guard nowadays, even here, nestled behind the walls of the highest tier of the city, hidden in the depths of the palace.

When he peeled the under-mask away, she smiled. To actually see him... his broad nose, his close beard and dark eyes crinkled at the corners. Smiling, as he would when mother was alive. But there were more lines than she remembered. She stroked his cheek, stubble rough beneath her fingertips. "I miss your face."

"It is our way..." he began.

"I know – Secrecy is Safety."

Silence again. He held his empty glass, running a thumb along the rim. "Sofia, things must change now that Tantos is... gone." He kept his voice gentle. "You must take his place as Successor."

A chill crossed her body. "Father..." She opened her mouth and closed it. She tried again. "Even though I'm a carver, and a woman?"

"Not every man sees women as carvers and mothers only."

"But all I know of weapons and poisons are what little you and Tantos have shown me! And I don't know anything about the Greatmasks. How can I take his place?" She shook her head. "And I don't want to argue with you."

"Argue?"

"Like you and Tantos did sometimes. About his training."

"That won't happen. And Tantos was never angry for long, he understood his duty."

Sofia frowned. How could she even begin to take his place? "The Mascare won't accept me."

"They will. You're Falco." He paused. "You are strong, Sofia. And King Otonos demands a Successor. I know he would give Argeon to another house to serve the greater good. That is his duty."

"What? But Argeon is ours."

He smiled. "Long have I felt the same. But we can't own the Greatmasks, not truly. Nevertheless, I've tied Argeon to Falco blood, to protect us. It would be extremely difficult for another house to use him now."

"But not impossible?"

"Arduous. Dangerous even. I made certain."

"So if I'm able to become Successor, the king cannot refuse me?"

"What I've done is forbidden. He doesn't know. Nor can he." He paused. "Sofia, the king will see who you can become. Who you need to become. Especially now that it seems Casa Cavallo's Greatmask has fallen silent."

She gasped. Osani was silent? Had that ever happened to a Greatmask in the history of the city? "What does that mean for House Cavallo? For the city?"

"If the rumours are true, and Osani has stopped responding, then Cavallo will lose much of its standing. But what worries me, is that Anaskar will have but one Greatmask left to defend its people. Argeon."

"You are its defender."

He took both her hands in his own. The calluses from years of knife work were rough against her hands. "Not forever."

Her shoulders slumped.

"I will help you, Petal. It will be difficult, but you must do this. With your mother gone and now your brother, we are the last of Falco House. You must take up Argeon and protect us. There is no-one else I can trust."

His face was set and there was a note of worry to his voice.

Sofia bit her lip. There truly was no-one else. And Tantos would have taken her place, had their roles been reversed. Father needed her. The whole city needed her.

She would learn. She would bear the weight of the new role. Become Successor, then eventually Protector... She would be the first woman in a hundred years to do so. She would make him proud.

Sofia squeezed his hands. "I will do my best."

"And I will be here for you."

CHAPTER 4

A cruel wind played in the mountains, lashing at her robe where she stood with hands gripping the parapet, Pietta at her side.

How long before the city below would be hers to protect? Perched on the mountainous coast, steep peaks sheltered Anaskar on three sides where the city stepped down to the harbour, three tiers each with formidable walls.

Nestled behind the walls of the First Tier sat the palace, its carefully arranged grounds a home she'd left but rarely – the last time to stand before the ocean, clinging to Tantos as mother's funeral pyre glowed on the horizon. In the Second Tier, a mixture of mansions, markets, shops, homes and gardens that even the palace folk sometimes visited. And finally, crammed behind and sometimes against the walls of the Lower Tier, warehouses, shipyards, slums and factories, from which grey lines of smoke climbed, and where the scurrying figures became antlike. The masts of dozens of ships, their sails rippling, were black against the sunset.

If she ran down and tried to book passage on one of the ships, would they allow her? A rueful smile for a child's thought. No. Abandoning her father was no option.

Beside Sofia, Pietta put her back to the harbour, shielding her face from the sun and closing her eyes. They'd both been up since dawn trying to finish Sofia's quota of masks. When her father woke her and explained she need not work, Sofia shook her head. "I want to. It will keep my mind busy." Only it hadn't. Images of Tantos, his dark hair slipping beneath choppy water, lurked behind her eyelids.

"Are you sure you can do it, Sofia?" Pietta asked.

"I have no choice." She straightened. "Father believes I can."

"I do too, Sofia."

She smiled. "Then I'd better start training. Tantos was two years before he took the Mask, and another year before he came close to learning the role of Successor to Father's satisfaction. I bet I'll have to prove myself in less time."

"Lord Danillo has high standards, doesn't he?"

Sofia sighed. "He once had Tantos pronounce a word in Neutral Voice near to a hundred times before he was satisfied. I remember because I had to count."

"And that's something you'll have to do, learn to speak that way? The same as all the other Mascare?" Pietta made a face.

"What's wrong?"

"I don't like it. I never know who I'm speaking to."

"That's the whole point, Pietta."

She frowned. "Won't it be hard to disguise your voice? You're a young woman and they're men."

"Very hard."

"Oh." She paused. "You know, I once saw one of them save a woman in the street from criminals. He was like a whirlwind of knives. Will they teach you to do that?"

"They'll try." Sofia shrugged. "But I think I'll end up spying on visiting dignitaries. I'm hardly built like a soldier and father won't risk the Successor." She fell silent.

"At least wearing a Greatmask will be fun," Pietta offered.

"I'm not sure of that. Argeon scares me."

"But the Greatmasks are meant to protect us – aren't they always watching, you know, if we're attacked by the Medah or something? Aren't they good?"

"Some legends say a Greatmask can wipe out entire battalions." She gave a wry smile. "Doesn't sound that good."

"But they are, deep down, right?"

"Father used to tell Tantos that Argeon had a will, but that the wearer was the one who decided whether the mask was used for good or ill."

An arch look, "Well, you can always have Captain Emilio protect you personally if you get into trouble."

"Pietta!" Sofia blushed.

Someone cleared their throat.

Prince Oson leant against a stairwell wall, black hair caught in the wind. His thick cloak was thrown open and he toyed with a dagger. "Good evening to you both – though I regret to say, Pietta my dear, that you must leave us now."

Pietta was caught with her mouth half open. She shut it and performed a deep curtsey before slipping away.

The Prince strolled over. "Ah, sweet Sofia, have you thought upon my offer?"

Not again. And not that honeyed tone. She suppressed a shudder, controlling her features. "I have."

"And?" He placed the tip of the dagger against his chin.

"And I cannot accept, your Highness."

"That is a... rash decision." He took a deep breath, leaning close to whisper, breath hot on her ear. "Imagine, Sofia, if our houses were joined, what we could accomplish for the city. What prosperity, what safety."

"That might be true, but we are not in love."

"Couldn't we be?" A slimy smile.

Polite but firm. "No, your Highness."

Oson moved to the wall with a shake of his head. When he turned to her, his eyes were narrowed and his voice grown cold. His moods were fickle. Like a damned animal or a madman. "You will regret such a decision."

She stepped back. "Your Highness?"

"I have heard your father's pitiful idea, Carver."

"What does that mean?"

He looked down on the city with a proprietary expression. "It means there's no way I will accept you as my Protector, Falco. You're simply not strong enough." He met her eyes. "And not only because you're a woman. Your whole family is withering."

Sofia flushed but held her tongue. How quickly his contempt resurfaced. For years he'd ignored her, but recently, he'd begun to court her. All political manoeuvring. He'd certainly had little time for Tantos.

If she lashed out now, Falco would be ruined. "And has the king said he will not allow it? The Heads of the Houses?"

He snickered. "We all know where House Falco stands on the matter. Those Falcos which are left in any event. I understand your brother is now fish food?"

She clenched a fist behind her back. Driving a chisel into his throat wouldn't fix anything. "Did you wish for something from me, your Highness? Because if not, I will be leaving."

She made to sweep by, but he caught her arm. His fingers dug into her flesh. "Not yet you won't."

"Let me go."

He shook her. "You will listen to me."

Sofia broke his grip, breathing hard, but stood her ground. "Say what you have to say then."

He sneered. "Very well. A warning then. Just remember, Mascare training can be especially... taxing."

"What does that mean?"

He turned and headed for the stairwell. "My father has called the Heads of the Houses to meet. You'll find out what it means then."

Sofia glared at his back a moment, then slapped the parapet with a curse. What was he getting at? Did the king know what his son was doing? Likely not. More important, did Father know?

Sofia ran to a stairwell opposite and took the steps three at a time, a guiding hand held close to the wall. She only stopped when she reached her rooms, mumbling a greeting to the Shields and bursting inside.

Charging into the study, she slid to a halt.

Her father stood before the fire, his shadow large on the wall. He stared up at Argeon, lips moving soundlessly.

"Father."

He turned to smile at her. "Sofia."

"Is everything well with Argeon?"

"Yes. I was explaining that you and he were to speak."

She shifted. "Now? Don't we have to wait for the

Successor's Ceremony?"

"Soon." He moved closer. "You are troubled."

"Father, the Prince came to me earlier. He means to block us. He said the king was calling a meeting tonight."

"Weasel." Her father's voice was hard. "Centuries of cooperation between the Houses, centuries of loyalty to the kingdom and now this upstart. I suspected he would try as much, but it is I who asked the king to call a meeting. He supports us, Sofia."

He stroked her cheek and the tension in her shoulders eased. "Good. But there's more."

"Oh?"

"He asked again for me to consider the union of our Houses."

"With your hand?"

She nodded.

"Never."

Sofia hugged her father. Let the Prince think he could stop them. Falco was stronger than he knew.

*

Rain pattered against tall windows lining the throne room. House tapestries hung between patches of darkness, illuminated by lamplight. The proud yellow of Casa Falco hung across from the throne, as did the Stallion and Sea Turtle – though the King's Swordfish dominated the entire back wall in a dark orange.

Each banner lay bold against dark stone. The few times Sofia visited the throne room they'd been part of the walls, nothing more. Now, seeing her falcon spearing the sky, it was as though the bird called to her. Its continued flight rested on her own as much as her father's shoulders. Everything was different now.

King Otonos looked around the table. His dark eyes were sunken and his beard grey – he was so different from his sneering son. Oson took after the Queen, a sickly woman Sofia had rarely seen. "Let us proceed." His voice had lost the boom that once startled her as a child. A pallor lurked beneath his tan.

Her father stood. He wore only his travel mask but his robes were those of his office, trimmed with silver. "Thank you, my King. I will be brief, as I believe my intention tonight is well known. In light of my son's death I would offer my daughter, Sofia, as candidate to the role of Successor. His strength is her strength. She will serve Anaskar and its King well."

From across the table, Oson raised an eyebrow, but said nothing. The two Mascare beside him were silent also. One would represent Cavallo, the Stallion, the other Tartaruga – the Turtle. All eyes rested on the king.

He leaned toward her. "Sofia, this is a grave responsibility. The guardianship of a Greatmask, of my family and our city, is nothing you can accept and then walk away from. You must be certain, above all else."

She lifted her chin. "I am ready to learn, your Majesty."

"A fine answer." A smile flicked across his lips. "Know that I have no objections. I trust in your father and believe that you will become a fine Protector for my son."

"Your Majesty, if I may?"

Sofia wasn't sure which House the Mascare spoke for, but his voice was the same, unemotional tone his kind spoke with. Soon to be her kind.

The king waved a hand. "You may, Solicci."

"I've no doubt Danillo's daughter has merit, but it's an unorthodox move which may cause her trouble. Regrettably, Sofia might face undue opposition from her fellow students."

The other Mask murmured his agreement.

"It's been over a hundred years since a woman took the robes, Father." The Prince's tone was entirely reasonable, moving into mock apology. "I fear the Mascare might take offence, but I say now that I suspect they would sooner accept Lord Hosan's ridiculous notion of allowing common folk to enter training, before accepting a woman. Such is the state of things."

Sofia clenched her hands together, keeping them beneath the table. Eels, the three of them. They were hardly concerned about her, and without use of Osani, Cavallo would find it difficult to put forth their own candidate. Not without first sullying her ability.

Her father offered no response, waiting for the king. Otonos glanced to the banners a moment. "That is worth considering. But as heads of your Houses, I've no doubt you will be able to adequately prepare your flocks. If there are no other speakers?" His expression did not encourage further discussion. The Prince straightened, but at a bare flick of movement from Solicci's hand he was still. The king did not seem to notice, speaking to her father.

"Train her well, Danillo."

"Of course, your majesty."

"Now." He spread his hands on the table. "To matters of an equally pressing nature. Renovar. What have you discovered?"

Her father answered, his voice even. To Sofia, there was a strain but his bearing was firm. "Storms have kept ships from returning even as near as the Far Islands, so I cannot confirm what is happening in Renovar at present. But the last report spoke of a powerful weapon, held by an ambitious new Conclave. It bears watching, and in fact, I maintain a full Quarter ought to be sent to Renovar."

"A different Conclave? That is new," the king said.

"Yes. Former leaders were replaced due to an 'unpatriotic stance.' If word of a weapon of power is true, then I wish to know more."

"And I still disagree, my king," Solicci said. "We cannot afford to waste time and risk the lives of four Mascare on a fishing expedition based on rumour alone. Or further, risk our standing with Renovar. They have long been among our closest trade partners. It's unlikely they would become aggressors."

"Ambassador Lallor remains evasive, Sire," her father said. "He claims not to know of any changes in the Conclave, yet he is clearly concerned about his homeland. I see it in his eyes."

Solicci shook his head. "The Ambassador has been in Anaskar for years – what would he know of any developments in regards to the Conclave?"

"Messenger birds do leave the city."

Solicci snorted. "And few return in winter. Lallor's fear is just that – fear. He has heard rumours and fears they will impact trade and so he talks them down."

"Perhaps."

The rest of the conversation washed over her as they began talking in circles.

Oson scowled at the tabletop, barely acknowledging questions directed his way. Sofia hid her grin. The prince wasn't going to make anything easy for her, but she would be ready. She would carry the honour of her house.

Become Successor.

CHAPTER 5

Sofia sidestepped.

Her opponent's wooden knife met air, stirring dust motes in the morning light. She snapped her hand over his extended wrist and twisted an arm behind his back, placing her own knife against his throat.

"Be still," she told him between lungfulls of air. Sweat trickled down her throat. She was getting the hang of the footwork, but a handful of lessons didn't make her a master. For an hour now they'd sparred in the training hall and she finally had the better of him – but was it enough?

"Stop." Her instructors rose from their perches, red robes swirling as they crossed the floor.

She let Ritorio go. He snickered beneath his mask. "Whatever you say, Carver. No Falco, no woman, will get the better of Casa Cavallo."

She'd never seen his face, but it would have been plastered with sneers. And that blasted voice, so smug. "Shut up."

"You're only here because your father's Protector and

your brother's dead," Ritorio hissed. Sofia squeezed the handle. If only it were steel.

Luciano placed his large frame between them. He glanced over his shoulder. "Leave."

Ritorio bowed and scurried off.

"Sofia." Luciano's voice was heavy. "I saw your body language. You let him anger you. Remember, a Mascare is calm, he is the chill of steel. The whisper of night."

"Or she."

He shook his head and beside him, Uche waved his hands, a sigh in his voice. "In Neutral, Sofia. And with at least a modicum of respect."

"I will control my temper." She lowered her voice and kept it even. But it was nothing like the Neutral, plain voice everyone else used. She sounded like a young woman, only worse – a woman trying to conceal her gender. "It's useless, Uche. Everyone knows who I am, and I can't get the voice right. And even if I do, they'll see my build."

"You will not give up, however."

Luciano stepped forward. "Enough. She will pass those tests as best she can. Let me finish. Sofia, again, your left hand, be mindful of it. Your aim remains shaky."

"It's so different without the proper feel of steel."

"Granted, but that is not something you are ready for. You did well today, however."

"Thank you for your trust, Dirratore Arms."

"If I may?" Uche asked. Luciano stepped back so the poisons master could stand before her. He presented her with strapping to be worn beneath her robe. A linfa-belt, each slot contained a coloured vial. Poisons and powders to be used in shadow, where she would probably spend much of her life. As had father. "Borrow this and practise filing vials, according to potency and purpose, with your eyes closed. Feel the weight, the shape. You never know under what conditions you may need to access the vials." He winked at her. "Just don't let anyone but your father see you with it. A Novice ought not to carry the linfa."

She accepted the belt with a bow. "Thank you for your trust too, Dirratore Poison."

He smiled at her. "That's enough for today."

She left the training room, lined with dozens of sets of knives, staves and wooden practice swords. So many of which were simply too heavy for her wrists.

Closing the door, she leant against it a moment, breathing a sigh of relief. She'd held her own this time. Now she could tell Father –

"That's not what I meant." Luciano's raised voice cut through the wood.

"Then what did you mean?" Uche asked, his own voice heated.

"Only that Danillo underestimates the Mascare's progressiveness. You know she won't be so easily accepted as Successor, let alone Protector one day. He expects too much of her. A woman as Protector? You saw the Cavallo boy, how he acted. He's not alone."

"That I know. It's how your House acts too, Luciano."

"Well Danillo won't have the king's ear forever."

"I believe she can handle it."

"We'll see." He paused. "Now, her brother, there was a man fit to follow in his father's footsteps..."

Sofia pulled away from the door. She didn't need to hear any more about how Tantos had been better. What did they expect? She'd been training half her life to become a carver.

She stalked the hallways, heading for the Lord

Protector's rooms, breezing past the guard when she arrived.

Inside, her father paced the study. He wore no under-mask and held Argeon at arm's length. He stopped when she entered.

"How were your lessons?"

"I'm improving."

"Good, good."

"Is something wrong with Argeon?"

"No. But I think it is time for you to meet him formally."

Sofia straightened. Another chance to prove herself. "What do I do?"

"Simply open yourself to him." He raised a hand when she made to speak. "I know that is vague, but trust Argeon. Do not fear. He will lead. It's confronting at first, as there will be darkness only. But in time, you'll see beyond the dark and wear the mask as any other, and Argeon will rest on the edge of your awareness."

"That doesn't make much more sense, father." Sofia held out her hands, palms up and her father lowered the mask.

A shiver ran up her arms at the touch of cool bone on skin. Argeon was heavier than she'd expected. His surface was not a bright, bleached white like the new masks she made; it was yellowed with age, with smudges and a nick in one of the cheeks, and tiny cracks around the edges. He was more than old, he was ancient. The mask had been in her family for over four hundred years, since before the Great Landing. He radiated something. Was the hard line of his mouth about to pronounce judgement? The black space of his eyes were as hypnotic as they were chilling.

She'd never been allowed to touch Argeon. The mask

was always too old, too dangerous for her – for anyone – to play with as a child. Not that anyone but her father and brother were able to lift it from the setting anyway.

"But why is it dangerous, Father?" she would ask.

He'd pick her up then, rest her on his knee. "Many reasons. We might use a Greatmask to compel others to act in a way to protect us, our city, our people. But also because sometimes, some people might be influenced by the masks themselves. Do you understand?"

She'd said she did, but she hadn't really.

That was when Father wore Argeon often and when mother would shake her head if Sofia asked to touch the mask, dispensing a few stern words before returning to her carving, robe sleeves pushed up and fingers covered in bone dust. Carving. Even now, standing in Father's dim chambers in her own grey carver's robe, she could still hear the scrape of steel on bone, the coughing fits her mother would fall prey to while doing women's work.

Important work, Father always said.

Argeon gave off a faint glow – he absorbed the firelight whereas the dark, polished furniture that filled the room reflected it. Sucking in a shallow breath she placed the mask on her face.

The room disappeared.

Argeon floated before her in a black void. Every mark on his face stood in vivid detail and the sockets of his eyes burned with... not hostility, but a tangible disinterest. He negated her in a way even Oson couldn't manage. As if every possible choice, every moment of her life to date, her life to come, was as nothing.

Sofia groaned. Had he refused her already? Or was it simply Argeon's way?

And then Father was there. His stern presence held

no shape yet he 'stepped' between them, freeing her from the mask's eyes. Somehow he communicated with Argeon and then the mask's attention, while divided between her and what felt like thousands of others, was no longer cruelly uncaring.

Argeon looked at her and she did not quiver. A flicker of acknowledgement. The flash of feathers streaking across blue sky.

The study flicked back into focus, her father's concerned face before her.

Had Argeon recognised her? She let out a breath and handed back the Greatmask. A shiver lingered from his disinterest. "Did I do something wrong? He didn't seem to like me, father. He didn't speak." Sofia looked down. "I thought I'd do better."

"I'm sorry, Petal. It was wrong to rush you. But he saw you, he knows you. Worry not." He stared into the fireplace and she stood beside him, following his gaze. The yellow tongues of flame were frantic but somehow soothing.

"You expected more?"

"Perhaps. I was certain you would be able to speak with him right away. But there is time enough for you to spend with him before the Successor's Ceremony. It would do well to impress the king. We will try again tomorrow."

"Will it become easier?"

"In time."

Her Father returned Argeon to its setting above the mantle and she met the mask's eyes again.

Darkness.

CHAPTER 6

"Notch?"

He started. Flir stirred in his arms.

"I'm here."

What woke her? It didn't matter. What mattered was escape. Especially if more creatures lurked beneath the city.

"I can't feel my face." She struggled to stand. "I can hardly move, what happened?"

"Let me." He helped her up. Even in Flir's weakened state, her attempt to use him as leverage nearly drove him down. "Something attacked us."

"What was it? My mouth tastes like sewer-fish."

He laughed, tension in his muscles easing. "Mine too. Nothing natural."

"Feels like tiny insects are crawling all over my body. What happened back there?"

"The creature did something. Your face was covered in slime." He rubbed his own jaw, the echo of a tingle still present. "I think it paralyses. You might have drowned otherwise."

"So that's what I can taste?" She paused. "Gods, it's even in my ears."

"It nearly covered your head." He paused, ears straining in the dark. Nothing. "It probably wanted food, though I've never heard of anything like that living down here."

"Nor I, but I'm glad you stopped it."

He could sense more than see her stretching her limbs. "Can you walk?"

"I can. I'm more worried about the lamp."

"I couldn't find it."

"Then we follow our ears." She took several slow steps forward, boots squelching. "I marked one of the access tunnels not too far from here, at a point where the channel divides. Harder to find without the lamp but we'll manage."

Notch followed her uneven footfalls, one hand trailing the wall. "We should visit the Queen's Harper."

"Clearing your name won't be that easy."

"It's a start. Seto will have ideas."

She stopped and he bumped into her. "You're just a mercenary now, Notch. Don't forget that, or it'll get you killed."

"You think I should leave Anaskar?"

"I do. Forget about your name. Find a new one. You've done it before, you could do it again. Besides, the Royal Family want you. On principal anyway; I doubt they care about the girl."

"That was different," he said, frowning. His old name was of no use to anyone now, and he wasn't giving up another one. But she was right about the palace. None of them cared about the girl. Just the perceived blow against whatever House she'd worked for. "And I didn't kill her."

"Save it, Notch. You know I believe you."

"Well?"

"Well what? Are you angry?"

He spoke through clenched teeth. "I don't want people to think that about me, Flir. It's not who I am. Is that so hard to understand?"

"It's not," she said. "But no-one will ever believe the best about us, Notch. That's who we are."

"I'm going to see Seto."

"And I'm going with you."

"Thank you."

*

Flir's escape route took them right to the harbour. The squawking of gulls slipped through the wooden doors and gaping windows of a rundown building. Its floor was muddy and the walls covered with spider webs. Shouts from dockworkers and sailors mixed with the slosh of water against stone. The scent of fish was strong, even inside.

A child in ragged clothing appeared, his face shadowed.

"Spots. Good work." Flir flicked him a silver piece and he caught it with a grin, slipping away.

"I have something for you, Notch. Then it's back to the Second Tier." She pulled a cloak and hood from a pack resting by the door. "No good breaking you out just to have you recognised."

"True." He donned the garment.

He followed her outside, blinking against the sun where it lanced down over the wall. His first step lodged in a grate. A chip of cobblestone flickered into the black, tiny splash following. Though covering a deep shaft, the bars of the grate were narrow enough to be safe. He ignored Flir's snicker. Such grates served the city well enough in rare times of flood.

Men in canvas pants crowded the streets, the flash of earrings and a swelter of voices, all bouncing off the massive walls. The loudest were those of laughter. Or anger. A noble kicked his horse into a crowd by the Harbour Master's Offices, curses bouncing from his cloak as he rode up the street.

"Wait. I want to ask after the Blue Lady," Notch said.

"Someone might recognise you."

"Then we'll be quick. You can do all the talking and I'll wear my hood. Just ask after the ship."

He slipped into the flow, jostling a man with a crate on his shoulder. The dockworker grunted, but didn't stop. Notch climbed the steps to the Harbour Master and entered a room presided over by a wide desk carved from bone. At it, Harbour Master Michai, a man every captain and merchant knew well, wrote at a ledger. His bald head glinted in torchlight, despite light streaming through open curtains. Flanked by a pair of Shield, the harbour master ignored a woman and man who stood before him.

By their fair skin and hair, both appeared to be from Renovar, Flir's homeland. Neither wore an expression of patience.

"But we were not told," the man said.

Michai did not look up. "Your captain ought to know better. No red items of clothing are to be worn in the city."

The woman placed her hands on the bone. "But it is only a scarf. Surely that is no crime?"

"It is indeed, madam." Now he raised his head. "Only the Mascare may wear red. Now remove it or you will be returned to your ship." He held out his hand.

The Renovar exchanged glances, then looked to the Shield, and back at each other. Finally the woman removed her scarf, tossing it at the Harbour Master with a sneer before storming from the room. The man trailed.

Flir stepped forward. "Harbour Master?"

"Wait." Michai finished writing, then squinted up at her. "Yes?"

"Has the Blue Lady left the city?"

He didn't even consult his ledger. "Of course. And it will dock in Whiteport within three weeks, if the weather holds."

Notch kept back near the door. Flir muttered a curse. "Trouble is, I was meant to be on that ship."

"I see. Were you looking to book passage to Whiteport? If so, I suggest you try Captain Melosi. His ship is the Hawk."

"Thank you."

"Of course."

Notch dragged his feet on the way out. It had always been a futile hope but it was his father's sword. He'd needed to know.

"Satisfied?" Flir asked when they stood before the crowds.

"No." He started toward the open gates. "Let's find Melosi. He's meant to be one of the best."

"Gods, why?"

"I want to ask him a question." He passed the gates, boots clapping on the stone, tread changing to a thump when he hit the boardwalk. It's trunk-like boards were crowded with sailors and merchants with handcarts, slow wagons and pairs of the Vigil, their blue and silver uniforms bright under the sun. Notch kept Flir between he and the guards but no-one gave him a second glance.

A cold breeze tugged on his cloak, flying in from across the glittering sea. Glimpses of water stretched beyond rocking ships tied off at the moorings, their huge hulls caked in green and black barnacles.

He stopped a smiling sailor, the man chewing on an apple. Sails snapped and Notch had to raise his voice over the throng of shouted commands and cursing. "Ho, sailor. Do you know from where Captain Melosi sails?"

"Aye, friend. The Hawk ain't far. Green flag up the crow's nest." He pointed to a two-masted ship down the harbour and moved on with Notch's thanks.

"Notch?" Flir had a frown on her face. "This isn't bright."

"We won't be long."

She shook her head but followed him.

At the Hawk, he hailed a sailor and was sent to one of the taverns built up against the city walls. A flimsy building, it was little more than three walls with a door, and inside, a bar. Rosemary oil burnt on the bar, but Notch still found himself swatting at mosquitoes where he stood. A bald man poured drinks, two street toughs positioned across from the door, eyes watchful. Clubs hung from their belts.

Conversation and bodies filled the tap room, but Captain Melosi was easy to spot, thanks to the description Notch had been given. The man sat alone, nursing an ale, his giant beard woven with tiny bird skulls and silver buttons bright against his black coat.

"Captain Melosi?"

"So I am. You?"

"My name is Marco, and this is Asa. I wish to hire your services."

He shook his head, not offering a chair. "You can ask,

but I don't take passengers unless they pay handsomely, and I have to say Marco, you don't seem the type."

"I'm not looking for passage."

Melosi eyed him. "Maybe you should sit down."

Notch sat and pulled a signet ring from a pocket sewn into his tunic. He slid it across the table, the single mountain peak quickly covered by Melosi's hand, who held it up, squinting. "My sword bears the same insignia, but it's bound for Whiteport on the Blue Lady. If you know its captain, I would have you seek it out."

"The Hawk might be heading east on the morrow, but I'm no errand boy." He placed the ring back on the table and waited.

Notch nodded. "Forgive me if I don't indulge you in the game, Captain. How does twenty gold pieces sound?"

Flir made a choking sound, but the Captain's eyes lit up. "Most agreeable. But what guarantee can you offer? I'd hate to come back here to find you gone and my time a wasted."

"We both know you're already heading there, what do you waste?"

The man waited.

Notch sighed. "Take my ring as a token."

He rubbed his forehead. "Not worth much. A Mountain family?"

"To me, it's priceless." Notch held the man's eyes.

Eventually the captain extended a hand over the table. Notch took it.

"A deal then. The Hawk will return before the deep of winter."

"A deal," Notch said. He stood. "Thank you. Call upon the Queen's Harper when you return."

The captain grinned. "Don't thank me yet."

"You sail the East Oceans in winter?" Flir asked.

He shrugged. "I'm the best."

"Thank you again, Captain," Notch said, pulling Flir from the tavern. "Let's go see Seto."

"And tell him he has to hand over twenty gold pieces?"

"I may just save that conversation until after Captain Melosi returns with the sword."

"Notch, you might never see your ring again. You know that. Or your father's sword."

"He wants the gold."

Flir said nothing.

Notch followed her up darkening streets toward the Second Tier and the Antico Gate, weaving by taverns and warehouses, small market squares full of bustling colours – no red – where people shouted their promises; fresh fish and plump lemons popular, and up to the open gates, where the emblem of the King's Swordfish lay on each wing. He couldn't keep a sneer from his face at the sight.

Flir flashed a carven bone pass and the guards waved them through, giving Notch a look but not challenging them.

"Where did you get that?" Notch asked, some distance from the gate.

"I happened across it some weeks ago."

"Happened?"

"In a purse I found in a tavern. On a man's belt. He was sleeping something off."

He shook his head, but couldn't stop a smile.

The streets of the Second Tier were quiet. Evenly spaced lamps, well stocked compared to the torches of the Lower Tier, barely illuminated ornate street signs carved into walls of multi-storey buildings. A statue of the old King appeared on a corner, his shape little more than a black outline against the last dying light in the sky. Pinned to the plaque was one of several reward notices.

He took one down. His likeness was fair, though the artist had given him squinty eyes and a sneer – no doubt to suggest a more criminal appearance. "Thought I'd be worth more than that."

Flir shrugged. "You only killed a noble's Broann slave. That's the way they are up there. Though the palace does work fast, I'll admit that."

"They're indentured servants, Flir." He rubbed his cheek. "But I agree. That's exactly the way the palace is." He dropped the notice.

The Queen's Harper lay close to the Antico Gate, which had once granted entry to the city, many years gone, before the Lower Tier grew toward the harbour. Seto's inn was always open – all Notch had to do was reach it and he'd at least be able to change his clothes, and hopefully figure out what to do next.

Flir's idea of leaving the city shouldn't have been tempting. At the least, he could chase down the Blue Lady's captain in the Far Islands himself, retrieve his father's sword. But he had to make it known that he wasn't a child-killer. That he wasn't the scum of the earth. Every other name he could, and had worn. None of them mattered. But the last one had to go.

The clump of booted feet echoed up an intersection. Notch ducked into the recess of a candle maker's shop and Flir pressed her slight frame against him.

"Extra patrols?" he whispered.

"Fugitives are bad for city morale, I guess."

A small group of Anaskar Shields came into view, swords out, orange uniforms dark in the lamplight. More impressive than their matching tread was their bearing. Heads swivelled and eyes were bright, shoulders loose. They were either just on shift or particularly dedicated. But why not use tier troops or the Vigil?

Maybe all three forces were out there, looking for him.

"Go," Notch said when the men passed, heading down a musty side street. He crossed another park where he accidently trampled the contents of a flower bed, then paused half a street from the Queen's Harper. A three storey building, graced with a balcony on the top floor, towered over surrounding homes and businesses. Black roofing tiles glinted in the moonlight.

Beneath the latticework sign, shaped as a harp, a pair of Shields and a single Mascare stood in the pool of yellow light pouring from the windows. The Mascare's crimson robes were without crease or fold and his white mask glowed in the light, exaggerating the darkness of his eye slits. He gestured to one of the soldiers as he spoke, his words too soft to make out.

"What in hell is he doing here?" Flir snapped. "How'd they know you'd come looking for Seto?"

He grunted. "Maybe they're guessing? But that's what the Mascare do. They ferret out secrets."

She snorted. "Of course, how else can they protect the king from his own people?"

"But out in plain sight?"

"I know."

"Maybe he's a decoy."

"What now then?"

Notch scratched his cheek. There were other places he could go. Safer, quieter if colder, places. But he wanted the Harper's warmth and food, he wanted access to Seto's mind. Their sometime employer might be difficult at times, but he was a well of knowledge, a demi-God of the Second Tier. "Distract them."

"Quite an idea, Notch."

"Thanks." He rubbed his neck. "A fire might be a bit much."

"And I could start heaving flagstones at them but we'd still draw too much attention."

"Then we circle round, go in through the stable yard."

"The back wall's quite high."

"Yes."

"I see."

Notch slapped her shoulder. "You're strong enough."

"Fine. Get a move on then, I want to bathe."

Circling to the rear of the inn, Notch slowed when they reached the alley leading behind the stables. A wide door without a handle faced them. Seto's men never opened it for someone who didn't first walk through the front door. He couldn't start thumping on it anyway, the Mascare and the Shields were out of sight, but any disturbance might reach them. Flir stepped over a pile of trash and gestured up, her hand movements half-visible in light cast from the mouth of the alley.

"Ready?" she whispered.

It was high. Notch frowned. If he'd misjudged this, and Flir couldn't get him up, there'd be quite a racket when he crashed back down. He placed a foot between her hands and steadied himself, tapping her shoulder once he was set. Flir heaved him into the air.

He caught the top of the wall with a grunt of surprise and effort. The stone was cold and sharp beneath his hands, but he was already pulling himself up, boots scraping. He lay atop the wall and held his breath. No hurried footsteps from the front of the inn. Good.

Notch tapped the stones twice, softly, and reached down to Flir.

She leapt to catch his hand and he pulled her onto the wall. For Flir it was effortless, the height of the wall was nothing to her, but she'd nearly dragged his arm from its socket when she pulled back for leverage.

She sniffed. "It's not so high."

"For you at least." He looked into the stable yard. A square of light from an open door showed dusty flagstones and the openings of quiet stalls. A water barrel lurked in a corner and beside the door rested large crates marked with the Royal Swordfish. Fire-lemon was too expensive to be stacked in the yard. The bottles themselves were doubtless in the cellar. Always the best for Seto.

Flir chuckled, lowering herself then dropping lightly to the ground. Notch followed, but with less grace, the impact jarring his bones. "By the Ocean Gods."

"Come on, Notch. You're not old yet."

"It's a high wall." He limped after her. His ankle was tender, whether it would hold up he'd soon discover.

The kitchen warmth rushed over his exposed skin, coming from still-glowing embers in stoves, the smell of fresh bread and leftover meat and sauce stinging his mouth with anticipation. The cook, a large man with scarred arms, ducked through hanging pots and utensils, meat cleaver in hand. Luik's ancestors were originally from the southern forests, though it wasn't easy to see at first glance – a tan concealed his Braonn heritage. It also served to prevent him from dealing with most of the prejudice his race bore from Notch's people.

When Luik saw Notch he beamed.

"Notch? Thought you were sailing for the Far Islands?"

He put the blade aside and took him in a warrior's grip. "What happened?" His nose wrinkled. "You don't smell very good."

"Something went wrong. I'll tell you about it once we see Seto." He grinned. "Flir wants to bathe first."

Luik turned to Flir, his smile becoming broader. "What, this mouse?"

"Mouse?" She threw her arms around his neck and Notch saw him wince, but he laughed.

Luik set her down. "How were the mines? I'm surprised Notch didn't go with you this time."

"He was hurt. And you know how he is about his family."

"I'm not welcome there," Notch said. "You know that." Hadn't been for years, and nothing would change the fact.

Luik raised an eyebrow. "Even your mother?"

"Luik."

The chef shook his head but left off.

Flir gave him a look but kept on. "I'd barely returned when I heard about Notch getting himself into hot water."

Luik chuckled. "He's good at that."

Notch rolled his eyes. "Yes. And I'll tell you all about it but I should speak with Seto first. Is he upstairs?"

The big man nodded. "Sleeping. I think he was quite the busy little bird today, trouble with his 'interests' in the harbour as he calls them."

"I'll wake him gently then."

"Come and see me after," he said. "I'll have something good for you to eat. Then you gotta cough up the details."

Notch climbed the narrow stairs at the opposite end of the kitchen, his ankle holding up well, where the low murmur of conversation snuck through gaps in the woodwork of the door. His stomach rumbled but he could wait.

"Think Seto will be glad to see us?" Notch said. "You did make bit of a mess last time."

"Don't worry. I'm his favourite."

Light came from under the door. Notch knocked, but Seto didn't answer. He tried the handle. "Locked."

"Let me." Flir nudged him aside and took out a lock pick. Within moments the door swung open, light from an oil lamp revealing a low bed set against one wall and a desk resting beneath a pair of shelves. Stuffed into the shelves were books, papers, little statues, tiny jars of coloured powder and in one space, a pin cushion and strips of ribbon.

Dominating a corner, a layer of dust obscuring its carvings, stood a tall harp. Notch had never seen it played, let alone wiped clean, in all the years he'd known Seto.

A thin man lay on the bed, spindly hands crossed on his chest, sunken eyes closed. He still wore a tight vest of red and soft shoes on his feet, as if he'd gone directly from dinner to bed.

"You both smell terrible. Get out."

"Seto."

He opened his eyes and sat up, unruffled. "If you wish to talk, go and bathe first. Especially you, Notch. And Flir?"

"Yes?"

"Don't pick my lock again, dear."

She hung her head, but Notch could see she was smiling. "No, Seto."

"You go first," Notch told her. "I'll be along shortly."

Notch stepped into the corridor at a wave from Seto. The old man smoothed silver hair back and began sorting items on his desk. "Quickly, Notch. I cannot tolerate your stench much longer."

"You've heard?"

He made a 'tutting' sound. "Of course."

"Well, I didn't kill the girl."

Seto glanced over his shoulder. "And now you wish for me to intercede on your behalf?"

"I want your help, yes."

He turned and spread his hands. "I'm sorry but you know I will never set foot on the priceless stones of the First Tier again, Notch. Not even for an old friend."

"That's not what I'm asking, Seto. I want –"

He raised a long finger and pointed. "Bathe. We will talk then. And shut the door after you."

CHAPTER 7

Sofia flipped the book shut with a satisfying thump. She couldn't prevent a sigh escaping. Her father turned from where he'd stood, lost in thought. As ever, the study was lit by lamps and the blaze in the hearth.

"Sofia?" His voice softened. "Do not despair. The text is dry, but it is important."

"I know, but I can't stop thinking about him."

"Who? The Prince?"

She glanced at the mask where it governed from the mantle. "No. Argeon."

He placed both hands on her shoulders. "It will grow easier, each time."

"I hope so."

"Both knife and poison master are pleased with your progress."

"But none of that helps with Argeon. Or what a Successor must do. And how. Father, I'm not ready."

"You will be. And you know the words, they are your guide. Say them with me."

She chanted, matching her voice to his. "To Protect

the Prince, to follow in my father's footsteps, to protect our Order from enemies within and without, to watch the people, to watch for our enemies." Just as Tantos once said. The First Protector's Oath.

"And I do all of that with Argeon's power?"

"With your own."

"Father."

"Just remember. Argeon is dangerous too. We must move slowly. I do not want him to overwhelm you." He came to stand before her. "Do the robes fit, at least?"

Sofia nodded, plucking at a crimson sleeve. The fabric was heavy but she was not stifled in the room. She'd pulled the robes on over her Carver's clothing as a test and not bothered to remove them. Surprisingly, they felt right.

"You will make me proud, have no fear."

"I hope so." She reopened the book, skimming the bold script. "You left early this morning, father."

He sighed. "I thought I had been quiet."

"Is something wrong?"

He did not reply. She leant back, looking up to his mask. Finally he spoke. "No. I visited the harbor... in case your brother had survived."

"Oh." Sofia turned back to the book but did not read. "Do you believe he did?"

"No."

She turned another page.

"Come, we must focus. Tell me, what does The Long History of Greatmasks say of Lineage? This will help with Argeon. He is like a library of our lives."

She flipped through the heavy tome, scanning the text. Much was familiar. The mask's carving from bones in the Old Land, over five hundred years past, to their careful transport across the vast oceans to the Landing at Anaskar. Or their dwindling number during the rule of the first kings, troubled by vicious attacks from the Medah and internal scheming, all the way up to the masks' eventual rise from powerful tool to sacred object, possessed only by the most powerful houses and now down to one, possibly two – Argeon and Osani. The King's Greatmask, Chelona, was said to have been lost at sea when his elder brother drowned, but when she'd asked, her father revealed he had his doubts about the story.

She pushed away the thought of drowning.

Her father was waiting. "Lineage. Do not expect to know a Greatmask without first understanding its lineage of custodians. Due to the fact that the men and women who wear them remain jealous, and remain opposed to the sharing of such a mask, they end up spending near to their entire lives communicating with their masks. In this, they impart as much of themselves into the bone as the Greatmask lends them."

She kept a finger on the page. Of her grandfather she knew only what father had shared. That he was a quiet man, prone to moodiness but nonetheless a stalwart defender of the crown. "Do you know Argeon's lineage?"

"Of course. Back to the Landing."

"And I need to know that to wear Argeon?"

"To become a Protector, yes." He sat. "Let me explain. Using a Greatmask is most like a conversation. When you wear it, you communicate with Argeon but he is also communicating with you. Or trying to. He is accustomed to speaking with those who have come before you. Me, your grandfather, our ancestors. You must be sure you are using the same words, the same thoughts."

"That doesn't make sense."

"Nor will it fully, for some time. We will try again. Remember, every time you wear him you will have to make him notice you, through your force of will. Argeon is busy with the ages I feel. Sometimes he will not listen even to me, no matter my call."

"Father, it's as if he's a mystery even to you."

"In many ways he is. Argeon has been in our family for centuries. He is unknowable in the whole." He patted her shoulder with his free hand. "Things will get better."

"I hope so."

Her father retrieved the mask. "This time when you wear Argeon, don't worry about which words you use. Call to him with more need. Draw his attention. He is aware of you, but it may help you to call to him, in your mind. What he will respond to I suspect, is your will, your strength, not your voice. Try, I will be here."

She raised the heavy mask to her face, the cool bone sliding against her skin, the scent one of age. Blackness came and then there was only Argeon. Her father, the fire, the whole room, the city of Anaskari, everything was gone.

Only Argeon's face remained.

To be looking at something she was wearing from the 'outside' was odd, but the thought barely registered. The force of his indifference hit her again, and she gave a small cry. Call to him. Hear me, Argeon. I am worthy.

"Argeon." She shouted into the dark – though who knew if she also spoke aloud? The Greatmask did not respond. He had to answer. If she was unable to draw his attention, unable even to complete such a simple task, then she was useless. She ground her teeth and called again. A flicker of interest? It passed but before she could try again, the room snapped into focus.

"Well done, my daughter." Her father held Argeon.

Sofia rubbed her temples. "My head. What happened?"

"The learning will be painful, but you did well. He acknowledged you."

"Even with such a small response?"

"Yes. It's early in your relationship. You are just as strong as your brother, have no fear that Argeon will continue to –"

The door to his chamber flew open.

Sofia flinched. Mascare, Shields and finally the Prince burst inside, crowding the study. The king trailed his son, wandering rather than storming into the room. He appeared confused, not at all like himself. Her father shot to his feet, Argeon still in hand. "What is the meaning of this intrusion? And worse, such carelessness? This is hardly the Open Chamber."

She stared. Several of the Mascare, those closest to Prince Oson, wore no masks at all. A matter of grave seriousness, that they would go without masks before so many. Reserved for the most secret trials of the Order.

The Shields were made up of the King's personal guard, each with the fin insignia emblazoned across their chests, and held drawn weapons. One was Captain Emilio, but he did not meet her gaze.

The Prince wore an expression of triumph, sending her an evil grin before his eyes strayed to Argeon. Beside Oson, the king's eyes fluttered. He leant on the arm of a Mascare without a mask. There were three such men, one with a hooked nose in a sour face, the other two with lips set in firm lines. They flanked the King.

"Protector Danillo, you are hereby accused of conspiring to murder King Otonos and overthrow the

Royal Swordfish," Prince Oson announced.

"What?" Sofia burst out.

Her father raised his hand. He turned to the Prince. "In that you are mistaken, my Prince. You act greatly beneath you, your father and your House in this churlish attempt to discredit me. I have never, nor will I ever conspire against the crown."

The Prince flushed, glaring across the room. Only her father, as Protector, could speak to a member of the royal family in such a way. Even so, faces blanched.

The sour-faced man responded in the Prince's place. Solicci. "No more lies, Danillo. We have evidence. Evidence the King must see with his own eyes."

Sofia frowned. Why bring the King to her father's rooms, to show him evidence of treason? Why not the Throne Room? And what was wrong with the old man, why hadn't he spoken? Last night he was a commanding presence, despite looking pale, but now he was barely alert.

"This is ridiculous. My father is innocent." Sofia directed her words to the Prince. He made no answer, only smiling back. Her father took a step toward the old King, who blinked back at him. Several blades were levelled at her father and Sofia edged toward him, pulse racing. She had to stay close. Whatever was happening, it was a lie. Father was no traitor.

"My King, you know this is not true."

King Otonos tilted his head. He moved his mouth slowly, but no sounds followed.

Her father turned to Emilio. "Captain. Surely you do not believe this?"

Emilio made no answer at first, though his eyes were wary. His breastplate reflected the firelight and when he spoke his voice was loud in the silence. "I am here at the Prince's behest to investigate claims that threaten my liege."

King Otonos nodded, lips pursed. "Danillo, yes...the man...that man seemed to be..."

One of the Mascare propping him up hushed the king, who complied without resistance, and Sofia felt her stomach turn. Had the king been drugged? He was old but he wasn't feeble. The whole thing was some cruel puppet show, a play for his benefit. And it was Oson's doing. No doubt all the scowling during the meeting had been an act too. The attempt to discredit her family was obvious. Pathetic even. Had the king been in his right mind, he would not have been fooled.

The Prince was still staring at Argeon. Sofia shivered. He wanted the Greatmask.

"Here, my Lords." A Mascare removed a letter from her father's desk. She hadn't even heard him cross the room. "It's written in their script."

"Show me that," her father said, but the masked man handed it instead to Solicci.

"It names you, Danillo of Casa Falco." He'd barely glanced at it. Sofia clenched her jaw. She couldn't fight them, they were too many and she untrained. But she couldn't convince the king that it was all lies either.

"What names me, Solicci? Have the decency to speak plainly."

The Prince took over. "It's a letter from warriors beyond the wasteland. From the west. Our old enemy has sent an assassin which you have paid for."

"The punishment for treason is death," Solicci added.

"I have not received nor kept any letter from the Medah." Her father suddenly had a knife in his hand, but she hadn't seen him reach for it. "Boy, what you have had your lackey plant is no evidence. Prince or no, you will detract your accusation or die by my hand."

Sofia drew a breath, her surprise echoed by many of those in the room. "No, father," she cried. "It's what they want."

"You're outnumbered," Solicci said. "Don't be a fool, listen to your daughter. She's quite bright for a Carver."

Her father's shoulders trembled. He was inches from rage. "I am outnumbered. But this cur will still be dead." The prince had gone purple but held his ground.

"And so will your daughter be," Solicci snapped back. Sofia inched her own hand for the big chisel at her belt. Her heart thumped, a thousand hooves against her chest, but she stood tall. Unprovoked, these men sought to shatter her father and sully the name of Casa Falco. Neither Father nor Tantos had done a single thing to hurt the other houses and never the King. Oson and Solicci deserved naught but steel.

Her father shook his head. "You need her. Argeon will not speak to a Cavallo." He looked to each unmasked face. "Nor a Pesce. Or a Tartaruga. I have seen to that."

Solicci puffed himself up. "You have dared to –"

"Enough." Her father roared the word. "You have dared to bring these false allegations against me, drawn weapons upon me and involved my King in your petty games. I feared you coveted Argeon, but I did not think you would stoop to such barren depths, Solicci. Am I wrong in guessing that Osani has abandoned you then? Or do you wish for both Greatmasks?" He paused, moving his gaze to the Prince. "Or worse, have you simply become a lapdog to this whelp?"

Solicci offered no response but Oson drew his own

sword. The King placed a shaking hand on his son's shoulder.

"No. Show me... the letter." His voice creaked in the silence. His head wobbled as he moved a hand in a circle before him. "Emilio, come."

Solicci handed the letter over and the king read slowly, the captain of his guard joining him. The Shields shifted in place but didn't lower their blades. Ten men, including the king, arrayed against her father. She kept her hand near the chisel. It was not much against swords, but she had nothing else.

Emilio glanced at her, then spoke, a trace of reluctance in his voice. "It is written in the Medah script."

King Otonos frowned.

"There is more, your majesty." Another mask-less man waved at the door. A dark skinned man was dragged into the room by two Shields. Sofia's stomach flipped. Hanging between the king's guard was a warrior from across the western desert, from Medah – a place where the old were taken into the sands and buried alive, where disobedient children were scalded with hot embers and women beat their menfolk if they disobeyed their wishes and where dark mages plotted and schemed to take Anaskar.

The old enemy.

How had the man crossed the desert? Survived the Wards? And worse, gained admittance into the city, let alone the palace!

A Shield pulled the prisoner's head back by the hair. Tears ran down his face and his blue eyes were wide. A large bruise swam beneath his swollen cheek. Solicci pointed to her father, speaking slowly. "Is this the man who sent you gold, who snuck you into the city?"

He nodded, eyes darting from face to face.

"And the man who asked you to assassinate King Otonos?"

"Yes," he managed, accent thick. "Please, don't kill me."

Her father made no response and she inched closer. His whole body trembled and he had not put his knife away. To the king, he spoke, voice quiet. "Your Majesty, you do not believe this, surely? Look at his eyes, they are blue by the Ocean Gods. He is no Medah."

The king's dark eyes flashed. Though he needed support, fury lent his voice power. "This letter... this man. It is a betrayal. Emilio?"

"Treason is punishable by death," the Captain said, his face set.

"No!" Sofia reached for her father. Something hot bit the back of her head and a moment later she was looking up from the floor, her father crouched over her. Had someone hit her? Argeon concealed her father's face but she could hear the rage in his voice, even as he whispered. "Through the fireplace, petal – on my word. They will lie."

He helped her up and Sofia flinched. A Mascare lay crumpled on the ground, blood pooling around the blade in his stomach. One of her father's knives. Oson was shouting from across the room where Solicci held him back. The Shields wore white faces and the Medah man was being pulled from the room. Her father radiated a power she'd never felt before. The air thickened around him and when he spoke, his voice resonated.

"This need not end in further bloodshed. I will spare the rest of you, if you stay your hands and let my daughter alone. I will accept your punishment."

She shouted. "No."

Solicci raised his hands. "If she cooperates –"

"No. She is to be given safe passage from Anaskar."

Oson spat as he stepped forward, pointing his finger. "No? You are a traitor, you make no bargains."

In the blink of an eye, faster than seemed possible, her father crossed the space between the two and caught the prince's hand, jerking the man close. He placed the knife against Oson's throat. "Stay," he barked, and the force of his word drove them back. Sofia took a half step back herself. It put her between her father and the fireplace – but with its flames she couldn't guess what he'd meant. It was large and the heat was real. What was she to do?

"Danillo, no more." Solicci held up his hands. "Give up the Prince and the Greatmask. If you do that, we will grant you your wish. On my honour, your daughter will be free."

"On your honour, Solicci? I do not believe you have any left."

"On my honour."

Still no-one moved.

Emilio whispered to the King, who straightened. "He is my son, Danillo."

Her father made no response, but the air changed again, becoming less oppressive. *They will lie.* Sofia looked from face to face.

"Very well. A son for a daughter. Swear it, my king."

"I swear."

A moment longer her father held Oson, and then he shoved him into Solicci's arms. The Prince wheeled on the captain. "Take my father away, you imbecile. Isn't he in enough danger?" Spittle covered his chin and his face was red.

"Honour the terms," her father demanded.

Solicci waited a moment, letting the old king leave before waving a hand. "Take them both."

"Now!" Her father leapt forward, knives flashing in the lamplight. Men fell back, even as others met his attack. None could touch her father. He wove among them, cutting and maiming. Oson backed away but Solicci and the other men without masks drew their own blades.

"Go," her father roared when he saw her watching.

"I can't leave you."

A soldier charged her, his blade poised to strike and his face a rigid snarl. There was no mercy in his eyes, no hesitation in his swing.

Sofia ducked, stumbling back as the blade whistled over her head. Her father appeared and his arms were blurs as he fought, cutting the Mascare to ribbons.

Spinning, he caught her and without pause, threw her into the flames.

CHAPTER 8

Ain placed a palm on hot sand and closed his eyes. The sun beat on his head and sweat slipped down his back. A familiar discomfort, and with no breeze running across the desert's god-like face, he might have removed his cloak. If he did, and the elders found out, he would be shamed. No Pathfinder let their cloak touch the ground by choice. Too precious, its entire length dyed a sky blue, each cloak was the work of a third of the settlement. More, it was not merely fabric. It was a symbol of the Ocean, a symbol of Medah's past. Or its future.

There.

Thumping from a pair of booted feet. The scuff of a lighter shoe on the sand, the plonk of camel feet. The bare tread of wild dogs, their pads sizzling. The hard lines of wagon wheels. Passage after passage trembled beneath his hand, vibrations played along his skin. The age of their passing was a collective thunder as they crossed the desert, filled his mind. It was an army, a history of the very land, in the form of every step any living soul had taken on the path.

He heard them all.

Ain raised his hand and the sound of their passage receded enough that he could resume his Pathfinder's Trial. He walked on, guided by the echo of footfalls. Water was close. With such a busy path to follow, one which resonated from deep beneath the surface, he had no doubts. His cracked lips told him it had better be.

If the Sands willed that he perish then it would be so, though his gift had never led him astray.

If the elders really sent an experienced Pathfinder along to shadow Initiates, then the man better be impressed. Ain had found every path, every water hole, every site of significance since starting his trial. And if it was Majid, Ain hoped his friend was watching closely. Once Majid left on the Search Ain would have no-one to measure himself against.

He'd have to think of a surprise for Majid. Payback for the pepper in his food. Maybe a nice big, sticky rock-lizard in the man's sleeping roll?

The echo of slowing footfalls brought him to a halt. Sand stretched before him, distant dunes wavering in the heat. A small collection of stones formed a cairn, beneath which would be a well. Ain hauled the stones to one side and slid the cover aside, revealing a dark opening and rope tied to a heavy iron ring. The ring was stained with age but the rope was new.

Pulling on it, the slosh of water rose from below and his throat gave a raw swallow of anticipation. When he lifted the bucket to his mouth, water spilled down his tunic. Wasteful! He put the bucket down and knelt. "Sands forgive me."

Cooling off was tempting but he only drank again, carefully. Next he stopped to fill his water flasks before resting against one of the larger stones. At repose, in a spot where so many feet had come to a halt over the decades, the rhythm of their moving was dulled to such an extent that he could barely hear them. Only when he slept, could Ain experience truer escape from the noise.

The sand was quiet. No other living creature visible, not even the scrawniest cactus, and only his own footprints suggested any one had ever set foot in this part of the desert. If an older Pathfinder like Majid was out there, he saw no evidence. To be Medah was to be skilled at concealing oneself in the landscape, but that was like saying the Sands were vast.

Ain was not convinced he wasn't totally alone. Upon sending him off, the elders would not answer his questions about whether he would be watched.

"You will be worthy if you return," was all they offered.

Ain would return. Faster than any Pathfinder before him. Then maybe they would take his request seriously, and allow him to shape his own future. Allow him to make Silaj a part of it. Even her mother would no longer object, once he was a true Pathfinder. Majid and Elder Raila believed in him, he would not fail them. He took another drink from the bucket before dropping it into the dark, covering the well and heading for the nearest dune. Beyond would be a new path, this one to civilisation.

With each step the sand gave a little. His legs were beyond aching but he kept on. If he travelled quick enough, he could reach the Cloud Oasis before nightfall. Paths spread around him like veins on the big leaves merchants brought from the far west. He'd tried to keep one as a child, but it eventually shrivelled to brown in the desert heat.

To his left pulsed a faint rhythm, an old, old trail

buried deep beneath the sand. It could have been for game or a regular road between settlements. This was overlaid by whispers of lesser paths, some that might never have been taken with any regularity, by any more than one or two people. The sand to his right was similar, the barely audible shuffle overlaid with stronger beats from more popular trails. The path his own feet trod was shifting, its power waxed and waned, as travellers past and present drifted on and off.

One such diversion, though faint, gave him pause. It sounded as no other path had before. Light, but sibilant. "What's this?" He placed a hand on the desert floor, then jerked his palm back at a sharp, slicing sensation. No blood. Frowning, he hurried along the side of the dune, its edges soft. The hiss of the path grew as he ran. No passage was meant to hiss, let alone cause pain. Feet had a rhythm, a step, a hard sound. Even the oldest trail he'd heard was the same, one of steps. The passage of feet striking ground. This was different.

A sharp depression appeared ahead. When he reached it, Ain leapt down its sides, coming to a halt in a spray of sand. A body, dressed in the remnants of Medah tans, lay in its centre. Half-covered in sand, it was a skeleton, bleached by the sun. He moved closer and the hissing disappeared. And then so did the murmur of other paths. All of them. Only in pre-wakeful moments had he experienced such quiet.

Who had died here, to leave such a strange trace on a path and then to create such powerful silence? Ain crouched. An outstretched arm was open, the other buried in the sand. How slowly had the wind uncovered this poor soul? The head was turned away, jaw agape. Ain brushed at the sand. There had to be a clue to the traveller's identity. He worked in the sun, pausing to drink but once, when he'd finished. Under the sand, a hint of familiar cloth was visible, hidden beneath the skeleton.

"Forgive me." He tugged on it. A large scrap came free, the portion which had been buried beneath both body and sand still held enough colour for him to recognise a Pathfinder's blue cloak.

"So. This is what happens when we fail." Had the man followed the wrong path or ran out of water? Was he attacked? Or was he a Pathfinder on his own Trial? Sometimes a young Pathfinder never returned, but it was rare. And cause for great mourning among the clan. When had it last happened?

The man was gone now, it mattered not how or when.

Ain straightened the limbs, flinching when the arm dislodged, and shifted the skull into place before tying the remaining scraps of cloak around the head, placing eyes, ears and mind to rest.

"Let the passing of feet go quiet now, your path is at an end."

He kept a smaller piece of the cloak, climbing the depression with heavy tread. The further he moved from the skeleton the louder the many paths became, mixing with and finally drowning out the swishing of the perished Pathfinder.

Somehow, the knowledge that the Sands willed it was not of comfort. Ain shivered. What did the Sands, with its restless shifting, have in store for him?

The noon sun slid across the sky, searing exposed skin, but he pushed forward. It was reckless, and he stopped barely an hour out from the skeleton. He'd been sipping too frequently from his water flask. Time to stop and set up camp. Travelling deep into morning was already a risk, his haste would kill him if he travelled into noon.

Setting up his tent and crawling into the welcome shade to take a long drink, Ain lay down and breathed deeply. Once he had a rhythm going, one counter to the hum of paths around him, he closed his eyes, blocking out the tan roof, the dark pole and the white orb blazing away beyond the canvas. Sweat trickled down his temples. He breathed deep and even until his heart slowed and his limbs grew heavy.

Hours had passed when he woke. The sun was heading for the dunes and a wind had picked up, beating against the tent. He'd lost too much time. There was a real chance he would no longer beat Majid's record of fastest Pathfinder to return to the Cloud Oasis. He rubbed his shoulder, which had stiffened as he slept. Did it matter anymore? Had it even mattered before? Proving his worth could be done, simply by completing the trial as required. Safely.

Driving himself too hard was not the right way.

Outside, the wind flung sand. He turned his back on it to collapse and repack his tent. Once set, he shielded his eyes with his hand and turned a slow circle. The horizon was clear, no chance of a sand storm yet. But the wind would be lashing his side as he approached the oasis. He pulled a blindfold out, wrapping it only once, and trudged on, cloak clinging to his legs.

When he finally crested a long dune, aflame in the setting sun, the wind had died down. The passage of countless feet converged at a point below, where low buildings spread around a glittering oasis. Partially screened by the ridge of a long, crumbling mountain range, faint lines of bluish smoke rose from the mud brick buildings on the north end of the oasis, heading for the scuffs of clouds. Scattered along the water's edge were larger tents and tiny cook-fires. At the south end of the oasis were yet more tents, these of a different colour, Sand-Snakes visiting from the Southern Oasis.

Ain paused his descent. The snakes were early. Had Majid's departure been brought forward? He ran to the bottom of the dune, leaping over small green plants that dotted the hardened earth, whose stones separated sand from water.

"Ho, Ain, slow down," a voice cried.

A white-haired warrior emerged from peach trees at the water's edge, waving his arms. Ain changed course slightly, and within moments stood panting beside the old man, whose muscled arms had come to rest on his hips. Jedda stood smiling through his white beard, long knife belted over his sleeveless tunic. A bow and quiver were slung over one shoulder. He enfolded Ain in a gruff hug then set him down.

"You've fared well, Ain – a Pathfinder in the eyes of all. Youngest in many decades." The man beamed.

He flushed, but couldn't prevent a smile. "Thank you, Jedda."

"Ha! Don't attempt modesty, what of your boast to me before you left?"

"Well, I was a child then. I am a man now."

"Ah."

"And I wasn't as fast as Majid."

"A week is very fast, and you are here," Jedda said, placing a hand on his shoulder. He glanced to Ain's belt. "As cannot be said for all. You found a Pathfinder?"

"Near a day from the Cloud. I guess the sands had moved? I performed the ritual and took a piece of his cloak." He handed it to Jedda. "I hope that was permitted."

"I'm sure he wouldn't mind. I wonder who it was. More than a few have been lost over the years," Jedda said, examining it and handing the piece back. "Why did you wish to keep it?"

Ain shrugged. The question was not one of judgement, but it was difficult to answer. He finally spoke. "I'm not sure. I want to remember him."

The older man squeezed his shoulder. "Then let's return now. Cloud Oasis has been waiting for you." He started back into the shade of the trees. Ain followed him along a narrow trail. Ahead, glimpses of water shone through the leaves.

"I saw tents of sand-snakes. Surely they are early?"

"Yes, a change for the snakes." He chuckled but his cheer soon faded. "This year's Search is not off to an encouraging start."

"What has happened?"

"The west clan is not coming."

Ain stopped. "What? Why?"

"They have turned away from our quest. From all that makes us Medah. They refuse to attend the ceremony, their messenger brought only the ill news."

"But the Search for the Sea Shrine... how could they turn their backs on it?"

"They no longer see it that way. Perhaps living so close to the Holvard in the far west has taken away their senses?" He paused to retie a piece of netting on one of the peach branches. "That is not the last of it."

"There's more?" The elders were probably fighting over what to do. Not even during the disastrous Glass War had the western clan broken pact. The oldest pact. The first pact, when there were no clans, no need for a pact. That alone was enough to swallow. What else had happened?

"Majid broke his leg the day after you left."

Ain stopped. "Is he well?" Majid's preparation for the Search lasted many months. Under the gaze of the elders his fitness and weapons training had been increased, as were his already formidable tracking and hunting skills. Perhaps most taxing, according to his friend, was learning the dirty language spoken by the Invaders, the Anaskari, and studying with the old Engineer. "And who will take his place? Isn't Yavil seeking the old wells?"

"Yes. I don't know who they'll send, but Majid is well enough. Furious that he cannot undertake the Search, but he will recover."

"Good."

"There's talk of the ceremony being delayed."

"For how long?" He had an important question to ask Silaj and there was no bigger night than that of the Leaving ceremony. He smiled. Was there truly any reason to wait? Even if the ceremony was postponed, he would ask tonight. He was a true Pathfinder now, what more did he need?

"The elders are discussing it."

By the time they reached the first mud-brick building, ringed by a low stone fence that sheltered an olive patch, his stomach was groaning. As if it'd been asleep and now woken grumpy. He could have snatched a handful of olives and gobbled them down.

In the large square men and women in yellow and brown hues carried rows of pot plants, which usually lined the building fronts, and arranged them into twin lines. The Searcher's path, through which the Oasis' chosen Pathfinder, Majid, would have left at dawn.

A voice shouted across the square. "Ain, Ain, you're

home."

Little Wim leant out a window to wave, squashing the riot of pink and red flowers on the sill as he did. "Are you a Path-man now?"

He laughed. "Why don't you come and see?"

Wim's mother gave a shout when she saw her flowers, shooing him out the door. The boy ran across the dusty square, leaping over the pot plants and flinging himself into Ain's arms.

"I'm happy to see you too, Wim."

Ain was soon surrounded by smiling faces and people slapping him on the back, children touching his cloak and somewhere beyond the group, women singing Homecoming, voices swelling. Dadel, his apron half-tied, grinned at him, dark hair still damp from the forge. "Well done, Ain."

Jedda too, smiled, but at a call, he moved away.

Wim tugged Ain's sleeve. "Can we play now?"

"What do you want to play?"

"Hide and Seek."

Dadel rolled his eyes. "You won't be playing anything, you two."

"Why not?"

"Look who comes with Jedda."

Elder Raila approached the group, Jedda in tow. His teacher's silvery head was bare to the sun and she adjusted her arm bands, the only mark of office the elders afforded themselves. More, the only mark she wore now that she had given up the cloak to become Elder.

At her approach, the crowd hushed.

Raila's face, barely lined for a woman of her age, was graced with a smile but her eyes held worry. "Citizens, let us finish preparing for the Leaving Ceremony, and make time to honour Pathfinder Ain this evening."

People left without complaint, Dadel offering one more whisper of encouragement and even Wim, who blinked up at Raila, slipped away. Ain went to both knees, sitting on his feet.

"Elder."

"No formalities today, Pathfinder. At least, not from you, Ain." She tapped his shoulder, beckoning for him to rise. He did so. "Congratulations from Cloud Oasis. We have been impressed with your conduct."

"Thank you, Elder Raila."

"I am aware that Jedda has explained some of the events of the past days. As you know, Majid is unable to continue the Search. He has asked to see you, will you come with me now?"

Ain glanced at Jedda, then back to Elder Raila. "He wants to see me, Raila?"

Jedda cleared his throat.

"Ah, I mean, Elder. And of course I will come. Forgive me." He sunk back to his knees.

Raila shook her finger. "None of that, Pathfinder. Let's be on our way, he is not far. Then we can get you something to eat."

Ain followed his teacher as she skirted the Searcher's path. He caught Jedda's eyes again but the man shook his head. What was happening?

CHAPTER 9

"You will take Majid's place."

Ain stood agape before elders from both his own and the Snake clan. They sat in their clan colours, Snakes brown, Cloud in tan, hands folded before them. The Snake had a dagger on the tabletop and a finger twitched, as if he wanted to fiddle with it.

No-one was smiling, and even Majid wore a far-away look. He ran a hand over close-cropped hair. His leg was trussed up in a splint where he leant against the wall of the cool room, his blue Pathfinder's cloak folded before him.

What had appeared to be a discussion with Majid was quite something else. The row of elders arrayed in Majid's home was shock enough, but this? The Sands were not mysterious, they were unfathomable. How could he be a faithful servant if they sought to surprise him so?

"I am not worthy." Ain fell to his knees and sat on his heels. He'd expected to be chastised for something. Or maybe asked about his intentions with Silaj. Sands, how to explain everything to her?

Raila motioned for him to stand. "You will have to be worthy. With Majid injured and the winter fast approaching, there's no time to train another Pathfinder. The desert will soon be closed."

"But I'm not prepared for the Search, Elder."

"Ain. I have trained you, like Majid before you, in the paths, and I know your worth. You may not know the language of the Anaskari and you may not be the greatest tracker here in the Cloud, you may not know the Search, but you are the strongest Pathfinder, Ain. You will accept your duty." She crossed her arms. The familiar gesture was enough for him to drop his head.

"Yes, teacher."

Elder Snake cleared his throat. "This boy doesn't speak the Anaskari tongue? Has not trained with the Engineer?"

"This young man," Raila corrected. "And I do not exaggerate, in spite of your concerns. He is the strongest Pathfinder we have produced in generations."

Ain flushed at her praise, but the Snake waved a hand. "I can have someone more able here in two weeks. It is best for all. Young Ain should not have to carry such a burden."

Kafik, who sat beside Raila, shook his head. His silver bands were scuffed from his battles in the Glass War and his heavy brow was drawn. "Even a week might be a risk, the sand storms will be too violent soon."

"That is so." Raila said. "Snake, trust my judgement, Ain is capable."

"If I might speak, Elder?" Majid glanced at Ain, offering a quick smile.

"Yes, Majid?"

"I would like to add my voice to that of my people." He

turned to the Snake. "Jedepa, we have hunted together. You know my measure. You know my word."

"I do."

"Then I will say now, Ain has been but a step behind me these past years. I may be more experienced, but that is only because I am a little older. Ain can make the journey."

Snake took Ain's measure, dark eyes roaming. It was difficult to discern exactly what the man felt. Was he displeased because Ain was young or because Ain wasn't Snake-clan? "He'll need a good Engineer, lad," the man said, not bothering to address Ain.

Raila nodded. "He shall be accompanied by Ibranu."

Snake grunted. "Well enough. But you ought to send at least one good warrior with him. I've been saying it for years, the reason we cannot locate the Sea Shrine isn't our Pathfinders. It's because they are not protected, but Sands forbid we buck tradition and actually provide for them properly."

Kafik shook his head. "That's not how it's done. Stealth is of import. If we are to drive the Anaskari devils out of Sekkati then it will be done at the Shrine, that is what the Engineers have always promised. It will not happen with arms. Down that road lies too much death, as well you know. The Glass War? The Years of Blood? Our entire history."

"All that might be true, but what's one more in the party, Kafik? And it's not tradition to send an under-prepared boy on the Search either, so don't give me lectures."

Ain stiffened but held his tongue. In another place he might tell Jedepa what he thought of the man's opinion, Elder or no. But not in front of Raila and Majid.

"Enough," Raila said, rubbing her neck. "It is not a

bad idea. At least until the Borderlands. There Ibranu and Ain can decide whether to brave the Wards alone or risk another life in addition to their own. Agreed?"

Kafik said nothing. Finally he threw up his hands. "What does it matter? The West Clan has not even come, the Sands can hardly be pleased. Send a Warrior."

The Snake was silent a moment, eventually nodding, though a frown remained. "Agreed." To Ain he finally spoke. "Good fortune with you, lad."

"Thank you, Elder."

Pride shone in Raila's eyes. "Congratulations, Ain. You are now the most important man in Cloud Oasis. It falls to you to unlock the secrets of the Sea Shrine, to restore the Medah to their rightful home, to Sekkati by the wide arms of the ocean."

He bent to his knees and came to rest on his heels again, bowing his head to hide his face. Shock was wearing off. Unpleasant truths sank in. He would have to leave Silaj. East, into the enemy's clutches. Crossing the wards. Risking his life. Sand storms. Anaskari devils.

He met Majid's eyes. The Pathfinder nodded.

Aloud he said, "It is my honour."

∗

His Feast of Leaving was underway when Silaj found him.

Tables laden with lamb and sauces, olives and bread, peaches and milk were shadowed by the crowd. Torches and standing lamps lined the trees in the Searcher's Path and around the square. Laughter jumped up and over the music and singing but he made no such sounds of his own, mumbling and forcing smiles as person after person came to offer congratulations. To let him know their hopes went with him.

Ain concealed his sighs. If the Sands willed it, he would prove worthy.

He'd eaten, and the food, usually delicious, was flat. Mush. Even Wim had not been able to get much of a rise out of him with his idea for pranks, and Dadel thumped him on the arm when Ain muttered about being forced to leave.

"I feel so sorry for you, having to go on an adventure while I'm stuck here pounding nails, arrow heads and sword blades. Or worse, those strange implements for the Engineer. You should see the old sketches Master Lusdeh has me work from. I can barely read them they're so faded. That's what I get to do."

"It's dangerous, Dadel. Few Pathfinders return."

"I know."

"And those that do are treated as failures. Barely acknowledged thereafter. Remember Naceh? How we found him in his home? His was face blue with poison. He still had the bottle in his hand."

His friend looked away, scratching at his stubble. "I know that too."

Ain sighed. "I'm sorry. I know I must leave, but it's not what I want. I thought, once I was a Pathfinder, I would be able to choose my path."

"I'm sorry too."

"It's not your fault."

Dadel grinned. "No, but I have the feeling you could blame anyone about now."

"I guess so."

His friend had slipped from the chair where Ain sat in the shadows, just out of the firelight, when Silaj approached.

Ain stood and went to her. Her mouth was set and she'd pulled her dark hair into a bun atop her head, as she often did when preparing for an argument. To keep it from getting caught in her mouth, she'd told him when he asked.

"You returned early."

"Yes."

"Ain, you have to tell Elder Raila you cannot leave."

No congratulations, no hello, not even a smile. He shouldn't have expected anything more than her discontent. It mirrored his own. "I didn't do this, Silaj."

Her voice broke and her combative stance softened. "Ain, please. You cannot let this happen, not now. Mother is weakening, I know it. This is the worst time to leave."

Couldn't she see he had no say in the matter? How was he to break hundreds of years of tradition? Simply run into the desert, take her with him? Hide and run from shame forever? Ain opened his mouth to retort but stopped. Her eyes glistened. He stepped closer, and when she didn't move away, he took her into his arms. "I don't want to leave."

"Then tell them you have a reason to stay." She spoke into his chest before looking up. "Our child will need you."

He gripped her shoulders. "Our child?"

"Yes. I wanted to surprise you... when you returned."

He stroked her face. "Silaj. They will not let me stay."

She smothered a sob. "I know."

Ain drew in a shuddering breath and held her. The celebration went on beyond them, dancing shadows and clapping hands washing against him.

*

Dawn dusted the buildings, trees and the line of Elders with gold. Ain stood before them, heavy pack pulling on his shoulders where it rested over his blue cloak. So soon after his own Trial, his head was stuffed full of sand. If he tilted it, half the desert would have fallen out. And he'd have felt no better for it.

But all night he'd lain with Silaj, talking, making plans. Foolish plans, dreams where he returned unscathed.

For their child.

When he left in the predawn, everything a mute grey, she made him promise to return. And he did, the words treacherous on his tongue. She saw his doubt and he looked away. He had to leave her with something, leave his child with her memories of a strong man. What else mattered but returning to his son or daughter?

The Search was important. Maybe it was only a symbol now after so many failed attempts over hundreds of years. But important still. Not only for Cloud Oasis, but for all of Medah. It would be wondrous to avenge his people, but how likely was success? A twig against the Sand Giant's rage.

"It is time," Raila said. "Searcher, Engineer and Warrior," she added the last title without pause, "you are about to undertake a journey that can only be successful if you agree pledge your lives to one another, if you act as one. This you will swear now."

"I swear," Ain said. Ibranu, and Schan, one of Jependa's Snakes, repeated his words from a pace behind, one to either side. One gruff voice and one flat, as if nothing in the sands could have been of less interest. What a team we will make.

"Then take our and the People of the Sand's blessings with you." She smiled at him as she and the others stepped aside. Ain led the way through the trees, a slow shiver spreading through his body. Beyond the square and the Oasis, the desert opened up before him, his home shrinking behind with each step.

Townsfolk and visiting Snakes lined the road, kneeling, faces solemn, eyes urging Ain on. Silaj had not come, as they'd agreed. He drew in a shuddering breath. It was better. He passed dozens of familiar faces, mostly mixed in with snake clan and even Peg, the visiting merchant from Holvard. The man winked at him. Further on, Dadel put his fists together in the old gesture for strength. Majid, supported by Jedda, broke tradition to step forward.

"You can do this, Ain."

"If you think so."

"Remember, when you reach the Shrine, you must Call the Ocean. That is what Ibranu and I have learnt from the old scrolls. It is the missing piece."

"But none of the legends speak of the Shrine that way."

"We don't know what it means yet. Ibranu thinks it will become clear when you find the shrine."

Elder Raila cleared her throat.

Jedda squeezed his shoulder. "Your parents would be proud, Ain."

Ain straightened his back.

Strongest Pathfinder. If Mother and Father could see him, they would believe in him. He could find the Shrine in Sekkati, City of Secrets, despite it being overrun with devils. He could pass the blazing Wards, find every water hole in the wasteland and slip through the stone walls. Where others had failed he would succeed. Why else would the Sands turn his path so far away from the one his feet had wanted to tread?

Climbing the first dune, he paused at the top. Beyond its smooth ridge waited countless other dunes, stretching into the yellow sun, whose light spread like a warm blanket. At least two weeks to the Wasteland and the Wards at their end. And then the Anaskar foothills and finally the city itself. Perched on the coast where the legends of the sea would come to life.

Ibranu clomped over. "What are you waiting for, boy?"

He took a breath. "I am pausing a moment, Engineer. I may be heading to my death and I have much to leave behind."

The older man shook his silvery head as he turned away. His squinting eyes and thin face had not been impressed. "By the Sands, they've given me a coward."

"I am not a coward," Ain said. He glanced at Schan, who shrugged. Unbelievable. Already alone and he hadn't even crossed the first dune out of the oasis.

Ibranu did not turn. "Well you're not half the man Majid is, Ain. You might be stronger, I'll admit, but you shouldn't be here. You're not ready."

Now Ain flushed. Where had that come from? He'd barely shared a dozen words with the man over the years. The Engineer had kept to himself, in his home. Especially of late, when he'd been speaking the cursed language with Majid and discussing 'machines' and other strange things. Old books, old stories, myths and legends from Before the Sand.

Information that couldn't be kept to himself. Ain would need to learn it all – how else would they find, and then use, the Sea Shrine to take their vengeance?

Schan watched on without speaking, his eyes drifting around the dunes. Weighed down with a variety of weapons, bow, sword and knife, he was prepared for attack, but barely appeared interested in events directly before him.

Bickering achieved nothing. He had no seniority in age or experience, but as Pathfinder he was to lead them. So it had been for every Search. Jedda's voice thundered in his ears. Lead with your body. Actions speak. Ain stepped forward. "But I am here, Ibranu. Either accept that or return to Cloud Oasis. Alone. See who people think is the coward then."

Ibranu whirled, hands balled into fists. "I won't be turning back, boy."

"My name is not 'boy' as you know, and I am your Pathfinder." He stood his ground despite a thumping in his chest. "Do you understand?"

Ibranu said nothing.

"Then find your own water." Ain started down the dune. He did not turn to see who followed.

*

The first night was one of silence. No-one spoke in the freezing autumn wind, huddled around a fitful blaze, eating the orange flesh of the white-bugs Schan had killed and shelled. Nor did anyone speak as they sought their tents, nor when dawn came and they set out. Not even when Ain broke his word days later, at the first well, where they refilled their water skins. Ibranu only nodded at the water and went back into his own shell. An old, grumpy beetle.

The Engineer travelled with a glower on his face and Schan appeared completely unruffled, still largely absent from proceedings. The only time Ain saw him become animated was at the sight of vultures in the distance, at which he made a rude gesture.

The sun beat down in the mornings and pounded its way into the tent at noon, while he shivered beneath his blankets and furs of a night. What poison had he been given in the form of Ibranu? The man threatened the Search with his behaviour, but most troubling, he threatened their lives. Perhaps not immediately, but once they passed the wards...

In the last few days, near to halfway across the desert, the man had begun to mutter. Even Schan took note.

"He is sun sick?"

"I will speak with him," Ain said, slowing to walk beside the older man. "What troubles you?"

He did not answer at first. Ain waited until Ibranu shook his head. "I ain't crazy. I'm practising."

"The Anaskari tongue?"

"What else?"

Ain kept a retort to himself. "Then I must learn some words, as must Schan."

"Later."

"Why delay?"

"Because I ain't ready, that all right, Pathfinder?"

"For now." Ain rejoined Schan. "He's practising the Anaskari tongue."

"That's a relief."

"I agree." His companion walked with dagger in hand, spinning and catching it, blade flashing in the sun. His tans were stitched with a pattern of scales, Ain held back a shiver at the image it presented, of a snake wrapping the man's legs. "Did you volunteer to come on the Search, Schan?"

"I did."

"Why?"

"I would see the Anaskari fall with my own eyes."

Ain understood. An old dream, of many Medah. One he'd shared. Once. Once he was going to be the greatest Pathfinder and locate the Sea Shrine and single-handedly bring down the Anaskari. Avenge his father, mother and uncle. Avenge his ancestors.

But did that matter now? It would be enough to return home. Sands willing.

Schan pointed. "What is that then?"

The sands were empty and the horizon wavered in bright blue. "I don't see anything."

"A dark shape, faint against the sand. Distant."

"Let's get closer."

A wind slithered the sand as he picked up the pace. The passage of feet, something he'd nearly missed during all the tension with Ibranu, grew louder. He angled toward a low point between the dunes, pausing at a yelping cry. Ahead, outlined against the sky atop a dune, were a pair of sand-fangs. Their mangy forms dropped out of sight at once, but Ain marked them. Any food scraps would have to be burnt or buried deep.

He followed the base of a dune to a wide depression. It stretched the limit of his vision, the sand at its bottom filtered with darker, thicker grains when he bent to touch it. The hum and scrape of feet had not lessened, it was a clamour in his head as the echoes grew. Horses, camels, boots, bare feet, pads, wheels, he heard them all. Each one driving toward the centre of the depression where something shimmered in heat waves.

"I think I see it."

Distant yet, the shapes resolved themselves into spires in rows, rising from the ground. Dark, each shaft had a curve. When he stopped at their feet, Ain whistled.

The spires were bones. Taller than a man many times over, the ribs were twice broader than he could stretch his arms. The beast would have been colossal.

He placed a hand against the surface as Schan and Ibranu circled the rib cage. Hard, like stone, and weathered. He moved to the next one, trailing his fingers across pits and ridges.

"Come see," Schan called.

The warrior was crouched by a smaller rib, still like a tree, Ibranu beside him. Ain joined them, the hum of the path intensifying. Along the base of the bone, words were scratched into the surface, doubtless with knife or even other fragments of bone. "Names." Each hand had some characteristic, either in neatness, height or positioning of letters. Some were horizontal, in the old script, while most played in vertical sweeps and curves – modern Medah writings.

Schan gestured. "Not all."

Where the bone met sand, a complex concentration of chisel marks, their edges precise and deep, peeked above as if from an ocean. He brushed more sand aside. The writing continued around the base and he took several steps, kicking at the sand to reveal more writing. It circled the entire bone.

"What is it for? Is it even in our language?"

Schan shrugged but Ibranu shook his head. "Nothing I recognise."

"Why carve it here, in the middle of the desert, where no-one can see it?"

"Got no idea," Ibranu said. He opened his mouth to continue, but instead slapped a hand against the bone, mouth moving as if reading silently. Just as quickly, he cursed and strode away.

"What's wrong?"

The Engineer did not answer and Ain bent to look at the bone. One of the names was familiar but he could get nothing but a grunt from Ibranu, and a demand to resume their journey. Ain agreed, fascinating as the markings and the bones were, they contributed nothing to the Search.

By nightfall the rib cage of the enormous beast was behind them and his first lessons in the Anaskari tongue had progressed as far as he could manage. Schan had given up on Ibranu's impatient methods, which seemed to be repeating difficult words at the top of his lungs and cursing. Somehow Ain learnt several phrases and words. Still the flat accent troubled him, but faint praise from Ibranu before the fire was doused surprised him.

"We are closing in on the first of the Wards," Ain said before the man sought his tent. "But I've been told so little of them. I know that after the Glass War they grew stronger, what does that mean?"

Ibranu squinted up at the stars, tracing a circular constellation, the Great Eye, with his finger. "No, the Wards are older. When our ancestors got forced from Sekkati and the sea they regrouped and sent another attack, very next summer. Too soon, the fools. It was a damned disaster. Those who didn't die, fled deep into the desert and learned the Ways of the Sand. It was they, their magicians who raised the Wards."

"But the Anaskari raised their own, didn't they?"

"Yes. But theirs was something foul. They twisted our own Wards somehow. Passing them is like gamblin' with your life now. Some get struck dead as they pass, others just enter the Wasteland beyond like nothing was even there. Don't learn much from the few who returned either. Hard to know why."

"That doesn't make sense. How did an entire army pass through, multiple times?"

"We destroyed one," he said. "As had our ancestors, but the bloody Wards grow back, don't they? Something about 'em, I don't understand it. But they don't stay broke. And destroying Wards is costly work."

"You fought in the Glass War. Can we pass them?"

"I reckon so. For you and the Snake, I don't know."

Ain shook his head. Another reminder of how he was underprepared. He should have known all about the Wards and what was beyond. "The Elders did not discuss this with me."

"You should know it already. It's our history."

"I'm not a warrior," he said. "My study was the finding of paths."

"No excuse."

Ain nodded. "True enough. I'll need your help tomorrow, when we face the Wards. And beyond, I know little of the Sea Shrine. Majid mentioned Calling the Ocean?"

He grunted. "You'll get my help, slight though it may be. And as for the Sea Shrine? If we find it I'll make it sing – I'll Call the Sea. Then Sekkati will be free. The Anaskar will perish." He made to duck into his tent.

"Wait."

Ibranu paused, a frown on his face. "What?"

"Back there, with the runes. Why did they upset you? Are we in danger?"

He grinned, showing a gap in his teeth. "No more than before."

"So the runes?"

"Recognised a name is all." He shrugged. "My father

and his Pathfinder. Good night then."

Ain looked away. "Good night."

CHAPTER 10

Bathed and wrapped in new, warm clothing, Notch stood before one of Seto's delicate paintings of the sea, a mug of ale in hand. The water was scattered with gold light, as if something magic rose from the depths. He'd always suspected there was actual gold mixed in with the paint.

Flir sat with Luik, arguing over the right amount of sauce for the slabs of fish. Gone were her street clothes, in their place she wore tunic and pants, both plain in cut and colour. The tunic left most of her arms bare, he'd never seen her express any discomfort from cold, not even with Anaskar's hard winters – which she called 'delicate.' Not that Seto wasn't a fine host; a generous fire lit his silver hair and warmed his private dining room.

"Is everyone at ease?" Seto asked. "Then welcome friends, back to my table. Do enjoy its fruits."

"Nice to be back, Seto," Notch replied, his sentiment echoed by Flir.

Seto sliced into a slab of whitefish with his bone-handled knife, inhaling before he took a bite. "Wonderful,

Luik. How did such a fine cook ever survive beneath the mercenary within you?"

Luik shrugged. "Folk have to eat."

"Indeed they do," Seto agreed. To Notch, he waved his fork, a frown creasing his brow. "Now. Tell me why you've surrounded my establishment with pesky Mascare and clumsy Shields?"

"Weren't clumsy in my day," Luik muttered.

Seto ignored the comment. "For I am not well pleased, Notch. There's even a mask in the common room, sipping at my finest. Tulio tells me he has nearly finished half a bottle of Fire-lemon."

Notch straightened. "I didn't do anything to you, Seto. And it's my name out on those posters."

"Yes, yes, and don't you just look lovely in them," he said. "But your actions, through fault or carelessness, have brought unwanted attention upon me. My affairs are grinding to a halt."

Notch placed his fork down. He didn't want to come between Seto and the man's quest to one day rival the palace for power. It seemed the only thing he'd sought, for years now, but that was enough theatrics. "You'll weather the storm, Seto. And I didn't come here to be interrogated. I came for help, remember?"

"With the unpleasantness near the harbour. About which you cannot recall any details."

"Yes. But I didn't kill her and I want that known here in Anaskar."

His expression softened. "Then you must answer my questions, you silly fool. Tell me your last memory, before waking."

"I was drinking at an inn."

"Which?"

"The Iron Pig, by the harbour." He sighed. He'd been over it before, with the guard, with Flir and within his own mind, dozens of times now. "I was waiting for a job, for a merchant ship sailing to the Far Islands the next day. It was a good contract too. Everything was fine."

"Go on." Seto's expression hinted that the name of the inn interested him.

"Everything wasn't fine," Flir interjected. "You were supposed to be with me and Silenna."

"Next time don't push so hard," Notch said. "I nearly punctured a lung on that rock."

She snorted. "It wasn't that bad. And next time I'll let the archer take out your eye."

"Children, please," Seto said. "Notch, carry on?"

He took another bite of fish. It really was superb, with a subtle tang to the sauce. Luik had a gift. Despite the cooking, it was hard to keep an unpleasant taste from his mouth. Seto had always lorded it over them. A bad habit left over from his time in the palace no doubt. But putting up with his manner was a tiny price to pay for what the man was capable of. "Afterwards I went and walked the streets, and that's all. Hours later, I woke covered in blood beside a dead girl. Her head had been… bludgeoned. People were screaming at me and before I could take half a step, the Vigil hauled me away."

Seto tapped a finger on the handle of his knife. "You walked the streets while drunk? Why? Why not seek your bed? You remain professional, as far as your lifestyle permits. I find that curious."

"My lifestyle?"

"Yes." Seto waved a hand. "You make no apology, as is your right, just as I make none for mine. Don't read things into my musings, Notch. Consider the question.

It will help."

Notch pushed a piece of fish through the sauce. The fat beggar from the street, was he even real? Or something his drunken mind produced from ale fumes? Leaving the inn too. Seto was right. He'd been offered a big job that paid well enough. Pirates barely bothered with the Far Islands, passage would have been easy. Why risk passing out in a gutter?

Or being hanged.

Flir put her knife down. "When did you start drinking?"

"Early. I meant to have just one, but the innkeeper offered me another, if I helped him move some kegs. He had a limp and couldn't do it himself."

Luik shrugged. "Innocent enough, Seto."

"Perhaps."

"I do remember one thing from the street," Notch said. "A beggar I think. He was quite big, so he might be easy to find again."

"We'll go at night," Flir said.

Luik nodded. "The Iron Pig is worth visiting again too."

Notch leaned back. "Sounds good. But I visited the harbour master and a tailor too. What about them?"

Seto shook his head. "Come now, Notch. Don't be dense. The inn is the last place you remember. The innkeeper..."

"You think my ale was drugged."

"Why else would your memory cease directly after drinking there?"

"But why? He's no rich lordling," Flir said.

Luik made a sound of displeasure. "Your food is getting all cold."

Notch shovelled a few more mouthfuls in. It was

growing cold, but still tasted good. "I don't know any enemies who wouldn't rather approach me with steel."

"Cegnar would be direct," Flir said.

"Exactly." The rival mercenary was an unforgiving fellow. Losing out to Notch and Flir when bidding on jobs, as he often did, hardly made him more pleasant.

Seto, whose plate was already clean, stood and moved to stand before the fire. "I feel you've been caught up in something larger. There's talk of a new criminal element working within Anaskar. They would be protective of anything they are doing, now, so early in their attempts to establish themselves in the city." He pursed his lips. "Especially since I have not yet approved of their presence. Now, what did you see in the inn's cellar?"

There was nothing to remember, and yet he couldn't summon any details. Holding a small keg beneath each arm, steps down and... He shrugged. "Nothing. I didn't see anything special."

Flir sighed. "You know they'd just kill him if he saw something."

"Perhaps." Seto was watching Notch closely. "You cannot recall, can you? The colour of the lamplight, the grain on the barrels, the size of the cellar? The quiet, the voices drifting down from above?"

"Not at all." Notch shook his head. "The whole evening is unclear after that."

"Even without the over-fed beggar you saw nearby, something odd in and of itself, I know of four murders within streets of the Iron Pig."

"Murder is hardly uncommon in Anaskar," Flir said.

"All within a week? And each bludgeoned, each a young girl? Granted, three were folk from the Lower Tier, but the last a poor half-blood?"

She hesitated, her expression thoughtful. "I'm not ruling out a strange coincidence."

"No. Someone wants attention on that inn. Ours or that of the palace, more likely."

Flir made no reply. The fire popped as a log fell, a buzz of sparks jumping then fading into the sooty recess of the fireplace.

"Tomorrow we go to the Iron Pig," Notch said.

"And our babysitters out front?" Luik asked.

Seto winked. "Let me worry about them."

CHAPTER 11

Notch paced.

Flir gave him a look. "Stop that, will you?"

He came to a halt behind her. She sat on a box in the abandoned building Seto had found them, feet resting on the window sill. Below, still visible through dusty glass, a busy street flowed. Dock workers and sailors swaggered along the cobblestones, their voices cheerful and brash. When a crowd of them met to talk on a corner, their conversation buried other sounds on the street. Womenfolk hurried back from markets, woven baskets in hand. Carts wheeled crates of fish up from the harbour, silver scales flashing in the morning sun.

Twice he saw a pickpocket at work. One boy got away with the purse he lifted, but the other was given a sound thrashing by his wary mark, then thrown to the stones. No-one helped the lad and it was a long time before he crawled away. The occasional pair of Shields would pass below their vantage point, hands on hilts, eyes roving. Notch didn't blame them. Anaskar grew ever-richer, its trade ships circling half the known world to bring back goods and the rarest luxuries for folk on the First Tier, but beneath it was no different to other cities. Plenty of dark places.

Did he stare down at one now? The Iron Pig was smaller than surrounding buildings, its upper storey built of wood, its foundation stones covered in grime, its sign faded. The door was closed and the windows dark, though he guessed it would open soon. The morning was wearing on.

He turned back to Flir. "I'll gladly stop pacing, if you tell me what's going on."

She frowned. "Luik is getting us something to eat."

"I meant what happened that night? What did I see? Why this place, Flir?" He rolled his shoulders, rubbing at the joints. "And what was the creature beneath the city? Why have four girls been killed here? Something's very wrong." If he'd been sober he might have answers. The girl might even be alive.

"I don't know, Notch. About any of it." She turned to face him. "We'll find out. Then you can clear your name and we can get back to how things should be. You can even go fetch your sword."

"Only if Seto's right."

"He's always right."

"Well I hate this waiting. I should just go in there now."

She shook her head. "Stick to Seto's plan. It's safer."

He resumed pacing. She was right, the old devil was usually too clever to be wrong. Seto had handled the Mascare and Shields simply enough. Earlier, he sent one of his men out as a decoy Notch. Next he slipped Notch, Flir and Luik out the stable gate beneath the cover of a mock brawl, one that spilt into the street in front of the common room.

At the thump of boots on the stairwell he moved to the door, sword drawn. It was plain and the balance didn't feel right, nothing at all like the masterful work his father's sword had been, but it was better than nothing, and more, it was all that Seto had lying around. His men preferred daggers for the most part. "It will have to do, Notch," the older man said. "I'm not running an armoury."

"It's me," Luik said through the door.

Notch let him in, accepting a pastry with thanks. Flir grumbled about it not being enough, but Luik ignored her, biting into his own. "Not bad," he said after a moment. He wore a leather vest and shapeless pants, a flanged mace belted at his side. Notch had once seen the man crush the skull of a full grown rock-fish with a single blow. Until he met Flir, it was the single greatest feat of strength he'd witnessed. "See anything?"

"No-one in or out the front yet," Notch said.

Flir rose slowly. "Hold it, look."

A pair of men in dark cloaks and hoods stopped at the inn's door, giving it a thump. After a short time they were admitted. Twice more, pairs of men in similar garb knocked before entering. Then the door was opened and people, whom Notch took for regular customers, began to drift in, mostly sailors and dock workers.

"This is strange."

"What?" Notch kept an eye on the street.

"All covered up like that," Flir said. "I think they were from Renovar. Newly arrived too."

"How can you tell?" Luik asked.

"They came from the direction of the harbour and one was sunburnt. I saw his forearm when he raised a hand to knock. I had the same problem when I first arrived here."

"You still go red as an apple when you burn," Notch chuckled.

"Well I don't burn as much anymore, do I? The whole world can't have your blasted Anaskari tan, can it?"

Luik suppressed a grin. "Any ideas as to why your countrymen are skulking about in the Lower Tier, Flir?"

She shrugged. "I've been away too long. The Conclave usually stays out of Anaskar's wars and skirmishes. They're more than happy to keep trading with the city of course, where else would they get Fire-lemon and all that fine Anaskari steel?"

"True enough. But something's afoot."

"Maybe we should visit the harbour after the inn."

"Good idea," Notch said. "But you'll have to stay here now. The Renovar will recognise you."

"The innkeeper will recognise you," she returned. "Besides, we need information and we can't risk having you make a scene."

"I can wear a disguise."

"So can I, and Luik can do all the talking. Besides, I know what to look for if the Renovar are up to something. You don't. I speak Renovas, you don't."

Notch folded his arms. "Fine. But don't stay there too long."

Too much damn sneaking and watching. If only he could get out there with a sword. In battle everything was chaotic but clear too. It all came down to survival. To fighting. Body and steel, that was all he had. All he had to worry about. Cloak and dagger and hidden motives were tiresome. Where was an enemy he could strike at, a clear target?

"Just watch for us," Flir said and she pushed Luik out

the door.

Notch went back to the window and resumed pacing. Soon enough Flir and Luik appeared below, cutting through the traffic. Flir let Luik do most of the work in parting the crowd, wrapped in a cloak and hood, keeping her hands within the sleeves.

Once they were inside, Notch stopped pacing and sat on the box, tapping his foot. Time limped forward. He counted carts of fish and crates of spice, these usually surrounded by heavily armed guards. A noblewoman prodded her Braonn servants before her, striding along while the girls struggled with their loads, resentment clear on their faces. He even spotted a pair of Mascare. They moved with ease, people unwilling to get close.

How long was he supposed to wait? Whatever was happening in the Pig was bound to be dangerous. Flir and Luik could take care of themselves but it paid to be careful. If he slipped around the back, maybe there would be –

Something crashed to the floor. He twisted to his feet, hand on his blade.

A trap door lay open in the corner of the room, dust swirling as a flow of children climbed out of the floor. They wore mismatched rags and had determined expressions, skinny limbs flashing as they ran across the room. Notch blinked.

Barely half a dozen had exited the hole when one saw him and gave a shout.

"Wait."

The line bunched in confusion, as those already out of the hole tried to scramble back inside, and those continuing to exit pushed forward. Notch took a step and a girl screamed, shoving at a bigger boy.

"Hush," he said, hoping the sound wasn't noticed from the street. "I don't want to hurt you."

"Go back," one of them shouted.

Even as he dashed forward, the children slipped into the trapdoor. He had to admire their organisation. But one boy had fallen in his haste, and now scurried at Notch's approach, only stopping when he hit a wall. A tiny paring knife appeared in his hand but the other snatched at a small cloth bag, gripping it in white knuckles. Peeking from its top were an assortment of fish bones.

"I'll cut you." He stammered, chest heaving. His face bore a slowly healing graze and his hair was uneven, hacked with a blade perhaps. "I swear it."

Notch raised his hands, resisting the urge to wrinkle his nose at the smell of old fish. "I won't hurt you. I just want to ask a question, and then you can catch up to your friends."

"Don't believe you."

"You can. All I want to know is your name. Will you tell it to me?"

The boy frowned. "Why?"

"So we can talk. Mine is Notch."

His knife didn't waver, still held between them. "I'm Tenaci then. Can I go now?"

"What was everyone doing here?"

"That's secret-is. Kael said we can't tell." He edged toward the trapdoor.

Notch tried a reassuring smile. "I understand. Did Kael say you couldn't talk about the trapdoor?" He fished a silver penny from his purse.

The paring knife dipped. "No. So I guess I could tell you, Mister Notch."

"I'd appreciate that, Tenaci."

The boy's eye never left the coin. "No one knows about it no more, it leads to a passage, except we haven't used it in a while. Sometimes we go the other way when we make deliveries for the witch but Kael said we had to use this one because the Shields have been snooping around our other path."

Notch pretended not to notice the boy's slip. "And this one leads onto the street?"

"Yep, and below it a bit further on. Comes out near the harbour. Kael says it was lucky he found it, but I think the witch told him."

"And the trail you take, does it go into other empty buildings around here?"

"It does but I can't say no more. Kael will give me a drubbing."

"Thank you, Tenaci." He held out the coin but kept his fist closed. "I just have one more question, then you should catch up to your friends. Have you seen me before?"

"You're the man everyone's looking for. The one who killed that rich lady's servant. Seen your poster."

Notch swore and took out another silver piece. "Let's keep this meeting between the two of us then."

"I swear it." He accepted the coins with an ear-to-ear smile and scurried down the hatch. Notch listened to his footsteps ring on metal bars and then fade, before moving back to the window. How long the boy would hold true to his word didn't really matter, Notch would be gone soon enough.

The extra attention was unwelcome, but Tenaci's talk of a witch was curious. There'd been no witches in Anaskar for decades, not since Otonos' father chased them away with violence. Or madness. It left only the

Storm Singers in the palace. Without them, the city was at the mercy of the Sea Beast. Which meant the blood line of a Storm Singer was to be protected at all costs – and they were so few in number, so inaccessible, that few people met one, let alone saw a Storm Singer outside the palace.

He'd been lucky as a boy. Heading home on roads outside the city he saw one. The woman calmed a wild boar with nothing but a song. His father had tried to conceal his awe but Notch simply stared as she rode by on a magnificent horse, surrounded by Shields.

Down on the street, the Iron Pig's door swung open and Flir led Luik from the inn, where they would eventually circle back to Seto's. In case the two were followed, Notch would take a different path. Flir told him he was being paranoid in taking a different route. He snorted. It was his neck, not hers.

Notch slipped down the stairs and exited the building, where he ducked into a side street. He strode along, taking busy streets only when needed, circling markets. Detouring a hole in the cobblestones, Notch waved off a cry from a pair of beggars, dried fish-head charms swinging on twine around their necks.

"Dipping Bastard," one shouted after him. Notch kept a chuckle to himself. The insult was typical. 'Dipping' suggested that he dipped his hands into the wealth confined to the Second and First Tiers.

Tall order for a mercenary.

Ahead, a figure in red robes crossed an intersecting street. Notch stiffened. The man's mask was carved into a deep frown. An unnatural expression. Not one worn by any true Mascare. They were too proud to tolerate imitation. And their whole reputation hinged on the populace being wary, even afraid of them, but not so afraid as not to turn to them for help. Awe through mystery, power through surprise.

Which made the frowning-mask an imposter.

He followed, keeping his distance. Had it been a real Mascare, Notch would have stayed put. They'd hardly bother imprisoning him again. He'd probably be executed on the spot. It was impossible to know how their search was going, though surely it was concentrated in the Lower Tier? And Mascare were not always striding about. Just as often they were in the shadows, dressed plainly, moving quietly.

But there was something afoot with this mask. And where had he gone? Into an alley or a building? He'd only been out of sight a moment. Notch shook his head. Too late to find out now.

He hurried up a wide set of steps. They ran alongside the main thoroughfare, which had been built wide enough to accommodate at least four wagons. Dust, brown leaves and dull scales had built up in the corners of the stairway.

He passed few people on his way up toward the Antico Gate.

A Sea-Priest in his deep blue robes and black gloves smiled at him as he passed, but Notch did not stop. The man's face was sincere but the chain of knuckle bones hanging from his neck was... not right. And if Notch let him, the man would probably talk his ear off. They meant well. Most of them.

The sky darkened as he made his way to the Second Tier. A cold wind rushed in from the sea, whose waves were a distant thump against stone. He kept his hood up, passing beneath an archway that led to the tier's curving wall. There he paused. The parapet offered a wide view of the harbour, ships making their way through the grey waves to dock. More importantly, it concealed him from the gate guards, though the wind buffeted him here. Moderate now, Notch had once seen it whip a man from the stone, during a particularly violent storm.

While there were guards placed along the parapet, those walking the western arm of the tier faced a long route; the wall stretched right around to stop at the mountain face, and Notch would be gone soon enough.

Carved statues appeared at regular intervals, set into the wall – usually bearded Kings, Ocean Gods or mythical creatures with giant teeth. He'd passed the three Kings of the Old Land when he stopped to crouch by a broad figure with a massive hammer. Celno, the Mountain God.

Notch stomped on the paving stones twice, paused and then twice again. After a time he repeated the pattern and the statue began to slide back into the wall, revealing a dark stairwell. Notch started down the narrow spiral, a hand touching the wall, the other checking that his hood concealed his face. Before light from the opening faded, a torch appeared on a landing and he was met by a tall man wearing a belt weighted down with keys, hammers and spikes.

"You're lucky," the man grumbled, pulling a lever set in the wall. "I'm about to seek my rest. 'Aint no-one manning the hole rest of the day."

Notch pulled out a small purse. The price was steep, but Seto could afford it and the privacy such a passage offered was worth every piece. Besides, the guards at the Antico Gate weren't going to let him through without a pass. "Sorry. In the past it was always –"

"Don't bother." He waved one hand, the other giving

the purse a heft. "Just keep on, friend."

Notch continued on until the stairwell ended at a door. Beyond was another set of steps and Notch ascended, calves straining as he spiralled up.

When he finally reached the exit point, sliding a panel open and stepping into another dim room, his muscles ached. He grunted as he pushed the panel back into place, even though it slid smoothly on tracks. A door opposite opened and a gaunt man peered in. "Hurry along then."

Notch joined him in a room where a single lamp sat on a desk. The gaunt man wrote at a ledger, but what caught Notch's interest was the pugnacious hand-crossbow beside it. The men who guarded the passage were many; Notch was yet to see the same man twice in the ledger room, and he'd used the secret path several times over the years. Each time with Seto's blessing, of course. The heavier weaponry was new.

"Trouble?"

"Nothing we cannot look after." The man flicked a quill at another door. "Out there and to your left. Once you enter the street, don't look back. Head for the circular park. Speak nothing of this place."

"Understood."

Notch soon found himself striding along the cleaner streets of the Second Tier. Wind whistled between gaps in the stonework and spots of rain darkened the cobblestones. He soon came across a low stone fence ringing well-kept lawns, the park's fountains trickling. He crossed a bridge that spanned an artificial pond, startling birds. In the depths of rippling water, mosaics of ships with full sails winked up at him, though all bore small chips and recesses where semi-precious stones would have rested. Notch muttered as he passed. To take from symbols and images of Anaskar's own heritage – it wasn't right.

The Queen's Harper was again staked out but Notch skipped the main entry, instead circling back to the wall behind and tapping on the stonework with the hilt of his dagger – another item he owed Seto for. A knotted rope dropped over the wall and he checked the mouth of the alley before climbing to the top.

Flir waited below. "What took you so long?"

"I had to avoid a strange Mascare and gate guards. I took the thieves' passage," he said as he started down.

"Ah," Flir helped him to the ground, her arms taking his weight without effort.

"What was strange?"

"His mask," he said. "It was frowning. I don't know if it means anything. He wouldn't be the first to try impersonating a mask." He headed for the entrance. "What did you learn? Is Seto back?"

"Something I can't figure out. And no, not yet. Luik thinks we should eat while we wait."

"That sounds good." He found a stool in an out of the way corner of the kitchen – only he wasn't out of the way. Luik's undercooks rushed about, knives chopping and pots simmering. A massive haunch of beef turned on a spit and shouted commands came from Luik's second – a man who ushered them up the stairs, hands flapping.

Notch glanced over his shoulder as they climbed. "So tell me about the Iron Pig. What were your countrymen doing there?"

"That's what I can't be sure of."

Notch groaned inside at the steps, though they were few compared to the passage between tiers. "Did they recognise you?"

"I wouldn't have been able to eavesdrop if they did."

He stopped before Seto's dining room door. "And?"

"They were bored."

"What?"

"Well, the new one wasn't. Turns out two at least have been in Anaskar for a good while, sun-burn had just arrived. The others kept complaining about being bored and 'wanting something to happen already.' One of them mentioned how 'slow' the Mascare were. It doesn't make sense. But it might support Seto's theory."

"Maybe. What do they think the Mascare are missing?"

"No idea."

"Did you see anything else?"

"No. The innkeeper wasn't there."

Footsteps creaked on the stairs and Seto appeared. Gone was his vest. In its place he wore patched clothing of a dull, unassuming nature. His hair was damp from the rain but he wore a grin. "We've located your fat beggar, Notch. With no small effort, believe me. But he's waiting for us in the basement. Shall we go down?"

CHAPTER 12

Flames seared her skin.

Sofia shouted as she crashed through the back wall of the fireplace and rolled into darkness, thumping against stone. She scrambled to her feet, the cool air of a passage tingling on her face and hands. A false wall and hidden passage. She exhaled. Of course.

She stepped toward the opening and shouted. "Father, I won't leave you."

A blade flashed through the flames, nicking her hand. She fell back as dark shapes crowded the fireplace.

Run.

Father had Argeon, they would not stop him. She could circle around and meet him when he broke free. Or better, help him break free. Escape first.

Sofia charged into the dark, shouts following. How many pursued her? She'd stand little chance in the shadowy passages. The Mascare knew the hidden ways better. She skidded around a corner and slowed as the light faded, moving forward until her hands slapped against a wall.

She ran on when footsteps followed. A yellow square of light appeared ahead, growing as she charged through a mess of cobwebs. Sticky strands clung to her face and hair and she tore at them, shivering at the brush of tiny legs on her skin. The square of light revealed a fork in the passage, with a slow-burning lamp set on the wall.

Sounds of pursuit still echoed. How close now? Could Father have won free? Sofia clenched her teeth and moved forward. The left fork had no webs.

She'd barely taken a dozen steps into the dark when she tripped, hitting the floor with a grunt. Raging heat spread through her foot and she clutched her ankle. "Gods be dammed." Using the wall for support, she pulled herself up and limped deeper into the darkness. Each step sent a jolt of pain up her leg but she kept on until she hit a door. The handle didn't turn.

"No." She ran her hands along the wall, stopping on a second handle. "Please."

It clicked. Sofia wrenched the door open, passed through and bent to jam her big chisel between the door and floor, thumping the handle with the heel of her hand. Anything might help. She limped on, finding herself in a series of twists and turns. Wherever she was, it was nowhere Tantos had shown her.

A sliver of light appeared ahead. How long had she wandered now? Pursuit seemed gone, but she couldn't risk slowing. Father was in need. She stopped a moment to rest her ankle at the sight, frowning and rubbing her eyes. The light didn't make sense. After so much darkness, she simply stared at the blade-like yellow glow as it sliced into the wall.

It was a door, left ajar. Beyond lay a well-appointed room with ocean views, its warmth slipping into the passage. A glimpse of a bed, sheets unmarred by any crease, was the only other sight she was afforded. Sofia hesitated, hand outstretched. No sounds came from within and no shadows crossed the light. She pushed on the door and exhaled.

Empty.

The bed was unused but a closet revealed rows of clothing in two sizes, almost all white, often silk but many of a cut not fashionable in Anaskar. The visiting Duchess Cera and her daughter Mila. But where were Lady and daughter? Not hard to guess. The open door was clue enough. Limping over to a bedside table, she found a small journal, but it was nothing more than a travelogue.

From the guest rooms Sofia could easily find her way around the palace but it was a risk. The Mascare hunted her. Was she too late to help her father? She refused to consider the alternatives. He'd fought his way free and was safe, on his way to bring Oson and Solicci to justice. And if anyone was left alive afterwards, Sofia would finish them. What she needed was information. And a disguise. What if... a mask. If she could find one and bluff her way through the halls, she might learn something at least, from a pair of gossiping chamber maids or idle guardsmen. Beyond that, she didn't know.

Voices raised in argument approached. Not from the passage, but the chamber adjoining the bedroom. Sofia spun and flew across the room, stumbling as her ankle buckled. She managed to reach a spot directly behind the door before it opened, concealing her. She'd nearly bitten through her tongue from the throbbing in her foot. She controlled her breathing and slid a chisel free, hand trembling. All they had to do was close the door...

"Idiot." A woman shouted. Lady Cera? "How did he get out of the city?"

Solicci replied, voice calm beneath his mask. "We have Argeon. Danillo Falco doesn't matter."

"He does. And so does that little brat of his." She spaced out her next words, as if conversing with an imbecile. "Only a Falco can use Argeon."

"So Danillo claims."

She gave a snort. "He wouldn't lie. And it is no more than you had done with Osani before you had your 'little problem' as you call it."

"We can break the bond with time." A change in his voice. Slight, but enough. He was not confident.

The sound of clinking glass preceded her response. "That I doubt. Catch him and his daughter."

"Of course, Cera. But even without the Greatmask, Danillo is best among us."

"Bah." Something tinkled in a dish – jewellery? "Be prepared to work hard, Solicci."

"I already have men on his trail. He fled south, toward the Bloodwood. If he slips into the Braonn Forests we won't find him."

"That I know. What of the girl?"

"Gone. She's disappeared, doubtless wandering the passages."

"Not good enough. Send more men inside."

"It's not simply a case of more men, the passages are –"

"Shut up." Footsteps crossed the room and Sofia raised her blade. Her hand wavered but she would drive it into Cera's throat nonetheless. The woman deserved it, as did Solicci. Plotting against her family to steal Argeon, to replace their own mask? Injured and undertrained, she might not have much of a chance, but she would try. The silence lengthened and she held her breath.

"What is it?"

"Hush, fool. The door to the passage, come."

Sofia peered round the door, catching a glimpse of Solicci's robes disappearing into blackness. Half-hopping, half-dragging herself into the next room, she headed for the nearest door, passing through a sitting room and into an empty corridor. Her luck held. Finding out more could wait for a safer time. Father was on the run, but alive. And the plot to discredit her family was becoming clearer.

All she had to do was find Argeon and get out of the palace. Nothing more. Sofia almost laughed. But there was no one else. Her father was running, her mother lost to illness, her brother lost to the sea. Last of the Falco? Keep moving.

Her ankle came first. A mask second. Then the rest.

Hallways in the guest wings were quiet, muscled statues of marble watching over them. Sofia made another painful turn, breaking into a sweat. The tapestries here were not grandiose, though they painted the old land and her ancestors as all powerful. A message to visiting dignitaries from other nations. They had no more beauty than a puddle of mud but they were a welcome sight.

It meant she had reached the rooms of Mayla the half-blood healer, a Braonn woman whose ancestors were native to the southern forest, and whose bloodlines had mingled with those of her people. Someone of Mayla's standing wouldn't normally have been allowed such quarters, but long ago the king himself demanded it.

Father had always taken her and Tantos to see Mayla whenever ill. Would the woman risk seeing Sofia now?

She knocked and waited. Still no sight of pursuit. Her ankle ached. Sofia rapped harder. "Healer?" She pitched her voice low. "I need help. It's urgent, I can barely walk."

The door opened. A woman with a careworn face and short grey hair stood with hands on hips. Aside from interlocking circle tattoos on her neck, for the most part she appeared as any citizen of Anaskari with her tanned skin, plain robe and long skirts, but her eyes were an unsettling shade of blue – so light! Sofia had forgotten, how long since she'd seen her?

Mayla's eyes were wide now. "You must leave, Sofia." Her accent clipped the words.

Sofia blinked. "Mayla, please."

"Word has already spread. It would be worth my life to treat you. Even to be seen with you." She began to close the door but Sofia caught the edge.

"But surely you have the king's protection?"

"And what is that worth now?"

"Something, surely?"

Mayla turned away, muttering to someone in the room. She spoke in Braonn, but Sofia caught enough. The Healer wanted someone to leave. A servant?

A young man with a thin beard, dressed in palace livery, appeared beside Mayla. He too was Braonn, and inclined his head to Sofia as he left, a bandage around his wrist.

Once the man was gone, Mayla took her arm, hauling her inside. Aside from the pouches, jars and medical supplies lining the walls, the room was a replica of those given to Lady Cera – save it had no ocean views. Instead, the windows looked into the green grounds with the mountains towering above. "Honestly, you are supposed to be bright," she snapped. "After what your father did,

I have not been called upon to tend the Mascare or the Shields. All know my reputation, yet why have I not been asked? Your Prince won't have a Braonn involved in Anaskari politics. King's Healer or no, I will not risk crossing Oson."

"I'm in pain, Mayla, please. Half the palace just tried to kill me and my father. Can't you help?"

"What have you done?" Her expression did not change.

Sofia lifted her foot. "I twisted it. It hurts to walk."

The woman muttered something in her own language, but did not move. Sofia opened her mouth to ask again, but Mayla waved at a divan with a sigh. "Sit."

"Thank you." Sofia did as she was told. "Will that man speak of me?"

"Of course not." With swift hands the healer got to work, removing Sofia's shoe and strapping the ankle in such a way that brought discomfort but support. Sofia flinched at the swelling, and winced when Mayla probed for signs of deeper damage. The King's Swordfish winked at her from a ring on Mayla's hands, a symbol of his favour. "You need to take care but there's no permanent damage." She moved to a sideboard and took down jars of dull powder. "Be still, I will return with something for the pain."

Sofia lay back. Who could help her? Casa Falco had a holding beyond the city, amongst the foothills, but their manor supported few servants – and even they stayed somewhere in the city with their own families during autumn.

She had her chisels, a row of poisons in her linfa-belt and a small purse of silver, but little else. Her fingers slid over the ridges of a bone charm, a tiny carven oar given to her by her mother.

"Drink this." Mayla stood over her, holding a cup of sweet-smelling sludge. Sofia took the warm cup and sniffed. Not bad. Her first taste was pleasant enough, but the texture was like drinking silky mud. She nearly gagged.

Mayla averted her face a moment, before accepting the empty cup. Was the healer smiling? "That will ease the pain for some hours, but do not push your ankle. It needs rest...though I don't know why I'm saying that. You won't rest it."

"Thank you," Sofia said. She put weight on her injured foot and was pleased to find the wrapping gave enough support that she could walk without too much pain and even make the motion appear normal.

"You must leave now."

"Wait, have you heard anything about my father?"

Mayla walked to the door, frowning over her shoulder. "Only that he escaped and is heading south, for the Bloodwood, as you Anaskari call it."

She ignored the last bit. Mayla was just proud of her heritage, she wasn't angry. "Thank you." Sofia walked, still with some discomfort, to the door and left. The lock clicked behind her and she pulled her hood forward and strode off in the direction of the servant's halls. Mayla was right to be so careful. Oson and Solicci had no honour, they would hardly think twice over silencing a half-blood healer if they deemed it necessary.

In the dimmer, narrow halls used by the servants, Sofia encountered no Mascare, no Shields. A pair of Braonn women broke off whispering at her approach, stopping to bow. Did one glare at her as she passed?

At the Carver's chamber she would find a mask. She crossed a hall, coming to the workshop. The place was quiet, it's embossed door closed but not bolted. The massive chisel, crossed over a Mascare mask, caught the lamp light. Was the chisel sharper now? Sofia slipped inside. If empty, as it ought to be at this hour, she could sneak a mask and be gone.

The familiar rows of chalky benches and stools, each with a folded leather toolset, stood empty, but a soft scraping drifted from a corner. Sofia crept closer. A figure in grey hunched over her tools, occupying the last bench in the furthest row. She worked directly beneath the pegs for completed masks. Many masks had been left to set overnight, the lacquer strong. Inhaling the sharp smell, she could see the hollows for eyes staring back up at her from the bench again. Always the same design, eyes shaped for sternness and a firm, horizontal line for a mouth. No deviations save for size and dimensions of the wearer. To carve otherwise was to break one of the oldest rules, that all masks should reflect most closely, the first Greatmask, Vitahu.

But all that had changed. Now she was not Successor, not even Carver.

Slipping away with a mask would be impossible now. She could sneak up to the carver, but how could she take the mask? Not by force – what if it was one of her friends? Sofia wove her way across the floor. Even with her injury she managed to avoid scraping the few pieces of chipped bone on the ground. Whoever had swept did a poor job. Two rows away now, the woman's slender back was twisted and her elbow moved in slow, precise movements. Working on the eyes. Sofia understood the concentration, such focus would aid her now. If she could reach the mask on the end...

Two steps from the woman and Sofia stumbled, ankle

faltering.

The carver spun, chisel raised, but lowered it as Sofia pushed herself level with a bench.

"Sofia?"

"Pietta."

Her friend gaped. She had dark rings beneath her eyes and when she hopped down and hugged Sofia her shoulders shook. "What are you doing here?"

"I need your help, Pietta. I need a mask." She spoke into Pietta's hair, then pulled back. "Oson is after me."

"I know. Everyone's looking for you, Sofia. They said Lord Danillo tried to kill the King, I can hardly believe it."

"It's not true, Pietta."

Her expression wavered. "They showed us all the Medah man."

"Please. You're my friend. My father would never plot against the king. You know that."

Tears came to her eyes. "I do. I just... what do you need?"

"Food and water. I'll find a mask." Sofia paused. "You're a good friend, Pietta."

"You too." She smiled and ran to a rear door, closing it behind her. Sofia checked the nearest mask. It didn't fit, and the fumes were so strong her eyes watered. Replacing it on a peg, she tried the next, and another, discarding three before finding one small enough. It wasn't a perfect fit but it was nearly dry. The lacquer was still sticky to touch but at least it didn't make her want to vomit.

Time passed. Sofia shifted her feet, trying to keep the muscles warm. What was taking so long?

Finally the door opened and Pietta stumbled forward. Two Mascare followed the carver into the room and advanced. They did not speak. Sofia stiffened, catching a glimpse of Pietta's tearful face as the girl slumped to her knees, and then the crimson Mascare filled her vision.

She fell back, shoving a stool at the nearest. The man dodged. Sofia tipped another and another, backing through the chamber as she did. Each obstacle was deftly avoided.

The entry was too far away. In her injured state she'd never make it, she had to fight and all she'd been taught were the most basic attacks. What chance did she have against two trained Mascare? Leaving a bench between the two as best she could, Sofia found herself herded toward a corner. Keeping both at bay was impossible, same as attacking one without the other taking advantage.

Sofia heaved the bench at them and broke into a uneven run. One was tangled but the other Mascare swooped after her. Before she'd covered half the distance a hand caught her shoulder, spinning her around.

The Mascare grunted as he tore the mask from her face. "There. Now don't move, understand? We won't hurt you if you cooperate."

She kicked his shin. He cursed but did not let go – instead he crashed to the ground as a stool smashed the mask from his face.

Pietta, eyes wide, stood staring at the motionless Mascare, the stool in her hands. "Go," she shouted when she looked up.

The second Mascare lunged for Pietta, knives out. She fell back, deflecting blows with her stool even as she was driven into a corner. Back against the wall, Pietta flailed at him with the seat. The Mascare kicked the stool from her hands and slashed down at her. The blades left deep slices in her forearms and she screamed.

Sofia tore a chisel free and leapt after him, driving

the blade into his back with a shout. He dropped to his knees. Sofia stumbled back, mouth hanging open as the Mascare crumbled to the stone floor, breath rasping.

"Go, Sofia, go." Pietta pushed her with bloody hands and Sofia's ankle wobbled.

Her stomach lurched and her hand shook. The man was dead. Dead. "I've killed him."

"They'll kill you if you stay."

The first Mascare groaned.

Pietta pushed Sofia toward the door. "Pietta, what will you do?"

Her friend rubbed her arms, smearing blood over her robe, turning in a half circle. "I don't know."

"Then tell them the truth."

She turned back. "What?"

"That I killed him. They can't blame you."

"I'll try."

Sofia held Pietta's eyes a moment then ran. She stumbled at the door, pulling herself into the hall where she sucked in a breath and clenched her muscles. Why couldn't she stop trembling? She'd killed a man. Driven her chisel into his back.

She retched.

Ahead, a small group of Shields skidded into view, swords drawn. Sofia forced herself down another corridor, biting her lip as she tried to sprint. The effects of Mayla's medicine had not worn off but the air tore at her lungs and her limbs were too heavy. Doors blinked by and a sleepy looking serving boy threw himself against a wall when she passed.

Tearing into a new corridor, she hit a wall of steel, sprawling on the floor.

Captain Emilio towered over her, jaw set.

She scrambled back. "Emilio?" He helped her up, but she shook his arm off. "No."

"Please, my lady. Let me help."

"Like you helped my father?"

His eyes glistened. "Oson would have killed me had I tried."

It was the truth, but she shook her head. "We needed you."

"You have me now." Footsteps echoed. "Quickly." Emilio dragged her down the corridor, boots thumping. She kept pace, gritting her teeth at the pounding. When Emilio finally tore open a door and pulled her inside, she cursed in the darkness as her foot caught the door frame.

"Hush." Somehow, his deep voice matched the dark.

Sofia steadied her breathing. Her ankle throbbed, small mercy that it wasn't being pummelled anymore. Emilio's grip was firm. Would they find her? She had one of her small chisels belted over her Carver's robe, hidden beneath the Mascare red. Little comfort, even with Emilio at her side.

Ocean Gods, what was happening?

The clamour of the Shields passed and Sofia waited until their footsteps and shouts disappeared. Emilio exhaled, long and slow. Sweat and steel mingled with leather in the room.

"What now?"

He let her go. "Now I take you to safety. Will you follow me?"

"Yes."

A tiny light bloomed. He held a snake's lantern, twin, narrow points of light hitting the floor. Furniture loomed but she kept close to Emilio's back, his orange tunic appearing a bloody hue in the dark, seeping from beneath his silver breastplate.

Blood was everywhere tonight.

He led her through the doors and rooms and passages without changing the light. The night was heavier here, so near to places and people she assumed were sleeping, than in tunnels she'd limped along alone. Or perhaps it was the light itself, so small.

Sounds of alarm were gone now, but she wasn't safe yet.

"Where are we going?"

"To the palace walls."

She stopped. "I need to take back Argeon."

Emilio did not halt. She hurried after him as he spoke, keeping his voice low. "You cannot. You are injured and alone, the Greatmask stays in Cavallo hands for now."

"Couldn't you try to –"

He stopped. "I have learnt the bitterest of truths, though I should have seen it sooner. Prince Oson thinks me a stumbling block between him and his ailing father, and the throne. I can do nothing. But I can save you, Sofia." The captain resumed walking. "Come, I have someone waiting."

"I feel like I'm abandoning Argeon." And Pietta.

Emilio's voice was calm. "You must if you are to live, if you wish to help your father. I know that none but Casa Falco can work with Argeon. I will get you out of the palace, the rest is up to you."

It was more than she'd expected. Emilio risked everything by helping, and without him she'd be dead or enslaved. He could get her out of the palace, more than she'd manage alone and injured. And she was alone. Mascare and Shields roamed the halls and her father was miles away, heading for the Bloodwood. If he was alive.

Hundreds of years of Falco history and she was too weak to reclaim it.

If she could escape and find help, real help, she had a chance.

"Who's waiting?"

"The Water Rat."

Sofia strode after him, the pain in her foot forgotten. Water Rat? How could someone with such a name be expected to help her?

CHAPTER 13

The beggar was a large man. He overflowed the stool he'd been tied to, a blindfold cutting into his head. He appeared as Notch recalled. A sullen expression. Dark hair, matted with blood and spotted across his stretched tunic. The single torch burning in the glistening basement cast more shadow than light. Supplies and crates of Firelemon hulked.

Seto gestured to the man, who'd raised his slumped head at their entrance. "Is that he? He was begging not far from the Iron Pig."

Notch nodded.

"Very well. What is your name, beggar?" Seto asked.

"Vinezi." His voice was tired. "Where am I, then? What do you want?"

"We wish to know why you're impersonating a beggar?"

Vinezi shook his head. His wide mouth was turned in a frown. It gave him a frog-like appearance. "I am a beggar."

Seto signalled with a twitch of his finger. Notch drove his fist into the man's stomach, twice in quick succession.

Vinezi wheezed and coughed.

"Thank you, Vinezi," Seto said when the beggar stopped. "I do so like to hear a man lie. Would you like to change your answer?"

"Gods take you," he snarled.

Notch delivered more blows, varying his target but steering clear of the man's head. For now. That was the way Seto preferred to start. That didn't make it easier and he swallowed a grimace, but it needed to be done. Notch had started to sweat when Seto raised a hand. He stopped. Vinezi was breathing hard and had cried out several times. It must have been worse, not being able to brace for the blows.

"Once more. Who paid you to pretend? What are you watching? Did you kill Lady Cera's servant? Take a moment to think."

"You got bones for brains?" he rasped. "I'm a beggar, that's all. Never heard of her."

"My dear?"

Flir stepped into the light. "Yes?"

"Fetch my needles will you?"

"Certainly." She left.

Notch pointed to Vinezi's shoes. "Look at his boots. They're only muddy, not old."

"My eyes aren't as good as yours in this light, but that he has shoes at all is a surprise."

"Stole 'em."

Seto raised an eyebrow. "Of course you did." He turned to Notch. "No matter. If he doesn't talk, we can simply kill him and dump the body – we might need help with the actual dumping – and then we'll pick up one of his friends."

"Good."

Vinezi shook his head. "I ain't afraid."

"That comes later." Seto's voice was very casual. Notch rolled his eyes. His friend was putting it on a bit heavy.

The beggar's chest strained against rope as he breathed, unable to make other movements. When Flir returned, the man was sweating, though the room was by no means warm.

"Ah, my needles."

"Needles?" Vinezi sneered. "You think needles will make me talk?" His bravado was telling. Vinezi was no beggar.

"That or kill you, as I plan to gradually drive them into your skull. Through your ear."

At Seto's words Vinezi flinched, wrenching his torso around and twisting his head away. Flir moved over to take his head, her grip light. Vinezi's muscles strained, bulging in his neck, but he couldn't move.

"Be sure to hold him still, dear."

"He's not going anywhere."

Seto chuckled. "True enough." From a small case, he withdrew a needle that spanned his open hand. Trailing it along Vinezi's shoulder then up along his neck, he rested it on the man's lobe. Notch was familiar with the routine. Few men had resisted the needle over the years. For most, it ended as Seto placed the point just inside the ear.

"Are you certain you have nothing to say?"

Vinezi's chest pumped in short, shallow breaths and he gave a shout. "Stop, stop. I'll talk."

Notch breathed his own quiet sigh of relief. Listening to a man screech until he died, in spasms on the end of a needle, was not a sound he wanted to recall.

"Begin." Seto removed the needle and nodded to Flir, who released the beggar's head.

Vinezi slumped against his bindings. "I'm paid to watch for people, people my masters might want to use. They need me to appear as a beggar so I'm not noticed."

"Hmmm. And what do they want to use people for?"

"They never tell me, but I get a different description each day. Sometimes it's a woman, sometimes a man. Young or old, it always changes."

"And who are your masters?"

Vinezi hesitated, squeaking when the needle grazed his cheek. "I don't know. Their accents are strange. I overheard them talking about the palace, when they noticed me they stopped. Started talking in their own language."

Notch glanced at Seto. "How many are there?"

"Six, maybe seven. I've seen them at the Iron Pig. Only one of them talks to me. He's the shortest, maybe their leader. 'Thalik' the others call him."

Footsteps interrupted and a man in dark clothing appeared. Tulio, Seto's second in command, gave no greeting, only leaning to his master's ear, whispering a moment and slipping out. Seto pursed his lips a moment. Notch waited, exchanging a glance with Flir, who rolled her eyes. Seto rarely shared such messages. To hear Flir tell it, the reason was simple – the old man loved his secrets.

"I must go for a time. Find out whatever else you can," Seto said as he swept by. "I will leave my needles. Finish up as you see fit."

Notch shook his head at Seto's exit. Loved his theatrics too.

"Think he knows any more, or should I just snap his neck now?" Flir said, flexing her fingers around Vinezi's face. Notch suppressed a groan. Not Flir too.

"Let's hear the rest, beggar."

"That's all. They don't tell me anything."

Flir turned the man's head from side to side, gently. "Find something."

"Well, there is one other thing." His face was pale. "I saw them speaking with the Mascare once. Inside the Pig. Wasn't for long and I didn't hear what they were saying."

Flir stopped and Notch pressed the man. "You heard nothing?"

"Nothing. One of them rushed me out of the room."

He frowned. Were the Mascare investigating or involved with the Renovar? Something much larger than the murder of a single, or even four, unfortunate girls was happening in the Lower Tier and he was in the thick of it now. And it didn't sound cheerful.

Time to gamble. He pulled the blindfold down, ignoring Flir's objection. "Have you ever seen me?"

Vinezi squinted a moment. "You're wanted for that murder. On the poster."

"Yes I am. What do you know about it?"

"Think I saw you that night but I wasn't paid to look for a man then, so I wasn't watching for you."

"What was I doing? Where did you see me?"

"Stumbling around by the harbour, near the big ships. You looked pretty happy."

"Was anyone with me?"

"No."

Notch replaced the blindfold and waved to Flir.

She joined him at the entrance to the basement, where he lowered his voice. "I doubt he knows anything else."

Flir shrugged. "That might be true, but something isn't right about him. I can't figure it out. He's no beggar."

"I agree." He glanced at the large man, mute in the

torchlight. "And what do you think about his claim that the Mascare are involved in whatever's going on there?"

"No surprise I suppose. They stick their noses into everyone's business."

"So do they know something about what's going on there?"

"Or are they involved?"

"That doesn't match their reputation."

She shrugged. "There's bad apples in every basket."

Notch motioned to the prisoner. "Well, what do we do with him then?"

"Dump him in the harbour."

"Flir."

"Seto will be mad."

"I'm not going to murder him, Flir."

"Fine. Why don't Luik and I drop him off at the prison? Stuff his pockets full of stolen goods or something."

"He could lead them back to me, he's seen my face."

"That's not my fault, you did that."

"I needed to know."

She shrugged slender shoulders. "Well, everyone's seen your face, it's on every other street corner. And Vinezi doesn't know where he is right now. Nor will he. He can't lead anyone anywhere."

"It feels like a risk."

"The harbour isn't all that far."

"Flir, I said no."

She gave him a playful shove, which drove him back a step. "You're a soft-hearted man, Notch. Unless it's on the battlefield of course."

"Take him then. Make it look good."

"I know. Where are you off to then?"

"Off to?"

She sighed. "Notch. You're planning something stupid. I know."

"I'm going back to the Iron Pig."

Flir folded her arms.

"It's no good me simply sitting here doing nothing. I won't go inside, but I'll be watching the building."

Flir held his gaze a moment. "You be careful."

"Every step."

*

He chose a different vantage point, this one on street level, in an empty doorway that gave him a clear view of the Iron Pig. It wasn't enough to lurk across the street behind a dusty window.

Fewer people passed this late in the day, the sun tinting the stones orange and casting purple shadows. Almost beautiful, though the stench of rotting garbage mixing with the harbour marred the effect. If only his hood was a mask as well. Or lined with smelling salts from the desert.

A pair of labourers, their overalls dark with grime, spoke in voices fuelled by drink. One fellow reeked of rosemary oil, the glint of it on exposed forearms a clear sign that his home or place of work was plagued by mosquitoes. Notch understood. He'd stayed in rooms near standing water, trapped between stone landings and street puddles, and it wasn't pleasant.

"No. I say he won't last the week," said the oiled man.

"You're wrong, Bac. The king will live for another month. More." He punctuated his words with arm waving.

Bac made a rude gesture. "Bah. You're thicker than a tree stump. The Prince says he's been keeping his illness secret for a whole year now."

"So he's not in a hurry, is he?" The other man's voice faded as they turned a corner. Notch liked the second man's odds. The sooner the old bastard shuffled off the better.

Notch swivelled his head. At the opposite end of the street, which ran into an intersection where a rundown warehouse sat with gaping windows, a small group of Shields strode along the cobbles, their boots loud. He kept his head down and waited for them to pass.

When the door to the Iron Pig opened and a man stumbled away, Notch straightened. The drunk was followed by a Mascare. A chance to get some more answers? Notch had tangled with the Mascare before and they deserved their reputation. Superior in close quarters, but if he could manage to surprise the mask...

He hurried across the street, keeping a fair distance from the mask but steadily closing the gap. The crimson robes fluttered round a corner as the Mascare entered an alley. Notch paused to draw his sword.

He stepped into the darkness and confronted nothing but emptiness. Two boarded up doors and a dead end, a pile of rotten fish heads and a hook placed above one of the doors. He checked each one, kicking at an apple core as he did. Both locked up tight. "Where did you go?"

"Found him."

Four men with drawn weapons crowded the mouth of the alley. One, the tall man who led them, sneered. Gaps winked between his teeth. He held a hooked blade, pointing it at Notch. "You shouldn't have come back here, Notch. Stupid. Very stupid."

Notch hefted his blade. "If I'd known you'd be here I would have stayed away, Cegnar." He spat. "I didn't think you'd stoop to this."

The man shrugged. "We're mercenaries."

"But not dogs."

"It's a very nice reward, Notch. What do you expect me to do? Now put your sword down and we'll make it easy, eh?"

"No."

Cegnar waved the weapon and his men charged. "We need him alive, hear?"

Notch remained still, sword ready. How long since he'd taken on four men at once? The narrow confines slowed them, but the first man broke from the press and swung his short sword with a snarl. Notch caught the blade on his own and dropped the man with a kick to the groin. Crouching beneath a slash from the second mercenary, Notch tore a knife from the fallen man's belt and drove it into his attacker's stomach.

Springing up, he shoved the wounded man into Cegnar and used his cloak to turn a stab from the third man, tangling the blade. Pain sliced the inside of his forearm. Too slow. Notch lashed out with his free arm, sword tearing through the man's throat, a spray of blood black in the air.

A grunt of effort from behind.

He spun, switching sword hands to catch Cegnar's wrist. The man slammed him into the wall and Notch growled. He dropped his weapon and caught the man's other hand as it snaked toward a dagger on his belt.

"Give up, Notch."

Notch squeezed Cegnar's wrists, then drove his head into the man's mouth. The mercenary roared, stumbling back. Blood covered Cegnar's chin and his lips were split. Another tooth was missing. Notch bent to snatch his sword as Cegnar leapt forward, weapon raised. Notch rolled, air from the blade whistling, and scrambled to his feet. Off balance, Cegnar tried to turn, but Notch was too fast, whipping his sword across the back of the man's neck. The mercenary slumped to the cobblestones without a sound.

"I wouldn't," Notch warned the man he'd kicked, who had now found his feet and stood locked in place, eyes wide. "Help your friend," Notch added, pointing his gleaming blade at the fellow who moaned, knife hilt protruding from his gut.

Notch turned to leave, wrapping his arm with part of his cloak.

"He's dying," the surviving mercenary cried.

"Yes, he is." Notch didn't bother turning back.

CHAPTER 14

Emilio paused at an ancient door heavy with bolts, fitting a key to its lock and motioning for Sofia to wait. Pale light coloured the stone beneath the door and a chill stung her hands and feet. She tasted salt in the air and distant water crashed against stones somewhere beyond. It was the third such door on their escape, each requiring a different key. The respite was welcome. They'd trudged through the secret ways of the Mascare for hours, or so it seemed.

Her ankle still throbbed. An ache gnawed at her stomach and her lips were dry, hours since her last meal and not even water to fool her body into thinking it had eaten. She swallowed her hunger when Emilio finally opened the door. Moonlight hit the white walls of low buildings crowded near the parapets of the Second Tier. Far below, the ocean crashed against stone but she heard Emilio, even with his voice pitched low.

"This is a fair part of the Second Tier but be on guard."

"I will."

"Head four streets over, to a cobbler at an intersection.

Knock on the rear door. Tell whoever answers that you have been sent by the Little Bird."

Emilio was the Little Bird? She could have laughed but her body wasn't willing. Everything ached, stung or weighed down on her. "Thank you, Captain. I'm in your debt now. Casa Falco too."

He smiled. Her cheeks warmed and she glanced away.

"No. It's a debt only partially paid to your father." He paused. "And by my honour, I would see you safe. Go now."

Sofia nodded but managed only a few steps before her legs gave way. Blinking from the cold cobblestones, she tried to stand but her knees wouldn't bend. Her vision spun. "Oceans."

Emilio scooped her up and she exhaled, relief soothing her limbs. The stars bounced as he walked along, hopping up from behind the rooves. The captain appeared to be in two or three places at once too. Holding her, but also appearing above her or off to the side. Sofia fought to keep her eyes open, stirring when she heard a thumping and then a voice, not Emilio's, speaking with some surprise.

And then the stars were gone and she was somewhere darker, with naught but a single yellow star. Gentle hands placed her onto a bed. Voices conferred a moment, before water was held to her lips. She gulped it down. It was better than any wine she'd had at the royal table. Someone told her, "Slowly" and she obeyed. The room had slowed its spinning and she turned away when something bright flared.

"Can you return?" someone asked.

The reply was lost in smothering dark.

*

Sofia jerked upright. A blanket slipped from her torso, revealing her carver's robe. Beneath the rest of the blankets her foot had been re-strapped. She shivered. Who had tended to her injury and where was her Mascare robe?

She needed a weapon.

The room was largely unadorned but clean, a dresser with a mirror stood opposite her cot. On the floor beside her was a cup of water, which she drank, and her red robes in a neat pile, half-covered by the blanket. She touched the robe. Clean and dry. Even her small chisels and her linfa-belt sat on top. "Gods, how long was I asleep?"

"Too long, girl." A tall man appeared in the doorway and she jumped. Dressed in a patched tunic and pants, he would have hardly been threatening, if not for the gaze that rushed out from deep sockets. She shivered when he spoke no more, only staring at her, expression thoughtful. Could she reach a chisel before he moved?

"I thought I was alone. Are you the Water Rat?"

"Of course."

"Then I must thank you for helping me."

"You should thank Emilio, it is he who puts his life in jeopardy to help you, girl," he said with a small smile. His speech was refined, unlike the street slang common from guards at the palace.

Sofia frowned. She was no 'girl.' She was to be Successor. Her House was the oldest house next to the king's, she was... she was alone. In a strange place. With no-one to help her. Father was gone and her future too, unless she could take it back. "Is the captain safe?"

"I believe so."

Good. "Emilio said you could help me."

He came closer and she realised he was older than he first appeared. His silvery hair was at odds with his stride, but he was still much older than her father. "For a price, I will do more than help you. I will both protect and restore you to the palace, Sofia Falco. I will ensure you are free of the insufferable Oson. You will have the Greatmask Argeon back and your father will be free to return."

"Who are you to promise all that?" She was unable to keep her eyebrows down. If he was making such unlikely claims, what would he want in return? "Do you know where my father is?"

"No, I don't know where your father is, sadly. And I don't claim it will be simple, but yes. I can arrange the rest. No doubt you miss your Greatmask already."

"I miss my father."

"Of course."

"And your price?"

"Your help. Through the power and influence of your eventual position as Successor."

"I can't guarantee that. Look at me. I'm hunted, my family scattered."

His smile returned, as if her acceptance was a foregone conclusion. "Entrust that to me. Will you accept?"

"If I did, what would you have me do with my influence?"

"For one, you must give me a ship. When you are restored."

"A ship?"

"A certain ship. The king's ship."

She couldn't stop a frown. An odd request. The Swordfish was the finest vessel in the Anaskari fleet, but it was hardly an object a thief could tuck away beneath a bed. "But why? And why do you think I'd be able to arrange that?"

"You'll find a way." His voice suggested the matter were of no consequence. "As to why, that I will keep to myself. Have we an understanding?"

"That's truly what you desire?" Sofia met his eyes. Resolve simmered beneath his casual attitude. There was more to his request than the ship. This man, this so-called Water Rat, was more than his name suggested. No simple thief. No merchant. And he didn't posses the bulk of a soldier. How had Emilio crossed paths with this man? From his speech, Sofia placed him in one of the Houses. But his attire, and surroundings, even his smell, suggested something else.

"Which house are you from? I would know with whom I deal."

"No house. I represent myself only." He waved a hand, as if to dismiss the whole notion. Or the question. What exactly was he holding back? It didn't matter. She couldn't afford to turn his offer down. By his face, it was unlikely he would even permit her to do so. Emilio trusted him and her father trusted Emilio. Was that enough? "Do you know my father?"

"We have met several times over the years. Our business was always mutual."

"So you claim."

"Indeed."

Could she be certain of him? "Very well, Water Rat. We have an understanding. You protect me, help me reclaim my place and retrieve Argeon and I will ensure you are given the king's ship in return. In addition to my help when I am Successor." She held out her hand to seal the arrangement, in the style of the street, something she'd seen soldiers do.

He clasped her hand after a moment's hesitation, as if such a gesture had not occurred to him. Definitely not born on the street then. Sofia smiled. "Partners."

"Partners."

*

Sofia chewed her bread and cheese, then sipped some of the lemon tea. It was not close to the quality or variety of food she was accustomed to, but more welcome than any banquet she'd attended. She was escorted, still limping, from the house to a carriage, its horses flicking their manes in the high sun. She wore bulky clothing and hood to conceal both identity and gender. The curtains remained drawn the whole time and the Water Rat said little, only that they were travelling to another part of the Second Tier, where he had access to more resources. If his manner was brisk, at least he was careful.

When the carriage rumbled to a halt, she stepped out before a three storey inn, but its true size only became apparent upon entering the common room. It could have seated near to a hundred patrons along its benches, tables and stools, all polished to a high shine. A stage for musicians was flanked by statues of the Ocean Gods.

Upstairs there must have been over two dozen rooms, though the inn appeared empty. Strange for noon. She'd seen no-one else in the building Captain Emilio took her to either. No servants, no visitors, no-one – in fact she'd only seen the one room. Had the Water Rat prepared her meal? Did he have the building waiting on standby for whatever he was involved in? Unsettling.

She could leave.

Sofia bit her lip. No. No matter his habits or his

business, no-one else was helping her. She would stay put, a little longer at least. Her ankle seemed stronger. For now, she would observe her saviour and his so called resources, then decide what to do.

It had to be better than cowering in the palace. And she still had her chisels.

"Why is no-one here?"

"Someone is watching my inn."

"But how can you afford to simply close?"

"For repairs. Did you not notice the sign on the way in?"

"I was surprised. It's almost grand."

"Thank you." He gestured to a stair opposite the long bar, its reflective surface dotted with clean glasses. "Why don't you take the room up the stairs and at the end. To the left. I'll be with you shortly, little Falco."

She frowned. Little Falco indeed. Sofia climbed to the upper storey, clutching the pack into which she'd folded her belongings, and counted doors, "One, two, three..." As she'd guessed, the inn had many rooms. The last door opened to a simple space; bed, chest and basin being its salient features. No window, but when she placed her pack on the chest and checked the sheets they were cool and clean beneath her palms.

"Sofia?"

A dark-haired man stood in the door. Perhaps a little younger than her father, he had close-cut stubble and an expression of concern on his face. A sword hung from his belt, his worn clothes gave him the look of a guard or mercenary. A bit of white – bandages, peeked from beneath a sleeve. She kept her hand near the chisel hidden beneath her clothing, eyes straying to the blade belted at his own waist.

"How do you know me?"

"Seto, ah, the Water Rat, said you need help? I'm Notch." He eyed her robe. "I didn't think he'd welcome palace folk, to be honest."

Her voice cooled. "Palace folk?"

"Well, you're hardly 'one of the people'."

"And that makes you what?" She snapped. Good. Stay angry. Stay on guard. "A thief? A mercenary?"

He stiffened. "Mercenary."

"Wonderful."

"And what did you need help with then?"

She threw up her hands. "It matters little. And I don't need help, thank you." What she needed was to find her father. He was probably still hiding in the tangled Bloodwood, hunted by Oson and Solicci's lackeys. Or by hostile Braonn.

No matter. None could match him, no man, no Mascare. Even if they found him, he would stop them. He would stop them as he always had. And yet...

"Wait, Notch." She stopped him from leaving. "What do you know about Bloodwood, to the south?"

Notch opened his mouth but made no sound. She could see his mind switching things around. He hadn't expected a question. Father taught her better. Never become predictable, it will keep those around you off-balance. Notch's brow was furrowed. "I've travelled it a few times."

She swallowed. "Maybe you can help me after all."

"I can try."

"I've heard it told that the forests are dangerous. That travellers who leave the paths are never seen again. That the trees within can drain a man of his blood and that the Braonn ambush good Anaskar folk."

"Good Anaskar folk?"

"That's what I've heard."

"I remember hearing all the same stories as a child and again when I first passed through the forests. They're lies. We travelled by day only and while we did keep mostly to the paths, no-one had their blood stolen by trees. Nor were we attacked." He paused. "Though we did lose one of our party. A boy."

"What happened?"

"He was reckless but cheerful. He used to juggle with whatever he could get his hands on. Stones, fruit, coins, anything."

"Was he killed?"

"I don't know. One morning he was simply gone. Perhaps he fled, tired of the life of a hired sword. We never found out, but no other strange thing happened. We all emerged unscathed. The Braonn weren't always friendly, but they let us pass. On other trips, nothing went amiss."

Sofia sat on the bed.

His expression softened a little. "You shouldn't worry. Everyone knows that Danillo Falco is –"

"That doesn't help, you know." How did he know who she was? What was the Water Rat doing, spreading her name around to anyone in the inn?

"Then many apologies, Lady Sofia." Notch muttered as he left.

He was just a mercenary. He didn't understand what she'd lost, didn't understand how dire things had become. She opened the chest and packed her Mascare robes away, leaving her Carver's robes on. She'd lost the mask during her escape, so only her belt and chisels were next. Two remained, now that one of her large ones were stuck in the back of some Mascare, another jammed beneath a door in the ways. She shuddered. How had the chisel become an implement of death, something with which to steal blood, not to carve bone?

She stood. Notch shouldn't know who she was. Even someone as prominent as her father was not widely known by sight – only by name. Certainly not by the populace. And now the Water Rat was sharing her identity about like a dockside whore. Safety through Secrecy. Silence is Safety. She'd heard Tantos chant it a thousand times. It only held up if everyone followed it.

The people of Anaskar would one day learn that their city was to have a female Protector, that was nothing she could control.

But the people should never know her face.

Storming into an empty hallway, Sofia strode to the top of the stairs and fell back when a short woman and a hulking man started up. The man smiled, green eyes warm, but the small woman, her features fine, skin pale and hair a whitish blonde, only raised an eyebrow. A Braonn man. And a Renovar woman from across the sea. Sofia knew of various envoys and Ambassador Lallor from the palace, but as a Carver, never had occasion to speak with either.

She moved aside to let the pair pass, but a voice called her name before the two reached the upper floor.

The Water Rat waited in a doorway across from her own. "Join us."

"Join who?"

"Us." The woman grinned as she passed. Her accent was slight, as if she'd been in Anaskar a long time. She wore a sword with ease, as though she knew how to use it.

The big man nodded, holding out a large hand. "I'm Luik and that's Flir," he said. "Seto told us about you. Welcome to the Queen's Harper."

"Ah, pleased to meet you."

"And you, my lady," Luik replied. "I guess you've already met Notch."

Sofia could only nod as she trailed along. Who were these people? Who else lurked behind closed doors? It seemed only the common room was closed. But what was important was whether they could help her. And for the Water Rat to stop sharing her secrets.

"I hope you were right to trust this water rat, Father."

CHAPTER 15

"Troubling things may be afoot at the Iron Pig," the Water Rat, or Seto, as the others called him, said as he lowered his cup. The dining room was quite plain but warm at least. "First, what do we know? Then, what I propose we do about it."

Sofia hadn't touched her wine, but she'd made a considerable dent in the roasted potatoes and beef – a delicacy, layering the gravy. It was near to as good as anything she'd had in the palace. Despite her misgivings, she'd almost laughed when Luik told her he'd cooked their meal, and he was beaming at her over the candles now, obviously pleased that she was enjoying it. Both Flir and Notch had empty plates, having already finished up. A cup of the heady Fire-lemon sat before Flir but Notch had no mug. From Seto, she knew about their quest to restore Notch's dubious honour – after his possible role in the death of Lady Cera's handmaiden – and something of the events leading up to the meeting. What she didn't know yet, was how or even if they could help her.

"We know that four young people have been murdered

near the Iron Pig and that Notch has been implicated in one of them," Flir said.

"And that there are at least six Renovar staying there. A man named Thalik may be their leader and he has met with the Mascare. In addition to this, he pays Anaskari street people to watch for certain types of citizens at different times, men, women, young or old."

"They have done what?" Sofia interrupted. "Who said that?"

"A beggar we collected, who claims to have been paid by the Renovar. He witnessed such a conversation," Seto explained.

"My father hasn't mentioned it. He would have told me." She hoped that was true. He was worried about the Renovar, why wouldn't he mention it to her? Especially if she was to be Successor. And now she had information for him that she couldn't deliver.

"Are you sure?" Notch said.

"He would have told me."

Seto nodded. "Of course, but what of those who disobey orders and edict? Solicci for one."

Sofia looked away. He was right. There was certainly no guarantee, simply because her father had been in a position of leadership, that all Mascare were honest. Or forthcoming. It was just one more betrayal. "Secrecy is Safety – the code works against us."

"What about the palace, who from Renovar is there?" Flir asked.

"Ambassador Lallol. Father thinks he's worried."

"As I thought. They're up to something," Flir said. "The Conclave would never slink into Anaskar on official business. There would need to be parades and banquets."

"Indeed," Seto said. "That's something I wish for you

to uncover. Be personable, Flir. Very well, what else?"

"Well." Luik rested his big arms on the table. "We don't know what they're up to. But we know that the Pig's innkeeper drugged Notch. So I guess the question is why? What did he see? Or nearly see?"

"Wish I could remember."

"Excellent question, Luik. That is something I wish for you to discover and to that end I have arranged for you to assist in the next wine delivery for the Iron Pig. Again, discretion is required."

"Wait." Sofia said. Their discussion wasn't leading anywhere hopeful. "What can I do? Can you help me retrieve Argeon? Locate my father?"

"You and Notch will eventually infiltrate the palace, with our help, of course. But not before we clear Notch's name. He's not as effective when he has to skulk about," Seto said, glancing at the mercenary's arm. "And more, if the Renovar here are up to no good, you would do well to learn about it."

"Why?"

"You are charged with protecting the Royal Family. Your position depends upon their health, does it not?"

Sofia shook her head. "Oson can rot at the bottom of the ocean for all I care, but you pledged your aid, Seto."

"We do have an agreement. But on my terms, Sofia."

What was the man doing? She needed his help, not obstinacy. Who had Father sent her to? "I can't just sit here, helpless, while you police the city."

"Unrest is bad for business."

"But how are you going to achieve all these goals?"

He waved a long fingered hand. "By the usual means. Brute force, cunning and stealth. Money and connection. Deception, murder."

"Murder?" Sofia stood. "I don't mean to murder anyone, Seto."

A man in a red robe lying prone on the floor, a chisel protruding from his back, flashed in her mind.

Flir giggled and Sofia glared at her.

Seto rose to move around the table. "Sofia my dear, you must understand. Lives will be lost in your struggle and you will be involved – did you think Oson and Solicci would simply leave or be slotted neatly into a jail cell? They will plot, scheme and undermine you. For what they have done to you, to your father, they must not be permitted to live. Moreso, for what they risk doing to our city. There is talk of a threat from the east, and yet they squabble amongst themselves."

She folded her arms. To the Depths of the Ocean with him, but he was right again. If only Father were here to guide her. When she'd vowed to take everything back, had she truly meant only to imprison Oson? He was the Prince, and had no issue. The king was too old to sire another. "I would end the Line of the Swordfish."

He shrugged. "Find a strapping lad and start a new line. One for Casa Falco."

Sofia blushed but did not sit. "Don't you see? My father's in danger, I need your help now, not later."

"That I cannot provide. But do strike out now, either for the palace or after your father. I will provide you with supplies and wish you luck." He paused. "But you will die, Sofia. Or be captured. That I believe."

She raised her chin. "Do you, Water Rat?"

He met her gaze. "Yes. I regret to say, but I do."

"Then allow me to prove you wrong." She pushed her chair in. "And without your help."

She strode to the door and closed it behind her,

calmly. Then she went to her room and began stuffing her belongings into the travel bag Seto had provided.

"Is this really what you want?"

Flir stood in the doorway, arms folded.

"Yes." She added another vial into the folds of her robe. But it wasn't what she wanted. She did need help – only it was clear she wasn't going to get it here. Emilio and her father were wrong about Seto.

"Don't be a damn fool." Flir snapped. "The palace isn't going anywhere and your father is probably safe. Just accept our help, girl – it's the best offer you're going to get."

She didn't look up. "I'm not without my own skills."

"Then add them to ours."

"You can't help me. A pompous innkeeper, a couple of mercenaries and," she glanced at Flir, frowning at the woman's slight frame and fine bones, "whatever you are."

Flir stalked forward, a grin on her face. "Whatever I am? Let me show you a fraction of what I am."

Sofia stood her ground but the woman only held up her hand, palm open.

"What are you doing?"

"Move me."

"What?"

"It's a simple request. Move me. Use your whole body if you wish."

Sofia scoffed. "What would that prove?"

"Try and find out. You won't be able to. You're too weak."

Weak. An echo of Oson's voice on the parapet.

Sofia clenched her teeth, then slapped her hand against Flir's, giving a good shove. She even used her shoulder. Only it was like shoving a mountain.

Flir chuckled. "Nice try. I nearly felt that."

Sofia pushed harder. Flir didn't even twitch. What was this woman made of? Was she a witch? Putting her whole weight into the act, Sofia strained, feet scrambling on floorboards. Flir rolled her neck, refusing to budge.

"Now it's my turn," the small woman said.

"Wait, I'm –" Sofia was flung back. She thudded onto the cot with a grunt and then screeched when Flir hauled her to her feet, again with no apparent effort. "Now, some more education. Notch, Luik and I fought the Glass War against the Medah when you were just a child dragging around a blanket. When you get back to the palace and your privileged life is restored, do some reading on it. See if you can figure out who turned the tide in the black sands. And Seto? He's far more than a rich innkeeper."

"I know about the Glass War, now let me go."

"No. You need to hear this. Ever wonder what happened to the king's older brother? Who should have been king? That wonderful musician with the fine fingers and charming manner, whose hair turned silver as a young man and whose curiosity sent him twice round the known world?"

"He died at sea. Everyone knows that."

"Do they? I'm sure Seto will be very disappointed to hear that, when I inform him of the fact. Now. You don't have to believe me, but I think you will. This is no band of half-wits you've been handed to. Do you truly think so little of your own father, that he would send you to Seto if he didn't trust the man?"

Seto was Oseto, the rightful king? What was he doing here? And how did he survive? She opened her mouth but all she could say was, "But, you're mercenaries, my father doesn't trust –"

"I'm sorry to say you don't know your father as well as you think. He trusts Seto. He trusts the king's brother – and Seto trusts us. You'll just have to deal with it, or I'll toss you out to the street myself. Right now." Flir gave Sofia a shake that rattled her teeth.

"Let me go then," she shouted.

Flir stepped back. "Good girl."

"Don't do that again."

"Gladly. If you take us seriously and help us. Then we'll help you."

Sofia breathed hard. Her hands shook but she stilled them and schooled her voice. "Fine. Just keep your word, Flir of Renovar. Casa Falco has a long memory."

The small woman gave a bow and left with the hint of a smile.

Sofia ran across the room and slammed the door, locking it. She slid down against the wood, unable to stop shuddering. Tears welled and she pushed her palms against her sockets, but they didn't stop.

"Oh, Father, what do I do?"

CHAPTER 16

A knock on the door.

She raised her head. How long had she sat there, slumped against the grain? Her limbs were stiff, joints cracking when she shifted. "Who is it?"

"Notch." He paused. "I'm going for a walk. I thought you might like to leave the inn."

"Seto sent you, didn't he?"

"Yes." He paused. "But I don't mind. I'd like to stretch my legs anyway."

At least he was honest. She climbed to her feet. Maybe it wasn't such a bad idea. Her ankle probably needed a stretch too. "Give me a minute." She moved to the basin and splashed water on her face then tried to arrange her hair into a semblance of neatness. Snatching her chisels, she belted them on and pulled a cloak from a peg before opening the door.

Notch stood in the hall, his own dark cloak over his shoulders. "Where to?"

"The wall."

He led her down the stairs, through a hot kitchen and

into a courtyard where he signalled to a black-clothed man standing by a gate. The fellow opened the heavy gate without a word and then they were on the street, heading for the Second Tier's wall.

Neither spoke in the afternoon cool. Sofia grimaced as she walked, but it was good for her ankle. By the time they reached the wall her muscles had warmed up and the pain dimmed. Even with the afternoon sun, it was cold on the wall, a breeze dancing across the backs of her hands where they gripped white stone.

She watched Notch where he leant on the parapet, facing the sea. How much was kindness and how much driven by Seto's request – what was the old man fishing for? Notch's hood was up, as was hers, but this close, his face was visible. His eyes were lined and his skin pale beneath the stubble.

He looked weary, as if he'd been dealt a blow, and one which might have been only one in a long list. Something she could understand.

"You're tired too."

"It's all the hiding. I'm sick of it."

"But we're in plain sight," she said. "Two people are holding hands a dozen feet away, anyone walking the walls today can see us." The man wore a bone charm tied around his neck. Hardly fashionable, but at least it wasn't a dried fish-head, like those in the Lower Tier.

"That's true. But all my life I've been able to walk my home without hiding my face."

"Secrecy is Safety."

"And prison, Sofia." He straightened and rolled his shoulders. Was he dismissing his own words? "Would you like to talk about your little argument with Flir?"

"No, thank you."

"She doesn't mean to be that way. It's who she is."

"Wonderful."

Notch chuckled. "I know it'll be difficult but you'll have to learn to trust us."

"It'll be very difficult, Notch." She frowned up at him. Perhaps he meant well, but simply trusting them wasn't an option. "I'm only letting Seto help me now, because I have no-one else. Because Oson, Solicci, Cera, they outnumber me. I don't trust you yet, any of you. I need you. There's a difference."

"Fairly said."

She let the silence stretch a moment. "Flir said that Seto is really the king's older brother. I don't remember him."

"So he is."

"Then you believe it?" If the Prince had survived, then why not Tantos? But then, her father had searched and found nothing.

"I know it. Prince Oseto never died in that shipwreck. It's a pretty unforgiving coast but he survived it and changed his name. When he recovered he became the man he is now. And when he heard his brother had declared him dead, and given up the search so quickly, and how he took the throne, Seto vowed never to return."

Such a callous effort didn't match the purposeful man she knew, but Notch didn't seem like the type to exaggerate. "He didn't search long? No-one speaks of Seto in the palace."

"To hear Seto tell it, even taking into account his love of the dramatic, perhaps a day or two. Not the search of a loving brother, but the search of a man who never took his eyes from the throne."

She scratched at the stone. "And you fought in the

Glass War?"

He tapped a finger on the stone. "Yes."

"Flir said you were important."

"Every Shield in the war was important."

"Yes, of course. But she said you saved King Otonos."

"We did." Notch's jaw was tight and he said no more.

The war was not a good topic. Sofia blurted out the next question that came to mind. "Is your family here in the city, Notch?"

"No. My brother... died in the war and my parents... I don't know if they're still alive. It's been too many years. They lived in the mountains, high above the city."

"You haven't seen them?"

"Not for a long time. My father made it clear, the last time we spoke, that cowards were not welcome there."

"Oh." She hesitated. "Do you miss them?"

"I miss my brother each day."

"I miss mine too. And now my father..." Sofia shrugged. Why was it easy to speak with Notch, a man she barely knew? A whole life of squashing secrets down, of speaking few words to people outside the palace, outside her family, of sharing little even with the carvers, even keeping things from Pietta. Learning to mask everything. Of all the people she'd met at Seto's inn, Notch appeared most open. More, he reminded her of Father somehow. Granted, she didn't know Luik, and Flir was too angry. Seto was more in line with Sofia's world, of nobles and games. But Notch was different. He didn't volunteer anything, but he'd answered her questions.

"We'll help you find him, Sofia."

"Thank you."

Notch leaned forward, eyes on the horizon. Black clouds boiled in the distance, growing large. She straightened when something big broke the ocean surface, a hint of black glistening. "Look," she pointed. "Is that...?"

"What?" Notch's hand strayed to his hilt.

"There, beyond the harbour. Breaking the waves now." A stream of water shot into the air. Sofia jumped. Large enough to disturb a passing ship, the water crashed down in a fountain-like spray. "That's the Sea Beast – surely no whale could do that?"

"Old Fury," Notch said. "It's been years. Those ships in the harbour are in trouble."

"The Storm Singer is probably already on her way."

The giant creature broke the surface again, sending waves that rocked ships already at dock. Not enough of it was visible to be sure, but Sofia had always thought the mysterious beast was at least as big as a full fleet. She'd only seen it once before, as a child. Where it came from, or what its purpose, no-one was sure. Her father's best guess was that it was an ancient creature from the blackest depths of the ocean. Legend said the beast was the first Anaskari king, cursed by the Medah as they fled their old city.

"True, and there you go." Notch pointed down to a stone walkway that extended out to the water. At its peak, small from her vantage point, was a stone chair. A throne, really. Lavinia, the king's Storm Singer, had shown it to her several times in calm weather. Slick with slime and droppings from gulls, the woman sat upon it in her fine robes without hesitation. Among the last of the magic-users in Anaskar, she lived a life of luxury and vigilance, though she too, had told Sofia that she was a prisoner. "Of duty," the woman said, her smile sad.

"It's her, it's Lavinia. See her hair."

"Like a flame." Notch was squinting against the rising wind, now bringing with it chill mist.

Sofia shivered in her cloak. "She'll still be able to calm both storm and beast, won't she?"

"She always does."

Lavinia crossed the walkway, waves lapping the sides, pausing once to hold her footing. By the time she reached the throne the black clouds had unleashed thunder and jags of lightning. People rushed to the walls to point and shout over the wind, or at Lavinia, but Sofia watched Old Fury. The Sea Beast lurked somewhere beneath the harbour, flashes of his inky mass now visible, now gone, now visible again.

And then he thrashed his bulk and people on the wall screamed.

An enormous wave tore through the harbour, capsizing smaller vessels and smashing into the big ships, tipping them and tangling their masts. Sails and rigging tore and snapped as ships lurched. People fleeing the harbour's boardwalk were swept from their feet and Sofia flinched when a figure was dashed against a wall. Others were sent tumbling up streets, while yet more disappeared, sucked into the harbour. The wind masked the screams. Sofia turned away with a shudder. Gods, how many had died already?

"Notch, it's never this bad."

He shook his head.

Lavinia remained on the throne, red hair streaming as she sang. At first it was just a suggestion of new sound, thin notes woven into the wind. Sofia closed her eyes to trace it better. Clear, beneath the wind and the thunder, like a brilliant bell, Lavinia's voice rang across the harbour. It slipped between other sounds and the world slowed.

Sofia exhaled when she opened her eyes.

The rain had faded, black clouds dissolved, as if blown away from below. But the only thing coming from the throne was Lavinia's voice. It filled the air and Sofia's chest resonated with it. Even the Sea Beast had sunk beneath the water. The harbour was calming as the wind fell away and blue sky peered through tattered cloud. On Lavinia sang and Sofia blinked at sudden tears.

She wiped them away, turning from the wall a moment. People beside her stood with tears in their eyes. A young man took her hands and danced a little jig. Before she could react, he'd turned to another onlooker.

Someone cheered. Within moments the entire wall was cheering. Sofia shouted her joy down to the tall woman, who was even now walking back along the spur, toward the private entrance to Anaskar. At its black iron gate she stopped to wave up at everyone and was given another roar of thanks.

Notch smiled down at her. "I'd forgotten."

"Me too."

"Beautiful." His voice was quiet. "And you've met the King's Storm Singer?"

"Many times. She'll be exhausted after such a feat, but when she sings, even softly to herself or even in a hall, it changes the whole room. Even her guards forget to frown."

"I'd love to hear that."

Sofia checked the harbour. Waves still slapped against the docks and ships with ragged sails still rocked. Men in orange and blue, both Shield and Vigil, rushed to help, but many people were already dead.

Elsewhere, fishermen would be rushing to ready those vessels able to sail. Each appearance of the Sea

Beast brought with it magnificent hauls, nets overflowing with all manner of fish – both rare and large. As if half the ocean couldn't help but follow the Sea Beast. For weeks after, the catch would be plentiful.

Once, the people of Anaskar had tried to slay the beast, long before her grandfather's time. To hear father tell it, no-one came close to hurting it of course, and once people realised the Sea Beast brought fish with it, no-one cared to try again and the city grew richer.

But was it worth it, when people died? "Can we help them?"

"We could but it's too great a risk. The Vigil and Shield are there."

The crowds jostled her, pressing in and sucking the air from the wall. "Should we return then?"

"Good idea. Seto might have something for us to do now."

"I hope so. I hate all this waiting," she said.

Notch nodded. "Me too."

Sofia led him from the wall and along the cobblestones, part of her glad to be leaving. "I hate to think what will happen if Lavinia can't find others to train. Only her children remain. And her brother, but he has no children."

"It'd be a disaster. Otonos should be protecting the line better." Notch let a wagon pass, its sides bulging with silks. "When I was a boy, I once saw waves, created by the beast during a storm, that cleared the lower wall. Imagine a whole winter of such weather."

"It's never that bad is it?"

"Not often but sometimes I'm surprised captains still sail here. They risk a lot for their profits – even with the post-beast bounty."

"Well, at least the Sea Beast isn't seen that often."

"True. And he's always left after her song. Once, back when her father was Storm Singer, there was a time the Sea Beast didn't return for ten years."

"Hmmm."

She wove through the thinning crowd. Music resumed, flowing from a street corner where men in blue tights with Swordfish headpieces bounced as they played. The costumes were silly but they pleased a group of children, who stood laughing and clapping. One even spun a little dance, her arms in the air. Wealthier parents tossed coppers into open instrument cases. Sofia smiled. The children's faces were alight.

One of the musicians smiled back at her before bending to place a sweet-cake in a boy's hand.

"The musicians play well," Notch said as they passed.

Sofia paused to listen a moment. "They do, almost as good as —" she choked on her last word as the smiling man, his blue costume damp with sweat, leapt forward. He caught her arm and dragged her from the street. Shocked onlookers made no move to help her, as the rest of the musicians stepped up to block them, their instruments silent.

Notch had not paused with her, and was almost out of sight.

She broke her captor's grip, driving her elbow into him. "Notch!"

The musician snarled, snatching at her. She swatted his hand aside and jabbed at his face but he dodged, twisting to deliver a glancing blow to her side. Pain ran along her ribs and she grunted, collapsing over his arm.

Someone caught her shoulders.

"Keep her still," a voice shouted.

Sofia kicked at the man holding her, but he turned his

thigh, absorbing the blows. Fingers dug into her cheeks and something was poured into her mouth. A bitter tang. Dormi, sleep-drug favoured by the Mascare. Tantos used it on her once, as a stupid prank. Father had been furious.

A hand clamped over her mouth before she could spit, and then she was tumbling to the ground.

A blood-splattered forearm lay on the cobblestones, weeping red.

Steel flashed in the sun and screams echoed along the street as Notch spun into the circle, his blade shearing another limb. His face was set as he slipped into a crouch, slashing with a knife and blocking a kick with his sword. He skipped forward, driving his shoulder into another man, who stumbled amongst his fellows. A small woman in blue leapt onto Notch's back, circling an arm around his neck. The mercenary spun with a roar, flinging her into the crowd.

Something clawed at Sofia's cloak and she flinched.

The smiling musician, his face now twisted in pain, drew her in with his single arm. His stub pumped blood as he struggled with her. Sofia drew a chisel and slashed it across his cheek, scrambling away.

"Sofia." Notch caught her arm. His tunic was splashed with blood and concern covered his face. "Quickly, the Shield will come soon."

"Wait," she gasped, jamming her fingers down her throat.

Vomit splashed across the stones, coloured with a bright orange liquid. She'd end up sleepy once the adrenaline wore off, but for now, she'd stay awake. Hopefully.

"Go," she said.

People fell back from Notch's expression as he leapt

over a crumpled musician and a shattered swordfish headpiece. He pulled her into a side street and Sofia glanced over her shoulder. Two of the men in blue were limping away.

The smiling musician lay still.

CHAPTER 17

"We weren't followed and we knocked at the stable gate. I don't know if the Mascare or even the Shield are watching the inn anymore. Tulio let us in," Notch said.

He dumped his bloody shirt into a washbasin, Sofia and Seto hovering behind. Pink clouds spread in the water and he shivered when a chill ran over his bare skin. The rear of the inn was a little too distant from the fire. Not as though it would kill him. Getting old, eh?

"You have so many scars," Sofia said. Her voice changed. "I'm sorry. That was insensitive."

He chuckled as he rinsed his arms. "Don't be sorry. I'm alive, aren't I?"

"And so am I. Thank you, Notch."

He turned, smiling as he accepted a towel from Seto. "And we're lucky too – there was only one mask. Don't know if I could have handled more than one at the same time."

Seto nodded. "The rest were likely Shields or Vigil, I imagine the palace has spread itself thin in its search for this little bird. Perhaps some more care is in order?"

Sofia frowned at him. "I'm too tired to tell you not to call me that."

"The drug will wear off soon. As I understand it, dormi is –"

"I'm familiar with it."

"Of course you are. Silly me."

Notch hid a smile. At least the two were talking. "I think we need to anticipate their next move. Solicci or Cera could be more direct next time."

"I and the other Rats will watch for them," Seto promised. "In fact, I have an exceptionally skilled young Braonn doubling as a manservant in the palace."

"Should we strike back?" Sofia asked. A hardness rested in her gaze.

"Until I can prepare something, you would be best served by remaining hidden."

Notch took a clean shirt and ducked into it. "That wasn't the only excitement we had, Seto. Old Fury visited. He flooded parts of the Lower Tier. It looked bad, even if it might have cleaned the place up a bit. Are Flir and Luik safe?" Notch rubbed his shoulder. "Do we need to go and look for them?"

"So eager. Trust my judgement, I'm sure they are well and will return soon. We're all cogs and our parts are not always to act. You need to stay out of sight."

"You could never be a cog, Seto," Notch snorted.

"That's true, old friend."

He massaged his neck. "Seto."

The older man gestured for them to follow, heading back toward the dining room. "I know you feel useless. But you're nothing of the sort. Besides, I have news of my own. I don't know if there is a connection between what I have to tell you and why the Mascare have left our doorstep. But since we reopened, I caught one snooping about."

"Where?"

"In your rooms. We would have found him sooner but I was attending to other matters."

Sofia glanced over her shoulder. "Where is he now?"

"Come." He led them down a narrow hall toward the basement. Sofia followed, a limp in her stride, Notch close behind. He'd have to keep an eye on her, not just her ankle, but to make sure she held up. She'd worn a brave face since Seto brought her to the inn.

"So we're still being watched?" he asked.

"I have extra eyes on the eyes upon us. If the Shields or the Mascare attempt something so bold again, we will have warning." He lowered his voice at the entrance to the cellar. "There's something peculiar about this Mascare, however."

Seto opened the door and took them to the centre of the room. A body lay beneath a cloth, unmoving in the torchlight.

"You killed him?" Sofia ran forward, tearing the cloth free. She gasped, looking back over her shoulder.

Seto knelt beside her. "Yes. You see what I mean about peculiar."

Notch felt his own eyebrows rise. A tall man lay in Mascare robes, a mask beside his head, hands at his side. His skin was quite pale – moreso than the Braonn, who spent so much time beneath their forests. This man was so pale as to be snow-like.

Renovar.

"An imposter," Seto said. "He attacked when I caught him. Regrettably, I was forced to kill him before learning anything of use."

"This is punishable by death," Sofia said. "Worse. Do you know what happened to the last man who pretended to be Mascare?"

"He was stoned before the city walls," Notch said. "In full view of his family." And a crowd too big to disperse. A hot day. Too hot for armour, but he'd been on duty and that meant the full gear. It might have shielded him from steel had he been on the field, but it couldn't block out the screams.

Seto covered the man. "Clearly he had not heard, coming from across the sea as he did."

"I saw an imposter myself. I lost him, but his mask was set in a frown."

Seto's own face creased.

"What does this mean?" Sofia said.

"I don't know. Trouble for certain." The old man stood. "But now perhaps I do have a task. One which we will all undertake. If you are able, Notch?"

Notch straightened and his pulse quickened. It was almost shameful, how easily the thought of action stirred him. Action led to the restoration of his name. Whatever was left of it. He flexed the muscles in his forearm. The stiffness was bearable. "Tell me."

"Two of my favourites – deception and misdirection. Are you able too, Sofia?"

Sofia sniffed. "Of course I am."

Notch sighed. "Seto, tell us."

A man in black cleared his throat, standing in the door. Seto met him and the two conferred a moment. When he returned he was smiling.

"First let us eat. By the time we've finished, Luik at least will have returned and I will lay out my plans." His mouth twitched. "I understand Flir had to swim some of the way back, but they're fine."

*

Notch ran.

Stupid. Bloody stupid. Why did he always end up going along with Seto? If there was ever a stupider idea, he had yet to hear it. And yet, he ran.

Stone walls, dark doorways and the surprised faces of onlookers flashed by as he skidded through a small square, turning into a street leading to the Iron Pig. Too far from the wall to have been flooded, the cobbles were damp from the rain. He nearly slipped several times and shouts from pursuing Shields were never far behind. A man stepped into his path, arms outstretched, as if to stop him. Word of his reward had made people bold on the Lower Tier it seemed.

Notch flattened the fellow with a single punch, barely breaking stride.

Crashing through the inn's door, he skidded to a halt, using the nearest table in the common room to slow him. His chest heaved.

At his wild entrance, customers jumped up, one spilling a drink and cursing. All eyes were on him. The bench seats were full, meals and tankards set before workmen and darker sorts, but it was the innkeeper, standing in an apron behind the bar with the most telling reaction.

The man's eyes widened and he spun, giving the wall a thump. An opening appeared, one that did not appear to be a regular door.

From the corner of the room, Luik stood. The muttering had grown, and Notch barely made it halfway across the floor when a man with greasy hair stood, opening his vest to show a knife.

"Stop there, friend," he said.

Several men joined him but Notch didn't pause, grabbing the first fellow and tossing him onto a table. The room erupted with a roar. Luik appeared, giant arms beating a path. "Hurry," he said, grunting when someone smashed a chair on his broad back. Spinning, Luik delivered a blow that slammed the man into the wall. He stomped on. The display of brute strength gave the patrons pause and Notch broke free, following Luik to the wall behind the bar.

"No handle. Sealed," he said.

"Try the kitchen."

Ovens roared and massive pots bubbled, but every person in the room lay groaning on the dirty floor. Except Flir.

"What took you so long?" she asked.

"They're right behind me," Notch shouted over new noise. He glanced over his shoulder. The group of Shields had burst into the common room with cries for order.

"Out back." Luik wrenched a door open and waved them into a small passage. At its end a stout door waited, crossed with two steel bars. Luik flipped them, kicked open the door and charged up an alley. There Seto waited with Sofia and an unhitched wagon laden with barrels.

"Flir," Seto called. She dashed forward, took the horses' harness and lifted, pulling the wagon down to block the door. Notch chuckled at Sofia's gaping mouth. It took time to grow accustomed to Flir's strength.

"Now what?" Notch said. "How long?"

"I don't know," Seto said. He waved to Flir and Luik. "Go back to the front of the inn." He turned to Notch. "We shouldn't tarry. I have men watching the streets, but there's no guarantee the Renovar are inside. We can only hope your arrival and the Shields have stirred things up enough."

It was a typical Seto scheme. Bold, brilliant, unpredictable. From the first stroll Notch took in a not-too-distant square, hood pushed back, attracting the attention of passing Shields, to the moment they pulled the wagon across the door, his heart had missed every other beat. But he grinned like a fool. If everything went to plan, Seto's stunt would flush enough rats out to really find out what was going on. Below the inn Luik had found weapons. A stockpile. Crossbows and bushels of bolts. Enough to arm a small force, enough to cause real trouble.

If the Iron Pig was the only inn being used by the Renovar. It made no sense, Renovar had never taken up arms against Anaskar. Merchants from both nations had been crossing the sea to trade for decades, bringing stability to both nations. Why would Renovar risk that?

Luik had been lucky to catch a glimpse of the stores. Even so, Notch was unable to shake off a chill. Something didn't seem right. And it wasn't just a leftover feeling from Vinezi, now safely behind bars.

Seto moved up the alley several steps, facing the entrance. In his hand was a small axe, the other held a long knife. "What did the innkeeper do, when you entered?"

"Took one look at me and fled through some sort of concealed doorway."

"I want that one."

Sofia turned back to face Notch. She too was armed, both hands held knives just like those used by Seto's men, each in a white knuckled-fist. "What if —"

A roar filled the alley.

Heat and light bloomed and he was cast into the air, cracking his head as he bounced from the wall. Something tore into his leg and he cried out, vision swimming with black and red, orange swirling. He could barely move. His ears were clogged, the crackle of flames and collapsing stone was muffled, as if at a distance. Heat seared his lungs, stealing his breath as he clawed at the ground.

Gods, what was happening?

Sofia. Seto. Luik and Flir, were they alive? He closed his eyes, turning from the heat. His chest tightened, struggling for air. Something took his hands and he fought, but was being dragged across the cobblestones, sockets straining.

Cool air hit his skin. Released, he gasped, sucking in great lungfuls of air. "Who..." he croaked. Notch blinked through tears. A flaming inn resolved from the mess of black, red and yellow smudges. Flames leapt from the doorway, visible over the overturned cart and tumble of barrels. A pillar of smoke rose from the inn's entrance, pouring into the afternoon sky. Just how big was the explosion? All the people in the common room... Notch reached his knees. One pant leg was no more than ribbons and blood coated his calf.

Reaching for a wall to steady himself, Notch made it to one leg and stopped. Again his vision swam and he had to cough and breathe deeply until his body could respond properly. Whoever helped him was gone. He staggered forward, shielding his eyes from the glare. The flames had died down, but still lit the alley. No dark shapes lay mute or smoking. Had Seto and Sofia escaped? They'd stood further along.

He limped back toward the opposite end, and sagged

against a wall. People shouted and ran before the burning Pig. It's windows spewed smoke and flame and the front door lay in wreckage across the street. Inside were the bodies of dozens of people, blackening as Notch stood and panted. What madman would do such a thing? It couldn't have been a personal attack. Notch swore. He wasn't worth that.

Someone with their head on straight had formed a line of buckets, heaving water onto the flames, but it was having little effect. They shouted to one another, urging each other on, calling for help. Notch coughed. More Shields and the Vigil would soon arrive, he'd have to leave.

Only he couldn't. Not without the others.

Across the street a large figure stepped into view. A man stood with arms crossed, a smile on his face as he surveyed the damage. He was big enough that his shirt strained over his bulk but he moved quickly when he turned to leave.

Vinezi.

Notch stumbled forward, but the man was already gone.

"Here, get out of the way, will you?" A member of the Vigil grunted, pushing past with barely a glance. Notch ducked his head and hobbled back to the mouth of the alley.

"Notch."

He turned, dragging his leg. Flir, her face covered in soot and her hands just as black, stood in the alley, waving him closer. He shambled forward and she caught him beneath the arm, wrapping her own arm around him and taking his weight.

"Faster," she said as he tried to keep up.

"What happened?"

"I don't know. I was watching the front, waiting for one of them to try and run, and then everything went red. When I could see again, there was fire and smoke everywhere."

"The others?" He was breathing hard.

"Luik's fine, but Seto isn't. I can't find Sofia."

He tripped on an uneven cobblestone, injured leg snarling. "We have to find her." He thumped his thigh for good measure. "Is Seto going to live?"

"I don't know."

"Where are they?"

"I broke into a nearby building. It's empty but there's not much inside. Luik's watching Seto. I'm going to try find the girl."

"I'll help."

"I doubt that," Flir said, taking his whole weight as they turned a corner and knocked on a wooden door. This far from the inn, the sound of the chaos was softer but the smoke still rose into an ugly column. "Luik."

The door swung open and Luik, burns on his face and hands, pulled Notch into the building, setting him down at a table and chair. The building Flir found looked to have, at one time, been a workspace for a carpenter or other craftsman. Dusty floorboards, big windows and generous space.

"Thank you," Notch said. "How is he?"

"Seto'll survive, he always does," Luik said, but his lips were tight. "Probably needs a healer though." Stretched out on makeshift blankets, face bloodied, Seto's chest rose and fell in an erratic rhythm. Notch shivered. Seto had never looked so vulnerable. If the old man died, the whole city would be lessened. And more. After the war, coming home hurt and disillusioned, the old devil had been the one to shelter him, to give him purpose.

"I'll return when I find her," Flir said. "Then I'll drag a healer back."

"Wait. I can help."

She shook her head. "You'd slow me down." Then she was gone.

"Hope you're not attached to your other pant leg," Luik said, even as he tore it. "Nasty cut." He kept tearing until he'd made bandages and wrapped Notch's leg as best he could, then returned to Seto.

"What happened, Luik?"

The big man shrugged.

Notch shifted his leg with a grimace. "Did you see anyone or anything?"

"Nothing. No-one came out. They're all dead."

"I saw Vinezi, the false beggar. He was watching. He enjoyed it."

Luik turned, eyebrows drawn together. "What? Flir and I put him in prison."

"I don't know how he escaped, but it was him. And he was very happy."

"He planned it."

"How could he know when we'd be there?"

"He couldn't."

Notch leaned forward. "You think he didn't plan it for us?"

He shrugged. "Could've been a big set up from the beginning." Luik took a damp cloth from beside Seto and mopped the man's forehead.

"But how? And why? He destroyed his employer's building, possibly killing most or all of them?"

"Got an idea about how, but I don't know how likely.

Or why."

"More than I have."

"Well, in Renovar, there's talk of a magic powder. I heard it off the ships, near months ago now. Supposedly it can break holes in castle walls. Only it isn't magic. But it explodes into fire. Like tonight."

Notch sucked in a breath. Such a powder, if they had enough, if it were real, could destroy a city. It had all been so easy, not too long ago. Capture some Renovar, get the truth out of them and clear his name, but now... "Is that what they're up to? They want Anaskar? What would they have to gain from war?"

"No idea."

"And does that make Vinezi a hero as well as a villain?"

"Nothing to say he didn't get his men out, wait for us or the Shields to go in first."

"True. And the powder?"

"No-one believed the rumours. Sounds like the magic of old, right? But if you put what just happened with the crossbows..."

"The king needs to know. Especially if we find more."

"He'll know soon enough."

Footsteps approached, and Notch fumbled for a weapon. His sword was still belted on but he couldn't draw it, instead pulling a belt knife.

"Luik."

Luik crossed the room on quiet feet, mace in hand – and admitted Flir, who held a comatose Sofia. Notch twisted his torso to better see, but the young woman breathed evenly. Her face and hair were singed and she too, was covered in smudges of soot. Notch fell back in his seat. She was all right. They both were.

"She needs water and rest is all," Flir said, placing Sofia

next to Seto and slumping into a chair. "How's Seto?"

"The same. What about the fire?"

"They're getting it under control." Flir rubbed her neck, rising. "I'll be back with a healer then."

"Wait, we were talking about Vinezi," Notch said, and rushed through an explanation.

"So he trashed the Iron Pig?"

"Possibly."

Flir narrowed her eyes. "Who did you see inside, either of you?"

"The innkeeper," Notch said. "He disappeared the moment he saw me."

"Just drunks. Didn't see the Renovar," Luik added.

Flir threw up her hands. "This will have to wait. Make sure Seto's all right." She left once more. Through the door, the street glowed orange and shouts clashed with the rush of feet. Notch moved over to Sofia, lowered himself to the floorboards with a grimace and placed a hand on her neck. Her pulse was steady enough. The fear and tension was gone from her face, lines between her forehead too.

He pushed her hair back from her eyes. "Do we have any water?"

"In here," Luik said, moving to an adjoining room.

His own throat was burning but Sofia's skin was red and raw in places, he could try soothe it when she woke. Notch tapped fingers on the floorboards. Flir was no doubt working as fast as she could, and finding a healer in the Lower Tier who made house calls was not easy. She might run into trouble out there, but there were few surprises for a woman like Flir.

The image of Vinezi, big cheeks set in a smile, mocked him.

That was a surprise.

Whatever the fake beggar was playing at, it was a ruthless game. Monstrous. The scale of his murder, Notch could only liken it to war. Deaths on the sands of the Medah deserts were larger by far, but hardly so cold. And no-one had enjoyed it like Vinezi. If the man was responsible. Was there was still a chance he was just a disgruntled lackey, enjoying the fall of his master? No. That smile had been prideful. As if he'd accomplished something. Yet where had the man been, during Notch's dramatic entrance? Had he been broken out of prison?

And how was the powder set off, without risking the life of the user? For that was surely what the barrels contained. And was the innkeeper and all his secrets, along with the Renovar, now smouldering in a blackened heap within the inn? If Vinezi was outside at the time of the explosion, and pleased with it, didn't that suggest that he was more important than he appeared? That Thalik and the rest of the Renovar strangers were also alive and well? The Iron Pig had been a front. A giant trap.

But if so, who was the prey? He or the Shield?

"Well, ain't this lucky? We've been looking for you."

A Mascare stood in the doorway. His red robe was singed at the hems and he held a thin dagger. His mask was wrong. Similar to the one Notch saw on the street, it had stern eyes but instead of the typical horizontal line of firmness, the mouth was set in a deep frown.

Imposters.

Notch surged to his feet, ignoring the pain and tearing his blade free. "Luik!"

The Mascare didn't react, save for a twitch in his blade hand. Notch barely took two steps when pain exploded in his head. He crashed to the ground, sword skittering away, then grunted when a boot lodged itself in his ribs. Crumbling over the shoe, he clawed at a set of legs but they kicked free. Another blow to the head and the room began to darken. He struggled to keep his eyes open as blood trickled down the back of his neck.

The first Mascare spoke. "Where's the other one, then?"

The second man had a faint accent, but Notch couldn't place it. "Out to it in the other room. I would have finished him but I heard you in here."

"Bones! Do it properly or don't –"

"What?"

The first Mascare raised a hand. "Someone's coming. Quick."

From where Notch's face was pressed against the dusty floorboards, the second speaker stood out of his line of vision. Clinging to consciousness, he breathed a curse as shadows clouded one of the Mascare, who bent over Sofia, scooped her up and turned for the door.

CHAPTER 18

Each Ward thrust up from the point where sand filtered into earth. Around their bases grew stringy grasses from grey dirt and sharp rock. In the morning sun, the towering Wards cast long shadows.

That in itself was impossible.

The narrow towers, stretching for miles in either direction, caught and reflected sunlight in such a blast that each appeared as standing pillars of white flame. Ain could not look at them for long, the light throbbed within his head, pushing the blood through his temples. Patches of glass on the ground caught the light, reflecting. It was a dark, murky glass, where the sand had melted and congealed beneath the might of old magical battles.

Schan chewed on the inside of his mouth. "So, we'll be burnt alive, then?"

Ibranu grunted. "Those are our Wards, right, but I can't say what they'll do any more than the enemy's ones. They're meant to protect people."

"By killing us?"

"By turnin' us back."

Ain started toward them, still some distance away, waving his companions after him. "Let's not delay then. Water is on the other side." A path hummed beneath his feet, the first strong one he'd felt in days. Their water was low. Enough for a day, less. But a path this strong had to lead to water.

All they need do was pass the Wards.

He slowed mere feet away, almost blind. "What happened the last time you passed?"

The Engineer grunted. "Stumbled through, barely able t'see. You know you passed when you can see clear again."

Schan held up one of his knives. "Will your instruments and tools, or our weapons be safe? I've heard stories of steel warping in there."

"Won't happen," the Engineer said.

The answer gave some comfort. If Ibranu's pieces were lost, and even if the Sea Shrine was located, how could its secrets then be unlocked? Legends spoke of it as a marvel, both intricate and mysterious. Hence all the tools, cogs, keys, charts and writings in Ibranu's pack. An Engineer's life was given over to such things, just as a Pathfinder would always feel the passage of feet.

"I will go first," Ain said, but did not move. He pulled back his shoulders and squinted into the empty wasteland beyond. The Ward blazed beside him, casting no heat. If he stepped inside and died, Silaj would never know. He would never hold or speak his child's name. That last night together, they had chosen a name. Jali — the old word for 'ocean.' For a boy or a girl.

He would not return a coward, would not shame his child.

His first step was short, stirring dust, but he took

another and another. If it killed him, what would it do? Ibranu had been vague. Perhaps it was better not to know. Or maybe Schan was correct and the moment he passed the ward it would burn him to cinders. And he'd not know a thing about it. "Sands protect me."

He crossed the threshold.

Silent chaos reigned. The path he had followed splintered like a thousand butterflies and he was plunged into traffic to rival that of the largest gathering of the Clans. Could battle be much different? Countless shades passed, their forms grey with iridescent white outlines. All were lost. Many shouted or screamed to each other but their voices were mute. Men, women and children, even animals moved about within the ward, some in circles, some racing toward nothing. Their bright outlines had trouble keeping up, one girl's hand trailed her as she jumped and waved for attention. No-one came to her.

Ain took a half step before ducking reflexively, as a shade with a massive axe charged across his path. A bird shot through the mess of shapes, it's outline sizzling in the air as it swept down to catch a struggling mouse.

He tried to touch a nearby child dressed in animal skins, the like of which had not been seen in the Medah clans for centuries, but his hand passed through the shoulder.

"Can you hear me?"

The boy did not react. Ain walked deeper into the strange place. Perhaps he had already died, and this was the great Beyond. He pinched his arm and it hurt. Maybe the Sands had not forsaken him.

Another figure loomed up, greater than the others by far, a magnificent beast that walked on four legs, with the body of a desert cat. Only so much larger in scale, and with enormous fangs and claws the size of Ain's forearm. Where it stepped, other shades skipped away from its blue outline.

Ain stepped aside but the shade paid him no heed, fading as it passed where he guessed the ward boundary lay.

Schan walked near the boundary, one arm outstretched and another shielding his eyes. He was not moving fast and did not react when a pair of warriors dashed through him.

A mere two paces back Ibranu lay facedown in the sand.

"No." Ain dashed toward him, calling for Schan. He found himself alone when he crouched by the Engineer. The man's eyes were closed and his chest unmoving when Ain rolled him over. The Ward had taken him.

He flung sand at the world around him. "You let him pass before."

He hadn't liked Ibranu, truly, but the man had still died for his people. Ain began to shovel sand aside, to make a grave, but always the sand resumed its position. No matter how many armfuls he dragged away, the sand returned to a level surface, grains silent. Ain removed Ibranu's pack and arranged the man's arms on his chest, speaking the ritual words from where he knelt.

And then he stood to leave, lifting the pack. The water in Ibranu's flask was precious, so too the materials he carried for use in the Sea Shrine. Schan was gone but the frantic passage of the spirits, their cutting white lines turning the air before him into a ceaseless jigsaw of lines, raged on.

He stumbled into the shades.

Without the engineer his quest was doomed.

*

Ain waited beyond the Ward, shivering in the blazing sun. A little longer and he would carry on alone. The path which had shattered in the shade-world returned, strong beneath his feet.

Sweat trickled down his temples, gathering beneath his eyes. The moment he exited the dark world with its trapped spirits, his ears were free. The distant squeal of a bird of prey echoed above. Wind stirred the tufts of grass, hid a swish in his cloak.

Where was Schan? The warrior hadn't been far away. Ain shouldn't have beaten him from the Ward. The engineer's pack, much lighter, sat nearby. While waiting, he'd examined the contents and discarded much that was similar to what he already carried on his own back.

What he kept was mysterious. Two thin books, their covers worn, all written in an indecipherable script and full of strange pictures. A roll of scrolls, some cogs and several round, teethed bits of steel. A set of keys, each blocky and nothing like the slender tools used to fit the Elder's giant chests. What purpose any of the tools had was beyond him.

"Pathfinder."

Schan was jogging toward him, curved blade in hand, having exited from a point some distance away.

"Schan. Thank the Sands, are you well?" Ain smiled when the Snake stopped. Schan wasn't talkative, but he was company at least.

"My eyes hurt, but I'm upright. Ibranu?"

Ain shook his head. "I saw him in there. I don't think he made two steps before the Ward took him."

"Poor bastard," Schan said.

"Truly." Ain stared across the wasteland.

Ibranu claimed it was three days travel to the plains below Anaskar, a further two into the foothills before they would climb the mountain. And then finding a path, a secret path, into the city. But between them was the wasteland, a blasted place that had sickened after the Glass War. In only fifteen years it had become largely barren. Somewhere out here, his father and mother lay in fitful slumber, no Sand to cloak their bones.

An insult to the way they had lived their lives. Jedda told many a story of his parents being among the most faithful servants of the Sands and the Oasis.

Ain bent to pick up the engineer's pack. "We've been lucky no storms have come, but we must still find water."

"You have a path?"

"A strong one. We follow it north."

"Not east?"

"No. Hopefully it isn't too far out of our way. Even with Ibranu's water, we could not cross the wasteland."

Schan nodded and started forward, boots stirring dust. Ain followed, tread heavy. Looking too far ahead was a trap. Ignore the language, ignore the ignorance of geography and custom, ignore the lack of knowledge about the Shrine, let alone its location, ignore it all. Ignore everything but water.

A low ridge of rock formations appeared on the horizon as they walked, and by the time he and Schan drew alongside it, the sun had dipped, tinting the sand orange. He'd drank from his lightening water flask twice, and their supply of dried fruit and salted meat dwindled too. The last of the white-bug flesh lasted only to the Ward, and there would be none here in the Wasteland. Few animals beyond scavengers were said to live in such a dust-choked place.

"What's wrong with the rocks?" Ain asked. The stone was heaped and twisted, with black scars across the surface. "Was it burnt?"

Schan stepped forward. "I don't know, it looks –" He fell back with a shout, slashing with his belt knife as he hit the ground. Sparks flashed where he made contact with stone, and Ain jumped forward to drag Schan back.

The rock itself had attacked the man.

"What dark magic is this?"

Schan stood, dusting himself off. "The Glass War changed much. Let's keep moving."

Ain agreed. The rock face was still, but the pattern of scorch marks had changed slightly. He did not want to know what drove the very stones to strike out. They skirted the next few groupings of rock, and by nightfall, had placed their tents across from each other in the open, partially shielding a small fire. Fed by the dried remains of shrubs and the fragments of what must have once been a cart or wagon, they were warm, if hungry. The trail rations were not filling, nor did they cook well.

Schan toyed with a hilt he'd found in the dirt, a large topaz stone set in the pommel. So unlike the plain, curving swords and short bows of his people. No blade remained and the crosspiece was half-melted. Ain had held it and shuddered. The heat needed to do such a thing was not natural on a battlefield.

"This is the kind of weapon the filthy Anaskari used against us," the warrior said.

"What is the jewel for?"

"Show. Nothing more."

The man did not continue and Ain stood to stretch his legs. "I will take first watch."

"Thanks, lad."

Ain placed his back to the fire and listened. The wind had died down and once Schan finished arranging his blankets and fell asleep, there was only the hush of the night to contend with. Twice Ain completed a circuit of the camp. Once he thought a pair of yellow eyes glowed in the distance, but when he peered closer, he found nothing.

He mentioned it to Schan when he woke the man for his shift.

"I'll watch. Probably a scavenger-dog, if any live here."

Sleep came slowly, but when he drifted off it was dawn too soon. He drank the last of his water. That left Ibranu's flask and whatever Schan carried.

"Hope we find water soon," the man said as he slung his pack onto a shoulder. It was something of a question.

"As do I." No strong trails split from the path they travelled. A few wandered, their footfalls fading, but none rivalled the age or frequency of use, of the path he trod upon now.

By noon Ain's mouth was so dry he could barely swallow. Dust caked his face and hands; he had to tie a blindfold when the wind picked up again. Schan followed suit and they paused to take shelter in the first copse of trees they'd seen. Stunted, the leaves were not green but a sickly grey and the bark was mottled. Everything about the wasteland was unpleasant. Even the sound of his tread was not the soothing hiss of sand, but a hard clumping on dirt.

He sipped from Ibranu's flask, just to wet his tongue before handing it to Schan. The warrior did the same before returning it. "What do you feel, are we close?"

"The path is strong still. We must trust it."

"No choice."

The land beyond the trees grew rockier. In places it was so uneven that some of the dips were deep enough to fall into, others simply nasty traps for unwary ankles. Ain increased his pace. Such a landscape would capture rainfall, though standing water was a risk. He stopped when the path split. One trail headed east and the stronger continued more to the north, putting them further off course. But it was the stronger path.

"What is it?"

"The path forks. Some travellers, many, head east from here."

"And the rest?"

Ain moved a dry tongue with some difficulty. Had he made a mistake? The paths didn't lie, and yet, many were long. Was he out of his depth? "Carry northward. More."

"North it is then," he said, moving forward.

Noon came and passed, and when finally Ain saw the sun begin to sink, he found water. A small puddle, tepid and clouded over, a mess of tiny bugs skating across the surface, lay between two outcrops of stone.

It was hardly fresh but he marked it. He lowered himself to his knees, thanking the Sands for watching over them. "We are close."

Schan slapped his hands together. "Good. About time too."

The landscape changed again, rock formations grew from the wasteland's floor, many creating man-high ridges and grooves in the land, as if hewn by a cosmic gardener in the dawn of time. The furrows cast shadows and twice he had to detour large holes that were more like craters, their mouths concealed in shadow.

"I hear something," Schan said from behind, as Ain

paused to wipe his brow.

A faint rushing sound, as water on stone. "It's close."

"This way."

Schan ran around one of the larger craters and lay upon its edge, hanging his head over the side, plunging it into shadow. "There's water down there," he rasped when he raised his head.

"Finally." Ain's smile stung his cracked lips but it didn't matter. Water at last. Gift of life. Time to find it, dunk his head and gorge himself. The murmur of the path faded when he stopped at the edge. Orange light flashed on the water in the crater, it was a steady flow and did not seem deep. It was a narrow fissure in the rocks, one that disappeared beneath ground.

"The hollow looks deep," Schan said. "It probably extends beyond where we stand now."

Ain shifted his feet. "How do we get down?"

"Without these," he said, removing his and Ibranu's pack. Working quickly, Schan unpacked his own bag, taking out a coil of rope, then repacked it. Ain placed his own near the small pile and collected the water flasks. "Opposite side." Schan walked around the crater, which was large, and slapped one of the irregularly shaped rock formations. "Tie off here and down we go."

While Schan worked on the rope Ain removed his Pathfinder's cloak. The edges of the crater were uneven, there was a chance they would tear the rope. He knelt by the edge without thinking, folding the cloth to use as a buffer, but a hand fell on his shoulder before the fabric touched the ground.

Schan held his own cloak. "Use mine."

"Thank you," Ain said, shaking his head. What was he thinking? Sun-sick already? Or delirious with thirst?

Nothing around him was unreasonably amusing. Grey and black rocks slashed with orange and a darkening sky.

"Ready?" Schan asked.

"Ready." Ain took the rope and lowered the warrior into the crater. When the man reached the bottom he tugged the rope. Ain moved to the edge and threw the flasks down, kneeling as Schan rushed to the stream, where he dunked a flask, filled it and slapped the cork in before tossing it up to Ain.

Ain tore the cork free and drank, the water spilling down his neck and soaking his chest. He paused, cupping his palms and washing his face. From the crater Schan's great sighs of pleasure drifted up.

"Better than Holvard wine," he shouted up.

Ain laughed. "Better than any wine."

He drank again, emptying the flask. "Schan, catch." He threw the flask. The warrior caught it and crouched by the water. Ain slid down the rope, burning his hands enough that he soaked them when he joined Schan in the shadows.

The stream was barely two feet wide and the bottom not past his forearm. It was smooth from the passage of water. "So. It travels beneath the earth not far from here."

"And starts from the rock wall there." Schan gestured with his chin.

Ain walked to the wall and examined the shadowy opening. It was regular, set with stonework and even had a symbol above the mouth. "This is man-made."

Schan joined him, cursing when he brushed dirt from the symbol. "That's the mark of the Mazu Clan."

"The Mazu Clan is a myth."

"They are no myth. And to drink from their streams, they will punish us with death."

Ain touched the symbol, a curved outline with two triangles inside. Mazu Clan. Called the Death Clan in children's stories, but the word 'mazu' in the old language was closer to 'Sleeping.' The Sleeping Clan of the southern desert, a Clan supposedly wiped out during the first war between Medah and the enemy, and who returned as ravenous darklings during the second.

Beings which lived in shadow and which collected blood to boil for soups to give them their magic. Beings which, according to Jedda, kept the hands of their victims. The man would never tell him why. He shivered.

But that was all. Stories, nothing more. "Schan, you don't believe in them, surely?"

He stood. "I have seen one, when I was a boy. It snuck into our camp and my father scared it with a torch."

"And this is truly their mark?"

"Yes. We must flee this place, Pathfinder."

Ain collected the water flasks and dashed to the other side of the crater, looking up to the fading light in time to see the rope slither to the ground in a coil. Dark shapes gathered round the crater's edge.

"The Mazu," Schan hissed.

Ain trembled.

CHAPTER 19

Black sand sprayed from his feet.

Almost within reach, the king floundered, driven down the dune, his sword throwing off sparks as he fended blows from curved Medah blades. Bodies lay at the king's feet. Blood stained the tunics and breastplates of the Honour Guard.

"Hurry." Medoro couldn't see, but his brother ran behind him. Their father's sword was slick in his hand and Medoro's chest heaved as he ran. The sun blasted his head and hands, catching on the blade as he swung a terrible arc.

Notch woke to darkness, grasping at nothing. Sweat trickled down his temple and he squeezed his eyes shut. "Damn you." Old dreams. How long had it been now, since the war snuck into his nights once again?

A blanket covered his body. The murmur of voices and music, faint, rose from below. A slip of light from the moon through heavy curtains revealed enough of the room that he lay back a moment. The Queen's Harper.

Sofia. Seto.

Notch swore. The explosion and the false masks.

He threw the blanket aside, cursing when his leg protested, and fumbled with a lamp. Once lit, he ran his hand along a bandage on his leg. The wound throbbed but it was bearable. He collected his tunic and a new pair of pants, dressing quickly and belting his blade on before leaving. Whoever patched him up did a good job. He sucked in a deep breath, head clear.

Tulio, a small man with a hard face, met him in the hall. Seto's second in command and a more nimble fellow than Tulio Notch had not met. "Notch. Flir and Luik are waiting for you. How do you feel?"

"Much better, thank you. Have they been waiting long?"

"A little. They're in the dining room."

"How's Seto?"

A shadow passed over Tulio's face. "Recovering."

"Good."

Tulio led him to the room and waited outside. Within, Flir and Luik spoke together by the cold hearth. Flir appeared unscathed but Luik's head was wrapped in a bandage. Notch touched his own head. Tender, though he had no bandage.

Bread and cheese sat on a plate between the two.

"You look dashing," he told his friend.

"How about I make you one to match?"

"How do you feel, Notch?" Flir asked as he sat.

"Well enough. Tulio said Seto is on the mend?"

"He's holding on," Luik answered. "Flir's healer got him here alive, which is more than I expected. He's not awake yet."

"He got you all here alive," Flir said, an eyebrow raised.

"You're right."

She exchanged a glance with Luik. "Notch, Sofia is gone."

"I know." He gave a heavy sigh. "We've failed."

"You saw her?"

"Two Mascare took her. They were looking for her. Someone scared them off though."

"Wasn't me," Flir said.

Luik pushed the plate to Notch. No cooked meals now. "If the Mascare took her, that's the end of it. We won't be able to rescue her."

"It might be worse," Notch said around a bite. "The Mascare. I think they were fake."

"What?"

"Their masks were wrong," Notch said, trying to sort the spinning images. "The faces were despairing. The mouth had been set in a frown, it looked as though someone with some skill carved it. And there was the Renovar imposter Seto found here in the inn. The body's in the cellar now."

Flir's brow creased.

"They're as good as dead if they're found by real Mascare," Luik said. "They don't like no-one playing with their toys."

"That's an understatement, Luik," Flir said. "The last craftsman who made a mask on the sly had his head dumped on his table, phoney mask and all."

"That's just a story."

"Is it?"

Notch slapped the table. "This isn't helping. Sofia's in danger. It could just as easily be the Mascare up to something," he said. "Either way, what do we do?"

"What can we do?" Flir asked.

"If they were real masks, we break into the palace

somehow and take her back." He lowered a piece of cheese. "If that's where she is. And if that's who took her."

"We know the palace is looking for her," Luik said. "With her father on the run, they'd want a Falco for bait."

Notch leaned forward. "And Seto once told me the houses tamper with their Greatmasks, to make sure no-one else can use them. Another reason the palace needs Sofia."

"But if they're fake, what are they after?" Luik nudged the plate closer to Notch, miming that he keep eating.

"The same. A bargaining chip?"

"Then we better ask around. See if anyone saw something. The fire at the Pig's memorable enough. Two Mascare, real or not, carrying a girl should be even more memorable. And we might want to do something about the fire too. Might not be the last."

Flir had folded her arms partway through Luik's suggestion.

"What's wrong?" Notch asked, another piece of cheese halfway to his mouth.

"You won't like this."

"Flir."

"We're wasting our time. We shouldn't look for her at all."

"What do you mean?"

"She's gone now. Whatever deal Seto struck with her is void unless she can return. The girl's no longer our problem. We should focus on finding out what's happening in the city. Where have the Renovar gone? Where will they strike next? There could be another explosion anywhere, anytime."

"I know. But we can't abandon her."

She leant forward. "And I know you like to help people in trouble – but we have to be practical now."

"I am. We could use Sofia's help with these Mascare whether real or not. And Seto offered her his protection, something he entrusted to us all, Flir. We failed her, we failed him. He'd just send us after her."

She did not uncross her arms. "Maybe. But that doesn't change anything. Whatever my countrymen and that piece of scum Vinezi are up to is a bigger problem."

"Tulio can help with finding the Renovar. Or we go to the Shields, tell them what we know."

"You think they'd listen to me, Notch? Soon as I finish the story, they'd take one look at my skin and they'd slap the chains on. Or try to."

"Give them some credit."

Flir shook her head. "No-one tries to kill me and stays around to grin about it."

"This isn't about Vinezi."

"For me it is, Notch."

Luik spoke quietly. "Sure your countrymen murdering dozens of innocent people isn't the real problem, Flir?"

"I don't like that either, you lump," she said. Notch thought she was fighting off a fond smile, but the expression was fleeting. "We aren't interested in war or chaos, or whatever it is that's going on in the Lower Tier. It's not what the Renovar believe at all. Or it wasn't when I left."

"That's a long time ago," Luik said. "What, ten, fifteen years now?"

She nodded.

"So has something changed?" Notch asked.

"I don't know. It makes no sense. Our trade lines would be cut. We need each other too much." She ground her teeth. "Listen. I don't like it, right?"

Notch sighed. Her family was in Renovar, and despite all the silences she kept about them, she would be worried. How could she not be? The Anaskari naval fleet would overwhelm the island nation of Renovar in a matter of days. "I'm sorry, Flir."

"Me too."

He stood and leant on a chair back, stretching his leg. "We need to be smarter than this. Treat it like a battle."

"Split up," Luik said.

"Exactly. Why don't you and Flir chase down Vinezi and the Renovar? I'll take Tulio and ask around the Pig."

"And what does Tulio think about this?" Luik said.

"He'll want to help me find her. It helps Seto."

"And if no-one saw anything?"

"Someone must have seen something." He hesitated. "If not, I have an idea." Tenaci's mysterious witch might be able to help. If she was real, and if he could find her. "That building across from the Pig will lead me to the Harbour Witch. She can lead me to Sofia."

Flir snorted. "She's a myth, Notch. Don't chase shadows."

"No, she's still alive. And I know how to find her." He explained about the children and the hatch.

"You're trusting a terrified street boy?"

"I took his measure. He didn't lie."

"And if you find the witch, if she exists, you think her magic will lead you to Sofia? No-one knows for sure what the Harbour Witch can do."

"I don't think the palace has Sofia. You know how the Mascare all speak the same? These two didn't sound right. They were faking, I'll bet my sword on it. Sofia might be anywhere if imposters have her. This is the quickest way."

"If it works. If you even find the witch. And if she agrees to help. Otherwise you're better off helping us. The false Mascare are connected to the Renovar. They're likely working together, which would lead you to Sofia."

"I can ask about the Mascare as I search, Flir."

"With a price on your head?"

He grunted. "I never said it'd be a delightful sail around the harbour."

She sighed. "Then I suppose we should get started, shouldn't we? It's nearly dawn. Luik and I will join you near the Pig, then you and Tulio are on your own."

*

Tulio shook his head, flipping a small blade up his sleeve as he straightened. "Seto needs me here, Notch." He'd been slouching against the wall, but he came almost to attention when Notch left the dining room and asked for help.

"I'd welcome your skills, Tulio. And this is important to him, there must be someone trustworthy you can leave behind?"

"No, but I think I can offer you someone better than me." He nodded to himself. "He usually works the palace but he's here now. I'll send him up."

"Thank you, Tulio."

Notch went to his room and added a knife to his belt, along with a heavier purse. He'd no idea what the Harbour Witch, if he found her, would expect in way of payment, but it wouldn't hurt to be prepared. And he could afford to be generous. Seto was paying. Pulling his cloak over his shoulders, he paused when the fabric caught on his cheek a moment.

His beard had grown in. Enough perhaps so that if

he kept going, he'd be harder to recognise? Especially if he had someone lighten his hair. Better than any disguise would be the assumption that he'd died at the Iron Pig. Was that a rumour worth fuelling, temporarily at least?

"Excuse me, Notch?"

A tall blond man, and not long a man at that, waited in the doorway. His hair was tied into a tail and he wore a thin beard much in fashion with the nobility, though his costume suggested otherwise. From head to foot he wore dark clothing, plain, much like Tulio. Only this fellow had a line of interlocking circles tattooed down his neck. The markings began beneath his ear and disappeared at his collar. A sign of his family's link to what the Braonn called the First Tree.

"Tulio sent you?"

"Yes. I am Wayrn, how can I assist you?"

Notch kept his voice kind. "Well, you don't have to be so formal."

"Very well."

Notch opened his mouth to try again but thought the better of it. It was probably the lad's training. "Who did you work for, as a child?"

Wayrn flushed. "Lord Biagio. I was three years old when my parents sent me here for a better life."

Notch frowned. 'Better life' wasn't always the case for young Braonn men and women sent north to the city. But maybe Wayrn was one of the lucky ones. He might have been happy, Lord Biagio might even have been a decent man. It wasn't Notch's place to question that and he didn't know the Lord. "But now you work with Seto?"

"I do. I wanted to report to him, actually, but he's been on another of his trips. The thanks I get for leading a double life."

"Something wrong?"

Wayrn hesitated. "He prefers I report directly to him."

"I understand. Seto trusts me, if that helps. I wouldn't be here otherwise."

"I do believe you, Notch." He sighed. "Among my instructions I was to listen for word of the palace's search for you and Lady Sofia. I know he values you."

Such a formal lad. "And I him. Is there news you can share?"

"Little. They are arranging for more Mascare in the streets, and scrambling after the explosion. Gates are watched, inns are watched, but for Sofia mostly now. They already believe you dead."

"Good. Do they suspect the Renovar of involvement?"

"No. Though the Renovar ambassador is upset about the rumours of war. He believes them to be false and seeks to convince Oson of such."

"A smoke screen?"

"From what I have heard, I could not be sure one way or the other, sir."

"We'll find out soon enough I suppose." He scratched at his beard. "Wayrn, don't feel like you need to stand on ceremony with me. In fact, it may draw unwanted attention. Can you relax while we work?"

"I think so."

"Then let's begin. I'll introduce you to Flir. I assume you know Luik?"

"Yes."

"Good. Down we go to meet her and then it's off to see the Harbour Witch."

CHAPTER 20

The Iron Pig was little more than a blackened skeleton with a hollowed centre. The scent of ash and char still filled the air and the edges of blankets, no doubt covering the dead, were muted in the dawn light. Notch sent a short prayer to the Ocean for their souls. How many would have been poor fools caught up in someone else's schemes?

He stopped an old man carrying a bag of oranges. "Excuse me, grandfather. Did you see the explosion?"

The man shook his head as he hurried on. "Don't know nothin-is."

A typical response. Notch didn't blame any of the people they questioned. The streets were rife with Shields and Mascare, even a few Sea Priests looking to help. The palace had probably been questioning people for hours. Notch avoided most of them by having Wayrn speak if they were stopped, and by keeping his hood raised. Many Shields were knocking on the doors to homes and businesses. The people who answered did not have welcoming expressions.

Having split from Flir and Luik earlier, and weary now of the silence and glares he received on the streets, Notch led Wayrn into the same abandoned building used on their first search, and up to the second floor. The window overlooking the street was dusty, as was the floor, though the passage of feet had only a light covering.

"Hmmm." Neither street boy, Tenaci, nor his friends, had used the trail for a time.

"What is it?" Wayrn called from where he was examining the other rooms.

"We're looking for a path to the harbour. It's used by children of the Lower Tier and hopefully it'll lead us to them. Or the Harbour Witch."

Wayrn re-entered the room, brushing dust from his hands. "Do you truly believe the Harbour Witch exists?"

"I hope. We need help. Sofia could be anywhere in the city, or even beyond it for all I know." She was probably unharmed at least. Too valuable as a hostage. That the weasel Otonos might have been behind her capture was not a good sign. But they needed her alive to use the Greatmask. Even if imposters had her, she was valuable. And safe for a time at least. But he still had to find her.

"It looks like the children aren't using this trail anymore. It'll be hard to follow."

"It leads to the hole in the wall in the other room?"

Notch pointed. "And down the hatch in the corner."

"Which way?"

"Down I suppose."

Notch pulled open the trapdoor. A square of white light glowed beneath the first few dark rungs of a ladder. He put some weight on one, then a little more. It held. The second rung snapped and he caught the edge of the flooring with a shout. Wayrn helped him out and he bent to examine the rungs as best he could.

"Rust."

"Shall we try the building?" Wayrn asked.

The floorboards creaked in the next room. A rotten table and empty fireplace, and a gaping hole in one wall. A nearby building was visible through the opening, a large hole in its own outer wall patched up with debris. If he leapt across the space between buildings, he'd only bounce back and crash to the cobblestones.

The path of small footprints led to the hole in the wall.

"So the children once leapt to the next building, but someone has blocked it?" Wayrn asked.

"Looks like it. The buildings are close."

"I should be able to get in," Wayrn said, kicking his legs and snapping his arms. He performed a short series of stretches. "Allow me a minute." Notch nodded. Once done, Wayrn moved to the edge and pressed on the jutting stonework. He climbed the wall with a grace that Notch should have expected from someone Tulio described as 'better.' Once on the roof, Wayrn backed up then took a running leap.

He made the distance easily, landing and rolling on the opposite roof. He was like a black flash of cloth, then his smiling face appeared, standing over the edge. "This bit will be harder."

"What are you going to do?"

"See that window?"

"I do." A small rectangle, empty of glass but a tight squeeze, and positioned in a spot close to the roof. He could not guess its purpose.

"I'm going through it, then I'll remove the blockage."

"How?"

"I just have to line it up properly. Watch." He stood with his back to the two storey drop and paused, rolling his neck. He inched across, checking on the window, then bent down to place his hands on the roof's edge. Notch stepped forward. What was he doing?

The young man bent his knees a few times before driving himself away from the building. Still holding the ledge, Wayrn's legs came down and flew into the opening, after which he let go, stretching his arms over his head and allowing the momentum of his leap propel him through the window.

He landed with a thump. In moments he had the space open, tearing back the hastily nailed planks and debris so there was a space large enough for Notch to pass through. While the distance between buildings was hardly great, Notch unbuckled his sword and threw it across first. Even as he paced his run up, he had to smile. Was there any point mentioning to Wayrn that the building opposite might have been accessible from the street? No. Besides, this was more fun.

Notch charged the opening, leaping across and rolling as he landed. It might not have been as impressive as Wayrn's efforts but he made the distance easily. He stood, brushed himself off and accepted his blade.

"Very impressive, Wayrn. Where did you learn that?"

The younger man beamed. "Tulio. He said I am by far his greatest student."

"He did a good job."

He sketched a bow with a grin.

The room was lined with steel structures, timber benches and heavy tools. Notch replaced a many-pronged hammer. The structures had a vaguely warlike look. Their large handles and planks made no sense to him, though the square stove with a broken flue standing beneath the window did. He bent to the floor. Any trace of footprints near the opening had been obliterated by his entrance, but further on he found the trail, faint here too, leading to one of the laden desks. Notch pushed it aside. The combination was heavy enough that he estimated more than a few children would need to work together to shift the desk.

Beyond was a dark opening, large enough to crawl inside. Notch grunted. His knees were going to be raw by the end of the search. "This better not get smaller in the middle."

"I agree."

Notch crawled into the dark. A torch would have been useful but he'd have to unpack it, and thankfully the passage was short. He discovered its end when his head thumped into a wall. Giving it a push, he heard a click and blinked in the light.

Another drab room, though this one had high windows and a staircase leading to the ground floor. The footprints of the children, still with a light covering of dust, led to the stairs and a grilled gate. Notch unhooked the clasp and stepped into an enclosed courtyard.

"What is this place?" Wayrn asked, eyes roving the yard.

Beneath tall walls, stone benches were spaced evenly around large hedge boxes of grey dirt. Uneven paving slabs created a walkway that once must have woven through trees. All that remained now were a few stumps and weeds.

"A garden I suppose."

"For who?"

"I don't know." He bent over the ground. "But I think

we've lost the trail."

Wayrn moved to the opposite wall, running a hand over the bricks. "What about another hidden door?"

"I'll start here."

He began his circuit of the garden, pushing on irregular bricks and kicking at walls. By the time he completed a lap, passing Wayrn, Notch was frowning. He sat on a bench, running a hand along the simple edgework. The white stone was cold. He put his feet up on a hedge box. "We're missing something."

"The door?"

He chuckled. "True. But is a door in the wall too easy?"

"There is only dirt, dying trees and benches left."

Notch stood. Something was out of place in the garden. "What about that hedge box?" The dirt inside was darker at one end. Small piles, almost like crumbs, were scattered around the box. He brushed the topsoil aside. An iron handle. "Ah-ha." He kept going until a circular trapdoor appeared. He wrenched it open, revealing a black pit. The sun glinted on iron rungs, mostly free of rust, that stepped into the darkness.

"How would street children find such a convoluted trail?" Wayrn said. "From the street, across the buildings, behind the desks then into this garden and I assume, beneath the city?"

A fine question. "Perhaps it was shown to them." Notch thumped the rung with the heel of his hand before stepping down into the hole. He was on the right path. Survival for scavengers like Tenaci relied on secrecy more than strength. "Ready that lamp, Wayrn."

The cool enveloped his skin as he climbed, and even before Wayrn's shape obscured light from the opening, he was relying on touch alone to guide him. Only the scrape of boots reached his ears.

"I hear water," he said after a time. It trickled, a faint echo. Half a dozen rungs later he reached the floor. The passage of water over stones was gentle and a strong mineral scent filled his nose. He waited for Wayrn to descend and light the lamp before moving too far from the ladder.

They stood in a chamber of smooth, dark stones of blue. Two openings allowed a narrow but deep channel of water to pass, slender walkways on either side. Above the openings, each large enough for a man to walk within, were indecipherable carven symbols. Medah markings? Or were they older still? One was a series of vertical lines in a tight pattern, but none possessed the familiar oceanic aspect to Anaskar, and nor were they crude as the scratched arrow marked to the left.

Wayrn held his lantern up to a symbol. "These are ancient."

"Do you know who made them?"

"No. But they almost trigger a memory. During my studies with Lord Biagio, I may have... I do not know."

"Well let's follow that arrow." He pointed. "The children won't have put it there for no reason."

"Indeed."

Notch took the lamp and started down the passage, sword drawn.

"Expecting trouble?"

"Last time I went beneath the city I was attacked by some... creature. So keep your ears open."

"What manner of creature?"

"I don't know. I've never heard of its like in Anaskar. Its slime was numbing and it was probably man-shaped, but I never saw the beast itself."

The channel flowed through the unchanging passage. Their footsteps echoed and the lamplight caught in the water. Notch kept one eye on the murky surface; the other was reserved for shadows beyond the lamp. He kept his sword point up.

"Do you hear that?" Wayrn asked after a time.

Notch stopped. From ahead, the echo of falling water bounced off the careful brickwork. He increased his pace, lantern high. Twice the passage turned at right angles before he came upon a sharp drop, the way opening out to a much larger chamber, dwarfing the one he and Wayrn had first entered. There was no walkway, instead water cascaded into the black, disappearing in a muddle of echoes and dying light as his lantern struggled.

"Do the street children leap into the abyss?"

"I hope not." Notch crouched by the flow. Set off from the water, partially hidden from sight, was a heavy chain, bolted into the stonework at intervals. It too, slipped into the darkness beyond the light. "Down we go then."

Wayrn grinned. "No problem."

Hooking the lantern to his belt, Notch lowered himself over the side, grabbing the chain and setting his feet against the stone. Hand over hand he worked backwards, keeping a good grip. From the sound of water hitting water below, it was a significant drop.

"Can you see?"

"Well enough," Wayrn replied.

Notch climbed, muscles in his arms straining. When his foot slipped, he found himself kicking air where there should have been rock face. The chain continued down, but he had to lower himself several arm lengths before his boot found stone again, the flat surface and regular opening suggesting a passage. "I've found another tunnel." He swung inside.

It was unlike the blue tinted stone from above. The stonework here was older, more time-worn, chipped and scuffed. The floor was scattered with debris, a belt buckle and a handful of fish bones. One of the markings was another arrow, which he showed to Wayrn when the man joined him.

The passage was not long. It branched several times, each with an arrow, before climbing rough steps and emerging through the ruins of a grate, into the aqueducts. A now familiar sound of moving water met his ears but Notch gave a start when he raised the lantern. Grim-faced children, holding blades, slings and even a pair of short bows, ringed the opening. Several, including those on the far side of the channel, raised torches that hissed when water dripped from the ceiling.

Notch put the lantern down, moving slowly, and raised his hands. Wayrn did the same.

One child, smaller than the others but a little older, crossed her arms. She wore a knife but had not drawn it, and her vest was almost clean. Its green was gaudy but she obviously took pride in it. "What are you doing here?"

"Searching for Kael."

Muttering came from the children but the small girl glared at them, before turning back to Notch. "Why?"

"I need his help to find someone. It's a matter of life and death."

"All matters are of life and death," she replied, small face grim.

"True," Notch said. "Can you help us?"

"That's up to Kael-is."

"Will you take us to him?"

"No-one sees Kael without his say so."

"I see." He had to tread lightly. He could feel the beads of the arrows on his chest. People were counting on him. Sofia especially didn't need him dead in an aqueduct beneath the city. Wayrn shifted beside him. "Then may I speak with Tenaci?"

"How do you know Tan?"

"I've paid him for information about those I search for."

The girl frowned harder. "And how did you find this place, then? Did he tell you about it?"

"No. We followed a trail left in an old house across from the Iron Pig."

"That so?" She turned to a nearby child. "Buckets, get Tan." The child called 'Buckets' ran off, and Notch exchanged a glance with Wayrn. The man's face was calm, but his eyes were marking the positions of youths who held either bows or slings.

Angry voices floated up the channel as Buckets pushed Tenaci into the light, the boy rubbing his eyes. His hair rested at odd angles. Upon seeing Notch he gaped. "Are we claiming the reward?"

The leader grabbed Tencai, her face alight. "What reward?"

"The one with the rough beard. He's Notch."

"So?"

"He's the one the Vigil's looking for, Dilo. Did we capture him?"

Dilo turned to Notch. "No. He walked right in, said he was looking for Kael. Said he spoke to you before."

Notch kept his hands in sight as he stepped forward. Things were getting out of hand. "I can offer more than the Vigil if you help me."

Dilo stared at him a moment then shrugged, waving at her fellows. "Take their weapons. We'll see what Kael has to say."

CHAPTER 21

Sofia woke in a warm room, bound to a chair. Her face stung and dried blood flaked to heavy carpet when she moved her head. Her temples ached and a faint ringing filled her ears. Even her chest was tight beneath the ropes, muscles afire. There was little she could do about it. At least the room was warm.

Drawn curtains covered the windows and an empty chair sat opposite. Bright lamps were set on the walls, and somewhere, a fireplace crackled. So much like Father's study.

He would be disappointed. Caught like a mouse. Sofia sneered at herself. "Wonderful job, Successor." How was she to live up to his hopes now? How could she find him, or take back Argeon? What Successor in hundreds of years had been forced from the palace and snatched from the street? None. She was not fit.

The explosion.

Were Notch and the others alive? She'd been close to Seto, still gaping at Flir's display of strength, when a deafening sound and blinding light, and heat, tossed her to the ground. She clenched her teeth, wrenching her torso to no avail. Escape was the only option. Survive, prove Oson wrong, find her father. She kept struggling but the ropes were too tight, locking her arms at her side. Her chisel might as well have been back in the palace. If her captors didn't have it already. "Gods be damned!"

A door creaked and she twisted with a grimace, blind to whoever had entered.

Who was it? They weren't moving, not saying anything, barely breathing. Mascare. "What do you want?"

Nothing. Was the silence now touched with amusement?

"Who are you?"

Soft footsteps. A red robe came into view and a man sat across from her, hood raised and hands crossed within the sleeves. A sigh escaped the hood as her captor reached up and pushed it back.

A frowning mask of bone greeted her. Sofia drew back as far as her bindings allowed. The eyes were dark, turned at the edges as if in anger and the mouth was all wrong. From the right eye, a single black line ran down to the cheek.

"Sofia, successor, survivor." His voice was deep, carrying a resonance seldom heard outside a performer's troupe. Was there a slight Renovar accent, one he tried to hide? All her life she'd been around people who worked hard to control their voice, he was a fool if he thought he could mask his origins from her. "What fortuitousness." He savoured the word.

"I would know the name of he who held me captive."

"My, aren't you formal? Call me Lupo." Was he smiling beneath the mask? He spread his hands. "And all I wish is for you to help me."

"Lupo? There's no Wolf House."

"For now." Both hands gripped the arm rest. Healthy skin, not an old man then. And sun burnt, as if unused to the climate. Renovar, without a doubt.

"For now? Ha. You're just an imposter from across the sea. You can't even attain Neutral Voice."

He chuckled. "An apt description perhaps. And yes. I do have an expressive voice, don't I? Instead, Sofia, consider me a man of my own destiny."

"Untie me. I'll hear what you have to say." Then jam a fist into your windpipe.

"I appreciate that, but certainly not."

She lifted her chin. "Then find someone able to make such a decision, if it's beyond you."

He rose, moving behind her chair. The clunk and hiss of a log hitting the embers followed. "Few things will be beyond me soon."

"But you need me."

"You're important." He rested his hands on the back of her chair and lowered his voice, speaking into her ear. His closeness sent a shiver along her shoulders. Meat was heavy on his breath. "You know things I must know. And unless you're willing to help me, the little surprise at the Iron Pig will occur again. And again, and no-one will be able to predict where, Sofia. From tier to street, no-one will know."

"You did that? You're a madman," she cried.

His tone remained amused, indulgent even. "Not mad yet. But you've witnessed what I'm capable of. It's not truly in Anaskar's best interests for you to refuse me."

"Then what do you want?"

"I want you to reveal where your father has hidden the tabella. It does not lie within his room in the palace."

Sofia stared. Her arms twitched but there was no way to fold them. The table of names was not something this man should have in his possession, let alone know of. With it, he could trace the identity and location of any Mascare in Anaskar. The whole order would be at risk. Considering his mask and robe, which had a weave that looked authentic, the Mascare were already at risk. If the people connected this man to the explosion in the city...

"I don't know where it is. And someone like you shouldn't even know it exists."

He laughed. "Come now, Sofia. There are always those in high places willing to sell secrets... to those in possession of the right currency."

Who? Solicci or Lady Cera? She wouldn't put it past either. They'd shown how desperate they were. Sofia glared at him. "I don't know where it is."

Lupo tilted his head, dark holes empty. "As you might have guessed, I expected some reticence. To that end I'm granting you until dawn, Sofia, after which I will return and you will either tell me where the tabella lies, or which tier you wish me to strike. Or if you prefer, I can target your friends. If they survived." He reached out to place a hand on her shoulder again, bending down. "Consider well what the people of your city mean to you. Be their saviour," he said and left the room.

Sofia clenched her jaw.

*

Her hands were numb.

Dawn light slipped through the curtains. At one point in the night, another imposter had doused the lamps, held water to her mouth and left, all without speaking. Her stomach had burned in the darkness. Between hopeless plots to escape and useless, fitful dozing, she ran what she knew of the tabella over in her mind.

And it was little.

There was no longer an old list on parchment, written in several hands, sealed in a locked box and placed in the vault concealed behind her father's bed. Even such measures were still folly, her father told her. It existed only in his mind now. What she could tell Lupo, then, was nothing he'd want to hear.

Not that her captor would keep his word. If she actually knew the names, he could take information he needed, kill her and strike the city despite his word. She could lie, refuse to answer and he might do the same. In either case, she would be dead. Lupo was yet to threaten her directly, but that was no guarantee. And if Notch and Seto had survived, they were in danger.

Misdirection. She had to buy time, find a way to force Lupo to take her out of the room. And get feeling back in her limbs. She shifted on the hard chair, cursing Lupo again. There was no relief. Flexing her muscles periodically was as much a hopeful act as one to occupy her mind. At least she could move her fingers and feet.

The palace was a bad idea. Leading Lupo there would only create more bloodshed, and while the idea of a bleeding Oson appealed, if she escaped there was every chance it would be into the arms of her enemy. Lupo might be clever and ruthless, but was he a match for the entire palace? Unlikely. Going there would be a fool's swim into dark water. And she didn't want Lupo in her father's rooms again.

Seto's inn was out of the question too. Wherever she took Lupo, it would have to be isolated. Away from innocents. But somewhere he would believe the tabella might be hidden.

The door opened. "Good morning, Sofia. I trust your night was unpleasant?" Lupo sat and crossed his legs at the ankles.

It had been anything but pleasant. Her neck ached and her limbs were stiff, even though she'd long since given up trying to escape her bindings. "It was tolerable."

"And have you taken time to think?"

Sofia glared at him. "I'll tell you. But there's a condition."

"How wonderful."

"I'll show you where it is, I'll take you there."

He made no response.

She straightened her back as best she could. He had to believe her. "Either take me or kill me. Those are my terms."

After a time his mask shifted a fraction. "And where is 'there' exactly?"

"My father's manor in the Western Foothills."

He rose and swept a bow. "Very well, Sofia. Let's prepare for our trip."

*

Lupo's men were organised. It was almost impressive. At least a dozen, all in red robes and distorted masks, rushed about in the grey light, filling a courtyard beneath her room. She looked up at it, a box hanging off the edge of a two storey building. She'd seen little of the structure on her way down, Lupo directing her by a leather leash, tied to a collar on her neck.

It chafed. Being able to raise her hands and tug at it should have been a relief after all night tied to a chair, but it still irritated her skin. Worse than the stiffness in her knees, the ache in her ankle or the vicious tingling in her soles.

Lupo had her chisels and linfa-belt, so no-one paid her any heed, unarmed and leashed as she was, instead readying horses and loading supplies into wagon beds. Tent poles, water barrels and crates of food were being loaded, but nothing that looked like it could create the same damage as had been visited upon the Iron Pig.

"What are they doing?" she asked Lupo, who'd donned a true mask earlier. He wasn't fit to wear it.

He turned to her from where he'd been studying the gates. Beyond waited the rustle and thump of traffic. A bright blue sky presented its face in a mockery of freedom. "First, moving. We never reside in one place very long. Second, visiting with the good people of Anaskar."

"What does that mean?"

"Nothing as impressive as last night. Only that they should make themselves seen. Sow seeds of doubt in the minds of the people. Let them wonder about the mighty, dutiful Mascare."

"They'll be seen for imposters."

"That I would be most pleased with also," he said. "And how long to the manor?"

What was his game? Sending false Mascare into the city with their sad-faced masks would do nothing... unless he meant to link the Mascare to the explosions? But why? Perhaps something greater was afoot. The first steps toward war? Insanity. Renovar merchants might be a little bold, greedy even, but not warlike. No. It had to be personal. Whatever was happening, was all about Lupo.

He was waiting. Focus, Sofia. Escape first. "It's a two day return trip."

He waved and a figure emerged from the shadows behind a wagon. Sofia frowned. More Renovar, the pale skin of his hands and wrists an obvious tell. Just how many of them were from across the sea? Worse, were any Anaskari?

"Ready our mounts. You and I are taking a trip into the foothills."

"Yes, my lord." The Renovar's voice was younger than she'd been expecting and his mask trained on her a moment, before he made a quick bow to Lupo and ran off. His accent was also slight. A strip of flaxen hair slipped free as he ran.

"What are you Renovar doing here? Do you truly want war? Our navy would crush you."

He made an expansive gesture. "What we do here is the creation of a future."

"That's not an answer, Lupo. You're worse than a back alley mystic."

Lupo jerked the leash, hard enough to make her stumble and she choked, clawing at the collar. "Careful, Sofia. Do not expect that my tolerance for you is boundless. Now mount up." He propelled her forward and she bumped into a horse's flank, shock casting her mute. The horse snorted but stayed put. The young Renovar boosted her into the saddle then tied her leash to a lead rope, which he handed to Lupo, who was already mounted. Next, he lashed her to the saddle. She shook her head. Where did he think she was going?

"Westward then," Lupo said, before shouting to a man on the gate. It swung open and he led them out. A sea mist had rolled in and the empty streets were cool. Breath from the horses' nostrils steamed, as did her own. She said nothing. Swallowing was uncomfortable and her hands trembled on the pommel as they climbed the Second Tier, passing dark windows with sleeping flower pots.

Instead of noting information she needed to plan her escape, Sofia glared at Lupo's back. At every unexpected move from him she tensed. The collar continued to chafe her neck as horseshoes clapped down the cobblestones. She rubbed her mount's back as best she could. His outburst... she shivered.

In a way, she'd been a prisoner before. Of the palace and of her role as Carver, rarely leaving its grounds, or even the palace. Never leashed, true, but she'd been so long in the company of her father, carvers and the Mascare, the routines and rituals, the work, the familiar halls of the palace, that she'd grown complacent. That was part of her fear. With Seto too, she had understood the terms of their arrangement, known what was expected.

Even after Oson's betrayal, meeting Notch and Seto, running on the streets, the explosion, she had not felt this. Had it all built up? Was she so fragile that a few harsh words from her captor would set her limbs trembling?

No.

It was Lupo. He was unpredictable.

She had to watch him. To become her namesake, to be ready. To be strong where he expected weakness.

The Mountain Gate loomed in the thinning fog. Massive bolts crossed thick iron, they were so heavy that a mechanism was required to open them – the gate guards stood arranged in pairs before it, yellow light blooming in the gatehouse. Could she use them? Would they help her if she cried out? Each was heavily armed and they outnumbered her captors.

But would they believe her? A 'prisoner' of a Mascare? No-one challenged the Mascare but royalty. Or perhaps a man in Emilio's position, and then with little expectation. Certainly not a gate guard. Nor would she risk their lives. Wait a little longer. Strike when he's alone. Isolated.

"Open up, men," Lupo called.

One of the guards stepped forward, breastplate catching the light. "Not before full light, you should flipping know –" he stopped, eyes widening when he saw them. "My Lord, I apologise, I meant no offense. It's just that so many –"

"No trouble," Lupo interrupted, pulling his mount to a halt while the guards jumped to action. Some cast glances at the odd mask on the young Renovar, but no-one dared mention it. And if they detected his slight accent they did not mention it either. A grinding followed as the gates swung open, revealing an empty mountain road. Dark stone walls rose up to one side and a sharp drop waited opposite.

The Mountain Gate. One of the only access points to the city outside of the harbour, certainly the only one of size. Heavily guarded since the first Medah attack, hundreds of years ago. And the quickest route to her family's manor, not that Father used the home much anymore. Secrecy meant Survival.

The wind was colder, whipping up the gorge beside the road. She shivered, her cloak a poor replacement for her Mascare robe, which she had been told was being cleaned. Another shudder ran through her body at the thought of Lupo, of any of them, dressing her.

Far below, dark trees grew on the slopes. Her view grew considerably as they wove their way lower, at times she could see down to the pale green of the foothills.

"Is your manor a modest place then?" Lupo asked after a time, speaking over the rhythm of the hooves.

"I don't know what you think of as modest, but wealth is not to be flaunted."

"Ah."

They rode on and the sun rose, its rays weak. Sofia coughed, her breath wheezing. She needed warmer clothing. And yet, her face was warm, skin hot to the touch. If a fever was building, it couldn't have chosen a worse time. When Lupo pulled them into a wider space beside the road to eat trail rations at noon, the young Renovar approached her, a scarf in hand.

"You seem cold," he said.

She said nothing.

"My name's Veddir. Will you take this?"

It looked warm. A token gesture, perhaps, but inviting. Veddir held it out, mask sockets impossible to read.

"Thank you." She wrapped it over the collar. The fabric cut the wind and she almost sighed as a slow warmth spread.

He held his torso half-turned, as if expecting to be dismissed. Or even struck.

"Are you unwell?"

"No."

What did he want? An offer of friendship would be a front. Was he trying to lure her into a false sense of security?

He averted his gaze. "I hope it helps." He walked back to his saddlebags.

Sofia rounded on Lupo, who stood watching. By his posture he could have been smiling beneath his mask. It was in the set of his shoulders, at ease. Familiar too, mocking. People like Oson stood the same way and it troubled her. It could have been his lack of concern over his prisoner. She had no-where to run. Yet. The wolf had not eaten, but simply waited for them to finish before motioning to mount up.

The horses carried them down the mountains and temperature climbed, her body warmth rising. Up ahead, a heavy cart, laden with wool packs from the lowland farms, trundled toward them. The driver pulled his team up against the wall to let them pass, despite there being ample room. He pushed a boy back on the bench, bowing his head as Lupo passed. The driver's eyes flicked to Sofia's leash but he made no comment.

The imposter inclined his head to the herder, as if royalty.

Sofia snorted.

Near nightfall the darkening foothills rose around them, green grass bending in a breeze. Domes of moss and stone peeked from the earth and sometimes low walls cut through the hills. At a marked fork, a turn she could have made even without spotting the rough bird she and Tantos had cut into the base of a stump, Sofia directed Lupo up a winding trail that passed through groves of dark pines. Their needles littered the path and blocked the setting sun. The singing of birds faded.

"We're close then?" Lupo said.

"It's not far." Still she had no plan for escape.

Beyond the grove a low stone wall ran around a hilltop. A single hole in the masonry sat beside the gate, which was closed but not chained. Lupo opened it and led them along a path that curved up to her mansion. Lined with trees, many of which she'd climbed as a child, it obscured the building until they dismounted out front, its many windows catching the last of the sunlight. 'Modest' compared to the palace, it was nonetheless large. Three storeys and a stable around back, with grand double doors resting over a landing, it had once hosted dinner parties for well over a hundred guests. When mother had been alive, and father cared about such things.

A place of comfort, more so than her rooms in the palace, here she had been allowed to play, before the grind of the carver's life took over, before day after day of shaping bone, hands aching over chisel handles. Here she had imagined her life as similar to her mother's – she would have a handsome husband and beautiful daughters. And then, when she got a little older, a life as the greatest carver the palace had known.

Sofia could have sprinted to her room. In other circumstances she would have.

"It looks empty," Veddir said.

"It is. The servants have returned to the city," Sofia said, trying to breathe deeply. "Winters can be hard here."

"Very well." He untied Sofia and helped her down. "Stable the mounts, Veddir, and meet us inside." The man led the horses away and Lupo continued. "Sofia, I have some news you may wish to hear."

"About?"

"Oson has asked that the populace assist in your capture. There's a significant reward. Casa Swordfish has certainly wiped its hands of you."

Typical of the slimy weasel. She glared at her captor. "Why tell me this?"

He said nothing a moment. "To remind you that your only path is with me. Forget your father, forget your old life."

"No." She snatched the leash and wrenched it. He stumbled but caught the rope. "Help me and I spare you.

That is your path, Sofia."

"Damn you!"

He took her leash and removed it from the collar before binding her hands. "There. Does that help your breathing?"

She glared at him. Was he taking his lead from Veddir? Toying with her emotions? Loathsome. He wanted the tabella. Desperately. What else would he try to keep her off balance? "Gods take you and your blackened heart."

He started up the steps to the landing. "In we go, Sofia."

She growled. "It'll be locked."

"Worry not." He produced a key from his robes with a flourish and placed it in the door, giving it a turn. It clicked and Sofia glared at his back. How much had he stolen from her father's rooms?

The foyer was splashed with light from the many windows, twin staircases beside another set of double doors. The stairs led to balconies and other closed doors, access to the third storey from a second set of stairs. Empty lamps flanked each stair and a cold chandelier hung overhead. Beyond the double doors was a ballroom, it had not heard music or felt the clap of hard shoes for years.

"To your father's study then?"

She said nothing, but at a gesture from her captor, led him up the stairs and through the nearest door. Her breath came a little hard at the top, and sweat gathered at her temples. Still a fever threatened. Lupo kept close behind in the darkened hall, the leash alternating between slackness and a tugging on her wrists. Even the weight of the rope was a reminder that she was captive. Inspiration had not struck. She couldn't even slip something into his water – no dormi, no linfa-belt, nothing. She'd managed to separate herself from the city at least. No innocents were in danger, but the leash was something she hadn't counted on. Foolish.

She stopped at the door.

"Inside, Sofia."

"What are you going to do with it?"

"Read it, little successor." He pulled her into a small room. Across from open curtains stood a deep desk, papers in neat stacks and quills and ink pot nearby. Shaped as a falcon at rest, Sofia almost smiled. Once she'd dropped it, spilling ink all over his documents.

She knew what to do.

"In the desk. There's a page hidden throughout each of the documents, sealed within other pages. You'd never know."

"That seems... insecure. Unlike a Falco."

She shook her head, mind racing. Outwardly, she kept her face composed. "He wanted it out of the palace. He suspected the other houses were plotting against us." She looked away. "And he was right."

Lupo tugged at a drawer and it slid open. "Hmmm." He began heaping stacks of paper onto the desk, looping the leash over his wrist as he worked in the darkening light. Outside the sun began to slip out of sight.

She did not join him.

Sofia stayed across the small room, standing by the window, leash near its limit. She took a shuddering breath and held it. Time it right. Wait, wait, wait, watch his arm. Wait for the right moment. There! Lupo lifted another stack of documents from the bottom drawer and Sofia jerked on the leash, smashing the window with her elbow. In the same motion, she dragged the leather cord over the jagged edges of broken glass, slicing her forearms. Blood slicked her hands but the leash was cut.

She sprinted for the door.

"Stop," Lupo shouted. He lurched forward, his reactions slowed by surprise. Sofia dove, avoiding his outstretched arms. She rolled into the hall, gaining her feet and hurtling toward the opposite end.

Thundering footsteps followed and she slammed through a door, back onto the balcony, breathing hard. With hands still bound, her gait was not smooth but she took the steps two at a time and dashed across the foyer, Lupo's shouts falling behind. She twisted her torso as she shouldered the front door open. The wolf leapt down the stairs, robe flying.

And then she was charging around the manor, away from the stables. Shrubs flashed by her legs as she ran, using the house as a screen, crossing the tall grass that separated manor from tree line. Twice she nearly tripped on the leash. If she could stay out of sight long enough she might escape.

She slipped between tree trunks and spun, crouching down, gasping for air. Beneath the canopy her hand on the trunk was a pale smudge, smeared with blood. Her lungs had shrunk to half their size, or so it seemed. Blood pumped in her ears and her face was aflame. She thumped the tree. Not now.

Lupo and Veddir were moving around the house, converging on the spot that would lead them to her, the moment they marked her tracks in the grass.

She wrapped the leash as best she could and stumbled through the copse. Trees thinned where the hill sloped and she half-slid, half-fell to the bottom, collapsing to her knees with a curse. A stream, in some places no more than a puddle beneath grass, meandered through the gully. The black shapes of surrounding hills closed in as she dragged herself to her feet and splashed forward.

How many times had she played 'hide and catch' with Tantos here? Or her father, joining in to laugh and pretend he could not see her. It had always been a safe place, something about the hills... they would protect her. If she could locate the old cave before collapsing, Lupo would never find her. Not in the dark, the opening was hard to find even in daylight. Lupo would pass her by.

Sounds of pursuit were distant but a faint glow might have been visible between the trees. Torches? She followed the water, still panting, detouring a large boulder and feeling her way up a game trail. Overground, it made for footing near as treacherous as the streambed, but she knew it well. The path turned with the hills, which still concealed much of the sky, and she was forced to slow as the last of the daylight disappeared.

A light bobbed along her back trail. Lupo's rich voice echoed in the night as he shouted commands to Veddir. Sofia moved as fast as she dared, stumbling often. When she tripped, she broke her fall with her hands. Blood trickled down her arms but there was nothing to be done for it. Rising was agony. Her ankle throbbed and her chest was afire. Each breath tore at her throat.

The cave mouth was close. She ran her hands along stringy grass on the wall. To the right of the game trail, somewhere not too far beyond the boulder, was a second path, a fork. It was marked with a shrub and a depression. Her feet would probably find it first but she slowed to catch her breath, or try to. She could only manage shallow breaths through the pain.

Damn you. The curse was for the rising fever, for

herself, for Lupo, it didn't matter. She crept forward until her feet found the depression and to her right, as she remembered, the shrubs. Shuffling around them she continued along the new path, moving deeper into the hills and the darkness.

"Finally," she gasped when her hands lost contact with the grass. She stopped to trace a narrow opening, partially grown over. Shoving an arm inside, she tested for obstructions before crawling in. The cold from the stone floor seeped into her skin, soothing even as she collapsed into shivering. She crawled deeper, putting her back against the walls and catching her breath.

The opening was a lighter shade of black, nothing more. At any moment, light from Lupo's torch could arrive and if he noticed the cave, she would be caught. Would he kill her then? Unleash the temper that bubbled beneath the indulgent exterior? Not knowing was terrible. She found a loose rock, a pitiful defence.

If she could remain undetected until morning, and if she survived the fever, there was a chance she could forage for food and head back to Anaskar. A tear squeezed itself from her eye. Damn him. She would not be caught. She was Falco.

Light grew outside the cave. A pale bloom at first, quickly joined by Lupo's voice. She scrambled back, trying to make herself smaller.

"Continue looking. I need her," he was saying.

"She could be anywhere by now." Veddir's voice had risen in pitch, almost to a whine. "I think we've missed her."

"No. Those were footprints back there. She's here somewhere. Look again." Lupo's voice was flat.

The light grew as Lupo walked into view, pausing

before the opening at a sound from Veddir. "What now?"

The young Renovar rushed his words. "Wait, I hear her heartbeat. She's close by, Lord Lupo. I'm sure of it."

Sofia put a hand over her chest. How in the name of the Ocean Gods could Veddir possibly hear her heart? She froze. The thump of her heart was suddenly magnified, slamming into her chest, as if it fought the fever. Having Lupo and Veddir mere feet away, discussing her heart, doubled its beat. Was it some strange Renovar magic she'd not heard of? No Anaskari could do such a thing. Not even the Storm Singers.

Lupo took another step. "Here?"

"Yes. The sound is very close," Veddir said. "She's here. Wait, what's that?"

"Ah," Lupo said as he bent down by the opening. He pushed his torch into the cave and looked around, mask bright in the torchlight. His gaze swept across her twice before he backed out. "She's not here," he snapped.

"But I hear her heart." Veddir cried. "Even the pump of blood in her veins."

A slap echoed in the night. "The cave is empty. See for yourself."

Veddir repeated Lupo's actions, lighting the rough walls with his torch but seeing nothing when he looked at her. He crawled back out.

"But, I can still hear it." His voice rose again. "I've never been wrong."

"You are this time. Come, continue searching," Lupo said, steps moving on. "And keep your voice down." Veddir followed with his own torch, and it wasn't until the light faded that Sofia released a fit of gasping.

CHAPTER 22

Sofia frowned in the darkness. What happened? Lupo stared directly at her. Backed out of the cave and walked away. Left. And Veddir made the same mistake.

Did it even matter? Since they'd left, her heart slowed and her breathing came easier. Her clothes were damp with sweat. She tugged on the collar and adjusted her scarf. It was cold in the cave, best to keep them on.

Escape was possible. If she could wait until dawn she would have a chance, so long as they had given up.

Soft clicks came from the opposite end of the cave. Sofia straightened. A lavender glow slipped from a fissure in the wall and a tiny figure holding a cane clicked toward her. No bigger than her hand, the small man crossed the cave floor to remove his hat and sweep a bow. His coat was tight and his pants billowing. He smiled up at her and she gaped down at his glowing form.

"Welcome back, Sofia."

"Ah..."

"It's been a few years, hasn't it? I hope you've been happy."

Sofia swallowed. "Who are you?"

"Excuse my poor manners," he said, bowing again. "We haven't actually met, have we? My name is Padin di Mente and this is my home. Or, part of it."

"Are you real?" She was still only half in control of her jaw. Maybe the fever was inducing a hallucination.

He sniffed. "I am quite real, I assure you."

"I'm sorry. But, ah, what are you?"

"A Mente. What are you?"

"A Falco, I suppose."

He lowered himself to the ground, crossing his legs and laying the cane across his knees. "What brings you back to the Payvesa Foothills?"

"Payvesa? These aren't the Western Foothills?"

He nodded. "I've heard you Falcos call it that. Even your curious friends from before are thinking of it that way. They walk across history, blind as moles. Payvesa was ancient before your ancestors built your home."

Sofia waited. He stared up at her expectantly, the glow from his body lighting the whole room. It was so powerful that the walls responded, traces of purple swirling beneath the stone, as if looping patterns had been drawn there and were slowly waking. Beautiful, and yet, would it be visible from outside? If Lupo returned... "Ah, Padin, your glow is very bright. I worry that men looking for me might see it. They are not my friends."

"Oh, don't worry. They cannot see us."

"So, you helped me?"

"I must admit, you appeared in some distress."

"I was. Thank you Padin."

"It was my pleasure. I have missed watching over you. And do not worry. They won't see you should they return, not so long as I am awake."

She exhaled. That at least, was a relief. "Do you sleep often?"

"I sleep much of the time you Falcos are awake. I was in fact quite surprised to see you here. It has been many years since I last saw you – hiding and giggling in my reception room."

"This? It seems a bit bare. But still beautiful," she hastened to add.

"Bare only to your eyes, Sofia. This room does not appear to me as it does to you. You see the necessary illusion."

"Your magic is very powerful, Padin."

"Thank you, but I am a mere student."

Sofia stared at him. If he was a student, what could a master do? "Do you live in this hill? By yourself?"

He waved his cane around his head. "All of them, actually. The Payvesa Foothills are my home and while I do live alone, I have many visitors. Some of which are even welcome, such as you."

"That's a relief, Padin. What do you do here?"

"I watch and when I do not watch I tend to the hills."

"For who?"

"No-one has instructed me to watch. It is the di Mente way."

"Ah, I meant..." Sofia stopped. Maybe it didn't matter. The fact that she was speaking with a miniature man who glowed, who'd watched over her in the past, and who'd saved her life, did. "I have to thank you again, Padin. Can I repay you?"

He smiled. "No, but you are a kind Falco to offer. In fact, I'm glad you returned. I have something for you, wait here a moment if you please?" He rose, dusted off his pants and strode to the fissure in the wall, slipping inside and taking his lavender light with him. In the utter dark Sofia waited, sweat sliding down her temple.

When Padin returned, he was dragging a ring into the room, which he urged her to wear. The slender ring was a perfect fit for forefinger, the band carven with feathers. "It's beautiful. Whose is it?" she asked, turning her hand.

"A warrior queen once wore it. She died defending her people in Payvesa, many years ago. Her hair was quite golden, even at night. You might know her name, though I cannot recall it."

"I can't remember her." She said before twisting the ring off and laying it in an outstretched palm. "But I am not worthy to wear it, if what you say is true."

"It is indeed true. And I'm giving it to you, it is well that you wear it, Sofia. I have no use for it. A Mente watches."

"Thank you." She replaced it, finding that her breathing had eased but that her eyes were heavy. "Padin, may I sleep here? Safely?"

"Of course. I will watch."

She leant back. "Thank you again. I'm in your debt, Padin."

"That you are, but the price is not to be paid yet. Sleep for now, Sofia. We will meet again, I am sure."

"I'd like that," she whispered, closing her eyes.

*

The day was wearing on when she woke. Sunlight poured through the grass edging the cave mouth, splashing onto the floor. Despite sleeping on stone, Sofia's limbs weren't stiff, nor did a single ache trouble her. The cuts on her arms were healed, the blood gone and only thin, white lines remained. All trace of fever had been banished, she drew in a deep breath and felt her lungs expand. Her old wounds no longer troubled her, ankle free of pain. Even her bonds were cut, the scraps of rope and collar missing from beneath her scarf.

She stretched. "Padin?"

The little glowing man was gone. She held up her hand. The ring. In the day it was bright, the feathers delicate and unmarred by signs of age. Which Queen? And where in the hills had she died? None of Sofia's history books mentioned a golden warrior queen, though with such a description, how could she be forgotten or overlooked?

"Goodbye, Padin. And thank you." Sofia crept from the opening of the cave. No-one walked the trails. The breeze was cold and the sun warm enough that she almost enjoyed the walk to the stream, despite her parched throat. Bent at the river, water cold on her teeth, she drank her fill. It didn't take the place of food, didn't much ease that ache, but it would have to suffice. She had nothing and the stores in her mansion were inaccessible. Or as good as. Lupo could be anywhere.

If she circled the building and returned to the road some miles away, she could be well on her way to Anaskar and away from Lupo. And Veddir with his strange claims of being able to hear her heartbeat and blood. Was it true? She shivered. Time to move on.

Sofia wove through long, swaying grass, cresting the hill in the same grove from the day before and keeping the mansion in view. Inside were supplies and equipment. A water flask, food and heavier boots and cloak, a bedroll or at least a blanket and tinderbox. It was only a day's travel, but she was starting late. Night would catch her in the mountains. Thanks to old games of hide and seek, she knew of one trail near to the road, but not how far it went. She'd be a fool to try the journey without real planning.

Life in the palace did not prepare her to travel alone in the mountains, but going into the mansion, even approaching it, was madness. To walk directly back into Lupo's clutches, she might well have never escaped.

Yet if she followed a trail back to Anaskar, and walked through the night, there would be no need to risk recapture by sneaking into her mansion, where her heart might give her away. How close did Veddir need to be? Could he hear her even now? Keeping her distance was the best thing. Even now, the two were probably lying in wait and what did she have? Nothing. She might be able to subdue Veddir, but Lupo? He was bigger. He probably had more ability than she gave him credit for.

No, don't go back.

Sofia crept around the hillside, keeping the tip of the mansion's roof in sight. Her heart thumped, despite efforts to measure her breathing. If it made things easier for Veddir, she was caught. A bird squawked overhead and she flinched.

When she finally ducked into the cover of large stones growing from the earth, and started up a trail, Sofia exhaled. Her path ran parallel with the road, she was heading in the right direction at least. With each step she moved a little further from recapture. By the time her knees and feet started to ache, she'd stopped looking over her shoulder. She'd given them the slip, no doubt Lupo was searching every nook of the mansion for the tabella. She ground her teeth and kicked at the earth as she walked.

He had no right to be in there, touching everything.

She climbed on. Her stomach had twisted itself into

smaller and smaller shapes, starting after noon. None of the shrubs or stringy plants bore fruit or berries. Her footfalls echoed between the stony walls, deep blue and green moss crawling in the shadows. Not even a trickle of a stream reached her, and when she finally stumbled onto a plateau offering a clear view of her surroundings, Sofia cursed.

Her path had diverged, angling north. By the dusty road she could make out below, still heading east, she was also higher in the mountains. Nor did she have any idea of how long her trail was reliable for; she'd already climbed over one landslide and taken one right hand fork before having to double back and head left.

She bent to scoop up a few rocks and cast them at the glimpse of greying horizon. Each one sailed down to disappear with only the faintest of clicks. The day was wearing on and she hadn't managed half the distance she imagined she would need. Her throat was scratchy, and after a vicious throw, she paused to catch her balance.

The light-headedness passed. She wasn't turning back.

Sofia climbed higher, her steps slowing when a light rain began to fall. She stood with her mouth open, the relief slight. After a meagre mouthful she walked on. The scarf was of small comfort now. Hungry, thirsty and wearied with a whole night of travel before her, the vitality she'd woken with was gone. Had it been a gift from Padin? If only he were near. A wind picked up and she drew close to a wall, squinting in the rain.

When the trail finally sloped back down, Sofia increased her pace, sky clearing overhead. She shivered in the wind. Her path curved around a gorge, inside which dark trees grew on the slopes, the bottom lost in shadow as the sun began to set behind clouds. A hawk or falcon crossed the sky, its call shrill, and she lifted her legs higher, despite her fatigue.

The moment of renewed strength was brief. By nightfall she no longer knew if her path ran parallel with the road to the Mountain Gate. Another shower, this one heavier, blew in from somewhere, pelting her face, but she moved ever forward, repeating the same actions. One heavy foot ahead of the other, then the next. Do it over. Look around. Do it over.

The moon was strong, casting the rockface and occasional tree in a rain-slick silver. Rain still fell from scraps of cloud, beyond, the sky was like a deep blue ocean that threatened to spill. Shivering so much that her jaw rattled, Sofia paused beneath overhanging rock, clutching her arms to her sides.

She shivered until the rain stopped.

The moon had not left the sky. She set out again, her clothes and shoes wet and her heels blistered. She had to be close. Earlier, she'd climbed an outcrop and stared down at the moonlit mountain, trying to discern the road. It might have been a pale strip cutting through a distant gorge, but she couldn't be sure.

On she stumbled. The moon faded from the sky and the trail before her widened as it reached another fork. She took the lower path, hands held out before her when the walls narrowed and the darkness grew. She still stumbled, crying out when something sharp sliced into her knee. Rolling onto her back, stones digging into flesh, she gripped the cut, biting her lip and squeezing her eyes shut.

When the pain faded enough that she was willing to move, Sofia tore strips from her hem and bound the wound, probing with her fingers first. It was deep.

Gaining her feet, she limped forward, knee protesting with every step. The path was blocked. Jagged rock and stone lay scattered before what must have been another landslide. More light and she'd have avoided it. Now she limped along in the dark, dragging herself up the path to take the other fork. Which would probably take her further away from the Mountain Gate, wherever it was.

"Fool," she snarled. "Damn fool."

She'd barely taken half a dozen steps when her knee gave way. She fell, reaching for something to hold and finding nothing. She hit hard, slipping on loose gravel, and then she was falling, a scream splitting the night.

Sofia bounced off something solid, her body flung into another unyielding object, and then she was scraping along stone and rolling down a slope. Searing pain flew up her leg and the skin of her hands and forearms tore as she tried to halt her fall. A crack to the head stopped her and she wretched, curling into a ball where she lay in some sort of depression, struggling to breathe. Saliva ran down her chin and she spat, face pressed against chill stone. How far had she fallen? Where was she now? Her limbs didn't respond when she tried to rise. Another drop could be mere feet away. Moving might be a mistake. Turning her head caused her to gag again.

Soft spots of moisture hit her face and she blinked as the rain returned.

Gods!

She was going to die in the dark, somewhere on a mountainside. Soaked through. Either from her injuries or exposure. She was a speck, invisible. No-one would have an inkling of where she was. Sofia groaned. Worse, she'd failed Father. Wherever he was now, when he heard of her disappearance, he would be disappointed. He would no doubt deny the news at first. He was convinced that she was Tantos' equal, but he was wrong. And he would have to accept it, even as it broke his heart.

"No."

There was no answer, only the dark.

CHAPTER 23

Kael was the eldest child standing before Notch, nearer to Sofia's age if he had to guess, though the grime and wild hair made it difficult. He sat on a large chair that looked to be salvaged, which was in turn set before a row of spears, each having been thrust between cracks in the stone. Makeshift braziers burned; one appeared to be an urn on stacked crates. Notch counted three separate check posts on the way into the children's lair, which was spacious but near empty. Sleeping pallets lined the walls of what was once some sort of station for the aqueducts; and moving around beyond the light, some dicing, some wrapped in thin blankets, were perhaps a half a dozen youths.

"They seem quite organised," Wayrn whispered. His eyes clouded. "And many are Braonn."

Notch nodded. Runaway Braonn servants who could not return home often ended up on the city streets. Several boys still trained weapons on them, while Tenaci and Dilo spoke in low voices, gesturing back often. Kael placed a bottle of Fire-lemon aside and tied laces on his ragged cuffs as he listened. He stood without a word when they finished, approaching Notch. A thin sword swung at his side, but he did not draw it.

"You will offer us more, if we help you?" His Braonn accent was heavy. He gave Wayrn an appraising look. "Delam ma sorr?"

Wayrn smiled. "Da lirka."

Notch waited. His Braonn was passable; the two were discussing where home was and how long each had been away, but their speech quickly became too rapid for him to follow.

When they stopped, Kael repeated his question. "You and the Water Rat can offer us more?"

"Yes."

His eyes narrowed. "Then what do you wish for, Notch and Wayrn?"

"A friend has been taken from us. We need to see the Harbour Witch and ask for her help."

Gasps filled the room but Kael held up both hands, turning in a slow circle. "Stay calm." To Notch he shook his head. "That is not possible."

"What do you want?" Notch countered.

"First, what you claim you can offer. More than we would get from the Vigil."

Notch hoped Seto was good for another loan. "That can be arranged, Kael."

"And more."

"Yes?"

"You must kill the beast that hunts us."

"Which beast?" Was it another of the things that attacked Flir?

"Three of us he has already taken," Kael said before lowering his voice. "Their bodies were empty when found."

"Empty how?"

"Yes, empty. No insides, empty of blood and heart, empty of..." he waved to Tenaci, and spoke a few words in the Braonn tongue, pointing to Notch.

"Empty of organs," Tenaci translated, unaware that Notch had been able to follow. The boy's voice was tight. "No heart, no lungs, no liver. Barely any flesh left on the bone."

Notch glanced at Wayrn. He wasn't a monster slayer. Whatever was out there might be worse than the creature that attacked he and Flir, and that thing was bad enough. But what choice did they have? "We'll slay the beast. Then will you take us to the Witch?"

Kael did not answer at once. "Yes. If you agree never to see her again, never to speak with her again."

"Agreed. We'll need torches and bowmen." He pointed. "And your bottle."

Notch held out his hand and the youth took it, grip firm, a smile on his face. "Agreed. Tenaci and Dilo will aid you. Bring its head as proof." He handed the bottle over.

Tenaci paled but Dilo puffed herself up as the two obeyed, leading them from the chamber.

"Slaying the dragon," Wayrn muttered as he followed.

*

Exiting a narrow tunnel, Notch set out across a causeway. It spanned the widest channel he'd seen in the aqueducts. Light from the torches hopped across the water but failed to illuminate much on the far side. Water rushed beneath them, several feet below, passing between grates set in regular openings.

Wayrn followed close behind, but before Notch made any real progress, Tenaci hissed after him. "Come back."

Both children were waving from the mouth of the tunnel, Tenaci pale in the glow and Dilo's eyes scanning the walls. "What is it?" Notch asked.

"It attacked us here." His voice squeaked. "The causeway takes us to different parts of the harbour, but it's blocked now."

"So what is this thing and who has seen it?" Wayrn asked.

"We both have," Dilo said, pushing back a sleeve. A large purple welt ringed her forearm. "That is what it did to me. With its tongue I think. I stabbed it hard as I could but I don't think I hurt it. We drove it away... but some of us died."

"I'm sorry, Dilo." Notch put a hand on her shoulder. "How large is it?"

She spread her hands, an oddly adult gesture. "It's fast so I don't know. Three times as big as a man I think."

"More," Tenaci said.

"And it attacked you here?"

"Each time." Dilo pointed to the opposite end of the causeway, where a series of openings ran along the path beside the water. "It's hard to see but it came from one of them on the left."

Notch took the bottle of Fire-lemon and his torch. "Then we draw it out, into the open. Shoot straight, can you?" He gave them a look. Tenaci nodded and Dilo sniffed. "Wayrn, watch the other openings."

"What are you going to do?"

"Start a fire."

"Will that work? I mean, is it even attracted to fire?"

"I have no idea."

"If it doesn't work?"

"Then I'll go into those tunnels."

Notch dashed across the causeway, bottle held ready. It was a fool's plan. Not as though he could drink the creature under a table. But nothing else came to mind, it was act now or wait who knew how long for the monster to emerge. His heart beat in earnest and he grinned. Stupid. Not as stupid as going in after it would be, but stupid enough. At least he was no longer slinking around spying on people.

Slowing, Notch chose the second opening and hurled the bottle at its mouth. Shattered glass rang across the water and the liquor glistened on the stones. The bitterness of the dark liquid was strong, even standing over it. Notch turned his face away and thrust the torch down. A flash lit the room and he jumped back. Steady flames hissed in the damp, revealing a trail of muck leading into the tunnel. Notch ran back to the causeway and firmer footing. No doubt he would need it.

Torch held aloft and sword ready, Notch thumped Wayrn's shoulder when the man joined him. "Now we wait."

Wayrn swallowed. In his hand he held an axe and his own torch. "I've just realised what I'm doing. I'm not trained for this, Notch. Nor is Seto paying me enough."

"I've been saying that for years," Notch said. "You're agile. Use that."

The passage of water followed. Some distance away, the fire from his bait still burned but the monster did not appear. Water flowed.

Time passed.

"There," Tenaci shouted.

Notch followed the boy's finger. Something large

crawled or maybe slithered along the roof, speeding at them from beyond the puddle of fire.

"Tira's Shade," Wayrn said.

Notch spread his feet, putting a sword's distance between them as the thing approached. It leapt down near the fire, splashing into the water. Too fleet to be seen clearly, all Notch could be sure of were scales and long tentacles, a blue hue and the fact that its body alone was wide as a man was tall.

"Watch the arms," he shouted.

It splashed onto the causeway and reared up, droplets spraying. Its face was indistinct, he had only an impression of teeth and a wide, glowing eye before it charged. He swung his sword and severed a limb as the beast slipped between them. The arm twitched, leaking slime. He gagged on the wet stench as it slithered back into the water. No humming – a different creature to the one that attacked he and Flir then.

Quiet. Notch took a few more steps along the causeway, motioning to Wayrn for silence. From the opening to the tunnel leading to the children's chambers, one much too narrow for the creature to use, Tenaci breathed hard. At the sound Notch raised a finger to his lips but the boy couldn't stop. His knuckles were white on the bow, torch thrust into an old ring in the wall.

"I hear it in the water," Wayrn said, turning.

Notch spun. The beast sprang from the channel, limbs flailing as it charged. The hiss of arrows passed his ear, but they bounced off its scales. The thing's tentacles wrapped his sword arm and leg. Fetid breath steamed over his face as the jaws snapped inches away as he struggled. The pressure on his arm grew and he gritted his teeth. The beast tried to drag him closer, but again, its stunted neck prevented it from biting him. It gurgled, squeezing harder, as if in frustration.

Notch roared as he shoved his torch at the eye. Another tentacle batted his hand aside. The light was gone, darkening the causeway. Scrambling at his belt for a knife, Notch drove it into a patch where no scales covered the beast – only to have the blade and handle disappear into the bulk.

Wayrn gave a shout, axe flashing as he hacked at its arms. One blow sliced the limb holding Notch's arm and a spray of blue liquid covered his clothing. He bent to tear at the tentacle around his leg. His fingernails were useless, and Wayrn had been driven back, ducking and weaving.

Dilo appeared, a long bladed knife in both hands. She hacked at the tentacle, only to be knocked to the stones by another arm, and then the creature was moving, leaping for the channel. Notch barely had time to take a deep breath before being plunged into cold water and dragged along in a maelstrom of bubbles. He kicked and struck out at the beast, chest tightening, but landed no blows, being torn this way and that.

It burst from the water again, and he bounced into the stones, jarring his hip. The sound of air and water rattling in its lungs neared and he twisted, jamming a boot into its face. He managed to keep the creature at a distance, even as the tentacles that held him tried to draw his other leg into its mouth.

"Help me," he shouted.

The creature slid backwards, dragging him across the stones. The scent of Fire-lemon was strong, the crackle of flames nearing. It was trying to pull him into its lair. Already another tentacle had caught his sword arm, his free hand scratched for a weapon.

His fingers stopped on something smooth.

With a circular opening.

Glass!

Notch slipped a finger into the broken bottle neck. He heaved himself upright and jammed the fragment into the glowing eye.

The beast convulsed. Gurgling followed and it released him. He thumped to the ground as it shied away. Notch struck again, gashing along an unprotected flank. Mottled skin tore, a wet mess spilling out. A flailing limb knocked him from the ledge and he splashed into the water. Bubbles surrounded him once again, as he thrashed his way through the chill. Unable to stand, he broke the surface and grasped for the lip of the walkway. Wayrn had reached the creature and was fending off limbs, a torch in one hand, his hatchet in the other. The man lived up to his training, spinning and rolling, fending off tentacles.

It couldn't escape into its lair.

Notch hauled himself from the water and jumped onto its back, dodging the few remaining arms. Blinded, it was unable to ward off Wayrn's blows as effectively. Wayrn stepped back when Notch leapt.

The creature stumbled and half-collapsed against the wall. Notch flung out a hand. "The axe."

Wayrn tossed the weapon. Notch caught it, got a grip high on the handle and drove it deep into the thing's eye socket.

Blood and slime sprayed from its mouth and the creature fell still.

Notch slid from its carcass and stumbled back. Wayrn caught an arm to steady him but said nothing. The thing twitched as gases and more blue slime leaked from its bulk. Patches of the creature had no scales for protection and stout legs, many of them, with clawed feet, were half-visible. Tiny fins protruded uselessly from its body, some even growing from the arms, most of which were halved. Or stubs.

Notch wiped gunk from his face and arms. It had no numbing effect, but smelt and tasted foul. His clothing was covered in it.

Wayrn's eyes were wide in the light of his torch. "What was such a creature?"

"Something unnatural."

"Truly."

Notch turned to the causeway. "I'll get my sword. We need its head."

CHAPTER 24

"Who are you?"

The harsh voice echoed in the crater and Ain raised his hands. "Pathfinder Ain, of the Cloud Oasis. With me is the Warrior Schan of Snake Clan."

The dark shapes moved closer together and voices conferred. He could not guess their number, darkness was falling too quickly. Schan held one arm out of sight. Not the one holding his knife, but the one which held water.

"Leave your weapons and climb up. You first, Ain of Cloud Oasis." The man waved a hand and Ain finally bent to take the rope. He glanced at Schan. The snake was removing his weapons, laying knife, bow and sword on the stone. The water flask was nowhere in sight.

Ain shed his own weapons and threw the rope up. Was he climbing to his death? Whoever was up there spoke well enough, if slowly, and had no accent Ain could place. "What do you intend to do with us?"

"Here." A rope followed his voice down. "That depends on the truth of your words."

Ain took the rope, rough against his palm. "I am a Pathfinder, I am sworn not to deceive my people."

"I know the oaths. Climb up, Pathfinder."

Schan nodded at him and Ain gave the rope a good tug before starting. When he reached the lip of the crater, arms pulled him up and he was held in place. Schan soon followed and a torch was lit, raised by a man dressed in Medah tans. His head was completely shaven and he wore a necklace with flashing jewels.

Ain squinted when the torch came closer.

"So, you are speaking the truth," the man with the torch said. Before Ain could reply the stranger turned to those visible, dressed in a similar fashion and all with shaven heads, and waved a hand. "Back to Mazu-Kam. Prepare food for our guests."

"Guests?" Ain had tensed at the word 'Mazu' and he heard nothing after it until the mention of 'guests.' He looked over his shoulder to where Schan stood, open-mouthed.

The man with the torch, obviously the leader of their captors – or maybe it was hosts – clapped Ain on the shoulder. "Someone will bring your belongings, don't worry. I am Tanija and you are both welcome here."

*

Tanija's home rested within a series of caves beneath the earth, accessed via a curling path that ringed a large crater. A series of torches carried by the men who'd found them lined the path. At the rear, Tanija's boots crunched along beside them.

"The caves extend back some distance but we only use the rooms closest to the surface or the openings," he was saying. "Smoke usually escapes from cunningly cut holes in the rooves of the kitchens. No idea who made 'em either, but they're a blessing."

"Wait, then you aren't Mazu Clan?"

Tanija burst out laughing. He slapped Ain on the back and gestured at his face. "Do we look like darklings to you, lad? No, we aren't Mazu Clan. Though I don't doubt that's who built this place."

"The caves are man-made?"

"Not all of them. Some I believe are natural."

The closer they came to the bottom, the more doors appeared set into stone. Not all fit perfectly, as if they'd been built as an afterthought. Light slipped from beneath some doors, while others were dark. He was still unsure of Tanija and his people, but there were no overt signs of danger yet. At least no-one had asked for blood.

At the crater's floor waited several large openings, within which many doors were set between passages. Old paths led inside, stretching deep beneath the earth. Men and women went about their business without paying the visitors much attention, and it wasn't until Tanija led them to one of the openings and into a large room that Ain got a close look at one of the residents.

A woman arranged cutlery and mugs around a broad table, long dress swirling around her legs. She wore a necklace similar to Tanija's and her head was shaven too. Ain stared, a hand moving up to his own hair. Short, but nothing like the people who dwelt in the caves.

"Hello." Her voice was sweet and she smiled at him, but when she turned to Tanija the amusement in her face turned to fondness.

"Husband."

"Ashia, we have guests tonight. Ain from the Cloud and Schan from the Snake Clan. Have we room at our table?"

"Of course, welcome to you both. I hope Tanija has been a good host."

"He has," Ain said as he was shown to a seat. Ashia went to a small water barrel and removed two more mugs and plates. As she set them down, she called two names in quick succession, unfamiliar names that ran together. A moment later two children, dressed only in pants, skidded into the room. At the sight of Ain and Schan, the boy blinked. The girl pointed at Schan.

"Who are you?"

The warrior's mouth twitched. "Schan."

Her finger moved. "And you?"

"My name is Ain."

"Mother, father, what are they doing here? Will there be enough food?"

Tanija laughed, then stepped over, scooping her into his lap. "Of course, Sae. They are guests. They come from the middle of the desert."

The boy gasped. "Beyond the white gods, father?"

"Yes. They're searching for something to the east."

He lowered his voice. "In the secret city?"

Sae shook her finger. "No, Bemn. Sekkati."

"Time to eat." Ashia spooned ladles of steaming brown sauce onto hunks of meat.

Ain swallowed saliva. His mouth tingled and even Schan sat with cutlery in hand. "It smells wonderful," he said.

"Well said." Tanija smiled. "Ashia is the best cook in the caves."

Ain finished half his plate, smiling as he listened to the children squabble and their parents indulging them. Even Schan put his spoon down to play clapping games with Sae. Despite the pang in his chest, he sat back in the chair. Perhaps they were safe for a time. A fat, pot-bellied stove in the corner of the kitchen pumped out warmth and though the night was not cold, it was comforting. Even the reddish walls and roof of the room were softened by the sounds.

Once the meal was finished and the children were abed, Schan lay his eating implements down and thanked their hosts. Ain added his own thanks and checked to see the children had truly departed before asking about the Mazu Clan. "You said they built this place?"

Tanija gestured to the walls. "Deeper into our caves are chambers with their symbol, rooms carved with columns and benches, recesses set into walls that remain a mystery. We rarely use them."

"There is no need, as we have enough room for our people without them," Ashia added. "Though our grandparents explored them at length when first we arrived."

"Then you settled here only recently?" Ain asked.

"Yes. Few travel this far north any more. Once it was people like us, who left their clan or even were banished or lost."

"Now it is mostly Pathfinders or stray Anaskari folk," Tanija said.

"You have seen others like me?"

"Yes. All searching for the Shrine." He met Ain's eyes. "They do not come back."

He fought the urge to swallow. "I will be different."

Tanija said nothing, but Ashia patted his hand. "I hope so."

Schan leant back in his chair. "You said you also see the Anaskari?"

"It is rare, but they come at times. If they pass at a distance, we let them. If they come too close, we kill them."

"Can you tell us anything of them? Or their land?"

"Not I," Tanija said. "I have never travelled there, but tomorrow you may speak with Ashia's father. He remembers."

"Would that trouble him?" Ain asked when he caught her sending Tanija a look.

She shook her head. "No, no. He will be fine."

"You both must be tired." Tanija stood and led them from the kitchen and into a passage opposite his home. Halfway down, the darkness thick, he opened a door and fiddled with something on the wall. Sparks jumped as flint rasped and a torch crackled into life.

A small room with two beds and a water barrel was revealed, their belongings placed neatly at the foot of each bed.

"Here you are, men. Rest tonight. I will wake you at dawn." Tanija nodded as he left. Ain went to the water barrel and splashed the worst of the dust from his face before sitting on the bed as Schan repeated his actions.

"We must be better off now, surely?"

Schan chuckled as he sat on his own bed, pulling his boots off. "We aren't dying of thirst."

Ain sighed. That was a positive summation. "Hopefully whatever Ashia's father can tell us begins to make up for losing Ibranu."

"You think it will?"

"No."

Schan snorted in agreement.

"But it has to be better than nothing."

*

After a breakfast of warm bread and goat's milk, Tanija led them to a cave set high along the curving ramp, where he knocked and waited. He'd told Ain only that the old man was 'never in a good mood.'

"Ho, Wilatt, are you awake?" The words had barely left his mouth when the door snapped open. A short man in a creased robe stood with a glare, his head shaven except for a long strip of white running along the middle. He tapped his fingers on the door where he held it.

"Hell on water, what is it?"

"Wilatt, these men have come to speak with you about Sekkati." Tanjia's voice was level.

"Eh?" Wilatt's gaze narrowed at Ain before waving an arm. "Off with you two, I'm busy today."

"You're busy every day, Wilatt. Can you not spare a moment?"

He narrowed his gaze. "Boy, I put myself up here so no-one would bother me. None of you three look like 'no-one' to me." He slammed the door.

"He'll come around," Tanija said, and opened the door to a large room cluttered with benches, scrolls and shelves. A bed was buried beneath a mound of paper. Before a small water barrel was a chair, free of clutter.

Wilatt stood at a bench, shuffling papers. He growled when he saw them. "Tanija, that better not be you."

"Please, just speak with them. They seek the Shrine."

Wilatt broke off a word, lowering his hands. "Do they? You poor souls."

"Good luck and keep him on track," Tanija said as he slipped out.

Hardly encouraging. Ain moved deeper into the room when Wilatt waved his hands. "In, in."

"Thank you for speaking with us," Ain started.

"You won't be when we're done, young man. Who's your friend, he looks old enough to have more sense."

"This is Schan of the Snake Clan and I am Ain, Pathfinder from the Cloud Oasis."

"A Warrior? Where's your Engineer then?"

"He did not pass the Wards."

Wilatt nodded, moving to the chair. He tapped his fingers on the arm but did not offer to find a space for them to sit. "Shame that. Do you have his keys at least, whatever maps he carried?"

"Yes."

"Good." Wilatt paused and shook his head. "Actually no, doesn't matter what you have. I won't draw this out. You're going to die, the both of you."

"What a relief," Schan said. "I was getting tired of all the anticipation."

Wilatt scowled. "Well it's the truth, Snake. I know. It's what happened to all the ones they send on the ridiculous Search. I was once a searcher."

Ain straightened. Ridiculous? Impossible maybe, but not ridiculous. "The Search is important. It is the only thing that will restore the Clans."

Wilatt gave a sad smile. "Are they broken then?"

"No. You know what I mean. To Sekkati."

"And why does that matter?"

Schan frowned. "It's our rightful home."

"You don't like your current home?"

Schan shook his head. Wilatt pointed to Ain. "What about you then? Unhappy in the desert?"

"It is my duty."

"Ah."

Ain took a deep breath when Wilatt didn't continue. Despite this unhappy man's nature, the Sands had blessed them, putting him on their path. No-one was supposed to return from the city. Wilatt had survived… reasonably intact. "You can help us. You've been to the city."

"Bah. Of course not. And no-one can help you, least of all me. Couldn't even help myself."

Ain's shoulders dipped. "Then can you tell us what you know?"

"It 'aint much."

"More than we have now," Schan said.

"Well, I don't remember so much." He rubbed his wrists. "That's the way of it now that I'm old." He looked up. "But I was a Pathfinder. Let's see, let's see. Everything went well enough, we both survived the Wards and both crossed the wasteland. I came here for water, just as you did, though it was a quieter place back then. Fewer runaways living here.

"We didn't hit trouble until beyond the foothills. We'd actually reached the outskirts of 'Anaskar' and had our path chosen. Before we left, there was talk of paths in the Engineer's texts. A hole in the wall, deep in the mountains, an old sea gate by the harbour or a bolt hole on the plain. Miles out, I'd felt the pattern of old feet, like a slight wave beneath my hand. We chose the plain. It was a long passage but we never saw its end. It might even be caved in, who knows?"

"What happened?" Ain asked. He leaned forward.

"Something found us. It stayed mostly beyond our torches, but it was fast enough to snatch my Engineer and begin its grisly work. He screamed for help but when the first spurt of blood hit me I fled. Dragged myself back here. There was no going home, not after what happened. What I did. All I can say is, I was young."

"I'm sorry," Ain said. Schan's face was set in its usual

mask of calm. "Is the bolt hole marked?"

Wilatt sighed through sudden tears. "You really want to die like that, lad, by whatever fell creature lives there?"

"No. But I must try, and I have no maps to those other places. The Cloud would not welcome me back if I gave up."

"I know it."

"Then you will help us?" Schan asked.

Wilatt was tapping both sets of fingers now. "A marsh, if that. Within a large swamp. It wasn't much then, might not be there now. But the bolt hole was a day's travel off the old road, near to two days out of the city – you will feel the path. Light, but there's an urgency to the steps. Like people had used it to flee someone." He met Ain's eyes. "Or some thing."

"You have our gratitude, Wilatt."

He shrugged. "Watch for the path, hidden in the marshland. You'll feel it. Watch also for the creatures which inhabit it. Their eyes, boy. Put out their eyes."

"Ah, you've been very helpful, Wilatt. We will be careful."

"I'd say fare you well, but I know better. There's a reason why our people don't return from the City of Secrets, those who make it that far."

He moved toward the door, Schan following. "I have to prove everyone wrong."

"I thought the same thing," he called after them. Ain closed the door.

CHAPTER 25

The old road between the Wasteland and the green foothills beneath the City of Secrets was quiet. They passed no-one and the landscape remained featureless until the edge of the murky haze of swamplands appeared.

Now they crossed into the spongy ground of the swamp, both prodding the ground with long sticks. Sludge with tufts of grey and reeds grew around firmer ground, with short, twisted trees standing like green islands. Insects chirped in ceaseless song, almost hypnotic in its brittle pattern.

The path pulsed beneath Ain's feet. There was a sense of urgency, but the trace of it didn't always stay with firm ground. "This is taking longer than I'd hoped." Ain wiped his brow beneath the afternoon sun. Three times now they'd detoured around wide pools of dark water, only to travel a dozen feet before having to do so again.

"Not a pleasant place to spend the night," Schan agreed. The back of his shirt was wet with sweat and he growled. "And where did this damp heat come from?"

Ain drank from his flask. "Wilatt's warning rings in my ear."

"We've seen nothing yet."

"True." Small sounds sometimes came from water being stirred, in the larger pools, and did not instil confidence in him. But nothing leapt out, no creature attacked. The path grew stronger the deeper they travelled into the swamp.

Ain froze at movement. A lizard crossed the path, the pale creature slipping into the shrubs. His free hand was never far from his belt knife, but by the time they came upon a low mound overgrown with weeds, a pair of trees growing from its peak, he'd forgotten Wilatt's talk of creatures whose eyes must be 'put out.'

"Here." The path led to an opening in the mound, its edges rife with yellowed tufts of grass. He bent down and tore a clump of weeds free. The dark maw beyond was just as Wilatt claimed. The bolt hole lay beside one of the widest ponds he'd seen in the swamp.

"We'll have to dig some of the opening free." Less than half the entrance was unobstructed, the build up of earth and weeds prevented easy access. The sun warmed his back.

Schan grinned. "You won first shift."

"And how did I do that?"

"You're just lucky."

"My blessings are many," he sighed, pulling his knife and digging in.

He stopped periodically to rake the loosened dirt with his arms, and by the time he and Schan had widened the opening enough, sweat cooled in the evening air. The sharp scent of turned earth filled his nose, pungent but somehow pleasant. In the desert nothing was comparable. Little white insects with dark heads curled in on themselves, shying from the light.

"Dark," Schan said.

"Very." While they had lamps in their packs, the oil was limited. How many miles from here, the bottom of the foothills, to the city? And what if the passage was collapsed, or worse, the creature still lurked within?

"Do you believe him? Wilatt?"

"No reason not to."

Ain did not move. His knuckles were white on the handle, he unclenched them and took a shuddering breath. What lurked within? The path beneath his knees, resting on the damp soil, was... flickering. As if those who'd trodden it were being forgotten by the path. Had it been doing that earlier? Impossible to explain it any other way. Or guess what it might mean.

"Then we better keep our wits about us."

Still he did not move.

Schan placed a hand on his shoulder. "If it's our fate, lad, nothing we can do to change it."

"I know. If the Sands will it." Ain looked to the grey hills, a mist of distant rain shrouding them. "Aren't you afraid?" Silaj. His child.

"Yes." He stared into the maw. "I fear I will miss a chance for vengeance."

"The War?"

He nodded. "Both my father and brother."

"But you survived?"

"If you call it that."

"What do you mean? You're here, alive."

"Sun-fever kept me abed. I never fought beside my family, as I should have. Instead, I will take my vengeance upon the Anaskari now, with you."

"If the Sands will it, it will be," Ain mouthed the words this time. When had their meaning changed? If the Sands willed anything, perhaps it was only death, one creeping grain at a time. For Ibranu, for Schan's family, for his own family, for so many others. "I do not know what lies before us."

"You will find a path. Come," Schan said. "Help me with this lantern."

Ain lit the lantern. He held it up and half-climbed, half-slid into the hole. The dark swept in around him despite his light and crawling things scuttled away as his boots crunched on loose dirt and stone.

"It's paved." He stooped over the floor. Regular paving stones, scattered with the soil he'd dislodged, revealed a familiar pattern. He recognised it from one of Ibranu's scrolls. Known as a Sword-Fish, it looked like a thin animal with a pointed nose.

Anaskar.

"That's a good sign," Schan said. "And these are support beams." He slapped a thick wooden beam, its surface glinting in the light. "Treated with something to keep the rot out."

"It has done its job well then," Ain said as he walked on. The way ahead was straight as an arrow.

The tunnel sloped down. Time passed in the sound of footfalls. Once they stopped to eat, crouched around the lamp, but there were no other markers. No sounds save for the many feet of an occasional insect. And the press of the earth above him, heavy like a blanket of black soil, suffocating.

Ain chanted the Prayer of Sand beneath his breath as he walked. "Sands willing, I will see another dawn. Sands willing, I will see another dawn." The more he said it, the more desperate he sounded. His shoulders grew tense and he stopped several times to breathe, though it was difficult to take deep breaths. Everything was moist and chill. The very air tasted of dirt.

The open expanse of the desert called to him.

Even Schan wore a troubled expression and Ain clenched his jaw, fighting the urge to hack his way to the surface, or flee to the distant entrance and its pale light. Go on. Forward was the only way out. Turning back now meant a long, maybe fruitless search for other paths, or even a direct approach and certain death.

At least here, under the earth, he was concealed.

And the path still whispered beneath his tread, sometimes strong, sometimes faint, as if only a handful of people had ever used it. But when it was strong it beat against his soles and the thunder of flight, of panic was enough to stop him. He even took a step back, bumping into Schan. Did the bones of Wilatt's Engineer lie beneath the earth?

"Ain?"

"It's nothing. The path... I haven't felt a path like this. Fear comes through the steps." He closed his eyes. "They're wide and hard. Running."

"Recent?"

"They're too muddled."

Schan shrugged. "We keep walking then."

"We do."

The tunnel began to climb. It was not steep, but the rise was steady. By the time they'd stopped again for another meal, and to split the watch, the path was quiet again. He sighed, stretching his neck. Now that the panic was gone, a comparative calm settled over him.

"How much oil is —" Schan trailed off and moved to

the edge of the light. "By the Sands."

Ain placed his pack aside and joined the man. "Have you found something?"

"There."

A wide recess had been dug between support beams, deep into the wall of earth. Cradled in the dirt were a pair of eggs. Each was larger than a human head, shells tinted gold. Small, rough mounds supported the shells and Ain shivered as he touched the damp walls of the tiny cave.

Claw marks. Gouges. Patches of coarse fur. Whatever made the opening was large. "We should leave them."

"Whoever left these eggs is surely between us and the city."

He froze, reply forgotten. A clicking drifted up the tunnel. Claws on stone. Coming closer, distant yet, but gaining in speed.

"Something comes."

CHAPTER 26

Shivering and not quite clean, but not as filthy after cleaning himself in the aqueduct, Notch stood with Wayrn, Tenaci, Dilo and Kael. Wayrn wiped the clinging blue gunk from his clothing and Dilo's small face now followed their every move, but Tenaci could not meet Notch's gaze. Notch knew why but the time wasn't right.

Kael's eyes lit up when he first saw the head. It still dripped foul blue slime where it sat on display, axe haft protruding. A small crowd gathered. Many spoke in hushed voices and some of the children came forward to kick it, little fists at their sides and faces twisted. Most kept their distance.

"Thank you again, Notch and Wayrn," he said. "You are mighty warriors both."

"You're very gracious, Kael. Can you help us now?"

"Of course." To Dilo and Tenaci he said, "Go quickly, take others. Harvest what you can."

"Harvest?" Wayrn asked when the two ran off. "Surely you don't intend to eat such a thing?"

"Fallok, no." Kael gave Wayrn a look, suggesting the

man was insane. "We are taking the bones."

"Oh. Why?"

"Do you know nothing of magic?" He pointed to the creature's head. "We take fish bones to the Witch. That is how it works."

No lands Notch had visited used fish bones for magic. Few seemed able to practice magic at all. Those in the Far Islands claimed they could read minds, but he'd never seen it. Luik had told stories around campfires about the depths of the Braonn forests, where certain butterflies could be caught and eaten, granting the diner magical powers. But those were children's tales.

Even the Storm Singers were few in number, and whatever strange magic the Medah knew, he had not seen. He'd only witnessed their flashing sabres. Heard the snap of their bows. Seen the hate on the faces.

The small pouch of bones Tenaci carried, that day in the abandoned building, made sense after hearing Kael's explanation. And why not? So much of the Anaskari way was the way of bones. The ornaments, furniture, the masks.

"You pay her with bones. Fish bones."

"Yes. We take them from the dead fish in the harbour or the trash," he said. "Or collect them from other places in the city. Metti takes them all. Big bones are best. Most powerful." He rubbed his hands together. "With what you have done for us, we will not be hungry for many moons. The beast will have large bones."

"Large indeed," he said. "Kael, I would like to take a bone for Metti, as further payment."

He waved a hand, an almost absent movement. His eyes were trained on the head. "Certainly. Tenaci will help you. He will guide you to Metti also."

"And the ransom?"

Kael held out his hand. "We have no need of it now. No-one will speak to the Vigil about you. Either of you."

"I'm not actually a wanted man, Kael," Wayrn said.

"That is well."

Notch grinned at Wayrn before taking Kael's outstretched hand. "We appreciate your help."

"Remember it, as we will remember what you have done for us."

*

Notch stood across from a small seamstress, its door a fading green in the afternoon light. In a quiet back street where tiny garden plots of lemon trees nestled between houses, he'd removed his hood a moment, out of sight of the Mascare and Shield. His own posters remained on a few street corners, but he'd snatched a fresh poster from an inn on the way to the seamstress.

Sofia.

In the poster, Prince Oson named her, both by title and House. The image was a close likeness, no one would mistake her fine bones and determined gaze if they saw her in person. The desperate need was clear. Oson wanted her, willing to completely destroy her chances of keeping her identity secret. She could never hide herself within the palace, within the First Tier, as all knew that the Successor was a young woman. That Sofia was no doubt used to.

But to unmask her to the people.

He would find her. Together they would bring the Swordfish down.

He exhaled, gaze drawn back to the green door. Notch shook his head. "I can't believe the Harbour Witch has been in the Second Tier all this time. A simple ploy. But clever."

"Hmmm." Tenaci said. Throughout their trip back to the surface, and along the streets, the boy said little. It was clear he wasn't going to mention the creature, Notch would have to do so. And before Wayrn returned with food.

"Tenaci, don't be hard on yourself."

His head snapped up from where he'd been examining the street, eyes wary. He'd made a fist by his side but didn't appear to notice. "What do you mean?"

"With the beast. That you didn't join it in battle, directly." The boy began to bluster but Notch held up a hand. "I'm trying to tell you I'm not going to judge you. A first battle is hard. Terrifying."

Tenaci's shoulders slumped. "It took my sister. I should've been able to fight. I wanted to. But I couldn't make my legs move. Even when Dilo attacked." He looked to the ground. "I'm a coward."

"I'm sorry to hear of your sister. But you're young yet and you're not a coward." The word 'coward' echoed in his father's voice. But it was never cowardice, it had been duty. Tell that to your brother. Father again.

"I'm supposed to be brave," Tenaci said. "For everyone."

"My first real battle, I felt the same."

"You did?"

"We were outnumbered. I had my sword and armour, I might have felt safe, but when the order to charge came, I didn't move. I told myself to go, to help my friends, but I couldn't move. Someone gave me a shove and it started me running. But without that push, I might not have left my place on the sand."

"Sand?"

"You're too young to remember the Glass War."

His face brightened. "I've heard of it. With the damned Medah. And you fought in it? All those years ago?"

"Yes." He didn't add that a little over ten years was not that long at all. And that some days, it was as if he'd just walked right off the sand.

"I bet it was exciting, Notch."

"Sometimes. Mostly not."

Wayrn appeared, his hands full of steaming packages. "It's spiced fish on rice." He handed them over. "It's all I could find."

"I'm happy," Notch said.

"To be honest, I'd prefer some venison, or anything else, right now." His lip curled when he flicked a piece of tentacle from a fold in his tunic.

Notch chuckled but set to work eating, licking his lips as he did. Tenaci tore into the food beside him. The spices burned but the rice was filling and the fish fresh – as it always was in Anaskar. Once finished, Notch wiped his hands on his pants and accepted a large rib bone from Tenaci.

"Pay her with this, it'll cover whatever you need," he said.

"You are not coming in with us?" Wayrn asked.

"If she knew we led you to her, she wouldn't see us anymore."

"Thank you, Tenaci," Notch said. "Remember what I said."

"I will," he shouted over his shoulder.

"What did you tell him?" Wayrn asked when they paused at the door.

"That being afraid was normal."

"Good lesson."

Notch opened the green door and stepped into a room awash with colour – all save red. Bold yellows and sea-blues mixed with dark greens and delicate pinks. Fabrics of all shapes and sizes hung from the walls, draped over the counter and rolled up in bolts that lined a series of openings resting behind a woman with an expectant expression.

"How may I help?" She wore a loose robe of a multi-hued fabric and her hands were covered in rings. She eyed their clothing but did not object. Wayrn shifted beside him.

The instructions were simple. Approach the woman on the desk, ask her if Metti was awake and hand over a silver penny, King-side up. Refuse to answer questions about how he learnt of the Witch, and reveal nothing about his name or purpose.

"I'd like to know if Metti's awake?"

Her expression darkened. "Who is asking?"

"I'd rather not say, though it's urgent."

"It always is." She picked up a heavy pair of scissors, cutting a piece of cloth. It melted away from the blade. "Who told you how to find this place, to ask for her?"

"I do need her help," Notch replied, placing a silver penny on the counter, the old King's stern brow visible.

She finished her trimming and scooped the coin into a palm. "I see. Follow me – only you," she told Notch.

"I will wait here." Wayrn folded his arms.

The woman led Notch into a second room, which had a small table and stove, in addition to a set of stairs. Leading down. Notch swallowed a groan. Not underground again.

The woman paused to check on a simmering pot atop the stove. "Go down and speak to Guingera. When you see Metti, you will swear an oath. If you lie, you will never see Metti again. But she will be able to see you. Any time she likes. Do you understand?"

"I do." He didn't but it seemed the right thing to say.

"Good."

At the bottom of the stairs waited a large man with a scowl. His eyes went directly to Notch's sword.

"Leave that with me, then."

Notch unbuckled the weapon and handed it over. "Should I knock?"

Guingera grunted as he rapped on the door.

"Come in, and don't let the heat escape." A melodic voice carried through the wood. Notch slipped into a warm room, closing the door behind him. A healthy blaze burned in a fireplace set behind two grand chairs and a small table, its flames greedy for air.

A white haired woman sat regarding him from lidded eyes. Her hair was cut close to her head and she wore a black robe over white skirts, neatly arranged. A kitten slept in her lap, its striped fur blending.

"Sit." She waved a bone at the opposite chair. It looked to be a jaw bone but it disappeared up a sleeve before he could be sure. Notch did as instructed, a slight gasp escaping. Up close, her face was a mask. Not a mask like those worn by the Mascare, but one of skin. Waxy smooth. No wrinkles but no natural movement either. When she spoke, her gaze passed over his face and to the bone he held. Her eyes widened, even as she asked his name. The corners of her mouth barely moved.

Tenaci said nothing of hiding his identity from the Witch. "My name is Notch."

She took writing materials from the table, wrote a moment and nodded. "I see. A new name for an old hero?"

Hero. The Glass War made no heroes. What he'd done for Anaskar was not heroism. What he failed to do would have made him a hero – in his father's eyes at least.

And maybe his brother's too.

"I'm no hero. I'm a mercenary."

Her laugh was a whisper. "You cannot hide your identity from one such as me, Captain. Though I will not press you, others must surely still recognise you as one of the men who turned the tide? And more, others may not have forgotten why you are not remembered with fondness at the palace."

"It doesn't happen often." He would not think on what the King had done. Bad enough that the dreams were coming back. "And thank you."

"Very well. To business." The kitten stirred in her lap and she stroked it before extending her arm. "Take my hand."

He leaned forward. Her wrinkled skin was hot, not just warm. Hot. He frowned at her unnatural-looking face. "An oath?"

"Of course." Her fingertips were like embers against his knuckles. "Swear now, by whatever deity you see fit, that you will never share what you learn of Metti the Harbour Witch."

"I, Notch, swear by Celno, Mountain God of Anaskar, never to reveal what I know of Metti the Harbour Witch."

She let go and he wiped a sheen of sweat from his brow. He felt no different. Whatever binding, if any, she had performed, registered not. The idea of her mask-like face watching gave him a shiver.

Metti's gaze dropped to the bone in his hand. "From where did that bone come? A fish?"

"Beneath the city, from a beast now dead. Must it be a fish? It had the look of one, in a manner of speaking."

"It must indeed be a fish." Metti opened her hand and he placed the bone within. The moment her fingers closed around it, the witch swayed in her chair. She placed it on the hearth, breathing with a hand on her chest a moment.

"I know its worth," he said when she turned back. Or at least, he had an inkling now. If merely touching it created such a reaction, and if she were actually a witch...

She raised a white eyebrow. "I doubt that, Notch." A smile. "And you believe I would cheat you?"

"I only want it to be sufficient payment."

"It is. But before we speak on that, describe the creature."

"Misshapen, with uneven scales and tentacles. Very fast. When we cut it, blue ichor or slime oozed from the wounds. It couldn't move its neck properly and it had useless fins."

"An efficient description," she said. "It certainly matches no creature I have encountered."

"Nor I."

"Hmmm. Very well, Notch. What do you require?"

"I need to find a girl. A young woman. Sofia Falco. She's in trouble."

Her tight face twitched, a slight widening of her eyes. "Danillo's daughter is in danger?"

"Yes. She's been taken by false Mascare, from the Lower Tier. Near the Iron Pig, only a few days gone. Do you know her?"

"I know her father. But that is not important now.

Wait." Metti took the bone again, lay back in the chair and closed her eyes. Notch turned to the flames. Her face, with closed eyes, was the perfect imitation of a corpse. Without the rise and fall of her chest, slight though it was, he might have been fooled.

He tapped a finger on the armrest while she sat and breathed. Then two fingers and then both hands. He moved from the fire, pacing the room. Beyond the shadows were small boxes in neat stacks, but he did not examine them, instead pacing. How far away would Sofia be now? Could he reach her quickly? She lived yet. That needed to be true. Else his efforts were for naught.

"Stop that."

Notch paused mid-step.

"Simply be still, Notch. And don't hang there."

He placed his foot down. "Do you see her?"

"I believe so." Smoke began to curl from her hands. "She has passed Mountain Gate."

Notch returned to the chair opposite. "Is she alone?"

"No. Her captors are two. Both wear the robe and mask. Sofia is collared and leashed. They travel west on horseback."

"What else?"

"It is day. A mansion lies in the distance."

"Has she been hurt?"

"I cannot see for certain but I think not. Wait... she is gone." Metti opened her eyes. Smoke still rose from her hands and when she lifted them, vivid scorch marks lay on the bone. The witch smiled. "My. That was the clearest picture I have ever experienced."

"So she's there now, near this mansion west of the Mountain Gate?"

"I believe so, though I did not expect to lose sight of

her so quickly."

"Was the bone –"

"No. It is more than suitable. She... passed into a place where I became blind to her. But that, I feel is geographical. There is something about the foothills to the west that has always been strange."

Notch stood. Something to go on at last. A destination. Evidence that Sofia was alive. All he had to do now was collect Wayrn, find Flir and Luik and set out. West of the Mountain Gate were few structures, and certainly only one mansion – the Falco Mansion. "Thank you, Metti. I have to go now."

"Wait." She did not rise, but her eyes bored into his own, hands moving of their own accord to stroke the kitten. "The creature you slew for this bone?"

"Yes."

"Now that I have touched it, I suspect it is a symptom of something wrong within the city. It did not come from a typical fish, perhaps not a fish at all."

Notch straightened. "Do you mean magic?"

"No." She shrugged. "Perhaps. I cannot be sure. But I do not wish for harm to come to those who would harvest such a creature. Especially if those doing the harvesting were... vulnerable."

"I believe such harvesters are in possession of enough bones to never seek such other creatures, should they exist."

"That is well."

"Though who knows if there are more or not."

"You are right of course."

"Thank you again." Notch headed to the door. He paused when she spoke again.

"And do remember your oath, won't you, Captain?"

A flash of heat ran over his hand. He swallowed. "I will."

CHAPTER 27

Notch led Wayrn into the Harper's stables. The scent of hay, dirt and horse combined to clog his nose. Sunlight filtered through a gap in the roof, upon which one of Seto's men had climbed to repair. His hammer beat a regular rhythm.

Seto, Flir and Luik waited. Luik still wore his bandage and Flir was pacing.

"Ah, Notch, you're finally ready." Seto said. His colour remained off, but he moved well enough as he crossed the yard to open the gate. Tulio had forced his employer to wear a large coat of fur, despite the warm autumn afternoon, something Seto had complained about. Loudly.

"I am. What now?" Notch rubbed his hand where the Witch had touched him. Was it unnaturally warm? She could be watching right now. He'd stretched the limits of his oath in delivering his news. Was she unhappy?

From above came a curse, then the hammering resumed. Seto grinned. "Hope that wasn't his thumb." He leant against the wall. "Very well, allow me to sum up what you have each learned. Even though Flir and Luik could not find Vinezi, they tracked his associates to a building – since abandoned – one which shows signs of great organisation."

"At least twenty or thirty men," she added.

"From traces they found in several rooms, it's clear they have enough of this powder substance to inflict much more damage."

Notch shifted. Had he made a mistake, focusing on Sofia? The city could be in real danger. And yet, Flir and Luik could manage. Sofia needed him too. "How much more?"

Flir shrugged. "No way to know. Enough to damage or destroy another half dozen buildings. Maybe less. Or twice as much. I'm just guessing based on what's already happened and what was left in their hideout."

Seto nodded. "But it is a grave threat."

Wayrn cleared his throat. "May I speak?"

"Certainly," Seto said.

"Is it time to inform the palace of all this? I could arrange it so that Lord Biagio 'stumbled' upon such knowledge. He returns from his hunting trip tomorrow and is in some favour with Oson."

Seto pointed with laced fingers. "It would appear so, my dear Wayrn, but I fear even he would not be taken seriously. In an incidental way I have tried to inform the palace already, using Notch as bait. As you said, there are now more Shields and Mascare on the streets. The palace is investigating, but I think we must assume they will not be as effective as we can be. We have more knowledge, even if we cannot share it with them easily. Later, I will send more direct word to other contacts within the palace. For now, I wish to disperse you, my flock, where most needed."

"And where is that?" Notch asked when Seto indulged in a dramatic pause.

"You and Flir to the Falco Manor." He went on to address Flir and Luik, summarising Notch and Wayrn's visit with the children, beast and witch. "I believe you can trust the witch's vision. Truthfully, I'm pleased to learn my father did not drive her out of Anaskar. At the manor you can retrieve Sofia and she will continue to assist me in my goal and Notch's. Luik, and Wayrn when your master has no need of you, will concentrate your efforts on locating the new hideaway of Vinezi and his Renovar. Wayrn, this is in addition to your usual duties for me."

"Yes, Seto."

"Begin with the area in the Second Tier where you found the last trace. I want them identified but not approached."

Luik nodded, but Flir shook her head. "Shouldn't I search for Vinezi and the Renovar? I'm the only one who can speak their tongue, after all."

"How quickly you forget my own skills, Flir."

"Are you coming with us then?"

"Certainly not. Tulio would never allow it in my present condition. But one of Wayrn's many talents is that of languages. He will be more than able to assist Luik there," Seto said. He raised a hand when Flir made to object again. "And I need you to help Notch. He may require your strength. There have been reports of rockslides to the west."

"But Seto —"

"No, Flir. The girl is more important than you seem willing to admit. The sooner you accept it the better."

"But why, Seto? She's not even a guarantee for your plans. She may already be in the hands of the palace. And what if she dies? Is dead already? Or worse, what if she can be returned but cannot help as promised?"

"Enough," Seto snapped. "I have a debt and I mean to honour it. Either assist me or seek new employment."

Flir crossed her arms. "So I'm just your servant, am I, Seto? Well you're not in the palace anymore, your majesty."

Silence dropped over the stable. Even the man repairing the roof stopped. And then, as if realising his silence was conspicuous, resumed beating.

Notch held his breath but Seto ignored Flir. "You have your tasks. My stores are open, take as you need." He swept from the stable.

Notch sighed. One look at Flir's red face was enough. He was in for an interesting ride to Falco Manor.

*

He spoke from behind the mask Seto had arranged, false red robes heavy on his shoulders. Although, knowing Seto, they were probably real. "This won't work."

"Of course it will." Flir's tone was tight. She rubbed her horse's neck as they approached the Mountain Gate. "We should have thought of it earlier. It'll save time, money and effort. What's not to be thankful for? You just have to say as little as possible. You look the part."

A bright sun with little warmth cast long shadows across the guards on the impressive gate. The men bowed and rushed to open the gate when Notch drew level with them. If they thought he was a pretender, likely the guards would turn him in. Or try to. The real problem would be if true Mascare caught them.

He waited until they'd started down the mountain road before answering Flir.

"Well I want to wear my sword. And the mask is making me sweat."

"We all make sacrifices, Notch."

He grunted as the rock face flowed by. It was a day to the manor and they were setting out late, somewhere along the way they'd have to set up camp. It was too slow. From the time he'd left Metti's, he'd felt a slug. Who knew what was happening to Sofia, and now he was trotting along a mountain road, unable to race. He clenched his jaw. At least he had a destination.

Near an hour passed before Flir spoke again. "Notch, can I ask you something?"

"Can I stop you?"

"No." She grinned, but it didn't last. Through the eye-holes of his mask her expression was apprehensive. "Have you have forgotten about clearing your name? You've taken a new name before, and it wasn't easy as I recall."

"No. I... don't want to be driven away again. By the King or anyone." Strange. It didn't gnaw at him as it had before, the need to prove himself to the city. It took him a moment to continue. Flir was being oddly gentle in her manner. "The city thinks I'm dead. Most of the posters have come down, replaced by those with Sofia's face. I still think I can live here, as Notch."

She nodded slowly. "That's well and good. But I don't want you to be disappointed."

"In Seto or Sofia?"

"Sofia. You don't know her. She's from the First Tier. They don't care about us. You know that, Notch. After what the King did to you, to Raff. How he repaid your loyalty. How do we know she's any different?"

He steered his horse around a hole in the road, refusing to follow her words to the memories lurking at the edge of his awareness. Threatening to break the surface. "Sofia is different."

"Just be on guard. If she weren't a young woman, you might not feel so protective of her. That's what it is, isn't it?"

He reached over and caught her reins, bringing both mounts to a halt. "Stop. What do you mean by that?"

"It means don't let your regrets cloud your judgement." Her voice softened. "She's not your daughter, Notch. You and Amina didn't take that path."

Amina.

No. Years, it had taken years to forget! He'd pushed her into a place of forgetfulness, but still he'd been a fool to think she'd stay there. He spoke through a clenched jaw. "It has nothing to do with Amina." Notch threw Flir's reins back before kicking his horse into a trot. She had no right to dredge up the past.

His knuckles were white around the reins.

Amina, pulling her hair behind her ears in the wind, the mountain's breeze gentle on the back of his neck as he leant in to kiss her, Amina planting seeds as he ploughed, her hands dirty and her smile bright, Amina and whatever dreams they'd shared before the war... dashed.

Enough. No use dwelling on it. Besides, all he was trying to do –

"Notch, look."

A giant tumble of broken stone and gravel blocked the road.

He swore. Just as Seto warned. Too jagged for the

horses to climb. What better time for the Mountain God to fall prey to such a colossal hiccup. "What now?"

"I could probably clear a path, but it would take hours. If it's unstable, longer."

"We could continue on foot. Send the horses back up the trail. The guards will hear them."

"We'd lose too much time once the path was cleared."

"Right." Notch dismounted, removing the mask and placing it in a saddlebag. He didn't look at Flir. "Then I'd better help you."

They worked until nightfall, managing to make a path the horses could navigate. Notch's hands were scraped and swollen and he'd not done half the work Flir had. It was a process. Much testing and prodding had to be done, to make sure the rockslide wouldn't continue if they shifted the wrong piece. Impressive as it was to see Flir toss large rocks and slabs over her shoulder, Notch groaned when they collapsed on the other side, moving some distance from the slide. Muscles in his legs trembled and his back ached.

"I never want to see another unconnected piece of stone again." He'd worked off his anger. It was enough to simply sit a moment.

Flir chuckled. "I agree."

"We should rest here." Cut for wagons to pass, the road widened enough for them to set up a small camp. Too dangerous to push on in the dark, with potential rock slides everywhere, he needed at least a short rest. He'd already been awake for hours, roaming the underground and battling strange sea-creatures, and now this. He pulled himself back up, legs weak, and removed his tent from a pack as the exhaustion of days hit him. Placing the tent aside, he affixed a feedbag to his mount's head, using his mount to support himself a moment. "Eat up, girl."

His own meal was cold, neither he nor Flir could find the strength to make a fire, let alone cook, and so when he crawled into his tent it was with another sigh. The urgency of the search slipped from his limbs the moment he touched his bedroll.

Tomorrow he would find Sofia.

Black sand.

A Medah fell beneath his blade, the man's scream cut short. The King was shouting, his voice hoarse. "Kill them!" An arrow protruded from the royal's leg. Medoro flung a knife across the space between archer and King, allowing his brother to step into the fray. Raff's sword was a blur. He cut through limbs and leather armour alike, scattering the enemy.

Medoro followed, deflecting a blow and backhanding a desert-dweller before whipping his blade around to drive it into the fallen man's chest. Two more steps, two more of the Medah down, and Raff had reached the king.

No more Medah stood.

"Your Majesty, we're here." Raff's face was set as he surveyed the dunes. More of the enemy would come soon, they had to get the king to safety. How had King Otonos and his Honour Guard been separated from the army?

"You do your nation proud. Both of you." The man breathed hard, sunken eyes blazing. His sword did not waver.

Medoro straightened. "It is our honour, Your Majesty."

A crashing, muffled.

Chaos woke him, a cracking of rock on rock, the very ground rattling his spine. Shaking off the dream – where it went next was not worth recalling – he stumbled from the tent into the night, calling to Flir.

Both horses pulled on their tethers, snorting. His head was heavy as he knuckled gunk from his eyes and ran to calm them. He stroked his mare's neck, speaking low. Flir joined him and he left the horse tied to the picket line, dragging himself up the road. A fresh slide covered the path, just beyond the original blockage. Dust settled in the moonlight, darkness cloaking most of the mountain, but the sharp edges of the new fall caught the moon.

"Lucky we weren't too close." Flir's hair was a mess and her eyes were wide.

Notch exhaled. The occasional stone still trickled down, clinking into the gorge. "Are we safe here?"

"I hope so."

He turned back to his tent but Flir caught his arm, fingers digging into flesh. "Torches."

He spun. Bobbing yellow lights converged on the slide. Voices hissed commands. A small group of men, faces indistinguishable blurs, worked at the slide a few moments before turning back. Were some of them carrying something away? Notch barely had time to snatch his sword and follow Flir when she leapt after them. They reached the slide in time to see the torches make a turn in the path and then their tread echoed and faded with the light.

"Who were they?"

"I don't know," Flir said. "It was too dark, even with the moon. We should follow them."

"The path's half-blocked again."

"It looked like they collected something."

"It did. Does that mater?"

Flir swore. "I don't know. How likely is it that a group of people with torches would appear near a rock slide, collect a stone and walk off with it?"

"True enough, but Sofia is at the mansion."

"We split up until I discover what they're up to. I can catch up to you, especially if you're planning to sleep until light. It's not that far away."

He hesitated. Flir could look after herself. But sleeping alone on a mountain trail? He was the one in danger, and yet... something was wrong. Whoever appeared in the night had conveniently arrived near the second landslide, which just as conveniently provided them with something they were seeking. Or had they simply examined the rock and turned back? Their journey foiled? No, they collected something.

He smacked his head. "Gods."

"What is it?"

"The Mountain Gate is supposed to be sealed after dark. How did the men with torches get through unless they left when we did?"

"Following us on official business then?"

If the palace had managed to set someone on their trail, it would pay to learn more. The same was true if it were Vinezi's men pursuing them. "Can you catch them?"

She grinned in the moonlight, almost bouncing on the spot. "Just you watch."

Notch ran for their lamp, lit and arranged it on a stable-looking part of the slide. Gentler than the first slide perhaps, it was mostly gravel crunching beneath his feet. The light cast more shadows, but it was better than nothing. "Can you see?"

Flir climbed the wreckage. "It'll have to do."

Twice she slipped, rocks clattering into the gorge but with her slight frame, she was able to leap to the road without any trouble. "Sleep well," she called, and slipped into the shadows beyond the lamplight.

Notch snorted.

CHAPTER 28

Sofia groaned. Every inch of her body was both on fire and aching, especially her chest, as if tiny demons hammered her bones and organs from the inside. Her eyes fluttered open to darkness around a bright moon. Moving her arm, something cracked. Heat seared through the joint and she froze. Something heavy lay on her legs and a sharp object dug into her side. Moving her other arm to her face, her fingertips came back slick with blood gone black in the night.

Was this the bottom of the gorge? Unlikely. But she'd survived the fall. More strapping pain shot through her limbs. By the Gods, was it even worth surviving?

Light blossomed at the edges of her vision. Slowly, she tilted her head, a rasp escaping her throat. Torches closed in and her pulse skipped a beat. Rescue! Someone from Anaskar was looking for her. Notch? Sofia blinked through tears, salt biting into her lips when the torches reached her. It had to be him, no-one else would be searching. Sofia squinted. Only dark shapes moved above her, one bending to lift her as another removed the weight from her legs.

"I still hear it." Someone muttered. It took a moment for the words to register. The Renovar language – but what were they hearing? They lifted her and began walking. The jostle of each step sent waves of pain through her body. She nearly bit through her tongue but clung to awareness.

The slight echo of speech from behind a mask.

White faces looked down on her and she croaked a single word.

"No."

They had her. Didn't matter who, palace or imposter. Escape, snatched from her grasp. She squeezed her eyes shut. All for nothing. Her injuries, all the trekking through the mountains, for naught.

She drifted in and out of consciousness then; the light never changed and the bumping continued for hours. Nothing else made sense. She was stuck in an endless, bright night, carried on invisible arms with white faces looming above. They never changed though sometimes they spoke.

"Can't you shut her up?"

"We aren't that far away. Won't be our problem soon."

"Look, just do something. I can't listen to her bitching no more."

A moment passed. Or even an hour. "You're paying for this."

"Whatever it takes."

Something was pushed between her teeth. In Anaskari, "Chew. It will make you feel better."

Sofia pushed her tongue out, trying to stop whoever held her jaw. Her tongue was ungainly, as if a dead fish replaced it in her mouth.

The voice sighed. "Just chew." Someone squeezed her nose shut, another hand covering her mouth, and only let go when she started to move her jaw. Cool juice flowed over her tongue and down her throat, soothing as it went. She kept chewing, the husk of whatever she ate sliding between her teeth as she ground it down. The longer she chewed the further her pain slid, until she actually smiled. The tiny bone-demons were gone and the air no longer tore at her skin. Her head cleared. Summer flowers filled her nose and she sucked on the last of whatever she'd been given.

Someone laughed. "She liked that."

The light had slowed, as if moving through water. "It was really good." Her voice was nearly as far away as the pain, and she lost any reply.

When she woke, it was to a twisting pain in her stomach, one echoed at various points around her body, but a pain somewhat distant. Turning her head wasn't too bad and her surroundings had lost their blurriness. A fire burned in a hearth, glowing on the tiled floor. Her bed was large where she lay propped on pillows, the canopy a thin white, and close by was a bedside table with steaming broth.

A closed door stood flanked by stands and vases.

Not the palace.

Tapestries hung on the wall that made her blush. In the corner was a large chest carven with lizards and Renovar runes. Her eyes skirted the tapestries. Even an envoy or ambassador would not bring such items with them.

"You're awake," a voice observed.

She flinched, crying out as the movement jarred her limbs. It set a throbbing in her head and a fire in her chest. Opposite her bed, furthest from the fire, a large figure detached itself from shadow and came to stand before her, taking up the broth and spoon. The man was heavyset but no sluggard, handling the spoon deftly. "You must be hungry."

"Where am I? And who are you?" If only she had a weapon. Or the strength to use it. She still wore her sweat-damped clothing beneath the blankets, but Lupo had her chisels.

"I am Vinezi and you are in my home." His smile was broad, rounding out his cheeks.

In the firelight it was hard to tell, but his skin appeared tan. Anaskari? What kind of traitor blew apart his own people? "Then you're Lupo's counterpart."

His smile held but his brows dipped. "We have common goals, certainly."

"So you mean to use me also."

"Most definitely, Sofia. You're extraordinarily valuable to our cause."

"I won't help you."

He replaced the broth. "You already have."

"Never."

"Lupo had a question for you, before he left earlier. You answered. Second Tier I believe."

Her mind struggled to catch up with his words. "That doesn't make any..." she trailed off, the pain in her stomach returning. Only now it was joined by a wave of horror. "No. I never chose that."

Vinezi almost purred. "Well, you had taken quite a large dose of lenasi, I suspect you might have said anything. In fact, I believe the deed has already been done. A building near a market as I recall. The blast was... impressive."

Tears stung her eyes as struggled with the sheets, but her muscles were watery. She hadn't chosen. Lupo did it. And would have done it without her. She collapsed, gasping. "Monsters... you're both monsters."

"And you have lied to us." He tapped the spoon on the bowl, as if chiding her for a minor infraction. "Lupo tore your manor apart and found no list."

"The list is gone," she spat.

He leaned in. "Where?"

"No-where you'll find it. It's the first thing the Protector takes in an attack or crisis." She breathed deeply before finishing, "And Father will never give it up."

Vinezi raised an eyebrow. "Debatable."

"Then you've found him?"

"We weren't looking."

Sofia sneered. "He would evade you anyway."

Vinezi shrugged as he moved to the door. "That has yet to be decided. Do be more agreeable when Lupo returns, won't you? He conceals a temper beneath that lovely voice of his, you know."

He slipped through the door, pausing to speak a word to someone, no doubt a guard, and then she was alone again. The scent of chicken broth was strong. She raised a hand to dash it to the tiles but stopped. Part of the ache in her stomach must have been from hunger, and she needed her strength. Sofia took bowl and spoon, her fingers just strong enough to hold them, and rested it on her chest, the warmth spreading beneath her skin.

She dipped the spoon but paused. If it were drugged, she was playing into their hands.

But they wanted her able to speak. Otherwise Vinezi would have ordered her taken care of the moment she lied about her father having the tabella. They wanted her for something else. Unless the broth were not drugged, but poisoned. She frowned. Equally unlikely. No point wasting poison on someone so helpless. On someone they had saved bare hours before.

Sofia inhaled deeply. The only scent she caught was one of deliciousness. Many poisons carried little scent, but she hadn't practised enough to detect them. She wasn't trained like her father or Tantos. Her stomach rumbled and she let her tongue touch the hot liquid.

She waited.

Nothing. A sip this time. Only the returning aches from her body. No symptoms, only a mouth-watering taste. Still she waited, and the broth had started to cool before she took another spoon. And then another, until she was suddenly scraping the bowl and looking for more. Placing it on the table, Sofia lay back, eyes heavy.

When she again woke, it was to light pouring in through a window opposite the fireplace. In daylight the tapestries were more vivid, and she had to keep her eyes averted.

Another bowl of broth sat on her bedside table, and she'd already wolfed half of it down before the bandage on her hands registered. Someone had changed her clothing and tended her wounds. Her left leg was in a splint, and her shoulder was strapped tight. A poultice was stuck to her temple and both her forearms and hands were bandaged. Her fingers had been left free but they were hard to move.

How many more times would she have to wake up in unfamiliar rooms, her wounds tended to by strangers? Pathetic. She was Casa Falco. And yet time and time again she'd been proven to be weak. Helpless.

The door swung open. A tall Braonn woman walked

to the bed, taking the bowl and giving Sofia a hesitant smile. "I hope you sleep well." The woman's accent was strong, and she kept her eyes on the floor. What was a Braonn woman, doubtless a runaway, doing working with the Renovar?

"I did."

"You are very bruised... very wounded. I worked long to help you."

"I appreciate your help." What did the woman want? Was her apparent concern an act? If she was the healer in Lupo's group of imposters then she would at least be concerned with her patient. But was that all?

"The pain will return, I warn you. It will be bad, you have suffered much in your fall."

"I am Casa Falco," she bluffed.

The woman nodded to herself, then looked up, blue eyes narrowed. She pressed something into Sofia's hand. "Take. Hide this. When pain is too many, chew."

Sofia opened her hand. A small green tube-like berry sat in her palm. It was glistening but dry. She gave it a gentle squeeze and the skin held.

"Called lenasi. Quick now, let no one see. Or see that I gave you."

"Thank you, but —"

The woman waved her hands. "I hear him."

Sofia placed the lenasi beneath her pillows as a heavy tread reached the door. It opened and Lupo walked in, his frowning mask in place and head swivelling to the woman, who was already crossing the tiles, bowl in hand.

"Hurry along now, sweet Miandra."

She bobbed her head and scurried from the room. Was Miandra a captive also? She certainly appeared afraid of Lupo.

"I applaud your resourcefulness, Sofia," he said. It seemed he meant it too, as no jibe followed, no anger even. He simply dragged the chair closer and stared, the black holes of his mask trained on her face.

"How did you find me?"

"Your heartbeat. Veddir traced it to the rockslide. I had set him to watch the road. You're ridiculously lucky to be alive." He paused. "And now your turn. How did you conceal yourself from us, in the hills?"

"A cave."

"That we searched."

"All of them?" Sofia asked. She would not give up di Mente so easily, despite her slip. Beneath the blankets she brought her hands together, finding the Queen's ring.

"Hmmm. And now we find ourselves in familiar roles."

"You're a man of your word it seems." She could not keep bitterness from her voice. Would it enrage him?

"You heard of the marketplace then?" He leant forward. "Merely a single step, Sofia. I will take each one after, and I don't need you between me and what I seek. You will obey me in the future. No more deceptions."

Her hands became fists. "You're worse than Vinezi," she cried. "He at least enjoyed it, you don't feel anything, do you?" She scrambled for something to hurl at him but found only soft pillows.

He caught her wrists. "Be gentle. You're needed yet. Whole."

"Why? The tabella is gone and you've killed innocent people again, what does it matter what I say or do?"

"The tabella was never all I sought."

She could not break his grip. "Then what, you coward, what?"

"You will grant me access to the palace, time enough

to win audience with the Prince."

"So you can kill him and take the throne, is that it? Very predictable, Wolf."

"And you'd truly object to that?"

She hesitated. How to answer? Oson needed to be punished, to die even, and be imprisoned at the very least, but to replace him with Lupo was no solution. "It won't make things the way they were."

"Nothing ever can," he said softly, and let her go, leaning back in the chair. His mask was still. After a time he stood. "You will agree to this now, or choose between the Night Markets tomorrow evening, or an inn called the Queen's Harper. I believe you know it? I imagine your friends will be there."

Hope flared but Sofia shook her head. "I cannot believe you." There was no way to know which was truth, and which a lie. Nor could she take his word on whether or even where he'd strike. "No matter what I say, you will do as you wish."

"Choose."

She held her mouth in a firm line.

He waited. Sofia glared at his mask. A long moment passed before he sighed, then turned to the door. "The Queen's Harper it is then. Listen for the sound, Sofia. It may even tremble the walls here."

"No." She leant forward, wincing at the pain. "I'll do as you ask."

"Much better. Our little visit to the palace will take some time to arrange. Recover well, Sofia and allow me to leave you in peace."

"Do so, Wolf," she shouted.

He made no response, closing the door as he left.

CHAPTER 29

The pain returned, just as Miandra said it would, and once again Sofia had woken to her own moaning. The fire was dark and sweat dampened her blankets. Throwing them off, she reached beneath a pillow and found the squishy object.

She placed the lenasi between her teeth.

Relying on the drug as she was, a herb or plant she'd not heard of, was a great risk. But the pain woke her most nights. She needed it, needed to rest to be strong if she was to escape. And there were few adverse effects. Sometimes her vision swam but her movement and thinking were not affected, her ability to reason and fence with both Lupo and Vinezi were not changed. She was safe enough – aside from being held captive again.

Coolness spread along her tongue when she bit down. The juice tingled, pain receding. Tightness in her muscles eased and the cloud of pain cleared. She sighed as she sunk back into the pillows, fumbling with the blankets, pulling only one across her legs and closing her eyes.

When she next woke it was morning. Miandra was

setting out her breakfast in the same routine they'd gone through for almost a week. The Braonn woman remained uneasy around Lupo and could not even look at Vinezi. Whenever the large man visited, she stilled herself, struggling to control a tremble. Twice now, she'd nearly been caught slipping Sofia the lenasi, after each instance she brought none the following night. Sofia sweated and swore through the dark, twisting her sheets.

"How you feel today?" In addition to the soup were chunks of bread and squeezed orange juice in a cup, a first. Sofia accepted the food with both hands, her shoulder giving her little trouble.

"Better."

"I am glad."

Sofia took a long drink. Was it only pity that drove the woman to help her? Miandra had once whispered of being 'taken' from her loved ones, but her story was interrupted by a guard, the man simply opening the door and looking in, saying nothing. But his look implied that Miandra was not to dally. Was Miandra's nature something Sofia could use? Probably not. Fear of her masters or captors did not equate to rebellion.

"And leg?"

"The same," Sofia replied. The lie came easily. Even one element of surprise could make the difference. Keep everyone guessing. Don't let them know the truth.

"Hmmm. Not little stronger?"

Sofia shrugged.

"The lenasi is many strong. I check after breakfast?"

"Thank you."

In the hours between visits and meals, Sofia was left to lie abed and plan. Nothing she had come up with was satisfactory, and none of her ideas were a magical cure for her leg either. While it did not hurt anywhere near as much as her first night, it was not healed. Should she somehow manage to escape, she would be slower than the long tide.

It was no use waiting and hoping that Notch or Seto would appear. If they still searched for her, they couldn't know where she was. If they even lived. She would have to pull herself out of trouble, and do a proper job of it this time.

Live up to her family name. Make Father proud.

Lupo entered without knocking, as he always did, coming to her bed and extending a hand. In it lay a blindfold. "Let's tour the city, shall we?"

"What?"

"I have a carriage outside. It's going to take us to somewhere with an ocean voice. I imagine you've been feeling somewhat... confined of late."

"My leg's broken."

"Indeed." He raised the blindfold. "Can you place this upon your own head?"

"I can." She affixed the cloth and folded her arms. "Now what?"

"Now relax." His arm slid around her back, the other lifting her legs, careful not to jar her splint.

"Let me go," Sofia demanded. He ignored her, lifting and carrying her from the bed, completing a dancer's twirl as he did. "What are you doing?" One arm caught his back for balance, but the other was free. His eyes would be protected by his mask, but she might jab his throat, even blindfolded. He'd drop her and she'd be free – for a flea's sneeze. How far would she get at a crawl? If that. And she was in the middle of an enemy stronghold, Vinezi's home, if the man was to be believed.

Even if she somehow made it outside, he could have Veddir track her heart and blood. And no glowing men of magic would save her now.

"Be patient."

He carried her along a corridor, through a door, down stairs and into the street. In the morning light, cold air brushed her cheeks and lips and she inhaled deeply, the taste of rain on her tongue. A frown followed. Lupo was right. She'd missed fresh air.

His boots echoed on the cobblestones as he issued commands. Another pair of hands helped lift her onto a soft seat. She stretched her leg and waited. The carriage, for that was what it must be, with the snorting of horses, rocked as someone followed her in. A door clicked shut and a rapping on wood followed.

The coachman's cracking whip started the horses, jostling her. Sofia reached for the blindfold but Lupo spoke. "Keep it on."

They did not move fast but she still strained to keep her leg from being jolted. As Lupo had obviously planned, she could not get her bearings. It was not hard to guess, however. Second Tier. Lupo and Vinezi would want to be in striking distance of the palace.

Wind buffeted the carriage when it came to a halt and she shivered, reaching a hand up to the blindfold.

"Go ahead."

Lupo sat across from her in an old carriage, its upholstery faded. With legs stretched across the seat, he gestured to a window. The view of the ocean from their position was impressive, distant lightning stabbed at the dark water with flashing whitecaps. A storm was passing, as if the heavens had held off just for her. Truly unlikely.

Most impressive was that she had such an unobstructed

view – without being on the wall.

"Where are we?" She strained her neck but saw no clues, only the hints of nearby buildings.

"There is a ramp off one of the streets near the wall. It leads to a building site. One of the more successful merchants is arranging for his residence to lie in such a way that he might see over the Second Tier wall."

She wound the blindfold around her hand. "This is all terribly transparent, you know."

The mask turned to face her. "Truly?"

"Yes. You can't win me over. All this effort. It doesn't change anything."

"It changes your view."

She sighed. Why did he bother with games? Lupo was in control, she had admitted as much. He didn't need to win her over. He was already forcing her to take him to the palace, and with her injured leg she wasn't going anywhere else.

"Sofia, I understand you feel this is a ploy. But this is who I am. I simply thought you'd appreciate time out of that room."

Speaking plainly had not earned her a swift death yet. He needed her. "You're a killer, without honour."

"Perhaps I'm those things in addition to being considerate."

She shook her head. "See? Still you attempt to sway me."

"How so?" He arranged his robes.

"With your calm. The way you turn aside my insults with apparent honesty. That you do not brutalise me for my behaviour, as another captor would. I see through it, Wolf – because none of it's needed. You already have me at your mercy. We both know that."

"Ah."

Sofia waited. "Well?"

"I have no need to convince you of anything, Sofia. Believe what you will. You are correct, certainly in one thing. I have all power over you I need."

"Then why the charade?"

He laughed. "You would not be confused if you believed me. It's no charade. You see me as I am."

"Then I've seen enough. Take me back to my cell."

"No."

Sofia turned back to the water. Only fools reasoned with madmen. Her breath would be better spent chasing away clouds. She flexed the muscles in her leg, trying to relieve an ache. After a time she broke the silence. "What do you get out of this, for helping Vinezi?"

"Vinezi helps me."

Was that his way of seeing things, or truth? If she knew, she might be able to divide them somehow. Both men were self-important, both confident and neither possessed much of a moral guide. But how was she to use that? What did Lupo truly want? "And once you're admitted to the palace?"

"We've gone over this."

She smiled. "Help me pass the time."

"It's simple. I will have the throne and a bargaining chip to use with your father."

She blinked. "Is this all about the tabella?"

"Not all. While there is someone I wish to find, beyond which, I need something else from Danillo Falco."

She narrowed her eyes. "He has nothing for you, and you know he's been driven away. What do you want from him?"

"That's between he and I. But for you, he'll give me

what I wish."

"He won't."

He shrugged. "That I plan to discover."

Sofia gave him an evil grin. "If you're thinking he has Argeon you're wrong."

"True. Your Greatmask is in the palace."

She crossed her arms. "Fine. But Argeon will only speak with a Falco. You won't be able to use him, Lupo. Not ever."

"Then it's fortunate is it not, that I currently possess a Falco?"

"I'm not a tame bird. You don't possess me." An empty claim.

He leant over and opened the carriage door. Hinges squeaked. "By all means, fly away, little one." And now he mocked her. When she made no move toward the open door he closed it and tapped on the carriage roof. A whip cracked and they lurched forward.

Sofia gave no answers on the ride back, despite Lupo's attempts at conversation, even after the blindfold had been replaced. A faint sheen of sweat grew at her temple, despite the breeze, and the pain in her stomach had returned. Dull aches snuck back to her body to take up familiar positions and she urged the carriage on. Miandra would have lenasi.

"Woah." A cry came from above and the carriage jerked to a halt at an angle, as if the driver had tried to turn the carriage but given up half way through. Sofia caught the window sill for balance, leg shifting on the seat. She cursed.

"What's your driver doing?"

He chuckled. "My, my. Speaking like a lady, Sofia."

A muffled voice called from above. "Lord Lupo,

there's something you should see."

"Stay here." The carriage door clicked open.

Sofia pulled her blindfold aside. Lupo strode down a street lined with expansive homes, robe fluttering in the wind. A single cry reached her as a man stumbled past the wolf. "Help me, sir." He cast glances over his shoulder as he went. A second scream came with the slamming of doors, and then Lupo was shouting for people to run.

He spun, taking his own advice. His body blocked her view, but something green scurried behind him, low to the ground. "Close the door," he called as he skidded to a halt, knife in hand, and placed his back against a wall.

Sofia stretched for the handle. Too far. A shrill scream rose from beyond the man and she gasped.

A mess of green things, whose spindly legs flicked liquid into the air as they flashed, scrambled from a hole in the cobblestones. Each left a trail of slime, their rounded bodies bulging with dozens of eyes. Several people lay motionless in the street, their bodies slashed with green. A scream burst from a person fending off several creatures, but whose arms were useless against the tide of green legs. He disappeared beneath them, a sharp hissing joining his cries.

Sofia strained for the door handle, but it was hopeless. Further along, a pair of women were smashing the creatures aside with their baskets. The green things splattered against the walls and Sofia urged the women on from the carriage. Lupo had already replaced his knife and was backing away from two of the creatures. The flow from the hole had halted, most disappearing elsewhere in the city. When the Wolf took a step, the lead creature mirrored it.

"Arm yourselves," he called without turning.

The carriage driver leapt to the stones, whip in hand. His legs trembled, but he advanced. Sofia gripped her splint, tearing the bindings. Even a plank of wood would be something. Lupo feinted and the green thing leapt at him but he was already twisting aside. A flash of powder shot from his hand, even as he raised the heavy sleeve of his robe to catch flecks of slime from its legs. Holes appeared in the fabric and he danced back. The creature he'd cast dust upon shrivelled to the ground, eyes popping as it turned black.

The driver's whip exploded the second creature, green flying, and he screamed, clutching his face. Lupo dragged him back to the carriage and tossed the man into the back, climbing to the driver's seat. The horses pawed at the ground until Lupo turned the carriage and pulled them away from the opening in the street.

"Are they chasing us?" she called.

"I don't know."

Across from her the driver shook, tearing his mask free. Sofia shrank back. Slime had eaten a hole in his face. The inside of his mouth was visible, teeth and wet, red flesh giving off a sizzle.

Veddir.

"Lady, help me please." The young man gurgled, reaching across the carriage.

She pushed him back with her strong arm. The Renovar slumped against the wall, tears streaming and chest heaving.

He was still when the carriage came to a halt.

Lupo shouted for help, ripping the door open and pulling the young man out, laying him on the street and checking him over. Sofia craned her neck, but only the sky was visible through the window. What was Lupo doing?

If the creatures had pursued them he was finished.

None came.

When the masked man rose, it was to step back and allow two of his fellow imposters collect Veddir's body. Sofia sat in the carriage without making a sound until the thunder of her heart eased. Only then did she call Lupo's name.

CHAPTER 30

The clicking neared and Ain strained his eyes. At the very limit of the lamplight only darkness remained. He waited, muscles tense. The clicking stopped. No figure appeared and the sound did not repeat itself.

"It's gone," Ain said after a long moment.

Schan waved his blade. "We should check. Best not to be caught unawares."

Ain returned to collect the lamp. He drew his knife and moved beyond the eggs. It did not take long to find another opening dug into the walls. Only this one was more than large enough to stand within and travelled deep into the earth.

"A passage."

"And who knows what made it?"

Ain shook his head. The clicking had stopped near the opening. It was clear, whatever made the sound was using the tunnels. Possibly made them too. "We need rest," he said. "Should we set a watch, keep the lamp low?"

"I am tired. And the oil should last, but I'm not sure."

"We have enough for two days and one more night I estimate."

Schan tapped his foot. "I think we move on. Put some distance between us and this opening."

Ain nodded. A much better idea.

He marched back to where the eggs lay and repacked his bags, helping Schan do the same. He kept an ear on the tunnel, but there was no more clicking. He paused at the shallow opening, bending before the eggs. Their gold-tinted shells were bright, even with the lamp turned low. He stared at them. Something about the shells... he reached out, running a fingertip across the grooves on its hard surface. His hand tingled.

They could not be left behind.

Such neglect. He would rescue them. "Schan, I'm going to take these with us. They are important."

"That's a bad idea, lad."

He did not look away. "They're connected to our path. I can feel it." It wasn't a lie but it was nothing he could prove either. Just a vague feeling. And besides, they were beautiful. The way they collected the light, the warmth they gave in reply.

"You sure about that? Because if whatever lives down here laid them, and can't find them later, we're on its list."

Ain paused. Schan made a fine point. And yet, the eggs could not stay. He smiled down at them. "They will be my responsibility, Schan." He lifted one. Heavy, cool. The tingling returned. Only sharper. And he nearly laughed. The path was stronger too. It no longer flickered – it pulsated, steady. The edge of panic was stronger too, but it no longer tugged at his emotions. Instead, a network of other paths stretched around him, running off into the earth in many directions. "This tunnel is part of a network. I can feel them all."

Schan put a hand on his shoulder. "Ain, I think it unwise."

Ain shrugged him off. "Can't you trust me?"

The warrior narrowed his eyes, then sighed. "I can. Just be on your guard."

"I will."

"And what of our path then?" Schan asked. "Does one lead to Sekkati?"

His mind flew along the dark tunnels, as if propelled on golden wings. "It goes through the lair of whatever makes these tunnels. There is a blockage ahead," Ain murmured, closing his eyes to feel it better. "It subverts the flow of old travellers, and now feet and claw, both use the new paths." He turned to Schan with wide eyes. "Sands, I've never felt it this strong before. What creature laid this egg?"

"I don't know, but I think we need to leave soon. And I still don't think you should take it."

"But it showed me more of a path than I've ever seen. It's powerful." Ain bent to collect the other. A flash of emptiness struck him. There was a crack at the base. The egg was light. Empty. "Just one then," he breathed.

"Let's move along," Schan said. He kept an eye on the shell, but waved for Ain to take the lead.

He strode forward, lamp in one hand, egg in the other. The path did not change, and despite many openings, now to either side of their passage, he ignored them until coming to a halt before a pile of rubble. At least an hour had passed but his legs had not wearied. Earth, stone and shattered wood poked from the tunnel and he pointed to a side passage, dug by claws.

"We must take the new path. Possibly into danger."

"Or turn back."

"Which I don't wish to do." Neither Silaj nor his child wanted a coward to return to the Cloud. Better that he die here. No. Better that he return champion of the Medah. What the elders wanted from him was impossible – but Ain would accomplish it and more.

Schan hesitated, and Ain tied the egg in his cloak and tugged at his tunic neck. It was no longer cold beneath the earth. The warrior waved his sword in a gesture of acquiescence. "It's a long way back for no guarantee I suppose."

"True. I feel Sekkati, if we simply pass this blockage we will be within... hours of the walls."

"You're certain?"

"I am."

Schan eyed the egg once more before sighing. "Lead on then."

The new passage was rough underfoot but spacious, enough for two abreast. The lamp, which Schan had refilled, cast craggy shadows from the earth. A large piece of stone grasping from the floor signalled a branch. The new path turned left and the first continued on. Ain passed the turn.

"Shouldn't we go left?"

"No, it's the next one." The brush and scrape of claws was stronger. At the next turn Ain touched the egg again, another tingle shooting up his arm. He glanced over his shoulder. Schan was lagging. Not too much, but the light had changed.

"Keep up, Schan."

He gave a grunt.

Another turn appeared and Ain took it, skidding to a halt. Something blocked the passage. He raised a hand

and Schan crept forward.

Fur. A beast filled the passage almost to the sides. Massive, clawed feet rested unmoving and a stout tail twitched. Ain swallowed. If it noticed the light, and was startled, it could well crush them. Or tear them apart — the fate of Wilatt's engineer?

"What is that?" Schan kept his voice low.

"I don't know. A burrow-creature?"

"Look at those claws."

Ain backed away, keeping it in sight. "This is the path. No other moves round the blockage."

"By the Sands, how do we shift it without getting trampled?"

"Drive it forward?"

"I suppose we could prod it. I know I wouldn't move backward if someone jabbed me in the rear."

Ain paused. "What is that?"

A clicking, still faint, echoed up the tunnel behind them. "There's another."

Schan drew his blade. "Let's move this thing." He crept to within a blade's length from the beast and paused. Reversing his sword, he gripped the blade between two hands and prodded the beast's rear, jumping back. A snuffling followed and the tail twitched but the creature didn't move.

"Harder," Ain said. The clicking grew louder. Schan gave another jab. The beast snorted and moved forward a step. The warrior jabbed again and the beast responded, shifting only a few feet.

"This isn't working," Schan whispered.

"The other one's closing in," Ain said. Stronger than the clicking of claws on stone was the pulse of the path.

Schan pursed his lips. "I didn't want to do this." He

flipped his sword over and took a breath before stabbing through the fur. Ain flinched. It wasn't a deep cut but the beast squealed. Poor thing.

It scrambled forward, tearing at the earth and flicking dirt into his eyes. He shielded his face with a forearm, following Schan forward. From behind, still there was nothing, but the second beast had made the turn, its feet rippled up the path.

Ain had to escape, had to protect the egg.

The moment the first monster made a turn, choosing right, Ain ran left. The tunnel walls shook, earth trickling down. His feet soon skidded onto stone and he charged on, Schan behind him.

The tunnel was long and his legs soon tired. They were climbing. Schan caught his shoulder, breathing hard. "It's given up."

Ain paused, panting. No claws followed and the rumble of the beasts moving through the tunnels was faint. "We have to keep going."

"I need to rest, lad. We've been travelling all day and I'd guess the better part of the night now." He sheathed his blade. "You should be weary too."

"We cannot risk it," Ain said. His own limbs were light. "And I don't know why, but I feel strong."

The warrior thumped his thighs. "All right. Let's get out of here."

Ain followed the path. It did not deter from the stone. Each opening, though containing many branches, was an unwanted distraction. Ignoring them caused a throbbing in his temple, but he pushed it down and pulled Schan along. Ahead lay the end of the passage and the secrets of Sekkati. No other Pathfinder had been this close.

"I see light," Schan gasped out.

Ain slowed, squinting. Their own lamplight was dim but in the distance, yes, a pillar of light streamed through the roof. He ran forward, the sound of Schan stumbling after him distant. Light came from the moon, pouring down from heaven through a pair of windows high above. He hadn't realised the roof had grown so much taller. A door in cool white rested above three simple steps.

He ascended and placed a hand on the steel.

CHAPTER 31

Black sand whipped his legs.

Medoro kept watch on the dunes. He'd tended to the king and now they would have to chart a course toward the battle lines, scattered as they were. Raff snuck up the crest, lying in the sizzling sand.

"What do you see?" Medoro called, pitching his voice low.

"Nothing. The wind has carried the smoke away, but if we head toward the sun we'll come across our lines."

"Did you hear that, Your Majesty?" Medoro turned, and choked on his next words.

King Otonos stood over the bodies, facing away from Medoro, hips moving in such a manner as to leave no doubt as to what he was doing.

The man was urinating on the dead Medah.

Medoro gaped.

"Animal," Raff roared. He flew down the dunes. Medoro stepped after him, slow to recover from the sight of his King dishonouring fallen warriors, even if they were the enemy, but Raff already had a hand on

Otonos' shoulder.

He spun his monarch round. "Stop this."

Otonos' face was a rictus. He shoved Raff away. "They are not human."

The two scuffled over Otonos' cursing. Medoro reached them just as his brother cried out. Raff fell to the sand, a knife in his chest. Otonos blinked down at his hands.

Medoro collapsed, gripping Raff's shoulders. "No!" His brother's eyes were already staring at the sky. "Rafiso."

Silence on the dunes.

Medoro raised his sword as he stood. Through the blur of tears, Otonos' face blanched.

War cries.

Medoro spun. A wave of Medah poured over the dune, weapons high. He leapt amidst them, his father's sword light in his hands and cries of rage on his lips.

Blood splashed across the black sand.

Notch woke to a hand on his shoulder.

"You're shouting."

He swallowed. "I'm awake."

Darkness filled the tent, only a slither of moonlight visible beyond the flap. Flir's shape blocked most of the light.

"The dreams are back?"

"They'll pass."

She squeezed his hand and he winced, despite her attempt at gentleness. "No, they won't. Not until you do something about it."

Flir was right. They always came back. In a way, they were never really gone. Nothing he could do about it. "So you've told me before." He stretched. "Did you learn anything?"

She didn't respond at once. "It was Sofia."

He sat up. "What?"

"I don't know how, but those shapes were Mascare. Or imposters. They were carrying Sofia back to the mountain gate."

He rubbed sleep from his eyes. His head was heavier than it ought to be. He hadn't meant to drift off. Foolish. But the bedroll was soft and his eyelids so blasted heavy...

"That doesn't make sense. You're sure it was her? Where did she come from?"

"They had quite a few torches. And I don't know where she came from, Notch. Come on." She hauled him to his feet and he stumbled from the tent. Their site had already been broken, Flir was only waiting on his tent, which she started collapsing. "I let you sleep a little. Seemed like you needed it."

"Thanks." He stretched his limbs further, then stopped. "Wait, how did they open the gate?"

"I don't know, but I found out that I couldn't do it by myself. I nearly had them too, Notch. They must have taken a hidden path, because I wasn't that far behind and then they were suddenly gone."

Notch shrugged, moving to lend her a hand. "This is the City of Secrets."

"Well, we've got a new one to uncover. A way into the city before dawn."

"With torches we might be able to see where they left the road."

"I had the same idea."

Once everything was packed away and torches lit, they led the horses over the slide. Losing his footing twice woke him the rest of the way, and by the time they moved along the road to the mountain gate, torches held close to the wall, his body was responding to the urging from his mind.

"There's nothing here."

"Keep looking."

He slipped from the saddle and examined the wall. "Well they didn't float down the gorge, did they?"

"I doubt it."

Walking the horses while they combed every inch of the trail by torchlight was folly. He lost track of the time that passed before the mountain gate appeared ahead, each moment giving Sofia's captors more time to escape, to disappear into the city. Or the palace. But what had she been doing here in the mountains when she was supposed to be at the manor? Metti didn't seem prone to error. Sofia must have escaped.

"This is useless. I've seen nothing."

"Nor I," Flir said. "And that's the gate."

"Then we have to –"

Thunder boomed. Somewhere in the city light flared, angry orange blooming in the black sky. "Is that...?"

"Another explosion."

"We're helping those people."

Flir gestured to the mountain gate, towering over them. Faint screams rose from beyond. "Open this for me and we can."

He shouted for the gate guard but no-one answered. Notch leapt from the saddle and snatched up a piece of rock, hammering on the gate. Still no-one came. He dropped the stone.

"Get some sleep, Notch," Flir said, her hand coming to rest on his shoulder. She'd already picketed the horses. "We're not going anywhere until dawn."

He kicked the gate. "Gods damn it. I thought we'd find her and now another attack."

"I know."

He paced until his legs grew tired. "Sofia was depending on us. On me."

"They want her alive."

Flir was right. And he probably could use some more sleep. He slung his pack to the ground and took out the bedroll. "Wake me when you're ready."

He lay on his back. The stars were bright though the moon had long since faded. Faint clouds scuffed the sky. He'd barely settled when he rolled onto his side.

"You can't sleep can you?"

He sighed.

"Take first watch then."

He switched places with her, leaning against the chill of the gate. Nothing stirred on the mountain trail and Flir settled quickly.

She'd been right earlier too. He was letting old feelings, long buried, sway him. He could keep pushing them down. Put Amina's face away again, as he'd done before. He was good at it. He needed to be. After all, few remembered Medoro the hero. Medoro the Shield, who, with help, saved half the Anaskar army with his bravery. Or to be honest, his rage.

Not Notch.

Notch remembered a mercenary who turned his back on the lies everyone believed, who cut his ties and took the jobs no-one else wanted, who stayed away from Anaskar until no-one remembered Medoro. Until only Notch stood in his place. Older and slower but still kicking. And blessedly anonymous. Something Seto had been willing to go along with. For all his faults, Notch's secret was safe with Seto. And Flir and Luik too.

Until that bastard inn keeper at the Pig and his Renovar masters pulled Notch back into the light. Each day Notch lived as a wanted man was another day, another chance for one of the older Shields to recognise him. Most of the Vigil wouldn't know him at least. And the posters were disappearing now, the explosion at the inn 'killing' him.

This explosion came from the Second Tier. Nothing else would make such noise and light. Who knew the damage? The screams had died down. Shouting drifted over the walls – but it was purposeful. Hopefully the City Vigil were helping this time. By dawn, there would be few traces, if any, left to find Vinezi. Or Sofia. The palace was an obvious place to look, but it was more likely that the Mascare Flir saw were imposters.

And to find them, he would have to rely on Seto again. Hopefully Luik and Wayrn had found the 'beggar'. It was high time the man was roughed up again. And then more. The bastard was responsible for how many deaths now? Perhaps death wasn't good enough for Vinezi. But it would have to do, Notch was no Sea Priest with watery promises of the Thousand Tomorrows.

He shivered as the end of the night stretched on.

He woke Flir with the rising sun. "They'll be opening up soon."

She stretched. "Good."

Charging through the gates when they opened, a clatter of hooves ringing in the street, Notch ignored the surprised gate guards and led Flir toward the Queen's Harper. The streets were largely empty as they rode. A few people scattered from his gaze and one woman even dashed back for her doors when he passed, an empty basket whipped after.

The first market they came across was empty. Not a single stall holder, not a single customer crossed the cobbles to haggle. Instead of the bustle and hum of voices, the rumble of distant wagon wheels, there was only a rising breeze, whistling between gaps in the stonework.

"What's happening?" Even shutters on the windows were closed up.

"The explosions must have spooked everyone."

"They spook me too."

Flir approached a woman who'd just opened her door, her voice pitched low. She was arguing with whoever was in the house. "I must go. Mare needs her medicine."

Flir leaned down in her saddle. "Excuse me, ma'am?"

The woman jumped but did not flee, closing the door with a firm hand. She glanced at Notch, noting his garb, then back to Flir in her hood. "Yes, my Lady?"

"Has there been another explosion?"

She placed a hand over her heart. "Yes. By the Artisan's Bazaar last night. Many were killed. I don't know if it's even safe to leave my home. The first explosion was in the Lower Tier, thank the Gods. But this one, it was only four squares away."

"You must be worried," Flir said.

"For days now. There's no way to know where or when they'll strike again. I won't even let my children outside now."

Flir offered an understanding smile. "That seems safest. Have you heard who's responsible?"

She shook her head, glancing at Notch again. "No-one's got a clue. Not even the Mascare, begging your pardon, my Lord, can figure it out. I don't understand.

Why can't the Greatmasks protect us like legend says? What's the palace doing – they've got three of them by the Gods."

An old promise in that legend. In times of trouble the Greatmasks were supposed to call forth some great power and 'compel the fates to smile upon Anaskar' sometimes by 'seeing to the city's bones,' sometimes by 'turning every enemy to dust,' but she'd be waiting forever. A child's comfort.

"I'm sure they're working on it," Flir said.

The woman's expression was not confident. "Some say the masks are involved, but that's obviously ridiculous." She trailed off, giving him another look. "Oh, I mean, well, I really must hurry." She bade them a good day and rushed off, shoulders hunched, as if expecting a blow.

Notch changed course, heading for the Artisan's Bazaar. "What does Vinezi want?"

"Fear. Chaos. Uncertainty."

"But what's it leading up to? You said yourself, you didn't see Renovar mounting any sort of attack."

"I still don't. He must have something else in mind."

"It sounds like the palace can't put a stop to it."

"Neither can we, Notch."

"Seto might be able to figure it out." He came to a halt, dismounting to walk his horse once the market square became visible. The woman took him for a Mascare, but the Shields and Mascare nearer the explosion might not be so easily duped. So long as none sought to speak with him he would be fine. He just had to keep out of sight, and sitting astride a horse in a red robe and white mask was hardly keeping hidden. He let Flir lead.

Flecks of ash drifted up the street, collecting in doorways and on windowsills. Char and ash stung his nose, the taste of it heavy even behind the mask. Through the crowd of bustling Vigil, onlookers and even a small group of Mascare with their heads together, were the skeletal remains of two shops. Blackened stone rested in a heap, by the look of the surrounding homes, some pieces had been flung from the square. Fragments of a charred frame stood in the centre of the blast and from end to end the square was lined with people shifting the debris, which was strangely colourful.

Using his horse, Notch kept out of the Mascare's line of vision, though they hardly seemed inclined to look his way, arguing amongst themselves. A grim-cart rolled out of the square as Notch and Flir stopped at the edge of the crowd. It was trailed by a member of the Vigil and a young Sea Priest, his face white. Notch shook his head. He should have recognised the colourful parts right away. Clothes. The colours were people. Many. No way to get an accurate count either.

This time the quick prayer he sent to the Ocean Gods didn't seem anywhere near adequate.

A young man in the thick of the mess climbed from the centre with a small shape in his arms. The child was battered and bloody, face covered in soot. The man had tears in his eyes and his jaw was locked as he placed the little victim on the grim-cart.

Notch glanced away. Wouldn't stay so empty for long. "No sign of Vinezi," he eventually said.

Flir's own face was set. "He likes to see it in the moment, doesn't he?"

"We'll show him a moment when we find him."

"Sounds good to me."

Before them, a pair of men spoke with crossed arms. Both stood in drab tunics, one with patches. The taller wore boots tied at the ankles with thick string. He spat, his bone charm rattling. "Look at them bloody Masks, then. Not doing nothing to help."

"Just ordering folk around. Haven't seen one lift a single stone."

"Bones for brains."

The other man snorted in agreement.

"And why didn't they warn us, eh? Should have seen this coming, especially after that last one."

"Not even safe in our bloody homes. See how much of the next shop it tore apart? I saw one of them new Masks slinking about before too. Worse than them water-priests."

"New masks, eh?"

"Yep. Them ones with the frown. Unnatural-is." He wiped one hand with the other, as if brushing dust away, an old gesture to ward off evil.

"Haven't seen them." The first man repeated the gesture. "Most of the dead ones look like southerners, bless the ocean. Could have been worse."

The second shifted. "Right."

"So how'd you think they got it under the shops, eh?"

"No idea, Bosi."

Notch led his horse away, glad they hadn't noticed him. "Did you hear those two?"

"Yes. Charming fellows."

"They raise a good question."

Flir tapped the ground. "Think Vinezi came up from below?"

"It might explain how no-one saw them coming and going. I don't know how much magical powder they need. Surely a large amount?"

"Could have just delivered it. Some of these artisan

stalls are furniture ones. They aren't small. No onlooker would notice a large delivery."

Notch cut short his reply when a figure stepped before him.

Mascare.

"What have you learned?" The man's voice was flat, calm.

Notch shook his head. A trickle of sweat ran down his cheek. Beside him, Flir remained silent.

"I too, have learnt nothing," the mask continued, a hint of frustration entering his voice. A great slip, the man must have been upset. "But there's continued talk of false Mascare, wearing frowning masks. Watch for them. In fact, give the Shield new orders, will you? Any false masks sighted are to be monitored but not stopped. I'm taking word to the palace."

Notch nodded and the man nodded back, apparently satisfied. Once the mask disappeared, Notch let out a breath.

"Well done," Flir said.

He laughed. "I suppose so."

Flir took his arm. "Look."

Luik waved to them from across the square before ducking out of sight. Flir was already leading her horse toward the big man. Notch hurried after.

Luik leant against a wall, his arms crossed. Bandage gone, his face and tunic were dark with soot, trails of sweat cutting a path down his face. A look of helplessness lay in his eyes.

"You look like you need some sleep," Flir said.

"I've been helping." He paused as shouts from a nearby stall swelled. "Didn't find her?"

"She's back in the city somewhere," Notch said,

explaining their night. He gestured over his shoulder when he finished. "Did you see that?"

"No. Got here quick enough to catch a glimpse of our old friend," he said. "Bad even then. Four grim-carts have been and gone since it happened. The place was busy. Another night market."

"The bastard had to gloat," Flir said. She thumped the wall, dislodging fine grains of stone. Her horse shied away but she soothed it.

"Do you have him?" Notch asked.

Luik shook his head. "Followed him and left Wayrn to watch while I came back."

"We should figure out a way to flush him out," Flir said. "Then we can beat whatever we need out of him. There could be a dozen more places he's targeted. Who knows?"

"I told Seto as much."

Notch put a hand on his shoulder. "What does he want us to do?"

"No idea."

"What do you mean?"

Luik drew a long breath. "Seto's gone."

CHAPTER 32

"What do you mean 'gone'?" Notch took a drink from his flask and handed it over.

Luik accepted it and tipped the flask to his mouth. He spread his hands once he'd handed it back. "Told me he had something to attend to, that it couldn't wait. Said I had to find Vinezi and wait for you two to get back."

"And then?"

"After that he ran to the stables. Tulio has no idea either," Luik said when Notch opened his mouth.

"Fine time for him to disappear on one of his mysterious trips."

"They don't last long," Luik shrugged.

"We aren't waiting anyway," Notch said. He mounted up. "Show us where Vinezi's hiding. We'll figure out what to do once we get there."

"Think Sofia's with him?"

"I hope so. Flir saw whoever took her, but not their masks."

"They have to be the imposters," she said as they skirted the market. "I can feel it. The Mascare wouldn't have been waiting near the Mountain Gate in a big group. And besides, now that I think back on it, their voices were..." she trailed off, coming to a halt.

Notch turned. "What now?"

"I finally realised something. It's been gnawing at me for a while, but I recognise it now." She cursed in her own tongue. "Vinezi's voice. It changed."

"Like a Mask's Neutral Voice?" Luik asked.

"No. Like dialects. At first he spoke like the street, then more Second or First Tier. I remembered when I heard the voices last night. The Mascare had a range of voices, I heard that much before they disappeared. They're fake, and so is Vinezi."

"Sofia is probably with Vinezi, but we already knew he was pretending to be a beggar. This 'Thalik' he mentioned is a lie too. Vinezi's the leader."

"I know all that you block head," Flir said. "But if Vinezi was behind this from the beginning, then why did he let himself be captured at all? Did he want Sofia all along? And this all had nothing to do with Notch?"

"Hmmm." A good question. Why would a leader risk himself? Seto had said it was difficult, but even so. If Vinezi was the mastermind he'd taken quite a risk.

"A trap," Luik said. "He meant to draw us in."

Notch scratched at his new beard. "But why?"

"To kill a lot of people? After all, we led a heap of Shields there."

"I don't know."

Flir leaned closer. "No, he's on to something. It was part of something bigger. He wanted the palace's eyes drawn to the inn as bait, maybe it's always been about Sofia for him? And we took her to the inn. Put her right within his reach." She shrugged. "Or maybe it was about her father... I don't know. But I doubt Vinezi's finished with the city."

Notch muttered a curse. If she was right, and they'd played into the imposter's hands... "Let's go visit him then."

His hand strayed to his hilt as he rode after Luik. He led them to a section of the Second Tier where new homes were being constructed on sloping grounds built up from the street. The owners would never see directly over the wall and their houses would not come close to climbing the wall to the First Tier, but Notch could imagine them having a fine view of the Second Tier as it sloped down.

A commanding house lurked beyond a high wall at a point where two roads intersected. The tops of trees were visible inside and a large gate with iron bands stood closed. The building was barely distinguishable from nearby homes, having only a slightly lower wall.

Luik nodded to the gate. "In there."

"Where's Wayrn?"

"Across the road. Paid the owner to let him sit on the roof. See?" Luik pointed to a three storey building, though the third was more of a box atop the second storey. It did not match the architecture of the city, which favoured sloping rooves. The kind Tulio jokingly described as 'slopes of death.'

"I can't see him."

"So? He's in there," Luik said. "What now?"

Notch drew his belt knife and slapped the hilt in his palm. His muscles were bunched, straining to strike out. Vinezi was so close. Probably laughing over a nice meal. A blight on the city.

"Think you could break that door down, Flir?"

"If I had to. Why?"

"What would you need?"

"I'm not planning on tearing up my knuckles, so I'd need something heavy to swing. And I left my best battering ram at Seto's, so I don't think we're going in today."

"Very funny."

"What are you thinking?"

"That we should break in, right now. Surprise them."

"Bad idea," Luik said.

Flir thumped his arm – gently. "Exactly. Stop being impatient. You don't know how many of them are in there, or what they're capable of. Or if Sofia is even inside."

"We'd still be doing the city, and the world, a favour."

"I agree. But we have to think this through."

Notch jammed the blade back into its sheath. "Well I'm sick of planning. I've been slinking around the city for days and it's gotten me no-where."

"Then let's do it properly."

"Fine. Any ideas?"

"Deception. And I don't even have to impersonate a Renovar either."

Luik grinned. "We'll need information. Numbers, location of her room. Routines."

Notch grunted. They were right and it was terrible. Just once, couldn't the scum-sucking imposters face him directly? He frowned at his friends. "I hope one of them is short."

*

Notch shifted on the bench seat, sweating beneath his hood. The innkeeper of the Old Guard – with its encouraging 'no Braonn' sign out front – placed another log onto the already roaring fire. Notch glared at the smiling man. The fellow was obviously happy to have such brisk business. Notch was surprised so many people were out on such a miserable night, especially after the explosion. Rain pelted the glass and wind rattled the door, patrons stumbling in as if given a shove by the weather.

Their targets were close. Luik sat across from Notch, eating his meal through his own raised hood, keeping Flir in his line of vision. She sat across from two Renovar in Mascare clothing, though they wore accurate copies of the mask this time. She spoke in a low voice, and from what he could tell, her act was working. They nodded along, seeming to buy her claim of being a mistreated foreigner keen to strike back at the city.

Patrons of the inn cast frequent glances at the group, but no-one was willing to confront a pair of Masks. Even if they didn't like sharing an inn with them.

"Brazen, aren't they?" Notch said.

"What?"

"Their disguise. Their game. If true Mascare were to discover them I could almost pity them."

"Think we're not risking as much?"

"True," Notch said. He paused. "I'm sorry, Luik. For bringing you here. Flir and I could have done this alone."

He shook his head. "You didn't bring me here, Notch, the Renovar did that. And none of it's your fault." He jabbed his roast beef with a knife. "Even if folk here wouldn't see it that way."

"Just keep your hood low." His friend was tanned enough, but his eyes were a giveaway.

He took another bite. "I will."

"You know, I could accuse them of being fakes. Then

we could haul them out of here right now. Find out what we need to know just as quick."

"Notch, it took a week to get these two alone, let's not make a mistake now."

"Fine." He toyed with his mug. "Have you heard from Seto yet?"

"No. I'm getting worried."

"He'll be fine, he's too crafty not to be."

"Hope so."

Laughter broke out at Flir's table. The small group rose and headed for the door. Just as they passed through, Flir paused, raising her voice. She spoke in Renovar, but Notch knew the translation. They'd worked it out. I forgot my cloak.

She closed the door and whispered to Notch as he and Luik met her. "Sofia's in there."

"You're sure?"

Flir pulled her cloak on as she spoke. "When one referred to someone 'upstairs' who they'd been forbidden to see, the other gave him a jab to the ribs."

"Hurry," he said.

She slipped outside and Notch counted a moment before following, Luik doing the same. The wind hurled rain at him, soaking his clothing. His boots splashed through puddles as he trailed Flir and the cheerful Renovar. Black shapes detached from the walls and kept a parallel course.

An uneven pool of light from another inn appeared ahead, and Notch clenched and unclenched his hands. Close now. Once the three shapes passed the light... there. Flir, who'd been walking closest to the centre of the rain-swept street, gave one man a shove.

He careered into the other and disappeared from sight.

Notch splashed forward, Luik and the dark shapes converging on the alley with him. Flir stood before an open door, pitching one of the men inside, a stern-faced Wayrn holding the door. The other imposter tried to scramble away but a second of Seto's men kicked him back to the ground.

Flir tossed him inside and followed. Tulio and another of his men, their dark clothing blending with the night, followed Notch in to take up positions along the walls. A bare room, save for two chairs and a lamp. Even as Notch paused to catch his breath from the final dash, Flir was lashing the two together, back to back, assisted by Wayrn.

"Well." She tied off the rope with a snap. "You two need to choose better friends."

"Why are you doing this? Who are you truly?" one asked. His Anaskari was good. More proof of their organisation. The imposter blinked water from his eyes while his fellow gazed round the room, head wobbling.

"You first."

"Pevin."

"And your friend?"

"Yalor. Why are you doing this? You hate it here."

"You have something we want, Pevin. Cooperate and I won't break you into small pieces, understand?"

His eyes widened. "I understand."

"Who do you work for?"

"Vinezi. Sometimes the Wolf."

Notch stepped closer. This was new. "Who is the Wolf?"

"A friend of Vinezi. He calls himself Lupo." He looked down. "He and Vinezi are the ones who tell us what to do."

"And did they tell you to go to the inn tonight?" Flir said.

"No, we were just hungry."

Flir held his gaze. Notch raised an eyebrow. The man didn't look away, he might have been telling the truth. She clicked her fingers and Luik stepped forward, handing over his mace. The weapon had a chilling aspect, even to Notch's eye, held so lightly by Flir.

"You're doing well, Pevin. I don't think I'll even have to use this."

"Th-thank you, ma'am," he said.

"How many men inside your compound?"

"Twenty, though many of us are on assignment now."

"Assignment?"

"Finding locations... and preparing them."

"You know where they are?"

"No, we don't." Pevin scowled at the floor. "We're not important enough to know."

"How many men inside, right now?"

"Only a few. It's early, perhaps only Lupo and his two favourites. Yalor?"

The other man opened his mouth but no words followed. He frowned at the ceiling.

"He agrees," Flir said. "Now, we are going inside soon, Pevin. Is there anything else we should know?"

Now he averted his eyes.

Flir placed the mace beneath his chin. She raised his face with it. "Speak."

"I cannot, they will kill me. Please."

"I will kill you. One bone at a time."

Pevin thrashed against his bonds. "No. He's an animal."

Flir slapped him. It looked a gentle blow, but his head snapped back, cracking into Yalor. The two groaned.

Pevin's head hung as he sobbed. "He will kill me."

"He doesn't know where you are. I do," Flir said. "Speak, Pevin, speak."

"You will spare us?"

"If I like what I hear, perhaps."

He drew in a breath. "The Wolf. He said we have to find people like you, Renovar who are unhappy here. Offer them safety from what is to come."

"Recruiting," Luik whispered.

Notch nodded.

"And what is coming?" Flir asked, crouching before him.

"An invasion."

CHAPTER 33

"There's no point waiting now. Invasion or not, we can take Tulio's men and find Sofia," Notch said, flipping his sopping cloak over his shoulder and re-buckling his sword. Better. "If there is some sort of invasion planned, then Vinezi or this Lupo will tell us more." The adjoining room was no brighter than where the prisoners sat, but it offered privacy.

Luik had his mace back now and was slinging a length of rope across his chest. Tulio and Wayrn stood ready, their men watching over the prisoners. Notch wanted this Lupo, or Vinezi, alive.

Flir crossed her arms. "I still think we should be sure. I can sneak in first and –"

"Might not be a better time," Luik said.

"You believe them in there?"

"Seemed like he wasn't lying to me."

"Maybe."

Notch moved to the door when she hesitated. "Speed's vital. I'm going. We could use your help with the door, Flir."

A moment longer and she nodded. "Fine."

Notch paused in the next room long enough for Tulio to give his orders and then he was back in the rain, charging across the street. Only two streets over was the wolf's lair, where he would finally find Sofia.

But if she'd been hurt...

He skidded to a halt at the gate, Luik close behind and Tulio leading Wayrn to take up positions either side of their small group. Their gaze swept the streets. Flir appeared a moment later, a bulky cut of wood beneath her arm. It was as tall as she stood and thicker than his torso.

"Where did that come from?"

"I found it in a neat stack between houses. Lots of people seem to be building things around here."

"The richer merchants like to call the top of the Second Tier the new First Tier," Wayrn said.

Luik snorted.

"Enough." Notch motioned for Flir to begin. She braced herself before the door, drew the hunk of timber back and swung. The gates shuddered, a boom echoing beneath the rain. Flir swung harder. The gates buckled in the centre. She swung again, and, with a mighty crack, blew one door clean off its hinges.

She dumped the log and leapt inside, sword in hand. Notch splashed into a dark courtyard. Two more doors stood at its end, one for the main building and another leading around its side.

"Wayrn, check the back." Notch ran to the main door, pausing to listen a moment, surprised to find it unbarred. Light from Luik's lamp revealed a wide room, with spiral staircases leading to a second floor and a series of closed doors above and below.

Empty.

Notch accepted a lamp of his own. "Hurry." He took the stairs two at a time. At the top, he shouldered the first door open. A row of three cots lay in flicking lamplight, nothing else. The next was the same.

Flir shouted. "Notch."

He found her inside a much larger room, standing by an empty four-poster bed. A bowl rested on a bedside table. He crouched by the dark fireplace and sifted ashes through his fingers. Cool. "They've been gone for some time."

"Seems that way. Look at this." Flir cupped a few green leaves in her palm. They were small, curled tight but bruised. He took them, inhaling sweetness from cupped palms. "Lenasi." The same drug soldiers used to kill pain in long campaigns.

"A powerful healer," Flir said.

"But too easy to become addicted to." Beyond was death. One mercenary he'd fought with in the Far Islands, who'd been using for years, became paralysed, one limb at a time. By the end, he was a useless lump, barely able to even speak. Finally, his body ate itself.

"Where was it?"

"Beneath the pillows."

A chill. "They've been feeding it to her?"

Flir shrugged as Luik appeared in the doorway.

"Top floor's empty. No clues to where they've gone."

"And the bottom?"

"Tulio's looking."

Notch took the bowl and hurled it into the fireplace. It shattered, but the tinkling sound wasn't enough. He grabbed the table but stopped. Stay focused, Notch. Smashing everything wouldn't help. "How do we find them now?"

"Keep looking. There might be something," Flir said.

"Wayrn isn't finished outside," Luik added.

Notch rushed downstairs, pausing in the large room. Lit only by a single torch and moonlight pouring through the windows, it lay empty save for Tulio. He crouched by the last unopened door, a lockpick in hand. "I couldn't break it down," he called, giving it a rap with his knuckles. "It was like running into a rock."

Flir started forward. "Let me –"

The rest of her sentence was lost as a grey shape burst forth, shattering the door and most of the wall around it, flinging Tulio into the stairs with its bulk. It landed with a crunch, four feet snapping floorboards. Notch pulled Flir back a step.

"Spread out," he shouted. Luik was already circling away from the creature and Flir moved in the opposite direction. Tulio had not stirred.

The thing looked blind. Its head extended on a horse-like neck, a round nub with naught but grooves for eyes and a long mouth that near to split the face. Its body was as if carved from granite, a bunching of muscles with mighty legs and forearms, which he at first took for front legs. It was something like a jungle creature he'd once seen in a book, though this beast had no fur. Had it straightened, its head would have brushed the roof.

The head swayed in a slow arc. Notch's hand was white around the hilt. Could it sense him?

Flir hissed across the room. "It traces movement. Stay back the both of you. You cannot hurt it."

The thing turned toward her voice.

"What is it?" Notch whispered back.

"Chilava. I can't let it leave the building." Her eyes

were intent on the creature.

The beast's body was still, moving its head in the same slow arc.

"You can't fight that thing alone."

"It's too dangerous for you," she said. "For both of you."

Flir darted forward, weapon raised. The chilava's head tracked her and even as she swung her blade, it brought a hand down to crush her. Flir threw her own arm up to block the blow.

A crack split the air.

She screamed, driven to the ground. Notch stumbled. Nothing had ever hurt Flir that way. Luik had already attacked, swinging his mace at the creature's flank. The blow tore a hunk from the flesh but the creature did not turn. It stomped the floor as Flir rolled and she rolled again when its fist smashed down beside her.

Notch finally leapt forward. He was a puny thing. A speck, a bare annoyance, but he hacked at its neck in an overhand blow.

Steel bounced from skin, a slip of pink left behind. Notch skipped back, wind from a massive fist passing his face. Luik too, had fallen away after his blow. Again, the creature beat holes in the floor, but Flir had crawled forward. She leapt up and wrapped a single arm and leg around its neck. She climbed, one arm hanging useless as the beast thrashed.

He signalled to Luik and they charged. Notch drove his blade into the chilava's rear foot, putting his entire body weight on it and snapping the blade. At the same time, Luik flung his mace behind his head, striking the area he'd attacked before. The beast shied away, flailing its limbs. Notch sprang back, too slow to avoid a glancing blow to the chest. Something cracked and he cried out, crashing to the floor. He struggled for air, rolling onto his back with a curse.

Luik crouched at his side. "Notch?"

"Help her," he wheezed.

A crash rocked the room. The beast was down. Flir rained blows on its skull with her fist. The creature was dazed, its head rolled on the ground but she didn't stop. Her chest heaved as she swung and the smacking sound of her blows echoed. Notch lay back, unable to watch, the strain on his chest too great.

The crack of a fist striking flesh continued and Flir began to grunt with the effort. Finally there came a roar, a final blow and then silence.

Luik's face was slack and Notch knew his own was a mirror.

*

Lying in the mess of flooring, with fragments of the wall and floorboards scattered around, the chilava appeared smaller. It wasn't, but Notch couldn't help thinking it. Death reduced everything.

Dark shadows had already appeared on the head, the chilava's wide mouth ajar. The rest of its body appeared untouched, save for the bleeding haunch and half a blade in its foot.

Tulio was lain across from the beast, arms at his side and Luik's cloak bundled beneath his head. Notch released a shuddering breath. The poor man hadn't been given a chance. The chilava's eruption broke his neck on impact. "Tulio didn't deserve this." Who would tell Seto?

"What was it?" Luik asked, one arm supporting Notch.

Flir, her own arm still dangling at her side, took a

moment to answer. Sweat trickled down her temple. Her jaw was set, as if she was masking great pain. "The chilava is an animal from the wilderness of Renovar. They're sometimes hunted. People take their heads as trophies."

"No ship would have carried that across the ocean," Notch said.

She nodded. "It's hard to see from here, but there are markings on the neck. I think it was drugged. There's no other way I could even conceive of it being transported. They're too dangerous."

"How do you hunt them?" Luik asked.

"I don't."

Notch shifted on the spot, taking another shallow breath. "You probably saved half the city, Flir. If it got loose..."

"I know. Lupo and Vinezi are mad to release one. I'm sure after a time, with enough people, it would have been stopped. But at a great cost."

"Could they have more?"

"Not here. When we disturbed this one, others would have been woken. They sense movement and sound."

"What do we do with the body? We should get back to –" He stopped. "Wayrn, where is he?"

"I'll see," Luik said. "You right to stand on your own?"

"I think so." Notch grimaced when Luik stepped away.

"Do you know what this means?" Flir waved a hand around the room. "It means we're fools. We walked right into this, Notch."

"The two at the inn."

"Yes."

"They gave themselves up, to send us here?"

"It seems so," she said. Her expression was dark. "They act well. I wonder if they know how to squeal."

"We need them alive."

"I know that," she snapped, turning away. "Gods, I know that, Notch."

He frowned. She wasn't usually so touchy – even if she did have a fairly short fuse, and was in pain, it was unlike even Flir. "What's wrong?"

"I don't like being led around."

"Me either."

"And I don't like not knowing what's happening at home. I've been away for a long time, but things shouldn't be changing so fast. Talk of an invasion. Mad men bringing chilava across the sea. Exploding powder. My people would never do this."

"They may not be. Bad apples, Flir."

"They're still my people."

Luik re-entered the room, the mute form of Wayrn held in his arms. Notch stiffened.

"He's alive," Luik said. "Found him at the rear of the property, out cold. Guess he tried to stop one of them."

Notch sagged in relief. He shouldn't have sent Wayrn off alone, that was stupid. And worse, if he'd not been so eager, so damn impatient to strike back at Vinezi, then Tulio might be alive. Idiot. Vinezi had a lot to answer for, but maybe he wasn't the only one.

"Can you help me, Flir?"

She took his arm. "Don't worry, Notch. I'll make the prisoners talk."

"Let's go then."

Luik started toward the door. "I'll come back with one of the lads to take care of Tulio."

Notch said nothing.

CHAPTER 34

Beyond the door, which had to be forced open on screeching hinges, Ain found a dim room packed with crates. The only illumination came via a breath of starlight from the windows behind him, cold air coming with it.

Thick dust and skeletal cobwebs covered crates. Nearest a second door were barrels, whose metal strapping was loose, the wood split and bulging. He'd never seen so much wood in one place. Whatever was inside had long since seeped out and gone to mould. Scattered amongst the boxes were droppings and on one crate, a hammer and steel bar.

"Where are we then?" Schan asked as he stepped inside. He raised the lamp, illuminating the reaches of the room and casting shadows. The crates were two rows deep, marked with strange angular symbols and the door had a large bolt and lock. It's steel was deeply pitted. Ain beckoned Schan closer.

"Someone doesn't want us coming up this way," Schan said.

"So how do we open it?"

Schan pointed to a crate. "There. The prybar." He took the bar and wedged it between lock and door before rolling his shoulders. Next he set his foot against the wall and wrenched the bar.

The lock gave a powdery snap and sent him sprawling. Ain burst into laughter and Schan shook his head from the floor, unable to keep a smile from his face. "Well, that was easier than I thought it'd be." He stood. "Let's try the door."

The bolt rasped as it slid free, but the door didn't budge. Schan stepped back and gave it a couple of good kicks. "It move much?"

Ain leaned in. "Seems to be, keep going."

Schan repeated his efforts, giving a grunt when the door crashed to the stone. Steps led up into blackness beyond. "That wasn't so bad either." He was breathing hard and his movements were slow as he started forward. "Let's keep on then, before the oil runs out. Or I drop."

The stairs were not long, leading to another closed up room. Much larger, the ghostly remnants of habitation remained. Rotted sheets lay in the corner, stretched over a narrow bed. Table and chairs crumbled into the wall and a double-chambered stove stood nearby, both stomachs cold. Few feet had trod this room in many years. He could never guess exactly how old a path was, and while this one wasn't ancient, he had a good idea how long it had been since anyone set foot here.

"Windows," Schan said.

Opposite the stove rested low shelves with stacks of dusty books and set high above was a window. Only a thin strip of light poured through, barely enough to see by, and obstructed by grime-caked glass. Had the windows been boarded over, leaving just a strip free at the top? No matter. He'd reached the surface. The urge to escape the underground, lost upon encountering the creature and the egg, returned. So close, he need wait no longer.

Ain stirred dust as he strode to the door. No lock on this one. "Let's see what's outside."

"Slowly, we could be anywhere," Schan said.

Ain turned the handle and pushed. Nothing. He placed the egg on the ground, making sure it didn't roll, then put his shoulder into the door. "It's not opening."

"Try inwards."

Ain got a better grip and tugged on the door. It creaked, opening enough to squeeze one hand in around the edge. The wood was gritty but he pulled until it split with a crack, a panel of wood coming free in his hand. Only darkness lay beyond the hole. As if the stars and moon were suddenly gone. Tossing the wood aside, he reached through and his hand came up against dirt.

"This whole room is buried," he breathed.

Schan still stood beneath the window but he sighed. "So we've got to dig our way out?"

Ain's shoulders slumped. "I'll start."

"No, we should rest first. We need sleep."

"But shouldn't we —"

"No way a beast that large will fit through those doors. Now no more talk, I'm tired." Schan dumped his packs and spread a bedroll.

Ain readied his own bedding, lying with his arm as pillow. He kept the egg nearby, closing his eyes only after being sure it was safe. Tomorrow he would find a way from the room and become the first Pathfinder to find the Sea Shrine. He would return to Silaj. Years later, he would tell their child the tale, and Sands willing, make Jali proud.

When he woke, a thin stream of pale moonlight fell through the strip of window not covered by earth.

Had he slept through the entire day?

Schan was already preparing a cold meal, hard bread and the last of Tanija's salted lamb. Ain wolfed it down, sipping from his flask. "Let me take first shift," he said. They were close now, he could feel it.

"All right lad."

The next hours passed slowly. They took turns digging and scraping packed dirt from the window. Since some light was visible through the glass, it had been the obvious place to begin. And if the house were buried, it was unlikely to be anywhere people were likely to visit. It was no risk to shatter the glass, sweep it away and hack into the earth with the steel bar. No-one would hear.

It wasn't until his second shift on the window, eyes blurring from long hours of focus, that he realised their position was not likely to be within Sekkati. Cities didn't have buried houses within their walls, did they? He paused. Maybe they did. He'd never seen a city.

Ain set his feet on the stack of crates they'd used to access the window, and pulled armfuls of dirt from the hole. It was getting harder to reach the soil. At least he'd let in enough light that the lamp, which had since flickered out, was no longer needed.

Ain paused at a swishing.

Schan had nodded off again, half in shadow, half in a patch of dawn light. The egg was safe near his bedroll but a discolouration on the stove was new. Had it always looked so? He wiped his hands on his pants and rubbed his eyes. No. Just the changing light. Or his tired eyes.

As he worked, Ain cast glances over his shoulder. The room was always empty. He'd obviously imagined the sound, and the stove appeared unchanged each time. Ain kept digging, back and arms burning, hands blistered. He hadn't dug a hole in years. He'd not missed the experience. Sand moved more, but dirt was thicker. Between the two of them, they'd almost dug their way free before the dawn broke fully.

Grumbling aside, he supposed he'd held up fairly well.

"How goes it?" Schan asked. He was sitting up on his bedroll, blanket thrown aside.

Ain gave a few more jabs, crumbling the edges of the hole and dragging more leaf-filled dirt inside. It had piled up on the crates and the floor and its rich smell spread across the room. "I think we can squeeze through. I can see the sky and tree tops."

"Good. Want me to finish?"

Ain shook his head. "Nearly done." He scooped the last few armfuls into the room and dropped the bar. It hit the floor with a dull clang. "I'll go and look around."

Schan tossed the bar back up. "Then take that, you'll want a weapon."

"You think we're near other people?"

"No idea, but I won't be far behind."

Ain accepted the tool and poked it through the hole before stepping up to the highest crate and reaching through the window. All the glass was gone but he still scraped his side trying to pull himself free. He muttered a curse, even as the fresh air on his face and in his lungs had him hopping up to a crouch.

Steel in hand, he kept low in thick grass. The scent was strong, nothing like the desert. He could even taste the tiny flowers, their white faces striped with pink, as he breathed in.

Dawn light greyed everything, from the earth and weeds growing on the building's roof, to the stand of trees nearby. Such wondrous trees. So unlike those on old scrolls. He stared, lips parted. Shrubs grew around the broad trunks and even now, colour was a fast blushing in the trees.

He shook his head, as if to break a spell, and ran around the building in a stoop. More trees, these moving down a slope that led to a white wall. Tall grasses stood in the growing light, paving stones winding up from a gate in the wall. He stood within a large, enclosed space, like a private wood with a house buried at its top. A blue bird flitted from branch to branch below, but other than that, the place was deserted. Who would build such a place? And then neglect it so?

Ain returned to the window. "Schan?"

"Here." He squeezed their packs through the opening. Most of Ibranu's engineer's tools and items came next, followed by the egg. Finally, Schan pulled himself through with a grunt.

"Come see," Ain said, after giving the man a moment to take in their surroundings. The sun climbed higher with each passing moment and the green was coming alive, touched with gold from the sunlight. He hopped up to the roof, climbing weathered tiles. Several slipped, but he kept his footing.

At its peak Ain stopped with a gasp. He'd been going to point out the wall and gate, but from his new vantage point so much more was visible. Beside him Schan breathed an oath to the Sands.

Beyond the wall was a building so large that it seemed to be its own mountain range nestled beneath a bigger, darker range. It spread across sprawling lawns in a white curve, glossed with gold, its walls strewn with balconies and flashing windows. From its four towers flew flags but the emblems were too small to make out.

"Sekkati." Outbuildings numbered many. Some were doubtless stables and other barracks, but as most of the buildings faced away, he could not be sure.

What took his breath, more than the jumble of stone buildings below the palace, was the ocean. The thing his cloak had been coloured for, the thing all of Medah longed to see again. It was so restless, even from a distance. Dark and vast, the tops of its waves were brilliant white and the nearer it came to the rising sun the brighter it grew.

"Jali. The sea."

He did not move. He barely breathed.

"It's not so different from the Sands," Schan said. "It stretches before the eye."

Ain nodded, not taking his eyes from the water. Finally Schan turned away and he followed.

CHAPTER 35

With Wayrn recovering in one of Seto's beds and Luik tending to Tulio's body, Notch helped Flir continue the interrogation. Pevin and Yalor remained tied to each other in their respective chairs, the latter who'd not uttered a word since capture and sat blinking in the new torchlight.

Notch breathed easier with chest bandages and a dose of something to dull the pain, but it was still difficult to draw deeply. The healer wanted him in bed, but he couldn't. It was back to the basement instead. Only now there were no needles. Only Flir's good arm, which she used to backhand Pevin when he laughed.

Dried blood covered his face, turning his skin even paler.

"That's right." He spat blood from a fresh cut on his lip. "You fell for it, just as you have all along. Vinezi is twice the mind of any of you fools. He's been leading you where he wishes. Hetha mal." The last words were delivered like a curse.

Flir leaned closer, arm in sling. "In the Anaskari

tongue, Pevin."

He grinned, mouth bloody. "Very well. To hell with you, bitch."

She held up finger and thumb, then moved them to rest on his throat, where she applied pressure. Only gently. And only until Pevin went blue. Then she rested a hand on his wrist while he fought to recover his breath, eyes wide.

"You... are dilar?"

She did not respond to his question. "Let's try again, Pevin. Where is Vinezi taking Sofia Falco? Where are the other targets in the city?"

He began to babble in his own tongue. Notch tried to pick up even a few words, not that he knew much Renovas, but the man spoke too fast. The word dilar was a mystery too. Flir had never used it to describe herself.

"Stop." She gave his wrist a squeeze and he cried out. "If you truly believe I'm dilar, you'll cooperate."

"He never told us."

She squeezed harder, and Notch heard cartilage rearranging. By the man's pale face, it must have been agonising. "You know. Tell me, and I won't crush each joint in your body."

"Release me, dilar." He pleaded. "Release me and I will tell you what I know."

"Your word?"

"By my word, dilar. I would never lie to you."

She relented and he shuddered before speaking. "The palace. They were headed there. It was our job to distract you then lead you to the chilava if you came. We've been waiting. Vinezi knew you were watching him."

Flir gave Notch a look before turning back to the prisoner. "Why are they taking her to the palace?"

"She's going to get them in, the people in the palace want something from her. And the Wolf wants something in there. He doesn't talk about it, but everyone knows that's one of the reasons we're here, dilar." He licked his bloody lips. "If I had known who you were, I would never have misled you earlier. That I swear."

Again, Flir refused to acknowledge what was fast becoming adulation in the man. What had she been hiding all these years?

"And the others?"

"Vinezi wants the throne. Says it will make things easier for the rest of us."

"The new Conclave's invasion?"

"Yes. It wouldn't be the largest force. But Vinezi has this city by the throat. You don't know how many stores of acor, the magic powder, he has made us set."

"What are the targets?" Notch asked.

He glanced at Flir first, who nodded permission. "Lupo chooses them, we never know in advance. None of us know what the others set either. That is why I could not answer before. I do not know them all – only the ones I have set."

"Then you personally, Pevin. Start with the last place you set this acor."

"A bathhouse on the Second Tier."

"When?"

"Two days ago, but I do not know the street. I cannot read the signs."

"You can take us there."

He looked back to Flir. "Then you will free me, dilar? I will become your servant, most humble, most loyal."

Flir turned away, conflicting emotions passing over her face. "No, I will not free you. But I won't kill you tonight. Let that be a beginning."

"Bless you."

She strode to the exit and Notch followed, struggling to keep up. He found her sitting on a barrel in the storeroom. Her legs did not reach the floor, giving her a childlike look. But the tears she wiped from her face were not.

"Not now."

He stood before her, eye to eye, thanks to the barrel. "This dilar business... I've never seen you like this."

"Believe it or not, I'm angry. More than I thought possible."

He waited. It never paid to push her.

"Pevin believes I'm a vessel of the Renovar God. A living embodiment of her, that I have holy strength."

"Don't you?"

"I don't know what I am, Notch. Nor where my strength comes from."

"Your mother or father?" He spoke softly. Flir had volunteered so little about her family in the past. Whatever mood had allowed her to open up might be fragile.

"No. They believed as others do, that I'm divine. They coddled me and catered to my every whim. As a young girl, well, it was fun." A small smile. "I had the whole village at my beck and call. But it was a lie. I'm not the spirit of Mishalar made flesh. At all. There have been others like me. I met one, years later. He taught me a lot about my limits."

"You have limits?"

Again, her smile was a mere suggestion. "Of course. Once I knew the truth, I couldn't return home, let alone stay in Renovar."

"And this Pevin believes you're dilar?"

"It's how he, along with many in Renovar, are raised to believe. He'll do anything I ask of him." She drove her fist through the lid of a nearby barrel and when she threw an arm up, droplets of ale flew through the air. "I thought I'd left this, this... madness behind. Not knowing when someone looked at me, or spoke to me, whether they were thinking of me as a 'vessel', rather than a person."

Notch spoke softly. "There's one good thing to come of it."

"That I can manipulate him? No, it's not good. It's wrong, though I'll do it for Seto, for you and for the city," she said.

"Thank you."

She took his hand. "You are sweet for listening, Notch. Now go and find someone to watch Pevin, and get Luik to round everyone up. I'll follow."

Notch did as instructed, pausing at the door.

Flir had not moved from the barrel.

CHAPTER 36

Sofia woke to a mask looming over her, firelight wavering beyond. She gave a cry, pushing at the figure, but it caught her hands. Lupo.

"Time to leave."

"Why?" she rasped, throat dry.

"Your pesky friends move ever closer to the bait we've lain, though don't expect to greet them." He slid his arms beneath her blankets and lifted her from the bed.

Notch and Seto were coming? Hope surged, but she squashed it. No. Lupo said they were close to a trap. They were in danger themselves, she was still alone.

The room was warm but not as warm as the bed. She shivered. Her head was thick and her clothing soaked with sweat. Being pressed into Lupo's chest didn't help, the man smelt sharply of sweat and something... unknown. Something that tickled her throat.

Was it the same powder he used to kill the green creatures from below the city? He had not spoken of the hideous things, rushing her to bed after the attack and leaving. Thankfully, Miandra arrived with lenasi soon after.

The drug's effects lingered, as her leg hurt less than expected. Usually, morning meant pain. But then, it wasn't morning. So hard to focus. Notch and the others were in danger. "They aren't going to be fooled by you, Wolf."

He strode from the room and into the hallway, saying nothing. They passed other men, imposters all in their stolen Mascare clothing and false masks.

"What have you done?"

He kicked open a door to the rear of the building. Night air blasted her face. "Invited them here, though we'll be long gone." A stone path wove through an enclosed garden, dark leaves flashing as he slipped between a pair of torches. Cut into the ground before the back wall was an opening, steps leading down into a tunnel of flickering torchlight.

Her vision swam and she clung to his robe. "Where are you taking me?"

"Home."

"No." She struggled. "Oson will kill me." Her leg throbbed and her arm was weak. His grip didn't lessen, but he laughed as they passed a single torch set on the wall.

"That's hardly my intent."

Sofia's voice stuck in her throat and she closed her eyes as another set of shivers wracked her body. An illness? She opened her eyes when Lupo spoke in Renovar, the words sounding slippery. He'd asked if the way was clear.

A man in a black hood replied in the affirmative, before leading them up a set of stairs and opening a door to the streets of the Second Tier. Sofia turned her head. Muscles were slow to respond, and she caught a glimpse of the light being cut off before Lupo swung her around. The carriage. She was placed inside, Lupo following.

"Well, Sofia. Here we are."

"Yes."

He exhaled slow and long. "Momentous things will follow."

"Momentous for you."

"Certainly. Who else has struck fear into the city of Anaskar as I have?"

She squeezed her eyes shut as the room spun and bit into her cheek. The flash of pain cleared some of the haze. "What's wrong with me?"

"You're addicted to lenasi. Your body craves more."

Addicted? It wasn't need, it was just... Sofia swallowed. He'd known the whole time? Gods. What a fool. To think it was a secret. Miandra... a ploy to keep her compliant. "You planned this?"

He shook his head. Black sockets were unreadable. "You needed healing. Lenasi is powerful, it's very name suggests it. A kiss from the Green Gods of Spring, or so the poor, enslaved southerners would claim. A useful side effect is the addiction it creates."

"Then I'll stop. You're not going to have another hold over me."

"You aren't that strong."

"I'm Casa Falco," Sofia said. She concealed her hands, balled into fists, beneath the folds of her clothing.

"Indeed."

"Don't mock me."

Lupo waved a hand. "Don't rest everything upon your house, Sofia. It will not serve you."

"Maybe for you, but my –"

"Enough," he snapped.

Sofia fell silent. A chink in his armour? Usually the man was more indulgent, but his family was a sore point. She'd not heard that Renovar families were any more harsh with their children than other peoples. Another dizzy spell hit her and she sat back, closing her eyes again.

The carriage came to a halt and she opened her eyes.

Lupo was already exiting. He turned back and reached for her. Even if she kicked him, she couldn't run. Helpless. The pain in her limbs had lessened, and her head was clear enough, but her hands trembled when she accepted his help.

"You'll stop trembling if you have more lenasi." His voice changed, as if he was smiling. Always smiling, always he mocked her. "And Miandra would love to see what her handiwork has done to one of her oppressors. For someone so bitter, she's quite the actress, wouldn't you agree?"

"I don't want lenasi." And she didn't need the Braonn healer coming to gloat.

Lupo did not answer, only lifting her free and heading for the palace gates. Constructed of heavy steel that surely no mere human could place together, let alone lift, they were covered in carvings of the houses. Even in the dark, the lamp-lit section of wall towered over Lupo and his men. Fifteen, maybe more, false Mascare stood quietly beneath the gates, waiting for the guard to answer Lupo's summons.

The imposters did not speak amongst themselves. Lupo gave no orders, the men did not even move. One caught her eye, a man more heavyset than might be expected of a Mascare. Vinezi.

A panel in the gate opened. From her position in Lupo's arms, she could not see the guard's face.

"My lords, King Oson has ordered the gate closed to all. Even the Mascare."

Hearing it put a bad taste in her mouth. Oson was no king.

"I commend your diligence, Shield. But the king will wish to see us," Lupo explained, speaking with pleasure. All trace of his accent was gone; Lupo wasn't a bad actor himself. He lifted her higher in his arms. "We have found Sofia Falco."

Silence followed his words. "I must verify this before you speak with the king's Seneschal."

"Of course."

"Open the gate," the guard shouted.

The massive walls of steel ground outwards, making a terrible sound. It must have woken everyone on the Second Tier. She cringed at the sound. When it stopped, an opening wide enough for no more than two men abreast was revealed. A group of Shields in their orange tunics and silver armour waited.

"A moment." All but the man who spoke before had hands on hilts. Lupo and Vinezi moved forward, the Wolf holding her out when he reached the lead Shield.

The man examined her. "I see." His voice was full of shock. "In you come then," he said, waving them inside.

Once again, she could have asked for help. The Shield were outnumbered, but maybe in the confusion... no. She could not run. All she would do by trying, is get them all killed. Whether they were loyal to Oson or loyal to the crown itself, she could not know, nor did it matter. Blood would not be spilled on her account. At least, not theirs.

"I'll escort you to the Seneschal, my lords."

Lupo's mask dipped in a nod.

No. Stay here, Shield. It's a risk. Still Sofia said nothing.

She twisted her neck to look up at Lupo's mask. There was no clue there in the white bone. In the dim light, cast from grass-lamps spaced along the lawns, it looked more authentic than the usual, more flimsy affairs she was accustomed to seeing on the false Mascare.

Once they crossed the lawns, the Shield led them into the palace, exchanging a brief word with the men on duty. No-one else questioned Lupo. The halls were darker but not empty, as servants went about their tasks. Avoiding the main passages meant there was little chance of encountering Pietta or Emilio. But if it happened, how could she keep them safe?

Were they even alive?

Within moments, the path became a covered walkway that overlooked an artificial pond, which was more the size of pools to be found on the coastline. Starlight glimmered in the surface, and Sofia shook off another spell of dizziness. Her stomach lurched, but it passed. Sweat beaded at her temples.

Finally the Shield stopped at an unguarded door, knocked once, waited and entered. Inside the reception room beyond, a man worked at a desk by candlelight. Seneschal Fratali set aside his quill and stood, giving a bow. "Captain? My Lords, what brings you here tonight?"

"The Mascare have captured Sofia Falco," the Captain said. "If I could take my leave now?"

"Of course," Lupo said, beating the Seneschal to it. The Shield left and Seneschal Fratali frowned, a bare crease in his brow. He stepped around the desk to study her face.

"I can hardly believe it. Where did you —" He gasped and Sofia flinched. One of the Renovar had slipped up to the Seneschal, and now caught the man as he slumped.

The fake Mascare cleaned a blade on the Seneschal's clothing before moving to the door and listening.

"All quiet." It was Vinezi. Sofia trembled but not from the lenasi. She would kill Vinezi with her own hands. She would find something sharp and drive it into his eye. Fratali had been a kind, if fussy man.

"How many more will you slaughter?"

Lupo ignored her, nodding to a pair of his men. "Go."

She beat on his chest. "Where are they going?"

"Hush." He caught her hands and followed Vinezi through the doors into the Royal chambers. A darkened reception room.

"No," she shouted. "I won't 'hush' and I won't let you do this."

He placed a hand over her mouth to muffle the last of her words, and she bit his hand. He cursed, and almost as a reflex, so fast did it happen, backhanded her. Sofia's vision blackened. Her lip stung when feeling returned.

The Wolf and his followers had already reached the old King's sitting rooms and were tying and gagging Shields posted outside Oson's bedchamber. Sofia frowned. Why hadn't they killed the guards?

"Bring light," Lupo ordered.

Men jumped to his bidding and when the group barged into the King's bedchamber, it was with bright torches in hand.

Two shapes lay beneath blankets in a bed that dwarfed her room in Vinezi's hideout. Clothing was strewn across the room, thrown over an armchair and dotted on the deep rug, a mighty swordfish embroidered on its surface.

Lupo handed her to another man, who said nothing, and stepped forward. "Wake, your Majesty," he boomed.

A groan.

Lupo kicked a post. The bed rattled and someone swore in a sleepy voice. A figure raised its dark-curled head, and large eyes widened. A scream followed. The girl scrambled back against the ornate headboard, a hand half-covering her naked breasts.

"Oson," she whimpered. She swallowed, eyes darting from mask to mask.

Sofia bit her lip at a surge of pity. How terrifying for the poor girl. To wake surrounded by impassive masks, to have no idea what was to come. Defenceless, shaking. Sofia linked her fingers, trying to stop her own trembling.

"What is it?" The King sat up, a frown on his face turning to outrage. "How dare you sneak into my bed chamber."

Lupo laughed. "I dare, little King. And if you wish to live, you'll follow my orders."

"You treacherous scum." Oson slid a hand beneath his pillow. The Wolf leapt around the bed and caught his wrist.

"No, Oson. Still your blade." He gestured with his free hand. "Look who I've brought you."

Oson straightened. A hunger kindled in his eyes, but he turned back to Lupo. "Who are you?"

Lupo did not release Oson. "I'll send someone to help gather your advisors, your counsel and other important folk, your majesty. They have a life-changing announcement to witness."

*

Notch hissed a string of curses, hands white around the back of a chair. Below, a line of Shields stood in the dark street. At regular intervals along the wall of orange and silver were crimson robes, white faces of bone glaring at the inn.

"What now?" Luik asked.

Flir thumped a fist into her palm. Free of the sling, her arm was already healed. Typical Flir, she recovered with God-like speed. The thought had new significance. "I break their line."

Notch shook his head. "Too many, Flir."

"Then we throw Wayrn at them."

The man blinked at her, half-rising from his position on the bed. "Ah —"

Flir laughed. "We won't do that. Come on, check round back with me." She pulled him up to the door. Her voice echoed down the corridor. "You can wake the others and keep watch."

Notch did not turn from the street. It was late and people were absent from the usually busy street. There had to be two dozen Shields – Palace Shields – and four Mascare. A potent force. With half of Seto's own team scouring the city for acor deposits, the odds weren't favourable.

"They're just waiting," Luik said.

"They know they have us."

"So how'd they track us down?"

"Does it matter?" Notch snapped.

Luik put a large hand on his shoulder. "Easy."

"Sorry." He folded his arms. "But it's our own fault, isn't it? We shouldn't have used the Harper, not after the fake Mask broke in."

"I guess not. But let's solve this problem first. Beat ourselves up second."

"All right. Any ideas?"

Luik grinned. "One. But Seto won't like it."

"I like it already. Let's go."

Notch followed Luik downstairs, chest still paining him, past the darkened common room with its silent Ocean Gods, and into the basement. The big man pointed at the crates. "There."

"Fire-lemon?"

"We can smash it at their feet, set it ablaze and run."

"Worth a try," Notch said. "Flir can help."

Luik left with a nod, and Notch put his hands on a crate. Something scurried over his hand and he flicked it away. He bent his knees and stopped. "Idiot." No way would his chest hold up.

He met Flir on the stairs.

"Do you think Luik's idea will work?" she asked.

"I can't think of anything else."

"Me either. And we're surrounded, so we might as well try it," she said. "I have Wayrn and a few more of Seto's watching the back and the side."

"Good. Can you carry mine?"

"Fine."

Seto's room had a grand balcony. The view of the ocean gave him pause, as it always did. Black in the night, the waves were a distant murmur.

"Quit slacking off," Flir said. She had a crate under each arm, and rested them beside Luik's with a grin.

"How many do we need?"

She shrugged. "Let's ask Luik."

It did not take long for Luik to be satisfied. They crouched behind a small stack of Fire-lemon, unlit torches spread between them. Wayrn still watched from downstairs.

"All right," Luik said. "Notch, you light the torches and Flir and I'll haul these over. Keep going until you're out. Then downstairs. Fast," Luik added, his eyes bright.

"You're enjoying this, aren't you?" Notch said.

"So are you."

He grinned. "Yes. But what if they don't break open? Or light?"

Flir glanced over her shoulder. "We'll throw Seto's bed."

Notch chuckled. "Sounds good." He thrust a bundle of torches into the fireplace, poking the embers until they caught. Shadows jumped as he moved behind Luik and Flir, who'd crept onto the balcony.

"Ready?" Luik asked.

"Try not to kill them," Notch said.

"Wait." Flir cracked open a case, grabbed a bottle and tore the cork out with her mouth. "No need to waste it all." Tipping the neck, she swallowed then gasped, handing the bottle to Luik. He took a drink and passed it over to Notch. The liqueur burnt his mouth but the blast of heat was welcome.

"Here we go." Luik stood and heaved a crate over the side. Flir's Fire-lemon sailed over right after, one from each arm. Notch was already lobbing his brands over as the first crates smashed across the cobblestones.

Roaring flames shot up. Luik hurled his second crate directly at the fire as Shields and Mascare stumbled back with shouts. Half the area before the inn was already ablaze, deep red shadows and greasy smoke choking the street.

Another of Flir's crates sailed over the railing and Luik hurled his third into the flames. Both exploded on impact, spraying burning liquid across the stones. Men fell back yet further, beating at their clothing. Notch pitched another brand at one of Flir's crates, then fell back – his own chest afire. He reached for another bottle and took a second swig.

Two more boxes of Fire-lemon shattered in the street, flames leaping.

"Go." Luik hurled the last crate down. Notch ran, gritting his teeth, down the stairs to collect Wayrn from the common room. He burst from the inn, heat searing his face. The wall of flames was high enough that the men beyond were unable to pass. They shouted to their fellow Shields, who poured from the same alley Notch had used to sneak into the inn.

He made to charge, but Flir was already upon them, deflecting blades as she slipped within the group. She gave a good shove with both arms and soldiers went flying into the dark, clattering to the stones.

"Hurry." Her shout echoed as she ran.

Notch slipped through the fallen men. Sweat stung his eyes as he staggered after. "Where's Luik?" he gasped.

Wayrn fell into step beside him. "Not far."

Notch skidded to a halt at a corner. Luik barrelled from the inn, casting another bottle into the flames as he did. Stray patches of burning Fire-lemon had latched onto the stones of the ground floor – but they weren't going to burn stone.

"Where are we going?" Luik asked when he caught up.

"I don't know. Somewhere else," Notch panted. "Where are the rest of Seto's people?"

"Going to ground."

"Which is where we should go I guess."

"How about Pistorio's?"

"Tell Flir," he said, falling back. "I need a moment." The darkened streets were empty for the time being. The sound of pursuit would not be far. The flames would die down, or be put out by the Shields, and someone would be sent to follow them. And even if Seto's men had locked up the inn, the Mascare would likely snoop around again.

Time for that later. Notch nodded to Wayrn, who'd stayed back, and took off again, feet scraping on cobblestones.

CHAPTER 37

Notch caught Flir's arm as she drew it back. Restraining a galloping horse would have been easier. "Careful."

"I know how to knock."

"But softly. You're all worked up," he said. "We all are."

She sighed, then rapped on the wooden door of the Second Tier smithy. Hinges squeaked. "Satisfied?"

"Very."

Pistorio, another ex-Shield, answered on the fourth knock, hammer in hand and narrowed eyes in a round face. "Notch? Luik? And Flir? What's happening?"

"Pistorio, we need help," Notch said.

"Come in."

Notch limped inside. The workshop was lit only by a lamp beside the door and embers banked at a giant hearth, tinting the room orange and red. It glinted on the polished steel of swords and knives which had been lined in neat racks. Hammers and tongs hung from wooden walls and a pair of anvils, spaced apart from one another with barrels of water, were cold.

Pistorio introduced himself to Wayrn then the smith

looked to Notch. "What have you done to yourself? And I thought with your posters disappearing you'd finally sorted everything out."

Notch waved a hand. "It's my ribs, but I'll be fine. We need to lie low a while, and then we need to get into the palace."

He raised an eyebrow. "That all?"

Notch grinned. Pistorio hadn't changed. "Any ideas?"

"Might do. Wait here." A moment later he returned, dragging a bench into the workshop. He waved a hand to Notch, who sat. "Sorted. Now, you know I've done well for myself here."

"So I heard," Luik said. "Not just officers, but noblemen ask for your work, don't they?"

"Exactly. And that's how I can get you in."

Notch straightened. "Delivery men?"

"Not quite. The palace wouldn't go for that."

Something thumped on the door. Notch put a hand on his sword, rising with a grunt to limp across the room. Flir joined him. Luik was on his feet and even Wayrn had his axe in hand.

"Who calls?" Notch asked.

"Seto. Open up."

The old man stood in the doorway, arms laden with papers and scrolls. His eyes were weary and the silver in his hair was matched by silver stubble. "Well? Get out of the way, Notch."

He stepped aside. "How did you find us?"

Seto's brow creased. "I used my head of course. Once I saw the fire before my inn, which I believe is now under control, I realised you'd have gone to ground. I do hope the Masks don't make a mess inside." He nodded to Pistorio, who nodded back. "Now. Exactly whose idea was it to burn up all my Fire-lemon?"

Notch shrugged. "We were desperate."

"I see."

"Welcome back," Flir stepped in. "So where have you been? We'd almost begun to worry."

He came forward and Notch and Wayrn helped him lay out the papers on a workbench, burying the tools, weights and measures, and even a statuette of an Ocean God, Banai, wrestling a giant sea serpent. The scrolls and sheaths of paper were varied in age and script. Much was in the ancient Anaskari text but there were also Medah runes. "In the depths of the city library. And I will say, while not as impressive as the palace library, I was surprised." He wiped his brow. "Wayrn, I'll need your help with some of these."

"Yes, Seto."

Seto glanced at Notch. "I understand you believe Sofia is held within the palace now? With Vinezi and a mysterious stranger known as Lupo, who is apparently in charge of our false Mascare?"

"Pistorio thinks he can get us inside."

"And then all we have to manage is the piffling task of taking Sofia back, of course," Flir added. "Now stop being coy, Seto. Why were you in the library?"

"Well, it didn't start in the library. Tulio updated me on the fledging crime lord of the docks, news that needed my immediate attention. His smugglers masquerade as spice merchants. They had quite foolishly tangled with The Slick Rat at the harbour, so I took some of my best and rectified the situation."

"The Water-Rat maintains his stranglehold then?" Pistorio smiled.

"He does indeed," Seto said. "Among their possessions

was a map that took my fancy. I pursued it through the library."

At the mention of Tulio, Notch's stomach flipped. Seto had no idea. He exchanged glances with the others.

"What's wrong?" Seto examined each face. Notch hesitated and the old man continued. "Come now. If you feel I ought to have been helping you, you shouldn't need reminding. I have many concerns to tend to, and many require my personal attention. Besides, you are each capable."

"No, Seto. There's bad news," Notch said. No use drawing it out. He steadied his voice. "We were attacked and Tulio was hurt. He didn't survive."

Seto's face paled. A piece of paper fell from his hand. "Seto?"

He said nothing until a croak escaped. "How?"

Notch opened his mouth but what could he say? Seto was always in control, never without a quip. A man who only lost his temper when it suited him. He had an answer for every question. He'd seen everything. He'd survived a shipwreck, survived the abandonment of his family. Rebuilt himself from absolute despair. He should have been King and instead he was the demigod of the Second Tier.

And now he was holding himself very still, jaw working beneath the stubble.

"Seto, he didn't suffer," Flir said.

"Just tell me," he snarled. Flir fell back. Notch glanced at Luik, who was coiling rope around his own wrists, hands moving on their own. Flir was Seto's favourite. He'd never shouted at her. Not once. Even after she lost an entire wagon load of silk in a single hand of cards.

"I'll let Notch tell it then," she said.

"Well?"

"We captured two of the Renovar. They confirmed that Sofia was in their quarters." He hesitated. His words weren't helping. Get on with it, Notch. "It was a trap. We'd been set up."

"Yes."

He took a breath. Seto's expression had not changed. "Tulio was trying to pick a lock but there was a creature. A chilava, a beast from –"

"I know of them," Seto interrupted.

"Well it knocked Tulio into a staircase and he didn't get up. Flir killed the beast and we took Tulio back to the Harper."

"When?"

"Earlier tonight. He's in his rooms."

"And you simply left him there for the Mascare to find? Did any of you even think?"

Silence.

Seto glared a moment longer, then turned away, head lowered. After a time he looked up but did not turn. "I'm sorry. Thank you each, for taking him home. And forgive me, Flir."

"It's nothing."

The old man crossed the room. He stopped at a long blade hanging from the wall and pulled it down. His expression was dark. "When I return from my inn, I will come with you to the palace. We will rescue Sofia together and I will hunt down Vinezi and this Lupo, and I will help you kill them. And their pitiful minions. All of them."

CHAPTER 38

The white gate at the bottom of the slope was locked. Ain sighed, he'd been a fool to expect otherwise. After all, everything else in the devil's Anaskar had locks, why not this gate to a disused hideaway?

Schan snapped the lock with the steel bar, as easily as the one beneath the earth, then jammed the shaft through the gap to break the outside lock. Clearly no-one was supposed to enter the place. Schan handed the bar over then drew his blade. Ain crept after him into the palace grounds. The passage of feet pulsed, gentle. He'd actually lost track of the paths in the moments exiting the buried house.

It was not yet full light but they were still exposed. Terrain between the white wall and the palace was open, broken only by small gardens and what looked to be a rock pool closest to the hideaway. Anyone could have been looking out from the windows, even now organising a force of olive-skinned killers to come and take them. A worse fate than to die at any other stage of the Search. To be so close and fail. Even as a part of the new sands, he would not forgive himself. Nor would Silaj if he failed to return.

"Is there a path?" Schan asked.

Beneath his feet were old paths. They more or less followed the trail leading up to the hideaway and its long escape route, coming from the palace. But crossing that path, further down the slope, in plain view of the palace, was an intersecting path. It wasn't a branch, but one older and stronger.

Ibranu's writings claimed the Shrine would not be difficult to find once inside Sekkati. The path leading to it was a beacon. As a central place of worship, the Shrine had been visited hundreds of times a week. Maybe even a day. For many, many years. That sort of traffic left its mark, an invisible one, but one that thundered, even from a distance.

Perhaps that was the true sound he'd heard before, when he fancied he could hear the sea.

"Thank the Sands, Ibranu was right. There's a path strong enough to be what we're looking for. Below."

"Good thing we didn't have to enter the city."

"We still might. Who knows what lies within the Shrine?"

"And there's all those windows too."

They would be visible, the closer they came to the path. In the Engineer's writings there had also been plans to purchase materials to counterfeit 'mask-dress' for disguises, but that was impossible now. "I know. And we cannot be caught now, so near to the Shrine." There was the egg too. The Anaskari weren't getting their filthy hands on it. He trailed a hand across its surface. So smooth, yet the grooves were deep enough to grip.

"Which way does the path run?"

He looked up from the egg, blinking. "Back and forth between palace and the mountain there." He pointed to a spot opposite their position. "Even if we use the cover, we will be exposed most of the way."

"Then let's go. Before they all wake."

Schan set off down the slope and Ain rushed after him, checking that the egg was secure and his steel bar tight in his fist. It would not be much against swords, but it was heavy and it was steel, which was more than he could say for his arms.

The lawns were well-maintained and they reached the first garden quickly, slipping through its hedges and flower beds and across the next patch of open ground without raising alarm. Ain cast frequent glances at the windows but no figure appeared on the balcony, calling for guards. No sentries walked the parapets either. Hopefully they were changing watch. He pulled his leaden legs across the grass, pausing for breath in another garden. This one had taller trees that oozed an amber liquid, which stuck to his fingers when he rested against one.

Bending to wipe his hands on the grass, he stopped when a nearby patch of ground darkened. Just like the stove. He froze, but the grass continued to darken and he looked up. Clouds passing the rising sun, nothing more.

"So far we're unnoticed," he said when he reached his feet.

Schan nodded, his own chest heaving. "Not far now."

The last stretch of ground was open. The path roared on beneath him, its thud like rocks crashing down in rhythm, but led only toward a featureless wall. The paths never lied. A Pathfinder's eye might fail him, but never the echo of where people had walked.

"Ready?" Schan was off again, racing for the mountain

wall. The ground grew rocky and Ain stumbled. He caught his balance and crossed the last few paces to slap against the rock face. Still cool.

"What now, Pathfinder?"

Ain ran his hands over the stone. "There must be a door or passage." He bent by the grass and stone, pushing and prodding for a sign of an opening. Nothing. He ran several steps along the wall.

"Ain, come."

Schan knelt by a rock pile smoother than others. Barely a foot from the mountainside rested a tumble of smooth pieces with jagged cracks. Several appeared to have once been circular. As if a pillar had stood there?

"Look at this." He handed over a smooth shard that had once been half-buried. In its corner were familiar runes.

"Old Medah." The same as those on the rib cages in the desert.

"We're close." Ain examined the wall, pausing when his fingers slipped into time-worn holes. Too regular to be accidental, they numbered four and were set in a top-heavy star. "Here, Schan. I've seen that pattern before."

He rummaged through Ibranu's possessions and withdrew a stone key, its teeth set in a similar pattern. It clicked into the wall. His pulse quickened.

"They've seen us," Schan said.

Shapes leant and pointed from a balcony. Their voices were distant but the urgency was clear.

Ain turned the key. A deeper click now. Stone ground across stone and a fissure appeared in the wall, its edges smooth. Ain touched one even as the stone panel continued to slide. Wider than he was tall, whatever moved such a heavy door had to be magic of some manner.

Beyond, morning light fell upon stairs leading upward, their edges worn in the centre.

"Inside then," Schan said. He added the last of the oil to the lamp before slipping into the dark. Ain turned the key again, collected the egg and followed. The door was already closing again, his last glimpse of the outside being green grass stretching before the white palace.

"Think they'll be able to open it?" he asked the waiting Schan.

"No. Without the key, nothing could move that door."

"Hope you're right."

Raising the lamp, Schan started up and Ain followed. The ceiling was lost beyond the glow but the walls were smooth beneath his hand, with small altars set in regular recesses. Each altar held a single round stone, rough hewn but streaked with a pink and blue quartz. Or it may have been a jewel; he wasn't going to touch them to find out. It might be disrespectful.

The stairs continued up, the path still like a sand storm vying for his attention. When he reached a landing he stopped. "Can you believe we are here?"

"No." Schan's usually closed face was alight. "No. But in a good way."

Ain resumed the climb with a laugh. The Search turned out triumphant. Luck had surely guided them. Finding Wilatt and the bolt hole, which led directly to the palace grounds, they were signs from the Sands. Destined for success. Nothing had been truly easy, his bones ached with each step, and yet – he was here. Alive. In the very heart of Sekkati – surely mere steps away from the Sea Shrine.

Though not everyone had been lucky. For Ibranu

there would be no moment of triumph. But he'd played a part. That would have pleased the old man, surely.

And a heavy part of his role dragged on Ain's shoulders still. The tools, keys and maps, charts and diagrams rolled into thin canisters, all of which he hoped would give him some clue of what he had to do once inside the Shrine, of what Majid meant by Calling the Ocean. Squinting at the scrolls by firelight after a long day's travel had yielded poor results. How exactly would the Sea Shrine banish the Anaskari devils from the City of Secrets?

But he would not fail. The Sands brought him here for a reason.

Light appeared ahead and Ain leapt up the last few steps, bursting into a giant chamber. Fractured light shone from high windows spaced along the ceiling. The room had been hollowed out inside the mountain, the work of years, the work of many hands. The chamber was dominated by a raised shrine that covered an entire wall. A pair of silent fountains flanked steps leading to a long altar.

The Sea Shrine.

Carved from the same blue and pink quartz from the stairway below, its luminescence bright enough to obscure parts of the room. He shuffled forward, Schan trailing in the quiet until Ain tripped. Flipping onto his back as he fell, he dropped the lamp to cradle the egg.

The lamp died, but he had enough light to see what had tripped him. A set of bones. Schan pulled him to his feet. "Look."

Turning from the brightness of the Shrine, Ain gaped. Scattered across the floor and lining walls were dozens of skeletons. Many lay flat on the stone floor, others were slumped against the wall. Some rested against one another, as if whoever had died chose to be near the remains of another person. A lonesome end.

"Who are they?" Ain crept closer. Sands, what now?

He crossed the floor, accidently kicking through an arm joint that caught on his foot. "Forgive me." He knelt by a pair of skeletons, one whose skull rested in the empty lap of the other.

The frayed remains of a blue cloak lay beneath the bones.

CHAPTER 39

Sofia recognised them all.

The Wolf had set her chair in the audience chamber of the old King. A healthy blaze filled the hearth, contributing to the sweat pouring from her body, and the large windows showed a gradually lightening sky over the sea. Her leg did not pain her, nor her arm or any of the other scrapes and cuts or bruises, but her pulse still roiled beneath her skin. The drug had healed her, but she was becoming its prisoner. She needed more. Soon.

Vinezi and his men lined the room, though the Wolf held the floor. A row of chairs faced the window, each containing a member of the ruling class of Anaskari. Oson sat between Solicci and Rittor of Tartaruga House. A girl with dark curls, Rittor's daughter, clung to her father's arm. Both men had schooled their features, in the Mascare way, though they wore no masks. Their robes were disarranged, as if they'd dressed in haste.

Other advisors were present, spindly men left over from Otonos' reign and who sat with wide eyes. If this had been council chambers, the place for the Seneschal would have been empty, as would be several other 'chairs.' Lastly was Lavinia the Storm Singer. Her jaw was clenched and her face white, hands gripping her knees. She was yet to make a sound. Lavinia's brother and children were nowhere to be seen.

"What is this then, Lupo, or Wolf, if that's what you wish to be called?" Oson said. He had glared at Sofia during the assembly of his council but she had refused to acknowledge him. Whatever happened, she hoped Oson and Solicci would feel great pain.

Lupo sketched a bow. "Assembled dignitaries. You have been brought here to bear witness to change such as Anaskari has never seen."

Solicci stood. "I thought you and your fellow imposters brought us here to bargain for Sofia Falco? Something to the effect of not being executed for impersonating Mascare."

"Oh?"

"What else could you possibly expect?"

"Since you ask, everything, Sol. Everything."

His brow creased. "What did you call me?"

Lupo stepped aside, so he was no longer standing before the windows. "Aren't you curious as to why you've been given this view?"

"No, we aren't. Now hand over the girl," Oson said. "I can have the Shield and Mascare here in moments."

"No, you cannot. I have sealed this room," Lupo said. "However, I may hand over the girl, on the condition that you hand over the throne, dear boy."

Sofia studied his posture. It gave nothing away, nor did his voice. He claimed no intention of giving her up to Oson, and yet... he could easily have said as much to placate her.

"What?" The King exploded from his chair. "You're an imbecile, surely? I'll never do that."

"Truly?"

Vinezi stepped forward, removing his mask and tossing it at Solicci, who snatched it from the air. A smile covered his face, cheeks flushed with excitement. "Are you perhaps familiar with the recent explosions in the city, your majesty?"

"What of them?"

"You should know we are the cause." He continued over gasps. "And there are dozens more locations set to explode, including one here in the palace. If you fail to agree, you'll bear the blackened fruits of your stubbornness."

Solicci waved the mask. "You have done this? By the Gods, you have killed hundreds. Have you no honour?"

Lupo clapped his hands together. "Oh my, you do make me want to laugh."

The head of Cavallo House glared. "What does that mean?"

"Only that I find it amusing that you would lecture on honour, in light of your transgressions in regards to Casa Falco."

One of the advisors, a man with a barrel chest, leant forward. "What is he talking about, Solicci?"

"Nothing, Brunetti." He kept his eyes on Vinezi.

Vinezi pointed outside. "Save it, gentlemen. Now, while you consider our generous offer, I would like you to watch the show. I hope at least some of you are familiar with the bathhouses west of the Second Tier gate?"

"No," Sofia shouted. Lupo pointed at her, then raised a single finger to the mouth of the mask, before tapping one of his men on the shoulder. She shuddered. The gesture was somehow inhuman. The imposter slipped from the room. Glass shattered and after a moment, while Oson and Solicci hissed to each other, a small light appeared outside. It was followed by another on the palace wall, then another deeper into the city.

"Not long now," Vinezi purred.

Oson stood again. "What is this theatrical heap of –"

Fire exploded into the sky, a deep rumble to go with it. A great column of flame and black smoke rose in the Second Tier and Sofia looked away as the room burst into shouting. Lupo flicked a finger at his men, who moved in to subdue the 'guests,' none of whom were armed.

Some of the advisors had tears in their eyes and even Oson looked shaken.

Lupo resumed the lead. "Further to your acceptance of our offer we will allow some of you to retain two things. Your positions and your heads. Be wise now."

Oson's face was red and his teeth clenched, but Solicci held up his hands. "The people won't support you as leader. You're not of the Houses."

"I highly doubt the people will care."

"And neither Mascare nor the nobility will accept an imposter."

Lupo raised his hands to his face, in an almost girlish gesture. "Then let's give them someone more authentic, shall we?"

With a flourish he removed his mask and threw back his hood.

Sofia let out a sob.

Tantos.

*

Another explosion rocked the city.

Notch ran to the courtyard door. The street outside remained empty, dawn light filtering down, but that would soon change. "Damn it," he shouted. He only hoped Seto's men weren't too close. "Feel that? We were too slow."

"We did our best," Seto said from across the room. His face was drawn, but he'd returned from the inn as vowed, a light burning in his sunken eyes. He said nothing of Tulio or what he found there, but there was blood on his boots and traces on his hands. A blade still swung at his side. Notch did not ask.

"I don't know if we did."

The old man didn't reply.

Pistorio waved from his wagons. "Nearly done, Notch."

"All right." Notch didn't move. His chest no longer troubled him, not after being rewrapped and having taken a dose of lenasi. "You owe me for this, Notch," Pistorio told him. "It isn't cheap." The explosion had rattled the whole building and already the screams were starting. He slammed a fist into a wall. He should have acted sooner. They'd known about the bathhouse and the latest store of acor. But they'd been too slow, even with Seto's men. Notch shouldn't have let the Shields, nor Seto's grief push it from his mind. More people were dead; who knew how many? Worse, Pevin wouldn't be able to help with many other locations.

He rolled his wrists, hand straying to his hilt. It was a problem for another day.

Sofia first.

Pistorio and Flir were reloading the wagons, making enough room for extra boxes to be slid into the beds.

Each box would contain a surprise cargo. Notch, Flir, Luik and Wayrn would slip inside the palace within one of the smith's deliveries.

"I could just as easily walk in," Wayrn said, during the discussion, "but meeting up with you would be difficult. Biagio has been upset at some of my lengthy absences lately."

Flir had favoured simply breaking in, but there was no way even her strength could open the palace gates. Notch had never seen anything like them, in any other city he'd seen in his years as a mercenary. The colossal gates were a singular achievement.

"Isn't there a better way?" Flir had one foot in a box. She wore her tunic and pants, no disguises this time. Masquerading as Mascare in the palace was too risky.

"Probably," Notch said. He jogged to his own case and gave a shudder. It was not unlike a coffin. Wonderful. A rough ride in a narrow box. "But Vinezi's already acting."

"Fine." She lay down, grumbling to herself.

"Just do it, Flir," Luik called from the nearest box, voice muffled.

Notch hopped into the wagon bed then the wooden box. He lay down, scabbard and sword in hand. How were Luik and Wayrn faring now? They'd been in their boxes for some time. After a moment, Pistorio appeared above him, holding a lid. "Ready?"

"Ready."

The top slid over and into place, a mere finger's length from his nose, bringing darkness. The smell of pine was everywhere. He placed his hands on the lid and hefted. The pine rose and Pistorio chuckled. "I won't nail it down, don't worry – but I will add something heavy to keep it down."

"Good idea."

"Here's Seto, too," he said.

Notch waited while the horses were hitched, Seto and Pistorio conversing. Their voices were muffled and once the wagon pulled out of the smithy, there was only the grind of wheels on stone.

By the time they stopped, hopefully at the gates, he was glaring at the wood. The bumpy ride seemed to have shaken his body into separate pieces. Indistinct voices drifted down from the front of the wagon. He held his breath. If the guards decided to search the wagon, things would become unpleasant. Quickly. Pistorio vowed that such searches were rare. After years of service, he was trusted. He was also one of the few artisans from the Second Tier with a pass. Everything would work out.

Unless Notch happened across Otonos.

Though there was little chance of that. If the man was as gravely ill as rumoured, he'd not be stalking the halls. And Sofia was counting on him. No time for personal scores to be settled. Besides, he should have settled it years ago. On the black sands in Medah.

Just as Father said.

Long moments passed and Notch tensed. He reached for his knife. It was the only thing he could get a grip on, sword on his chest. The new blade came courtesy of Pistorio, a much finer weapon than he'd been forced to use of late. For a change, he wasn't eager to use it. Shields weren't the enemy.

The wheels started rolling again and he exhaled. From the gates, the wagon would travel up to the outer buildings of the armoury and be unloaded, usually by Pistorio's men. Much rested on whether the quartermaster would offer to help. The blacksmith's livelihood, even his life, counted on delivering Notch and the others without being discovered. And that was exactly what Notch wanted. No-one else needed to die.

The wagon came to another halt and Notch strained his ears. Pistorio's voice. Tone reasonable. Someone answered. Silence. Finally, something slid along the surface of his lid.

Who would it be?

The wood lifted and light flooded in, Pistorio's face above him. Notch released a breath.

"Quickly."

He hopped out and into an open loading bay. Stacks and boxed supplies lined the stone walls. A broad set of double doors were closed.

"Where's the quartermaster?" Notch asked as he slid bushels of unfletched arrows from one of the boxes.

"He's gone to fetch men to help me. He won't be long."

Notch removed the lid and pulled Flir out. She jumped to work on the next box.

Once everyone was free, Notch sent them around the building and out of sight, thanking Pistorio before joining them. He crouched in a corner, avoiding a pair of windows and using the shrubs to shield him from the distant wall. Across the neat lawns was a sentry path, but as yet, no-one had appeared. It would be some time before the newly rising sun banished long shadows from the palace grounds.

"Where's Seto?" Flir asked.

"Looking for the best way in."

Luik rolled his shoulders. "Hope it's not another box."

"He'll have something good," Notch said. He turned to Wayrn to ask if he could stand watch, but the man had already crept toward the edge of the building. "And remember. Any interference, try not to kill."

They both nodded and Notch was relieved that Flir didn't fight him. He switched his sword between hands while he waited. If Sofia was still unhurt, he wouldn't have failed her. She would be restored and his name cleared. Even Seto would be happy then, he'd have his ship. What exactly that meant to the old man Notch couldn't fathom. But if it was important Notch would help. Just as Seto helped him.

"Someone comes," Luik said.

Moving along the wall in the distance, a figure kept low to the ground. Seto. Notch waved Wayrn back.

The old man paused to catch his breath when he arrived. "Two buildings along is the guest wing. I recall that a passage eventually connects it to the royal rooms. If we are swift, we can be in through a window while maids air one of the rooms."

"Lead on," Notch said.

Seto took them along the gardens by the building, pausing at the rear of a temple yard. A low stone fence was set with skulls in small, silver cages at regular intervals. Names were carved into the stone beneath the skulls — immortalised, or trapped, on the walls to their temple.

"Hurry." Flir pulled him along.

Beyond the temple stood the end of the guest wing, which stretched above them, shining balconies catching the sun. On the ground floor waited an open window. Someone's hands flapped a rug out the window, dust flying. Seto slowed when another set of hands appeared and a second rug snapped in the air.

By the chatting voices, they were Braonn women. One was running off a list of derogatory phrases directed at their masters. At a particularly loud curse-word, both girls giggled.

Once they left, Seto crept closer and peered over the sill. Sliding back down, kneeling in the garden bed, he waved Notch forward. "Be quick, they may return."

Notch followed him in and padded through the empty bed chamber to the door, closing it gently. From the next room he heard a window slide open and voices resumed. Flir was already in the room and Luik followed. Wayrn leapt inside after and Seto raised a finger to his lips. Footsteps. Had a maid forgotten something?

The handle turned and a young girl entered, giving a jump. Notch snatched her before she could scream, placing a hand over her mouth. "We won't hurt you," he said. "But you can't cry out."

Flir shook her head. "No, tell her to call her friend."

Seto moved over and smiled at the girl. "Call for your friend, dear. I promise no-one will hurt you, and no-one will be angry either."

Her wide eyes bulged and Notch started to remove his hand. She made no sound so he finished. "Go on."

"Rhia, I need some help," she called in fair Anaskari.

"All right." The other maid's voice carried from next door. The moment she stepped inside, Flir had her. Rhia struggled, chest heaving where she stood, locked into position by Flir's arms.

"Now, we're going to leave," Seto told the girls. "If you scream, we will be back and you won't like that. But if you say nothing, you will never see us again. How does that sound?"

The girl Notch held nodded, but the other had slumped in Flir's arms.

"Ah, I think you've held her too tight," Wayrn said.

Flir removed her hand and carried the maid to the

bed. "I'm sorry, I didn't realise. She's all right," she added after a moment.

"Can you care for your friend?" Notch asked.

"Yes."

"Good. Find her some water."

"And say nothing of us," Seto said as he slipped from the room. Notch waved the others after him and gave an apologetic smile.

"Sorry again."

The girl gaped at him.

He caught up to the others. Flir was shaking her head. "Seto, do you think that was wise?"

"Having you half-smother one of them?" He was counting doors as he strode along the quiet halls.

"No. Leaving them."

"By the time any of them says anything, if they do so, our work will be done." He stopped by a door that appeared the same as any other. "Ah-ha. Locked, but we go in here. Flir?"

Notch stood back. Flir gave the door a thump, shattering the lock and splintering the door and frame. She burst inside, but Notch saw only an empty room over her shoulder. The bed looked newly vacated but other than that, no clues remained to its owner.

"I meant for you to pick the lock," Seto said.

"I know."

"Can't you be more careful?" Notch said. "Anyone could have been in here. Not to mention the noise."

"Fine."

Seto had already opened a passage that resided beyond a seemingly plain piece of wall. Taking a lamp from the room, he lit it and led them into the dark tunnels. They walked through a series of turns and twists. Sometimes shafts or spots of light slipped through the walls or from the rooms, but mostly it was only the lamplight and Seto's back guiding him. He brushed cobwebs from his face several times, and lost his sense of direction halfway in.

Twice Seto stopped to inch open a door or peer through a hole, before moving on. "My memory is not immaculate," he said the second time.

He soon slowed. An argument was in full force somewhere, many voices adding to the clamour. Seto crept further along the passage and waited for a swell in the voices before sliding a door open.

A bedchamber was revealed in the dim light. From beyond, in an adjoining room, came the voices. Notch followed. A young woman was shouting.

Sofia.

He leapt for the handle but Seto stopped him.

"Wait. Listen first. Wait for the right moment," he breathed. Those in the room argued on until a rich voice laughed.

"Now," Seto whispered.

CHAPTER 40

"You were dead," Sofia shouted into the silence.

He spun. Time had changed little – and much. His eyes were still dark but they were lined now and streaks of grey marred his black hair. His smile stretched over a gaunt jaw, skin pale. "I'm still dead, little sister." His voice was no longer theatrical, but quieter – more like his own, more like Father's.

"No." The room spun but she charged him. Her leg was as new, only the ungainly shape of the splint slowed her as she crashed into him, beating his chest. "How? Everything you've done."

He caught her arms, giving her a shake. "I could do much more." To the audience he spoke over her protest, "And now to your concerns, which, I assure you all, are as dust before me. I'll say it again. Swear fealty to me. Work with me. Save your city. Become heroes in their eyes by stopping the explosions."

"He's lying." Sofia tore her arms free momentarily, aided by the sweat slicking them. "He'll betray you. He'll betray you just as he betrayed his house."

He caught her hands again, squeezing until she slumped against him with a cry. How did he live? And who had he become?

Tantos hissed. "I was the one betrayed, Sofia." To the council, "Well?"

Somewhere in the room Vinezi giggled. Sofia's stomach turned. Father needed to know. She had to tell Tantos how hard it was to take his place. She needed to kill Lupo, to strangle the Wolf with his own hair for what he'd done to her, to Father, to her house, to the helpless people of the city. He had to die.

Her brother had to die all over again.

Words stuck in her throat. What would she tell her father, if she killed Tantos? If she was even able? She stopped struggling when Solicci stood, staring at a point beyond Tantos. "I will swear."

"Traitor." Oson snarled as he rose, cutting off a council member. "After all we achieved, you're going to give in to this, this... ghost of a man? We can refuse him, Osani is close, I know it. Once we –"

Solicci roared. "Imbecile – didn't you see it? He has Osani."

Oson gaped. Sofia looked up at Tantos. His expression was expectant only. Just how long had he been in the city?

A councillor rose, arms crossed. "I will swear."

"Fine." Oson appeared to have recovered, though Sofia noted a tremor in his voice. He glared at them before turning back to Tantos, teeth clenched. "Give me a sword. I will challenge you for the throne."

"No," the girl beside him cried. Oson ignored her, standing tall.

Tantos laughed. "I have no need. I can merely –"

He broke off at commotion from an adjoining room.

Sofia barely had time to enjoy Oson's outrage, the defeat on his face, when Notch burst into the room. He grinned at her, just a moment, then a mask of concentration fell over his face and he swung his sword at the first imposter who ran to meet him.

The council scattered as Flir and Luik charged in on his heels, spreading out to engage the men around the walls. Hope surged up her throat, choking her cry of joy. Tantos kept his grip tight but Flir was already closing in, even as Notch was pushed back. He roared her name, sword flashing, but Flir was closer. She hammered one man aside with a single backhand blow, sending him crashing through the window. A second man she tore in half with her blade, the torso sliding to the ground.

Sofia fought as Tantos dragged her back with one arm, the other replacing the mask. He spoke a single word and the room went dark. A woman cried out, a long cry that grew silent – as if something had stepped between her and the sound. Sofia struggled on. While her leg seemed healed, she wasn't strong enough to break his grasp. His mask glowed above her. It was swallowing the light, bringing about a darkness so complete that even the dawn outside had disappeared.

He pulled her into a stumbling run, away from the shouting and into a quiet place. "Make no sound if you want to live." His voice was flat.

She swallowed a retort, struggling to keep up as he dragged her along what might have been a passage, the sound of her feet on stone enough to let her know they'd left the king's sitting room with its deep carpet, carpet now doubtless covered in blood. Who had cried out? Was it Flir? Was Notch alive?

Tantos gave another tug on her arm. When had he

become a monster? He had to be stopped. And more, he owed her an explanation.

"Stop, Tantos."

"No."

"Then tell me how you live? Your ship was lost."

No answer. A glow from Osani lit the passage walls. Webs climbed to dark corners and filtered light flashed by. Tantos paused at an intersection, his fingers still cutting into her wrist.

"Tantos, you owe me, be damned. You owe Father. He searched for you."

He flung her into the dark.

Sofia's head bounced off stone and she cried out, sliding to the ground, hands clutching her head. A wetness grew in her hair.

"I owe our father nothing, Sofia, do you hear me?" His voice echoed in the passage and his breath rasped in his throat. He was Lupo again, barely contained violence slipping out.

"I hear you," she shouted back. "But you make no sense. You're mad. Can you even see it?"

He hauled her up. "Be silent now."

Again he was off, tugging at her arm, cursing when she tripped, until he finally stopped and broke apart the splint, casting it away. She kept up well enough, but by the time he threw open the door to a well-appointed room, lit by a single lamp, the muscles in her leg were aflame. It only added to the sopping heat that wracked her body.

"Where are we going? Tell me that at least."

He heaved a chest across the ground and stepped over it, kicking through the wall. A soft covering made to resemble the palace interior crumbled to the floor. From inside, he tore a wooden box free and glanced at her, the black holes of his mask somehow bright.

"Here where Seneschal Fratali slept, and this is where they hid it. In a servant's room, by the Ocean Gods."

"Who? And what did they hide? Make sense."

"That fool Solicci and his runt. But they failed." He opened the box and she leaned in.

Argeon sat on a velvet cushion.

*

Ain whispered into the cool of the Shrine. "Let the passing of feet go quiet now, your paths are at an end." Had those before him uttered the same words? If the roar of the path wasn't so strong, he'd have sensed the hiss of a Pathfinder's last path. "Not only are we not the first," he said, dragging his feet toward the Shrine, "we're going to die here, just as so many who failed before us."

Schan hefted a bag that ripped as he stood. A jumble of tools and scrolls, exactly like those Ibranu had carried, clattered to the ground, tinkling. A cog rolled across the floor. "There are others too."

Ain counted four more bags visible in the light, the darkest corners hidden from him. How many tools had been forged, how many charts copied? How many years had the Elders been sending Pathfinders and their Engineers to die here, trapped once they failed? For surely, that is what happened. Each had failed to unlock the secrets of the Shrine, and had been unable to leave.

He would never see Silaj again. "Sands Below! How could the Elders betray us all?"

Schan shook his head, face dark. "Perhaps they do not know why no-one returns."

Ain unclenched his fists. When had he made them?

Schan had a point. "I don't know." He took the key from his pack and tossed it to Schan, who caught it, an eyebrow twitching. "We might as well see if the door can be opened from the inside."

Schan hurried down the stair. Ain placed the pack on the floor, adding the egg to the pile and approaching the altar. "I haven't forgotten you," he told it. The fountains were deep and dry. Caked with dust and flakes of stone, the spouts were arranged in a pattern that echoed the sun entering water, its rays shooting forth.

Not even the whisper of water's scent.

The paths beneath his feet were confused, broken. Turning. Moving nowhere. Making slumbering circles. They flowed up and down the stairs, pulsed in a desperate attempt to escape. The traces of older paths led down and beyond the door, but up here in the shrine there were no paths leading to anywhere.

Just the altar.

He climbed the steps and stopped before the quartz. Light that poured through the windows, themselves quartz by the fractured rays, struck the altar. He ran a hand through the glow, the cool surface appearing to ripple as his fingers passed.

In the centre of the altar were a group of quartz squares, their edges smooth. They did not move when he gripped one. He tried several more, but none would lift. Giving the last one a push, Ain jumped when a panel of wall behind the altar slid open with a rasp.

An opening twice as tall as a man, and many times wider, had concealed a giant bell. Polished to a sheen and covered in swirling patterns that evoked the sea, their deep lines tinged with blue, it would have crushed him like a scorpion if it were to fall. The bottom of the bell was marked with the same runes found outside and on the bones in the desert.

"Unreadable." He could check the scrolls, but what promise were they? Every other Pathfinder and Engineer had possessed the same materials.

Or had they?

Each Pathfinder might have known something different or less than the last. Maybe something more. He leapt down the steps and ran to the first pack, the one Schan had ripped, sorting the tools from the scrolls. They were fragile. He tore one and cursed as the edges of another crumbled. Several of the canisters were still intact, those he lay in a row.

Schan's footfalls approached. "What's all this?"

"Help me, can you? We need to collect all the Engineers' packs."

Pausing only once to drink and cram a few mouthfuls of travel rations down, Ain, with Schan's help, collected and ordered everything. In less than an hour he had the materials lined up from least to most deteriorated. The oldest scrolls had flaked away to nothing as he carried them in cupped hands, arms scooped, whereas the newer ones were usable.

"Now we look for difference," he said.

"What about the tools?"

"Let's organise them too. Though I see nothing as to where they might go."

"I'll check that great bell you found."

"Be careful." He didn't look up from where he crouched. "Anything could happen here."

"Thanks for the advice," Schan chuckled.

Ain waved in response. Between one scroll and the next, little difference appeared. But as he walked across the floor, slight changes leapt from the musty pages. A phrase or a word here and there. Most passages described rituals that made no sense. 'Washing the Stone' or 'The proper way to open the light' and 'Crossing the Eye.' It was all very formal sounding, bound up in permissions and chants. Nothing like life in the Sands.

The few scraps of the oldest scroll were illegible. Not just due to their age, but the writing. It was in an old script, no longer in use. Maybe Ibranu could have read it. Ain returned to an earlier scroll. One of the few that had been preserved in a canister, it mentioned 'Calling the Sea' and several lines down, 'the great bell in the Shrine.'

"Here." He tapped the scroll. "Majid mentioned this."

It was the answer. The scroll spoke of the sea and no other writing had alluded to the bell.

He opened his own scroll, the edges firm, unrolling to match the corresponding passage. There were few differences, mostly the forcefulness of the author's warning, that calling the sea was a 'final measure.'

"What better time?" he murmured. He read on, checking other scrolls often. The authors of the scrolls, or whoever the Medah scribes had originally copied from, described a simple process of striking the bell with a 'sanctioned hammer.'

"But what does that do, what does it mean?" he growled.

Schan returned. "Find anything?"

"I'm not sure. You?"

"I'm no engineer, but the tools don't look very useful. No-where to place them, and no way to squeeze behind the bell in any event. The altar is just a giant block and nothing in the stairwell seems of any use either."

"The scrolls speak of 'calling the sea' and 'striking the

bell' but we need a hammer."

Schan snorted. "Don't need no hammer." He skipped up the steps, leapt over the altar and drew his knife to smash the pommel into the bell.

Silence.

He swung again, then twice more before turning back. None of his blows made a sound. "Something's wrong with it."

Ain had leapt after him. Who knew what 'Calling the Sea' meant, but it sounded dangerous. Was it relief or disappointment, that nothing happened? Majid and Ibranu had believed it the answer.

"We need a 'sanctified hammer' whatever that means."

"I don't see any of them here."

"Nor I." Ain rubbed his eyes. How long had he been reading? The Shrine was darker, the altar less vibrant. His knees were sore from crouching over the scrolls. He sat on the steps to the altar and put his head in his hands.

The spark of hope given by the bell was dark. The whole journey, every step was for nothing. He looked up. "So is this what happened to all these others? They came all this way, found the bell and read their scroll and then died because no-one told us to bring a Sand-Blasted hammer?"

Schan did not answer.

CHAPTER 41

She reached out to touch Argeon's face but Tantos stopped her, gentle now.

"Somewhere quieter."

He led her back to the passages and within moments they were moving through the cold fireplace to her rooms. Even before he'd turned the last corner, she'd known where he would take her. She leaned against her father's desk.

"Don't you want him to know you're alive?" She tried to meet his eyes. Damn the mask. "What were you going to tell me?"

Tantos shook his head, then strode from the study.

It was her chance.

Even weakened and feverish, she might escape. Back into the passages, and lose herself in the shadows. If she could find her way back to the royal apartments... No. He would find her, he knew the ways better. And there was no way to hide from someone with a Greatmask. Besides, who knew what he would do next? He possessed two masks now. One of which belonged to another house!

He would find a way to kill more people.

Someone had to stop him. "Gods, I will try."

She followed him into their father's bedroom. Weak as she was, there was no way to strike him directly. Wait and watch, Sofia.

Tantos sat on the bed, box in hand. Argeon glowed, the rise and fall of his intensity matched to that of Osani. "They're speaking." He nodded to the box. "Osani helped me find Argeon."

"What?"

"All the Greatmasks know each other. It's only we humans who try to keep them apart."

Sofia blinked away the revelation, startling as it was. He needed to talk, but not about that. "Tantos. I want you to answer me now. Why?" She'd made a fist behind her back. There was no way to stop him. She ground her teeth. "Why, by the Gods? You've become everything we were raised to fight."

"I know that."

"And for what?"

"The tabella."

"What?"

"I must know all its names. Argeon will tell me what you cannot, what father did not."

"But why? You've killed hundreds of people for what, for the names in the tabella? For a list of Mascare?"

His voice wavered. "I'm close now, Sofia. Don't attempt to dissuade me."

"Will you stop, when you have the names?"

His head snapped up from Argeon. "You've had them all along? Father showed you?"

"No." She stood tall. "I'm asking, will you stop, Tantos?"

"Sofia." His voice was hard. "I've searched distant shores to try and stop. Help me now. Ask Argeon. He won't share them with me."

"Even if I wanted to help you, Father taught me so little."

He pulled Osani off with a sigh, rubbing his face. He stood, moving to take both her hands. She couldn't prevent a shiver at the race of his pulse, the heat beneath his skin. "Sofia, you must help me now."

Could she bargain with him? Unlikely, but she could hardly overpower him and she had no weapon. "Then you will stop? And no lies this time."

He drew a shuddering breath. His face lost some of its power, as if whatever fire burnt within had waned. He looked young, boyish with his wild hair. Vulnerable. He resembled her brother again. Tears built. Tantos had once helped her make a shelter for an injured bird. How could he be the same man who killed so many, who cared so little for life? Oceans, who was he now?

"I'll stop."

She wiped tears with her knuckles, growling. "How have you done this to me, Tantos? I shouldn't cry." She strode across the room, kicking at ashes in the hearth. "You're a monster. That's who you've become to me. A monster."

"But still your brother too, I hope."

"I can't change that, can I?" Still the older brother who'd carried her through the streets of the Second Tier when her feet became sore, or who'd snuck sweets from their mother's table, and giggled with her when they hid beneath his bed to eat them. "But you cannot think I love you now."

"I know."

She shook her head. What was he thinking? "Who do you seek? And why?"

"Derrani." He straightened. "Derrani is the father of Gianna, whom I once loved. I must find her, they have taken her from me."

Sofia stormed back to him. "This is all about a girl?" She swung her fist.

Tantos caught her arm. "Yes." He held her. "Yes, damn you. Everything I've done has been for Gianna."

"And she wanted you to kill for her?" Sofia's voice rose. A sweet girl with Braonn ancestry, Gianna always had a smile for those around her.

He threw her hand aside. "Enough. Take Argeon. Ask him, he'll respond to you where I have failed."

She stared at him. Finally she spoke. "Just remember your promise. A promise you made to family, Tantos."

"I will." She accepted the Greatmask. A chance to stop him. She couldn't make Argeon speak. She knew that. And yet... she placed the mask on her face. The room disappeared and only Argeon remained. His sockets were expectant, though his attention, the crushing force that it was, was split between her and another unfathomable force. Osani.

Father said wearing a mask was like communicating.

She would communicate. "Argeon, hear me."

Nothing.

Sofia tried again. Still nothing. Only Tantos' breathing across from her, beyond the void. Could she feel him because of the other Greatmask? There. He wore Osani, watching her. Bearing wary. If only Argeon would answer, she could ask him to stop Tantos.

"Argeon, I seek a man from the tabella. Derrani. Where is he?"

Did he even understand? She tried the Old Tongue.

More silence. What a fool she was. To think she could use the Greatmask to stop her brother. To think she could use Argeon at all. Untrained. Useless. Even if she did, somehow Tantos was able to use Osani. What happened when Greatmasks clashed?

Tantos' robes shifted as he leaned closer. "Ask, Sofia."

"I cannot make him speak."

"Truly?"

"Yes, I told you. I haven't been trained."

"You have to choose the void, you know that much at least?"

"Choose? I only ever see the void and Argeon."

He sighed. "Once Argeon grows familiar with you, the void will only come if you wish to communicate directly with him. Over time, even that becomes unnecessary." Some of his impatience eased. "You will see the world together."

"But for now?"

"Try again but listen to me."

What choice did she have? She had to placate Tantos. She replaced the mask and the dark returned.

Tantos spoke from beyond the ink.

"Try something for me. Try to show him, Sofia. In your mind, see the tabella. I believe Argeon will follow your intent."

Sofia nodded. The tabella. Old, its cover worn at the edges and inside, names scrawled across its yellowed pages, the handwriting of so many different Protectors – Sofia gasped. Names poured into her mind, Adaggi, Agua, Ainotto... and on until they stopped at Derrani.

Marochi Derrani, 'sleeping' in the Second Tier as a tailor.

It worked! If she showed Argeon another image perhaps she could –

The room snapped into focus. Tantos' expectant face waited before her. Argeon rested in his hands. He'd taken the mask, her mistake slow to register. Sofia smothered a sneer. How exactly would she have used Argeon to stop him anyway? She was a child, clutching at a bauble.

Tantos shook his head at her. "I think I will care for Argeon. Now, tell me."

"And you will keep your word."

"Yes. I swear it."

"What does 'sleeping' mean?"

"When a Mascare no longer wears the mask and has gone into hiding for protection. Or because they're too old or sick. Where is he sleeping, Sofia?"

"The Second Tier." She swallowed a curse. "I'll take you there." What did she have left? She couldn't overpower him and she had no mask, no weapon. Perhaps when he was distracted with Gianna, she could take the masks? A thin hope, but depriving him of them would be a start. Her leg was strong enough to flee. It had to be.

Tantos had them out of the palace quicker than she could have managed alone. He knew the passages so well. Part of her was coiled, waiting for Tantos to betray her again. If he did, she would kill him. Or try. She bit her lip as a cold knot formed in her stomach, counter to the sweat running down her back. Why couldn't he be her brother once more? No more Lupo.

On the streets, wind cut through her clothing. Thunder boomed and grey clouds darkened the morning sky, the scent of coming rain was sharp but none fell as they walked, keeping close to the buildings. Instead, the air almost stung her face, a sense of anticipation heavy.

Waves crashed beyond the walls.

"We turn here," she said at a small square, where few people shopped. Most stores were closed. She glanced at her brother. Argeon possessed a faint glow, as if drawing life from the coming storm. "Why is it so quiet? What's happening?"

"The explosions, the terror we created. The fear is meant to make it easier for..." he trailed off. "Maybe it has something to do with the strange green creatures."

Sofia pursed her lips. He'd changed what he was going to say. She would learn the truth later, now she had to deliver him to the tailor. Maybe even end whatever madness possessed him. And if not, to stop him. To take the Greatmasks.

Deep in the tier, but a stone's throw from the walls, a small shop with a tailor's needle hanging from a sign nestled between bigger buildings. The windows showed no light. It must have been too early for the man.

"You first."

She knocked on the door. There was no reply. At Tantos' insistence she kept on until sounds came from within. They ceased at the door. "Who's out there?" a voice rasped.

Again, at a wave from Tantos, who now wore Argeon, she took the lead. "Sofia Falco."

"Falco?" A key turned. A short man with thinning white hair was revealed in the open doorway, a smile on his face. "Whatever is Danillo's daughter doing on my doorstep at this hour?"

His smile vanished when Tantos pushed inside, dragging Sofia after.

"Shut the door Derrani."

"You." The old man gasped, hand still on the wood.

Tantos turned and batted Derrani's hand away, slamming the door. Argeon glowed again but Sofia stepped between him and the old man, who had stumbled back.

"Tantos! You swore."

He pointed at her. "Don't force my hand, little sister. I'm doing what I must."

She took a step forward. "What is this?"

He said nothing.

"Why have you brought him here, girl?" Derrani asked. His hand slipped beneath his clothing and came up with a knife, but he did not attack.

"Because I'm a fool," she shouted. "Tantos, you'll have to kill me."

He ignored her. "Where is your wife, old man?"

"Dead, Gods rest her. Dead." Tears formed in his eyes and his knife arm wavered. "You were wrong about Gyana, boy. She was lying to you, you never could see that."

"Her name was Gianna." His voice was a growl. "And our love was true, old man. Hers wasn't your life to take."

Sofia drew in a breath. "You killed your own daughter?"

The old man turned his head as if surprised, unable to take eyes from Tantos. "What in the name of the Gods are you talking about, girl?"

Another lie? "Tantos?"

His jaw was tight. He offered no answer. Sofia kept herself between them. Argeon bore down on her, implacable steps. Tantos' chest heaved and his own hands were white around his knives. Floorboards creaked beneath his boots.

"Move, Sofia."

She had to get to a mask. "No."

Argeon's eyes flashed darkness. She opened her mouth

to shout –

Sofia was sitting on a tree trunk in the wood behind the manor. The sun warmed her back and she was happy, but the apple in her hand was hard to grip. She kept dropping it and her father, no mask, his face unlined, hair dark and eyes twinkling, would pick it up for her and laugh when she dropped it again. The green apple rolled along the moss again and she stretched for it, feet dangling.

"Careful, Petal," he said. "You don't want to fall."

"I won't fall, that's silly."

"Of course, you're a big girl, aren't you?"

Somewhere the small part of her mind that had not been trapped in her memory heard screaming. Long, drawn out screams that twisted at the ends. She shuddered but her body completed the action as if moved by another.

From the manor her mother's voice drifted between the leaves, calling them for supper. Father helped her down and she took big steps, trying to keep up with his long stride. The green was dotted with yellow-faces and she bent to tear one free. The flower smelt like... nothing really, but the stains on her fingers were nice. A dark yellow. She put some on her face and smiled up at father, but he wasn't looking.

She tugged on his soft robe.

A man begged. Something sharp punctured something pitifully unresisting.

"What is it, Sofia?" When he saw her face, he scooped her into his arms and tickled her until she could barely breathe from laughter.

Something clattered to the floor and a man, a different man, called out. A woman's name. He wept –

Sofia snapped back to the tailor's shop. She lay on the floor. The fingers of one hand had brushed against feathers in her ring. Tantos knelt on the floorboards, empty hands red. Two knives lay at his side. His robe had soaked up so much blood. Argeon was only spotted, though a large splotch covered one of his eyes.

Derrani lay slumped against one of the walls. Gutted, his throat was slashed and his eyes were little more than dark sockets, slick with blood. She gagged. Two had died here. Derrani, a poor old man, and one of her most treasured memories, shattered by the echo of his pleas.

CHAPTER 42

Ain stalked across the front of the altar. "Anything?"

Schan rose from his examination of the bell's underside. With just enough room to slide his head beneath the rim, he'd been still for some time before rising with a nod. "There's something in there that seems to have been repaired. Or built."

"But what does it mean? Is it incomplete? Is that why the bell won't ring?"

"It looks complete to my eye."

"Then it should sound."

Schan grunted. "I agree, but I'm no Engineer."

Ain threw his hands up and leapt down the steps. He stood over the scrolls, edges weighed down with cogs and tools. Only one deletion in hundreds of years of the search. Why remove 'Calling the Sea' from the last few searches? It had to be the key. Either that, or it was what killed so many Pathfinders.

Did the Elders even know anything about the Shrine? Surely they wouldn't have generations of Blacksmiths preparing costly steel items that no-one needed? The

Elders wouldn't know the bell had been repaired. They wouldn't know what any of the rituals meant. No. One of the Engineers succeeded in repairing something within the bell, but now it would not sing. There was a missing step. And no-where in the chamber was anything remotely like a hammer.

Why had no-one brought a hammer before?

He paced the opposite wall, stepping over bones. He'd already searched the room twice. Only dead Searchers to be found. He paused, something in the wall was odd. A pattern, just like that from outside. A top heavy star. "Schan, do you have the key?"

"I do." He threw it across the room. Ain caught it and placed it in the holes, giving a twist. A long panel of wall slid across, light crashing into the shrine. He blinked against it, stepping back. When his eyes adjusted he gasped.

A wall of pink quartz. It was thick, though it was possible to see down onto the city and the ocean beyond. The view wasn't crystal clear, but he could make out the shapes well enough.

"Is it a way out?" Schan asked from the steps.

Ain examined it. No crease was visible and when he rapped on the quartz with the hilt of his knife, it rang solid. Without serious tools and a great amount of time, the window was not going to be their escape.

"No."

False hope. He kicked at a cog. The Elders had sent him to a death trap, just like dozens of his people before him. And those that reached the Shrine, who'd felt the same rush of triumph Ain had upon arriving, had all been betrayed at the last moment. "We don't even know if making the bell ring will do anything."

"The knowledge is supposed to come from the Mages."

"Wonderful," Ain said. "There have been no Ocean Mages for generations so we get to die here with that knowledge, like damn fools." He snatched up a cog and hurled it at the bell.

The steel bounced off without a sound. He'd not be surprised to learn it hadn't scratched the surface either. Schan skipped away as Ain threw another cog. He found another, and then another, hands scrambling for more objects as his vision blurred with tears. "Sands damn you." His scream echoed.

And the bell chimed.

Deep, it resonated in his chest. He staggered from the force, though it did not hurt his ears. Schan had fallen, but was climbing back to his feet, a hand on the altar. His face was comically surprised and Ain burst into laughter.

"How did you do that?" Schan asked.

Ain spread his hands. "I don't know, I just started throwing..." A skeleton he'd been unwilling to disturb rested near a row of scrolls. It was missing a hand.

"Ain."

Schan held a shattered hand of bone, the fingers broken and the palm cracked.

Throwing something, anything, at the bell, as if each object were one of the Elders themselves, wasn't supposed to include the bones of a poor Pathfinder or Engineer. He fell to his knees and arranged the bones into a position of repose.

"Forgive me."

Schan put a hand on his shoulder. "He wouldn't mind, Ain. Not if it helps."

"It's not right." Surely no other Pathfinder had done the same? Or had they, and failed at some other, unseen hurdle?

"Maybe not, but let's be sure it wasn't a coincidence."

Ain gestured to the skeleton. "What would we use?"

Schan bent to lift a thigh. "Here."

Ain took a deep breath, accepting the bone. The steps to the bell stretched. Had he trod them a dozen times or a thousand? Pausing by the bell he reached out to trace one of the swirls. It chilled his fingertips. "Time to Call the Sea. I hope."

He drew the bone back and swung.

A wave of sound flipped his heart but he did not fall. He'd been expecting it. The sound was much stronger standing beside the bell. He swung a little harder, bracing himself. The bell sang, its voice deep. A voice from darkness. He trembled but not with fear. Each note rattled him less.

"What's it doing?" Ain shouted over another dark chiming.

"Nothing here," Schan said. He ran to the window. "I can't tell. Keep going."

Ain struck again. Light through the window began to darken. The distant sound of thunder mixed with the chiming. He struck again. Something was happening. A chill fell upon the room. The hammering of rain started against the quartz, clouding it further.

"It's working," Schan called over his shoulder. His voice was barely audible over the sound, but the awe was clear. "Something's happening to the city, as if the sea is truly rising."

Ain gave a shout. The Sands blessed him. He would see his love again. "Then I will keep ringing, until it swallows the entire place."

*

Notch dropped to a crouch the moment darkness fell.

Unnatural, it pressed around him, trailing over his skin like warm breath. His body was slow to respond, but he brought his blade up when a woman screamed.

But it wasn't a scream.

It was a cry, a single note. The beginning of a song. Over the sounds of small movements, including a scuffling off to his left, where Flir had stood, came another cry and his chest swelled. His sword arm wavered. The singer's voice swam through the dark and he smiled. Wondrous.

The room slowed to silence. Even his breathing faded to a bare whisper. His sword point had long since touched the carpet when the darkness vanished.

Lavinia, stood before her chair, beautiful face alight and the final note echoing in the shattered room. Broken glass glittered on the floor by the window, through which Wayrn and Seto hauled a struggling imposter. Flir, her face set, held her stained sword and Luik stepped up to help Seto and Wayrn. Bodies continued to bleed. Most were imposters, but several council members were down too. A familiar face, Captain Holindo, the man with the scar, knelt over a body. Regret was plain on his face. Beside him, one of the imposters lay in a tangle, neck twisted.

The Prince – Notch recognised him by his dress as much as the resemblance to his father – was slumped against a wall. A young woman with dark curls clung to him, jaw slack. Oson's own face was still awed. Notch shook off the lingering effects of the song. Sofia was gone. Across the room stood an opening in the wall. Another passage. City of damnable secrets. He shot to his feet. "They've taken her."

Seto shook his head, standing over the imposter, who

groaned. "We finish here first."

He slashed at a chair. "It can't wait."

"It can. Didn't you hear? That was her brother. He isn't going to harm her."

Her brother was behind the imposters? Notch waved his blade. It didn't matter now. "You don't know he won't hurt her, and that's not the issue." They were disappearing into the maze of passages. Time was the enemy, not Tantos' blade. "We'll lose them."

"Enough," Oson said. The prince had regained his senses, standing by the body of a false Mascare. "I demand to know what's happening. Who are you, and who are these imposters?" He kicked at a pale hand. "Braonn?"

"Renovar," Flir said, and shoved the Prince into a seat. Too powerful, her push toppled the chair with the Prince in it. The young woman with curls gasped and Oson spluttered from his position on the floor. Seto nodded, a look of distaste directed at his nephew. Notch strode over to haul the young man to his feet, Flir at the Prince's opposite shoulder. He gave the girl a look and she fell back.

"Be still," Flir said. Oson swallowed.

"Is it him?" Notch asked. In devising their hasty plan, Seto and Wayrn had slipped outside to cut off any escape. The man struggling between them might have been Vinezi, but it was difficult to say. "Remove his mask," Seto said. Wayrn tore the mask from the man slumped at their feet. Seto swore.

A big man, but not Vinezi. His breath rasped and sweat beaded on his forehead. He bled freely from a wound in his leg and by the look of his robe, his torso or side.

"Find him," Seto roared, kicking the man aside and pacing the room. Wayrn jumped into action, leaping through the wreckage of the windows. The captain with the scar stood, looking from face to face.

"Holindo. What of Solicci?" Oson demanded. Flir nudged him in the ribs and he collapsed, struggling for breath.

Captain Holindo sneered. "He is unconscious. Though death is perhaps more deserving." To Seto, he swept a bow. "King Oseto."

Seto stopped his pacing, surprise on his face. "Do I know you, soldier?"

He straightened. "I served in your guard before you... disappeared."

"Wonderful. Very well, Holindo, I wish for you and Luik here to gather the Shields and sweep the grounds. Not a single foot is to be left unexamined, understood?"

"Yes, Majesty."

The two men left and Notch glanced down at the wheezing Prince, whose face was pale with shock. The young man stared at his uncle, as if just recognising him. Notch gestured to the Prince. "What do you want us to do with him? And the girl?"

"Bind them and post a guard."

"Flir can do that, Seto. I'm going after Sofia."

"Very well. First, please escort Lady Lavinia to her rooms." To her he smiled. "I do not wish for you to be endangered any further."

Lavinia had remained silent throughout the exchange, wide eyes on Seto. Her face was pale and she trembled. "I am well, but I would appreciate that, Your Majesty."

"Notch will help you, Lady."

Notch took a breath. "It'll be too late."

Flir tugged on a curtain, the whole thing crashing down. She tore strips and bound Oson and the girl, hands moving quickly. "It might be too late now," she said as she finished up, patting Oson's cheek. "I'll help you, Notch, then we'll find Sofia."

Seto looked to have dismissed the issue. After all, Storm Singers had to be protected. The old man bent beside the wounded Renovar, a thin knife in his hand. "Now. Let's see what you know."

Notch hurried Lavinia from the room, Flir close behind. He didn't have time for this. Sofia could be anywhere by now, the palace and its dammed maze of passages. He'd be lost within them but he had to try. She needed him. Her brother would no doubt be taking her out of the palace. Where to next? Underground? A watch needed to be put on the harbour.

First the Storm Singer. "Where are your rooms, my Lady?"

Lavinia pointed, struggling to keep pace. "Nearest the wall, to the east."

Flir tugged him back, being gentle. "Slow down, Notch."

"I can't." But he did, a little.

The halls were busy and several times noblemen or worried palace officials seemed about to question Notch, but Lavinia placated them. They reached her rooms in short order. Notch had collected a pair of Shields on his trip, not her usual guard by their insignia, and left them outside her door, escorting Lavinia inside.

The Storm Singer sat on a low couch, holding her head in her hands. A groan escaped.

"Are you all right?" he asked.

She looked up. "Yes, it's just... there is often pain.

After I sing."

"We haven't thanked you," Flir said. "For what you did back there."

She smiled, though her eyes were clouded with pain. "I simply acted."

"It was a good action," Notch said. He glanced at the door. Each moment was another moment lost.

She stood. "And I should thank you both for saving us." She stepped closer. "I hope you will forgive me for asking, but have we met?"

Notch kept his voice even. There wasn't time for her to remember him as Medoro. They had never met but she might have seen him. In any event, Medoro was no more and Sofia was in danger. "No, my lady."

"You are familiar to me."

"He was a Shield, long, long ago," Flir said. "When the mountains were fluffy little hills."

Lavinia smiled again, opening her mouth to speak but instead, gasped. "Ti and Calinzo."

"Who?"

"My guard." Her face fell. "I haven't seen them since the imposters woke me."

"We'll search for them," Flir said.

"Thank you. And thank Ana my daughters are safely tucked away at –" Lavinia doubled over, hands covering her ears.

"What's wrong?" He bent by her side. He hesitated, arm outstretched. Was it still inappropriate to lay hands on a Storm Singer?

"Can you not hear that sound?" she shouted.

Notch shared a glance with Flir. He heard nothing out of place, let alone a sound loud enough to shout over. "What is it?"

"A bell." She raised her voice further, falling to her knees and looking around the room. "Ringing so loud that I can barely hear my own thoughts."

He circled the room. Nothing. Out the window, only the windswept palace gardens were visible, grass rippling. No strange bells.

A Shield stepped inside. His broad face was concerned. "Is everything well, my lady?"

"I think you should find a healer," Flir told him.

He hurried from the room and Notch helped Lavinia back to the couch. Her eyes were wide. "Are you sure you cannot hear it?"

His impatience faded and he listened. A distant peal of thunder and another sound he could not identify was just audible, but no bells. Flir shook her head. "We can hear nothing. Has this happened before?"

"No, I don't..." she trailed off, swaying to her feet. She caught Notch's arm. "Wait, I can hear him."

"Who?"

"The Sea Beast," she said. "I cannot believe... he is attacking the very city."

CHAPTER 43

Lavinia took them beneath the palace, down what seemed like an endless flight of steps to Notch, whose head brushed the roof at times. Lit only by occasional lamps, some of which had gone out, cold air flew up the passage from the crashing sea below. It chilled the sweat on his face. Steps grew moist as they neared the ocean and the now perilous walkway.

"Is it really attacking the city?" Flir shouted when they reached a heavy gate barring entry to the Storm Singer's walkway and Storm Seat.

"His rage presses against me. Already he's flooded parts of the Lower Tier. Something calls to him. The bell, truly can you hear it not?"

Only the roar of the storm followed her words. She removed a key from around her neck, fitting it to the gate and opening the way. Spray from the wild water, which crashed over the stone walkway, drenched their feet and legs. Lavinia stood firm, stepping onto the path. A circle of stars embroidered on her clothing caught the light. "I will soothe him."

Flir jerked Lavinia back when another wave hit the grate. Notch kept one arm wrapped through the links. "It's too dangerous."

Lavinia shook her head, red hair darkened and plastered to her face. "Wait. Hold me, will you?"

Flir gripped her waist, linking her own leg through the gate as Lavinia leaned into the chaos.

Again the Storm Singer's voice cut through the discord. Not sweet, but strong. It rose to compete with the wind and her chest expanded as she spread her arms, as if to guide her song amongst the fury. Notch turned away. The song was too strong. The wind faltered. Waves receded, the swell of water lapping at his toes only, where before it threatened his knees. Her song intensified, this time making no effort to weave between the storm. She assaulted the storm, driving it back. A shaft of sunlight slipped through black clouds and Notch sucked in a breath.

She was pushing it back.

On Lavinia sang, her voice ringing out even as her arms trembled. A swell covered his boots and he gave a shout when a new wave roared up, burying the Storm Seat and crashing toward them. Over the new thunder and flashing jags of lightning, he reached for Flir.

The sea hit them and Lavinia's song was lost.

Foaming water slammed Notch into the wall and pain exploded in his chest, but he was not sucked back out. He'd linked his arm within the gate and white spots danced before him, but he kept his feet, jaw clenched at the burning in his arm. The ocean had wrenched his shoulder. Had the lenasi begun to wear off already? No surprise, the sea had the strength of a million Flir's. Angry ones.

"Flir?"

Stretched to her limit, the slight woman had one arm around Lavinia, whose form was limp, while the other clung to the gate, which had bent beneath her grip. He slid forward when the wave receded, helping to pull Lavinia in. Flir steadied him and they scrambled to carry the Storm Singer up several steps before another wave hit.

"There," Flir gasped.

"Further." Notch grunted as the crash of another wave tugged at his feet. Flir's hand shot out and anchored him. Together they carried Lavinia higher, Notch resting her head in his lap. "Storm Singer?"

Her eyes fluttered, and she coughed, leaning over to spit water. She looked up at him, her eyes wide. "I'm not strong enough – he is possessed of something."

"What now?"

"Take me... above," she panted. "To the walls."

Flir scooped her up and started climbing. The crashing of waves echoed in the stairwell.

Notch paused at the top, legs wobbling a moment. He huffed. His ribs were biting him from the inside, but it wasn't crippling yet. Luik would have nudged him, told him he was getting old. "Damned if I am," Notch said to himself.

Flir paused. Lamplight in the basement cast them in shadow. "What?"

"Nothing, keep going."

With the unrest in the palace, no-one was inclined to stop them. Had any servant or Shield attempted to do so, Notch would have sent one of them to get a healer for Lavinia. Which wasn't a bad idea. And wasn't one already on the way to her rooms?

"Do you need healing, Lady?" he asked.

"Just rest."

"Flir, we have to see what's happening out there."

She snorted. "Think you can stop this?"

"We better try something."

"I know. I know," she said. "But we can't leave her here."

Lavinia tried to turn her head, and Notch stepped into her line of vision. "Lavinia, we're going to take you to –"

"No," she gasped the word. The Storm Singer shivered. "I must see too. Only I know how to stop him."

"But you're exhausted."

"Take me," she said. "I command you, please."

Notch exchanged a glance with Flir, who shrugged. Something had to be done. And he wasn't going to say no to a Storm Singer. He nodded.

Flir set a brisk pace. It did not take long to find their way out of the palace, crossing an empty courtyard and wrestling with a gate. Wind tore across the grounds, whipping rain, leaves, dirt and even small stones in their path. Flir strode forward, cradling Lavinia as she approached the walls. Notch struggled to keep up, both the pain and buffeting of the storm strong enough to knock him off course several times.

Closer to the white wall, now grey in the storm light, a pair of Shields slipped from the gatehouse, waving their arms. Notch signalled to one of them, stopping close enough to see beads of water in the man's beard.

He shouted over the wind. "Sergeant, we must take the Storm Singer onto the wall."

The man's eyes widened. "My lady, forgive me. It's dangerous, you might be swept off."

Lavinia waved a hand. "That is my wish."

"She might be able to stop this," Notch added. Not that the Shield could refuse her, but he understood the man's concern.

The Shields ushered them into the guard tower. A long table stood before a fireplace, whose flames were whipped about by wind sneaking cold fingers down the chimney. A row of spears and bushels of arrows stood opposite. Two other Shields shot to their feet, a set of bone dice clinking between them.

"What's happening, Sergeant?" one asked. He noticed Lavinia. "My lady."

"They're going up. The Storm Singer is going to help us," he said. The Shields exchanged glances. Lavinia had barely stirred in Flir's arms.

"Quickly," Flir said.

The sergeant opened a door to a stairwell, the wood leaping from his hands to slam shut. He cursed and dragged it open again, waving them up. "Careful up there."

Notch thanked him as they passed. He slipped on the damp stones near the top and drew a bolt with a muttered curse. The moment it came free the storm ripped the hatch from his hand. He climbed up and caught it, crouching beneath the battlements and closing his eyes a moment. Damn ribs!

Flir followed, one arm easily holding Lavinia, and joined him.

He peered over the stone.

Wreckage.

The harbour roiled. Black water crashed into the Lower Tier as a mighty shape thrashed. The Sea Beast's body was a mess of darkness in an already shadowy sea. Lightning laced the water with white, but the wind and rain in his eyes obscured everything.

The wharves were in ruin. Half the Lower Tier looked to have been submerged, flotsam and tiny spots of colour swirled. Barely a single vessel remained, reduced to half-submerged blobs or so much floating kindling.

The Sea Beast gave another heave and Lavinia groaned. A thunderclap of water struck the lower wall, spilling into the streets. Great holes were visible in the section of wall. People scurried toward the safety of the Second Tier, where he imagined they would be beating on the gate in desperation.

"It's going to drown the entire tier," he shouted. "The harbour's already ruined, along with half the damned navy."

Lavinia tilted her head back and raised her voice. It was a clear note but it barely lessened the wind, so quiet it seemed. She squeezed her eyes shut and sucked in a shuddering breath. "I cannot."

"Then let it wear itself out," Flir said.

"It won't happen. It is not a being like you or I," Lavinia said. "I fear it will continue until it has covered the whole city. And the sea is endless."

"Then what can we do?"

"Only a Storm Singer can stop this."

Flir wiped her face with her free hand. "Then we find another singer."

"There are no others."

Notch's stomach lurched. "At all?"

"In Anaskar. My daughters are too young," she said, struggling to compete with the wind. "My brother is... not yet returned with them."

"There's no-one else?"

She squinted against the rain. "Even if there were, I

doubt they would be strong enough. Something calls the Beast, it interferes with my song."

Below, the Sea Beast continued to pummel the city with successively larger waves. People were dying, hundreds, maybe thousands. Tenaci and his fellow street children, who knew how they fared beneath the city? The aqueducts were probably flooded too.

"Take her down." He wrenched open the trap door. Flir climbed through and he followed, shivering with each step.

"Make space near the fire," Flir called ahead. A chair waited before the blaze, which the guards had banked. It still fought the wind, but the flames were strong enough to hold.

"Rest a moment," Flir said. Notch followed her across the room. "Let's send one of the Shields to get the healer, or a covered carriage at least."

"Good idea." He waved to the sergeant. "Soldier, attend to me."

He rushed over. "Sergeant Nolo, sir."

"Nolo, get to the palace. A healer or a carriage. Go."

He saluted and ran from the room.

"The rest of you, find your captain. Someone has to organise rescue for the Lower Tier."

The men hesitated. They were obviously torn. On one hand they saw a mercenary, on the other, a man who was obviously trusted by the Storm Singer. "But our post –"

"People are dying," he barked.

"What shall we tell the captain?" one asked.

"To take a look outside his window. Now go."

The Shields scrambled for the door. He shook his head, but Flir raised an eyebrow. "Feel good to be ordering men around again, Captain?"

"Don't call me that."

"I'm not ill," Lavinia said from her chair.

"You need warmth," Notch said.

She did not turn. Lavinia's hair fell over her face, but her head shot up and she tried to stand. "Wait. There is another." She flailed and Notch caught her hand.

"My lady?"

"He was the strongest of us. Abrensi. I do not know if he still lives. He was... taken out of the public eye."

Flir moved closer. "What does that mean?"

"The palace believed him possessed because he spoke to himself often. He was 'dangerous' to the reputation of the king."

Notch frowned. Something about the description was familiar. "Where would they have taken him?"

"The Lord Protector told me only that Abrensi was not dead."

"I know where to find him."

CHAPTER 44

Sofia launched herself at Tantos with a scream, slamming into his shoulder. He slipped in blood, twisting on the floorboards beside Derrani's body. Thunder crashed and somewhere, windows rattled.

"You can't understand." He reached his knees in time to catch her kick. He held her ankle in bloody hands. "Please, Sofia."

"No." She jerked free and snatched up one of his knives. Tantos caught her opposing arm, but she swung his blade and it glanced off his raised wrist.

He cursed and the room went black.

A hush followed. Her breath was a coarse thing. She kept the knife up and turned to the sound of his footsteps. She slashed but found only air.

"Derrani killed her, Sofia. In the night, while she slept in our bed. I woke to her cold skin."

She lashed out again, but his voice came from behind her now.

"And do you know what our father did, Sofia?"

A stab into the ink.

From another corner of the room. "He ordered her death himself."

"He'd never do that," she cried.

"How little you know father. Has he explained your duty, yet, Sofia? The Successor is a slave." A bitter laugh. "He admitted to her murder before he drove me from our home. He called it his duty."

"He'd never do that. He searched the coast for you, when word came. He found the longboat. You were dead, Tantos. We wept for you."

"Perhaps you did, Sofia. But not Father." His voice was directly before her. "He searched, but only to keep me from re-entering the city. To prevent justice. But I found a way to return."

She bit the inside of her cheek. "You're lying again."

"If it pleases you to believe as much, I won't stop you." From yet another part of the room.

Sofia tripped on something soft. Derrani. She scrambled back, hitting a wall and swearing. The tang of blood was sharp in the room. She climbed to her feet. "Tantos, I can't let you leave." Bluster. She was powerless.

"If I wanted to leave, you couldn't stop me."

"What does that mean?"

Something knocked the blade from her hand and Argeon flared in the dark, hovering before her. "I don't want to leave."

"Speak sense, Tantos!"

He gripped her shoulders. His breath rasped behind Argeon. "Did you know there's an island, beyond the Grave Sea where bones cover the whole beach and the grassland beyond? There are winding paths between them, they stretch on, ever deeper, feeding into a vast depression.

"At its centre is ancient bone. Bone that will never truly sleep, bone from which the First Masks were carved. Masks that make Argeon, Osani and the king's mask seem young. Restless even. In search of knowledge. Were you to touch it, as I have, you would see with wider eyes." He squeezed. "It is horrible."

"I don't understand." She tugged at his arms. "If you want to tell me something, then tell me. No more riddles."

He did not let go. "And those who carved them, Sofia. You would not believe. They look to us."

"Tantos?"

He grunted, as if struck a blow. "Do you know what happens to people who are addicted to lenasi?"

She struggled but he kept on.

"They need it all the time. And for a while, they feel wonderful. They forget the craving, the sweating, the chills and the pain. But after that, the real trouble begins. Before that happens, Sofia – find a good healer."

"Why are you telling me this, if it was you who poisoned me?"

"Because no-one else will tell you when I'm gone."

"Gone?" She wrapped her blood-slick hands around his wrists. "You have to pay for everything you've done. For your whole life, for all I know."

His body gave a violent jerk, but he did not let go. His laugh was unsteady. "A shorter life than I'd once hoped."

"What have you done?"

Now he let go. The mask fell through shadow. It struck the floor and was still. His breathing laboured. "No apologies, Sofia. It wouldn't mean anything coming from me."

She trembled in the dark.

"Tell father..." He heaved a breath. "Tell him he

shouldn't have kept Derrani from me. Tell him Gianna was no assassin. And tell him... tell him I would have come for him next, had he been here."

"What?" Sofia spluttered. "He's our father."

"Yes," he hissed. A hand pulled her down. "When you take Argeon, don't lose him. He has much to tell you."

"Tantos?"

He continued as if she had not spoken, voice softening. "Don't blame Father as I do. Keep your innocence, Sofia. Do not become me. Father thought he was doing the right thing. Even Seneschal Fratali thought betraying Gianna and I amounted to the right thing." He writhed, gasping for air. "As do we all, I imagine."

When had fresh tears come? She fumbled for one of his hands. His fingers could barely close around her hand. "This isn't right."

"Of course it is. But I had to avenge Gianna first."

She thumped the floorboards. "You selfish bastard." He was going to avoid justice. Somehow, he'd manage to take something and now he was dying. Still he manipulated her. "And what of all the people you killed? Is this all the justice you offer them? Or me, for the wrongs committed against your own family? Gods, I wanted to believe in you, Tantos."

"You'll share my end with everyone. Tell them about my cowardice."

Her shoulders slumped. "Then you never wanted to be King, never wanted to survive?"

"Vinezi wanted to rule from shadow. I only wanted you. Only you could help me find Derrani. Only you would have drawn Father back."

She flinched. All along, he'd used her to murder Derrani? And to bait their father? Every move but a move to build his revenge. All his indulgences as Lupo became clear. The way he'd stood while smiling behind his mask. So familiar because it was the way Tantos stood when he laughed. The way he'd produced the key to her father's study in the manor. And the trip to see the ocean in the carriage, had it been sincere then? It hardly mattered now. "I'm not responsible. You would have found a way without me, brother."

"Perhaps I wanted also to see you again." He gave another shiver. "See that you were safe."

"You can't do this." More tears came and she dashed them away. He didn't deserve grief. "What have you taken?"

"Nothing. I made a pact with Argeon to put an end to me. He works slowly."

She beat his chest. "Reverse it."

"Everything will be better now."

Better? For who she didn't know, Lupo or Tantos, but the last breath rushed out of him and he stiffened. Argeon went dark a moment, and then light returned. The shop was as before, though her brother lay dead before her, his traitor's robes bloodstained and his hands red, limp.

Argeon was black. Only a white streak remained. It ran from forehead to chin, not unlike a lock of hair.

CHAPTER 45

The head jailor of Anaskari Prison squinted in the torchlight. "Wait. Aren't you – "

Notch slugged him.

The man went sprawling. Before he could rise, Notch snatched both sword and keys from his belt. "Be silent now."

The fellow had a hand over his eye. "I'm going to –"

Notch lifted the sword. "No you're not."

The jailor paused.

"Now, chain yourself to the desk with those." He pointed to a set of chains that hung from the wall. Once the glaring man was done, Notch tore a strip of cloth from the man's tunic and stuffed it into his mouth.

Dumping the blade, he hurried down a set of steps, through a door and past a row of cells, one arm clutching his side. He'd pushed himself with the jump over the desk and he'd have to hurry, the jailor might be found at any moment.

Another guard met him at a second door. His face showed no flicker of recognition. "Yes?"

The man hadn't heard the commotion then. Notch jingled the keys. "I'm here to collect a prisoner, orders of the palace."

"I need to see authorisation."

Notch smothered a groan as he leapt forward, catching the man's wrist and spinning him into a headlock. He applied pressure until the struggling guard stopped moving. Notch lowered the man to the cold stone and placed a hand on his throat. A pulse. Good.

He strode inside. Few cells were empty. Shadows behind the bars barely stirred. When he came to his old cell, the sleeping bear opposite was still turned to the wall. Notch put a hand on the bars.

"Bren."

The man spun. Upon seeing Notch he started a jig. "Oh, Notch, well done. You're still out there."

"I am." Flir's cave-in had been repaired, the new stones cleaner than those surrounding. "I see someone fixed our cell."

"Yes, very kind. Yet, I never step on them." Bren hopped over the new stones. "I hear something, you know. Bells."

Notch fought down a bubble of excitement. Bells. This was Abrensi the Storm Singer. How far could he push the man? "I need your help, Bren."

He grinned, lips stretching. "Another murder?"

"No. There's trouble outside. Can you hear the storm?"

"Yes. But the bells are louder."

"Do you think you can come with me?" He held up the keys.

Bren shrugged, twirling a finger in his coat. Beneath the grime and food lurked what could have been a circle of stars, the same symbol on Lavinia's clothing. "I know my home."

"I need your help."

"We both do." He moved to the wall. A scratching began.

"Abrensi."

The scratching stopped.

"Not at all."

"I know that's your name. Lavinia says the Sea Beast is attacking the city. That it won't stop."

Bren turned. His eyes were less feverish than usual. "Abrensi is finished. Discarded. No-one wants that fellow. You'll have to leave, Notch. But nice to see you once more."

"Bren, we have to stop the beast."

"Then stop the bells." He slapped his hands together.

"We don't know where they are," Notch said. He took a breath. Had to control his voice. Keep it even, don't upset him. "Please, you have to help me. Help the city."

"I 'have to' nothing."

Notch thumped the bars. Damn him. "This isn't a game, Bren. It's serious, don't you –"

"No." His voice boomed. Notch fell back, hands covering his ears. People stirred and swore from the depths of their cells. A flash of Abrensi came through, as the unsteady man straightened, projecting his voice like a weapon. There was something magic in his tone, just like Lavinia's song. Within the sound was the urge to flee. Notch took half a step back.

He dragged a foot forward. "No. I'm not leaving without you, Bren."

"If I push too hard, you'll be dead, Notch. And I don't like to sing anymore, so don't make me."

"Then... then I don't know." He glared. "What do you

want?"

Bren wiped his hands on his coat. "A better question."

"I have the ear of the palace, of King Oseto. Does that interest you?"

"Oseto? Not Otonos?"

"Oseto."

A smile. "Ah, now that I like. Then turn his ear to me, Notch, turn it to me. There will be much to discuss after I help you. Much indeed."

*

He ushered Bren into the guard tower. The warm room seemed to shudder at the cold intruders. Bren shook himself down, not unlike a dog, and Flir grumbled at being flicked with water.

Lavinia turned from the fire, finding her feet with the aid of the chair. "Abrensi?"

"Lavinia." He crossed the room and took her hands. He giggled. "You're getting older, dear."

She laughed. "I know."

"Can you hear the bells? They are many, but one."

"Yes. Can you stop him?"

"It will hurt."

"You'll be fine."

"Not I." He began to pace. "The Sea Beast."

"Wonderful," Flir said. "He's worried about hurting the creature that's trashing his city."

Notch joined them at the fire. "But not us? Not Lavinia?"

"Not if you stay behind me. And cover your ears for good measure."

"What will that do?" Flir asked, arms crossed.

"Make you look silly."

Lavinia took his hands. "That's enough, Abrensi. Go. Sing."

His eyes lost focus. "It's been some years. I'm not sure that I should. They cried out, you heard them."

"I know, but you must."

Notch frowned. Who cried out? It didn't matter; Abrensi took off with a nod, leaving Notch to scramble after, Flir on his heels. Atop the wall the wind tore at his clothing and hair, rain biting his face. He crouched but Bren stood tall, his coat snapping.

"Ready?" He sucked in a breath.

Sound exploded. His voice shattered the air, a deep, commanding call that could not have come from human lungs. Notch clamped wet hands over his ears. Bren's voice grew louder, arms aloft.

The wind lessened as he sang, rain cutting back to a bare mist. Notch stood. Clouds rolled back overhead, patches of blue sky revealed. Below, the Sea Beast, still a giant mass of darkness, thrashed.

Except now it no longer leapt around in the bay.

Instead, it appeared to be doing its best to leap onto the wharf's ruins. Bren's song had changed. The initial fury of his voice cleared most of the storm, but now the tone was welcoming. It urged the listener onward. Below, a flood of people flowed toward the walls. They came from their homes or from the streets. Men poured from an inn holding tankards. In other streets people left houses half-clothed or still eating, their faces aglow with wonder. Did the song pull them forward too, or were they simply curious as to why the storm had passed? Notch fought the urge to clutch at Bren's legs.

The Sea Beast crashed into the wall and rolled back into the water.

Bren raised his song to a new height, true urgency in his voice now.

"What are you doing?" Notch cried.

Bren shook his head and Notch reached out but Flir caught his hand. "He knows what he's doing."

"Does he?"

"I think so." She pointed.

With a final wave of destruction, the Sea Beast hurled itself from the bay, breaching its massive bulk on the wharves and crashing through the wall of the Lower Tier, where it lay motionless.

Bren let his song fade away, then turned with a smile. "There. All done."

CHAPTER 46

Sofia collected the masks and left.

The cobblestones glistened and the sky above cleared slowly. Where was the storm? How long had she knelt before her brother's body? It didn't matter. And he could stay there with his shame. Let carrion-feeders take him.

She turned in a small circle. Garbage littered the streets. At one corner a statue of the Goddess Ana's face lay shattered on the ground. Inside Derrani's shopfront she'd heard nothing – though it had to have been a violent storm. No one walked the streets either; odd for such a clear noon sky, even with its watery sun. The cold chilled her sweat and she shivered, stomach churning.

What did it matter? Casa Falco was cursed. Tantos had lost his mind and if she dared believed her brother, Danillo had driven his own son away. And lied. Had he lied to protect her from Tantos, or to hide his own shame?

The Greatmasks were heavy. One, blackened and warm in her hand, the other cold and quiet. Osani she stuffed into her robes, and Argeon she carried from

Derrani's. And there the mask would stay for now. Who knew what Tantos' death had done to Argeon?

The clap of running feet raised her head.

A pair of young men, their clothing wet but their faces alight, ran down the wide street, shouting to one another.

"Come on, we won't see anything," the one in the lead said.

"Shut up," the second cried, pumping his arms.

They were heading for the harbour. Sofia turned down the same road and stopped. All manner of people, workmen, merchants, children and Shields, funnelled into the main road from other streets, alleys and homes. A cart stood unattended and a dog was tied to a post, tongue lolling.

She should return to the palace and help Notch. Vinezi was still up there.

A girl bumped into Sofia, opening her mouth to apologise. Instead, the child backed away, eyes wide.

"Wait." Sofia went to one knee with some difficulty. Another dose of lenasi wouldn't hurt. "Where's everyone going?"

"To the harbour, my lady." She cringed. "Am I in trouble?"

"No, not at all." She smiled. "Why is everyone going there?"

The little girl wiped the back of her hand across her nose. "'Cause the Sea Beast is dead-is, didn't you know?"

Sofia blinked. The oldest creature in all the lands, dead? "How?"

"Threw itself onto the wall and now it's dead." The girl spoke as if nothing simpler could have occurred. "I got to hurry, my lady," she said, with a glance at Argeon.

Sofia rose. "Of course."

The closer she came to the harbour, the thicker the crowd grew. Turning at a barricaded shipyard, masts peeking over the walls, she stopped. A strip of sun beat down between buildings, lighting the mass of people. The murmur of their voices filled the street but washed over her. Not a single word soaked in.

A dark mass had crashed through the wall. Scraps of stone littered its form, hiding half its bulk. The beast had smashed through the tier wall with such violence that its head must have lain beneath the ground, but the crowd blocked her view. Dust still rose from where the force of the Sea Beast's landing flung a massive portion of the wall into several buildings opposite.

They weren't inns, instead mostly warehouses, but people might have been inside. And anyone on the street during impact had little chance of survival either.

She pushed into the crowd. People grumbled and cursed, shoving as she tried to move closer to the beast. She couldn't break through with her size, nor go around, as people were piling up behind her. Someone shoved Sofia in the back and she crashed into a man before her.

"Hey." He spun with a snarl, hesitating when he saw her robe.

Sofia stared him down.

"This is useless," she hissed. No matter what might have happened to Argeon after Tantos, she had to clear the crowd. She put the Greatmask on, holding onto the image of the busy street – and froze. It worked. There was no void, yet she could sense Argeon.

Only this time, her ears were also filled with the sea. Or the sound of it. A vast rushing, from every corner of the world. It bore down with the roar and froth of giant waves and the vicious pull of tides, as if the Ocean Gods were dragging her through the black depths of the seas. The pressure buckled her knees and she cried out.

The roar of the ocean disappeared.

Oh, you can hear me, then? I did not think any of you were able any longer.

The giant voice in her mind was a whisper.

"Argeon?" He had never spoken before. What was different? Had Tantos' death changed the mask for the better? The crowd fell back, faces concerned. Shouting increased momentarily, but soon enough she was standing on the cobbles in a small space of her own.

My name is the world's name.

"Not Argeon?"

No, tiny one. Your chip of bone is not speaking with you. I am.

Sofia shivered as she whirled. The crowd had made even more room, and people were pointing. A voice cried 'magic' and she raised her hands. They glowed a faint blue. Even Argeon glowed. Sofia shivered – was the glow part of some old sickness? Some taint left over from Tantos' last pitiful moments?

"Who are you? Why do I glow?"

Do not fear. My name is not important. Come closer and do not tarry, for I am dying.

The Sea Beast.

She charged forward. "Move," she roared, and nearly faltered when her voice cut through the noise. It was like her father's voice in his study, only louder. Much louder.

People fell back, pressing each other against the walls. Screams rose and her way soon opened. Sofia ran, her leg stronger than it ought to be, giving the occasional reminder shout. Her voice startled people each time, bouncing from walls and buildings. She must have looked a sight. A Mascare in a black mask, glowing blue, running through the streets and shouting.

The beast appeared ahead, and she skidded to a halt in an open space, one perhaps made for her by the creature? A ring of people stood away from it, and Sofia slowed, detouring the debris that covered the stones. The Sea Beast was colossal. Near as tall as the wall it crashed through, it blocked most of the street. One of its multitude of fins, slick with slime, would barely have fit inside Seto's common room.

She was a mouse before it.

It was not graceful, not a thing of beauty. Its skin was a mixture of deep blue scales, some of which flaked to the stones even as she stared, black growths like sea moss and weeds, and oozing green ichors. Less sinuous than a snake, it had an approximate torso, which had breached the wall. Its tail rested beyond the city; she had no idea how long it stretched. A row of fins scraped the stones, chipping them as the beast gave a spasm.

Sofia dodged aside as a blue glob splattered beside her.

"Save us, my lady," someone shouted from behind.

"Keep back," she replied without turning.

The head, where was the head? She moved to a bare narrowing of the hulking mass, which had sunk some of the way below street level. Many of its limbs were bent or ragged. Huge holes covered its body, scars too, many of which had not healed evenly. Up close, she gagged on the stink of fish. One of the scales fluttered down, knocking her shoulder. The beast's surface was traced with fractures. Deep beneath the grime of its body a faint glow pulsated, but it was weak.

Are you near?

"Yes."

From deep in the hole a slit of blue appeared in the skin, growing until it was taller than she – an eye. Its pupil shrank in the light, still much larger than her head. A milky film covered the great eye.

Did you hear my song?

"I'm not sure, Old One."

Was it you? Someone heard my song and called back to me. Called me here.

Who would do such a thing? Tantos? Vinezi? "No, I'm sorry."

That is a shame. A trace of disappointment came with the voice that spoke in her mind. I had hoped someone would hear my final song, it was lovely. But you will be able to free me.

"Free you? How could I do that, Old One? Can you tell me who answered?"

I do not know. They sung from high above, a place I could not reach. It even drowned out the cursed bell.

Sofia frowned. "I didn't hear the bell either, Old One."

Nor would you. It was not made to chain you, but I. Long, long ago it was forged so that your kind might harvest of me.

Harvest him? No-one could possibly eat even a mouthful of the Sea Beast. "But you have always appeared in the bay and our Storm Singers have sent you away," Sofia said. "We have never even seen you fully."

It was well before your time. Or the time of those who lived in this place before your ancestors came to steal it. But I know your singers. Their voices are lovely. They have always freed me, at least, momentarily. At those times, I have roamed the oceans as I did in my youth.

The large eye rolled, as if in pleasure. Sofia wanted to shake the beast, gentle as it seemed to be, anything to have it speak clearly. "How can I help you?"

By searching. I cannot say where, exactly. But behind the city's palace, in the mountains. That is where the bell rests. It has always been out of my reach. Through you I might see it.

"Is that why you attacked the city?"

I did not attack. I am compelled by its ringing, to rise from slumber at the bottom of the great bay. I have lain there for hundreds of years. They only called me when they wished to harvest of me.

"Who called you in the past? And what do you mean by 'harvest'?"

Someone has rung the bell. They ring it even now. You must stop it for me, so that I may finally rest. I have been forced to decay within myself, long after my brothers and sisters have died, thanks to that cursed bell. If you free me, your rewards will be many. Take of my bones, but be wary of my flesh.

Sofia glanced at the crowd. She doubted any could hear her conversation, but no-one dared take a step toward the beast. "I will stop the bell."

With speed. The eye closed. I am near to death now, though that hardly seems a new thing. I would love to rest – for good. I thank you, youngling.

Sofia spun on those gathered. "Who has a horse nearby? Quickly." Her voice reverberated in the space as she ran forward.

A labourer stepped from the crowd, eyes wide. He rubbed a hand over his bald head. "You can use my mare, my lady."

"Take me to it."

A woman waved her down. "What will happen to the beast?"

Sofia took her hand. "Keep away from it, its blood is dangerous. And find some Shields, tell them to clear this place. Orders of Sofia Falco, Protector. Understand?"

The woman nodded, shrinking back. The whole street would have heard it, Sofia's voice rattled windows. She had no idea how to moderate it.

"What's your name?" she asked the labourer as they ran.

"Adamo, my lady."

"Thank you, Adamo. How far?"

"Not far at all." He took her down a side street, leaping over refuse, and into a yard behind a smithy. There a snorting mare stood by a trough. She was skittish at first, whether from the glow or the fact that Sofia was a stranger, but she stroked the horse's neck. "All is well."

The horse quietened. More of Argeon's magic? She had not felt a single trickle of awareness from him, but instead the attention of the Sea Beast willed her along. She kicked the mare into a trot, and started up to the Second Tier.

Those few people not already at the harbour kept out of her way. She tore through the gates of the Second Tier without acknowledging the cries of the guards. When she finally neared the palace gates she reined the mare in.

Two familiar figures ran toward her, faces set in determination.

She waved. "Notch, Flir, stop."

Both skidded to a halt. Both sets of eyes were wide, comically so. Like children who'd seen a ghost.

Sofia laughed until she could barely breathe. "Your faces," she gasped. "You should see yourselves."

CHAPTER 47

Sofia charged across the lawns behind the palace, leading Notch and Flir, who now rode their own mounts. She pointed to a corner of the grounds fenced off by white stone. "There. The First King's Solace. Maybe it's beyond?"

Notch caught her arm when they slowed, breathing hard. He was having trouble with his ribs, one arm pressed against his side. "Sofia, wait. You have to tell us what's happening. Properly this time. What did the Sea Beast tell you?"

"And how did it speak to you at all?" Flir asked.

Sofia spoke quickly. "I think Argeon allows me to hear its voice, because Argeon is made from the bones of the Sea Beast. Or another like it." She spoke over their gasps. "The beast is dying but there's a ringing bell that binds it to life. It supposedly lies beyond the palace. Have you heard anything?"

Two heads shook but Notch spoke. "Lavinia said something about a bell."

"Well, I think that's why it accepted the Storm Singer's

call. It wants to die."

Notch shook his head. "I have to believe it, because you're here, but it doesn't make any sense."

"I believe it," Sofia said. "We have to keep looking."

Sofia made to leave but Flir stopped her. "What of Tantos?"

Her stomach heaved. "Dead."

"I'm sorry," she said, and her eyes were sincere.

"Thank you."

Sofia looked to the mountains. Something shimmered on the rock face. "Wait. See the mountain there?" Beneath it stood a pair of Shields, their armour flashing in the distance.

"What are we looking for?" Flir said. "You mean the Shields?"

"No, an entrance." She took off, Flir's sigh following.

The Shields met them before the rock face. Both held drawn weapons, but one sheathed his blade when he recognised her. "My lady."

She dismounted. "What happened here?"

"Two men entered the mountain around dawn. When we got here there was no opening. Our captain left us to watch."

"Did you see them?"

"Only from a distance, I'm afraid."

"Continue to watch," Sofia said. She reached out and touched the stone, her glow flaring. A section of the rockface slid open.

"How are you doing this?" Flir asked once she and Notch had joined her. Her face appeared to be fighting awe.

A question she couldn't answer. Was it Argeon or the Sea Beast? "I wish I knew."

Steps led up into darkness. Notch put a hand on her shoulder. "We don't know what's up there. I doubt the two men are our friends."

"I'm ready."

He drew his blade. Flir's weapon gave an answering rasp. "As we will be also."

The steps were worn and odd spheres rested in recesses in the walls, but she climbed with barely a glance at them. Higher they led her until a suggestion of light appeared above.

You are in danger.

She stopped, Notch bumping into her.

"What is it?"

"I don't know." She closed her eyes, keeping her voice low. "How?"

Beings with ill intent wait in the chamber above. Use your Argeon as you call it.

Only she did not know how to. A wave of pain wracked her body, but it passed quickly. The Sea Beast drifted away from her. Its eye flashed in her mind and then Argeon appeared. In the dark he was not blackened, but still the aged bone she knew from before.

How had Tantos brought darkness down? And how did her father move so quickly? All she'd been able to do was put force into her voice. That wasn't going to achieve much here.

What good was Argeon if she... but there was a way. She'd shown him the tabella, could she try something similar? Sofia shook her head. What did she want the mask to do? How exactly would she – Argeon showed her without words.

She was two Sofia's. One stood with Notch and Flir, both who watched her, hands on weapons, while the other Sofia climbed the steps, knife in hand. The climbing Sofia was light, her tread a bare whisper on the steps. Her skin was pale, even her clothes and the blade itself showed the stone through its centre – as if the second Sofia was mostly an outline.

And then Argeon and darkness.

She knew what to do.

With Argeon's power, she split herself into two – was it her spirit? and glided into the chamber. A blade whistled through the air, slicing through her body. It tickled. Sofia spun. Her attacker had fallen back, sword slack in his hand. His skin was much darker than her own, and his clothing more suited to the desert.

Medah.

"Stay your hand and I will spare you," she said. Her voice echoed.

The man replied in his own tongue, pointing a trembling hand. She turned to see an equally stunned man in a blue cloak. He was younger, and his face was caught between terror and anger.

He shouted but she flew at him, pausing before his face. She raised a finger to her lips. Over her shoulder, she called for Notch and Flir. "Come and be ready."

They burst from the entrance, weapons drawn. Notch paused at her ghostly form, then leapt to wrestle the younger man to the ground. Flir already had the first man restrained, driving him to his knees by twisting an arm behind his back.

Sofia blinked.

The steps before her were touched with light. She ran up and found what she'd come for. Dominating the wall was a shrine, and in its centre, behind a glittering altar, a massive bell.

"Can you tie them?" she asked without turning.

"We'll manage."

Sofia climbed the steps, ignoring shouts from their prisoners. A human thigh bone sat on the altar top, but the bell was what she wanted. It was not ringing, but she'd not been able to hear it before either. Did that mean it rang without sound? She placed her hand on the surface.

"No." A heavily accented voice cut through the chamber. She glanced over her shoulder. Notch cuffed the young man and he struggled until Notch gagged him with a scrap of blue rag.

Sofia put her hands on the bell and closed her eyes. Argeon was closer now, and this time, being two Sofia's was easier. She passed through the bell's chill shell and found herself inside a lattice of cogs, pins and wheels, one of which had been constructed within the bell. Nowhere was it attached, but a hammer connected to the cogs sat poised to swing.

Sofia squinted at the device, reaching out a translucent hand. A pin winked up at her, though there was no light inside the dome. If she pulled it, the arm would fall. Inside the bulk of the machine, a cog flashed. If she removed it, the body of the structure would collapse.

But her fingers caught nothing. She tried again. Still they passed through the machine.

"Old One, can you help me?"

He did not answer. Was he gone already? The arm had stopped. Perhaps he was at peace. Or simply exhausted. And he'd told her, as long as it rang, he would be a prisoner.

Sofia was one again.

Flir and Notch waited together when she ran down the steps. Both prisoners were bound, with whatever materials were at hand, and both glared up at her. Mixed in with the fear was seething fury from one, and a flat, more dispassionate stare from the other. Too bad. They'd crept into her city and enraged the Sea Beast, leading to Abrensi's foolhardy move. And yet, what else could the Storm Singer have done? Notch had already explained, Lavinia was unable to soothe the beast. "There's a machine inside, but I can't break it from out here."

"Let me," Flir said. She leant down to her prisoner, shaking her head. The message was clear. Then she took the steps two at a time. "Give me some room, all right?"

Sofia helped Notch drag the prisoners further back. Nearby were a collection of bones, maps and more cogs, but at a grunt from Flir she gaped. The small woman gripped the bottom of the bell with both hands, feet set apart, and leaned back.

"Come on," Flir snarled. The bell titled on its hook, the top lost in shadow, but it did not come away. Flir let go and took a step back as the bell swung a little.

"Is it too heavy?"

Flir shook her head. "I'll get it." She performed a quick series of stretches and took the bell again. The younger prisoner shouted through his gag but Notch drew his sword and rested the tip on the back of the man's neck. The shouts stopped.

From the altar came the sound of the Renovar tongue, mostly curses. Flir rolled her shoulders and kicked out her legs. She took hold again, shoulders trembling as she strained against its weight. A slow cracking filled the chamber. Like some mythical giant crunching through rock, the cracking continued and Flir's voice rose to a scream as she gave a final heave.

Stone shattered, fragments spilling from the roof as

the bell clanged to the floor. It rattled Sofia's teeth. The bell rolled from the altar and down the steps, gaining speed where it hurtled into the far wall of quartz and lodged there with another mighty crack. Cold air poured in around its edges, more stone and quartz clattering to the floor.

"There," Flir said, dusting her hands with a grin.

Sofia could no longer sense the Old One.

CHAPTER 48

The rooms were those reserved for guests most favoured by the king. Not on the highest floor, but still commanding ocean views, the tall windows taking advantage of the bay and the glittering ocean beyond, its wave tops like chipped jewels.

Only now, the bay was a mass of destruction.

The enormous corpse of the Sea Beast lay across the Lower Tier's wall, sealed off by the Shield and Mascare. Beyond, the wreckage of countless ships and boats clogged the harbour in a floating wood heap. Seto was collecting dozens of reports on the deaths and the damage to the navy and Anaskar's shipping. The numbers were not encouraging.

Afternoon sun warmed the rooms, though a fire blazed somewhere too, and Notch breathed a long sigh of relief. Muscles eased across his shoulders. A long search had come to an end. Sofia was safe and his name was being cleared by order of once and rightful 'King Oseto.' The threat of the Renovar powder, acor, was, if not neutralised, being attended to – some of the locations revealed by Pevin's own investigations. The prisoner hung on Flir's every word, and shadowed her like a faithful dog. Notch had kept his laughter to himself about that one, at one look of Flir's face.

Even his ribs felt better, after being once again dosed up by a healer, the finest in the city according to Sofia. Mayla was a gruff Braonn woman who'd slapped Notch's hand when he'd tried to claim fair health.

"And the Medah prisoners, Notch? Flir?"

Seto presided over the meeting in an ornate chair, a bowl-like glass of wine in hand. Around the large table was a gathering such as Notch had never expected to see.

Sofia sat to one side, wearing the crimson robes of the Mascare but without a mask, Flir and the Renovar beside her. Nearby, his face drawn and bandages peeking from his clothing, a young captain sat with a pained expression. He'd been discovered in the cells deep beneath the palace, placed there by Oson for helping Sofia escape. Sofia in particular had been happy to see him alive. Across from them, Luik sat beside Notch's own empty chair, and then Wayrn and Captain Holindo.

A little further down, the Storm Singers, Lavinia and Bren. Both drew their share of glances from those assembled, some with awe, some curiosity. Bren had been cleaned up but still wore his knowing smile. What he would eventually demand in return for his services, Notch couldn't fathom. Something for Seto to deal with thankfully.

Markedly absent were Solicci, Prince Oson and Vinezi. He was the one Seto wanted most. Behind every decision he made, there would be an eye to how Vinezi could be found. Notch didn't blame him, Tulio had been a good man.

"Both imprisoned, Seto," Notch said.

Holindo cleared his throat. "His Royal Majesty."

"Sorry, Captain." Notch fought down a grin, ignoring Flir when she slowly raised a fist to bite down upon. "They are bound quite securely. They've also been searched and I have both Shields and Mascare on duty, Your Majesty."

"Good." He gestured to Luik. "And what have we discovered about Vinezi?"

"Escaped," Luik said, voice heavy. "Sometime during the coup he slipped out of the palace. Wayrn and I tracked him to the Second Tier where he disappeared, probably underground. I'd wager he's still out there, with about five of his men according to Pevin here. If we can learn where all the rigged sites are in the City, and I hope we can," he looked at the Renovar, who gave a hopeful smile, "then he'll be hamstrung. We just have to find the bastard."

Wayrn leant forward. "We're also searching the grounds. If there is any acor here, I will find it, that I swear."

"Thank you both," Seto said. "And what of the proposed invasion, my feisty little dilar?"

"Pevin swears it's coming, but he doesn't know when. We'll keep watching the harbour. If any ships are in one piece, we could send them out."

"Some few naval craft are escorting trade ships from the north, they are due any day now," Seto said.

Pevin raised a hand. "If I may speak?"

Seto raised an eyebrow. "I believe you just did."

"Ah, yes, Your Majesty. I am certain an invasion is crossing the sea even now. It will not be the whole of our armies. They expect to find a city subjugated due to the acor powder. They will have more powder, and I believe, means to deliver it by catapult. That is what the Conclave promised as we left."

A few gasps followed his words, but Notch had already heard as much. Seto wouldn't let him find and launch a cutter to investigate. The man was too preoccupied with re-adjusting to his role, catching up on years of his brother's 'mistakes'. As far as Notch knew, the two men had not spoken yet, something which surprised him. On the other hand, Seto had sent word to the ailing Queen. "I will see him soon enough," Seto had replied when asked. "Should he survive the week – I am, as you are aware, quite busy." His tone had been flippant but there was an old fury simmering beneath his words.

Seto was unpredictable if nothing else. For someone who'd spent years loathing the palace, he was taking to his old life well enough. But if the Renovar were attacking, they'd find a disorganised city, with or without the threat of Vinezi. What Notch really wanted to know, was why he'd been targeted in the first place. Had Flir been right, was it all a ploy to get at Sofia or Danillo? It sounded plausible. After all, no-one cared about Captain Medoro now, but Sofia and her father were important. They had access to the Greatmasks.

Seto calmed the room. "It is a threat we are preparing for, and one which Flir will be watching most closely. Pevin, I ask out of hope more than expectation. What does Renovar hope to achieve?"

"The Conclave did not confide in me, I apologise. My only guess is access to your mines, perhaps the gentler climate? Ice is an unkind master."

Flir shook her head. "That's not enough."

"Agreed," Seto said. "We must learn more. In the meantime, I believe all our stories have been told now, and despite the apparent ease with which the Medah entered the palace grounds, I'm not concerned about a Western threat. The wards hold, and I have a party confirming that.

"The link between this Sea Shrine and the Sea Beast, and what it all means I have yet to discern. But I am thinking upon it."

Notch noted that Seto left out the most startling discovery Sofia brought, that the Greatmasks likely came from the creature's bones. That made the beast's decaying body the most precious resource in any land. Possibly in the history of any land. It would be harvested, but first the people had to discover how to avoid the oft-times deadly ichors that oozed from the body. And the beast was connected to the recent influx of creatures beneath the city too. He'd bet his father's sword on them once being part of the Ancient One. Metti might be able to confirm and it would give him a chance to check on Tenaci too.

Seto was still speaking. "For the rest of you, I have tasks that must be completed. Sofia, as we have discussed, you will govern with me as Protector. Lavinia, Emilio and Holindo here, and with any surviving members of the Council and Houses we deem fit, will make up a new council."

Sofia said nothing and Seto continued. "Notch I will need you to assist Luik and Wayrn with the hunt for Vinezi. You are to clear any deposits we are as yet unaware of."

"What of Oson and Solicci?" Sofia asked.

"For their crimes there can only be death."

"I would speak to them first." Her face was hard. He'd little chance to speak with her since their return. Sofia had spent most of her time searching for Emilio, and then a carver friend. He had no idea if she'd succeeded with her friend.

"Of course, Protector. I wish to interrogate them prior in any event." Seto glanced at the window and the dipping sun. "Then until the evening meal," he said, "where we will continue to rebuild our poor city."

*

Ain railed at the soldier who'd dropped off their water, the man's face expressionless. Ain's curses echoed in the dark recesses of the palace dungeon.

"Devils be damned," Ain repeated, kicking at unyielding bars. The Anaskari offered no response, boots clapping up the stone. A heavy door boomed shut and Ain slumped against the wall. The paths in the dungeon were stunted, repetitive, without a flow of passage. Dead even.

Schan cleared his throat from where he crouched by the bowl. "Surprised it's so clean."

Ain sighed. "The water?"

"No, the cell."

"Your optimism is most unwelcome, Schan."

He chuckled. "Don't have much else, do we?"

Ain rolled his neck. By the Sands but Schan was right. Their weapons, tools, the key, even the egg, had all been locked away. Ain watched the precious thing every moment, flinching as it was passed between every clumsy set of Anaskari hands. First the terrifying ghost-girl in her mask, then the soldier with the close beard – but not the woman who'd destroyed the great bell.

That one he would have to find.

Then the egg went to yet more soldiers in breastplates

and orange tunics, crowding the palace as he and Schan were shoved down stairs, unbound and dumped in one of the cells, left with its quiet and chill. At least several lamps burned, and at least he could see the thick steel door concealing the egg.

It needed him.

If he could break out, find a way to open the door and then – Ain shot to his feet. Something had moved in the empty cell opposite. The empty cell opposite?

"What is it?" Schan rose.

"There." He pointed. A slender figure stood beyond the bars of their cell, its colouring mottled, changing with the light. Its shoulder and part of its face closest to the light were yellowed, but the sections of skin in shadow were black, or somehow blended with the surroundings.

It made no sound. No gesture as it approached. Nor did any voice speak within his mind, nothing at all. The figure only came on soundless feet. He knew what it wanted. Could feel it.

The egg.

CHAPTER 49

Sofia strode through the palace halls. Finally. Seto loved to talk.

It was all important, but Oson and Solicci had yet to face her. Everything else could damned well wait. She threw open the door leading down to their secret dungeon and accepted the bows of the Shield with a short nod.

The black mask still unsettled people, she knew that, but that was useful too. It would make them continue to take her seriously. Thankfully, it didn't seem to be tainted by her brother's death. More, somehow, it shielded her from the lenasi cravings. She'd only realised when she removed it upon leaving the mountain shrine. Within moments her symptoms began to return. Replacing the mask banished them. And they had barely lessened; she was already taking fiery seeds as a less vicious substitute at Mayla's insistence, her leg continuing to improve.

"I will see the prisoners," she told the Mascare set at the cell's entrance. "And your key."

"Yes, Protector." He opened the heavy door and

handed her his keys. She entered a row of cells, straw littering the floor. Torches burned at frequent posts, enough to see Oson and Solicci well enough to note raw skin beneath the manacles, heavy shadows under their eyes. Chained to opposite walls, they had naught but each other to look at.

Both appeared asleep.

Sofia slammed her dagger hilt into the bars.

Oson jerked upright and Solicci groaned.

"I hope you're both very uncomfortable."

Solicci's eyes fluttered but Oson managed a sneer. "If it isn't the Falco bitch come to gloat."

Sofia flashed him the key, before turning it in the lock. She moved to Solicci and took a vial from her belts. Not dormi nor something to encourage truthfulness. Something for pain. A pale yellow powder shifted inside when she shook it. "Do you know what this is, Solicci?"

He made an inarticulate sound. She reached up to peel his lids back. Giant pupils. Drugged. It was unlikely he'd feel anything she could do. His time would come. The prince on the other hand... Oson swallowed when she stood before him, moving the knife in a slow circle in the air before his stomach.

He glared at her. "My uncle wants us alive, Sofia, you won't do anything. You're just here trying to act strong."

"If you say so."

She drove the knife into his stomach.

*

Notch crept through the halls, knife in hand. The lamps were dark here, only two burned at a pair of double doors – the Royal Swordfish leaping across them. No guards. With all the commotion in the palace, maybe that wasn't a surprise. Though at any minute, they could return. Maybe Seto had pulled them from duty?

He rushed to the door and pushed.

Locked.

He knelt and removed a lock pick from his belt. The lock was stubborn, but when it finally clicked he slipped inside, pausing to close the door. A darkened marble entryway with a single banner, and another room beyond, lost to shadow.

Notch stepped into the hall, unhooked a lamp and slipped deeper into the royal chambers. The sitting room was empty, but in the bedchamber, complete with low fire and an entire table given over to medicines and washbasin, an old man with sunken eyes drew shallow breaths, head peeking above blankets. Otonos shared his older brother's features, though he was once more robust. Now, the man's skin had a sickly pallor, cheeks sunken.

A serious illness then. Good.

He placed the lamp on the table and moved to stand beside the bed. Was there any point to what he'd come to do? Why do it now, why take this chance now, when he had not done so in Medah? And should have. Instead of shaming Raff.

Notch's hand shook as he raised the knife. No. Wake him first.

"Your Majesty."

The eyelids fluttered.

He raised his voice. "Your Majesty, wake up."

Otonos wheezed but not until Notch shook the man, did his eyes snap open. Notch flinched. The whites of Otonos' eyes were thick with blood. Air rattled in his lungs.

"Who...?"

"Captain Medoro."

He shrunk back into the pillows. "Sands of Medah."

"Yes."

He waited while the old man coughed. Otonos fought with the blankets, gesturing toward the table of medicines. "The green one," he gasped.

Notch passed it across. The man drank half of it down with closed eyes, before letting the vial slip from twitching fingers. "I know why you are here," Otonos said, voice stronger. He was yet to look at Notch again.

"Do you?"

"To avenge your brother."

Notch swung his fist. Feathers burst into the air as he dragged the knife across the bed. The man flinched. Notch withdrew the blade. "Do you think that is all? You took my name. My name, Otonos! And with it, the future it had been tied to. All for your hatred, for your rottenness, all because you are not a man but an animal."

Otonos's head twisted around. "That is war, soldier."

He ground his teeth. "Dishonouring dead men is not war."

"Oh?" He was breathing harder now. "Then you never understood war, Captain. There is no honour in war. Only victor and defeated."

"And Raff?"

"That... I regret."

Notch clutched the knife. Death. It was what Father wanted for Otonos. And Father's rusty voice was never far when it came to the old King. Nor his face, crumbling in the firelight when Notch first came home. Then the rage and accusation, the shouting. "He was your brother!" Father had scattered bowls and cups from the table with a sweep of his arm. "Your family – that's where your loyalty lay, not with some greedy King."

From Raff, Notch could never ask forgiveness. He'd lost that chance long ago. And from Father, who could say? But perhaps from Amina? If he went home and tried to explain once more? Blood thumped in his ears. No. She'd not care. But he'd put this day off too long. Time to right an old wrong – for Medoro if no-one else.

Notch leant close. The tip of his blade halted before his one-time ruler's throat.

"Go. Deliver your blow, Captain," Otonos said. "All that is left to me now is suffering. You might as well end it."

Notch stopped.

Give him what he wanted? No. Only a fool would do so. No. Killing the ex-King would change nothing, make nothing right. And it would have been, ten steps ago, a handful of words ago. The kind of 'right' that built up over years. Lurking beneath every battle, behind every risk he took, every dark thought cast at the palace.

But killing Otonos wouldn't bring Raff back. Father wouldn't care, wouldn't forgive him. Notch pulled his knife back.

The ailing man coughed, red eyes rolling as he struggled to speak. "Damn it. Do what you could not all those years ago."

"No."

When the fit passed Otonos gaped up at him. Spittle flecked with blood covered his chin and blankets. A skeletal hand inched toward the green vial. Notch stretched to place the vial out of reach, rolling it with his blade. He did not break eye contact. Otonos's face blanched.

"I grant you this mercy," Notch said, straightening. "Something you were pitifully incapable of. Live as long as you have left, Otonos. I hope it is a long, slow time."

"The vial," he rasped. "Please, I must have it."

"No." Notch took the lamp as he left, a hissing from the bed lost in darkness.

*

Notch caught a glimpse of her in the street by chance only. Had he been two steps slower, he'd have missed her figure turn down an alley and head for the Lower Tier's wall. He needed somewhere to sit and drink, properly this time, and to get away from all the questions and attention. From common and high born folk alike. Word was on the move that not only had he never killed the girl by the Pig, but he was part of the effort to save the city from the explosions. He was being recognised a little too often. Just like after the war. Only this time he wasn't a fraud.

And still it was wrong.

More, he'd needed to get out of the palace. The King's haggard features, the man's bloody eyes, were dark in his mind. His hand had only now stopped shaking.

Notch had a foot in the door to a clean-looking tavern when he saw her. What was she up to?

He followed.

Sofia walked quickly, head high and shoulders back. Her feet scraped on the stone and her shadow flew out behind her as they walked into the spiked sun. The buildings were splashed with warm light, shadows deepening in alleys. He kept pace, but not too close. Not once did she turn.

A heavy pack was strapped over her robes and she

wore a short sword. Where was she going? Night was falling. She'd just seen the death of her brother, saved the city, and been given a ruling position. She should be exhausted, not preparing for a journey. He slowed when she stopped at the door to a tailor, raising a hand to knock. Instead she pushed, not bothering to close the door.

He dashed across the cobbles.

Inside, flies buzzed around a pair of bodies. One, slumped against the wall, had been gutted and disfigured. He'd seen worse on the battlefield, but not often. Sofia knelt before the other corpse. The man's dark hair was wild, his robe covered in blood. The still face was empty, eyes mercifully closed.

"Your brother?" he asked softly.

She did not look up. "Father sent Tantos from the city, months ago. Banished him, I think. To prevent him doing... that. I led my brother here because I believed he could be honest. That I could trust him. Worse, that I could stop him."

"Sofia... he was mad was he not?"

"Yes."

"Then no-one can blame you."

She stood. She wore Argeon, but removed the mask now. Her face was streaked with tears. "I can."

Notch hesitated before taking her into his arms. She stiffened at first, but then clung to him, smothered her sobbing in his tunic. "Everyone has lied to me."

He stroked her hair until she calmed, drawing deep breaths. She drew away, wiping her face and turning to the wall. "I'm sorry. You probably think less of me."

"No." He said, voice soft. "Sofia, where are you going?"

She gave a short laugh. "No-one was supposed to see

me, you know."

"It was an accident actually." He waited.

"I'm going to find my father." She turned back to him. Her face was set once more, though her eyes were still puffy. "And I don't want to hear you try and talk me out of it, Notch. You've been kind, and I know you tried to help me. And maybe you would have, even if Seto didn't expect you to. And I am glad for that, but I'm not staying here. I need to hear the truth about what happened between Father and Tantos. From my father's mouth. If he lives."

"I have responsibilities here." Notch held her eye.

She glanced away. "I wasn't asking you to come with me."

Someone needed to protect her. "I know the Bloodwood. Over the years I've picked up some Braonn from Luik. I can help you."

"I know Braonn."

"But not the paths in the wood, not all the customs, not all the dangers."

Nothing.

"I know I'm not as strong as Flir, or smart as Seto, but I'll watch out for you." He moved forward. "I know my way around a sword at least."

Finally she gave a small smile. "Very well, Notch. I don't think I can stop you."

THE LOST MASK PREVIEW

Book 2 of the Bone Mask Trilogy

CHAPTER 3

Seto rubbed at a spot of grime on the golden, gilded arm of his throne. Father had often let him sit on it as a child. A tiny step toward a typical preparation for a prince – preparation that not so long ago, he would have looked back on as pointless. No longer. Now he would be sitting on the throne often. And at the very least, he'd ensure it remained clean.

His father's unsmiling face loomed in memory.

"So, Father, is this not a triumph? Your son – your only worthy son – is King." King of two realms. One of deceit, and one of...deceit.

He snorted. How often Father came to mind, now when the clamouring of a thousand problems pummelled him. The shattered harbour, the poor tatters of the navy and the great, rotting intrusion of the Sea Beast. Near to two weeks since its breach and so little progress in harvesting its precious bones.

"No greater commodity," he whispered.

Footsteps approached. "Sire?"

He didn't turn from the Swordfish banner; an orange splash against grey stone. "Yes?"

"Ah, Luik requests that you join him in the city jail at your earliest convenience."

A Braonn page, dressed in yellow and grey, and beginning to sweat despite the cold hall, stood with arms at his side. Seto smiled. "Surely Luik didn't use those actual words?"

"That is his request, Your Majesty." A slight frown creased his smooth brow.

"Indeed." He rose and descended from the dais. He still had to meet with the council an hour after daybreak, but there was time if he hurried. What now, Luik?

He waved to the boy. "Off you go, then."

The lad swallowed as he bowed.

Seto swept through the corridors, the glittering trim on his robes catching dust as he slipped into the secret ways. How long before such freedom was denied? Already, the wet-nurses of the palace, or the council, if he was feeling generous, did their best to either curtail or at the very least, monitor his every move. How was he to run both his Kingdoms with worriers like Nemola underfoot all the time?

Seto slapped a hidden switch and crossed a corridor, its warmth rushing over his cheeks, then it was back into the darkness of the ways. Only twice since having the throne dumped in his lap, had he encountered Mascare in the passages, and each time, their challenge was answered with a royal response.

By the time he crossed beneath the walls and snuck into the cobblestone of the Second Tier, sweat had formed at his temples, even in the cool of morning. He exhaled and rolled up his sleeves. Most unbecoming. Dawn light softened the hard edges of the buildings, their upper storeys casting deep shadows. His footfalls echoed on the cobbles of the empty street and from afar came the crash of waves, a gentlemanly rhythm.

He passed two women drawing water from a well, their discussion hushed, arms straining. He nodded to them as he passed.

Anaskar City Prison was a squat building. Well-fortified, its heavy doors possessed twin steel bands and thick bars on the windows. He rapped on the door. A hatch soon opened and a face bearing a faded bruise blinked at him.

"Your Majesty?"

"I certainly am. Now do open up."

The door swung wide and Seto swept in. "Where is Luik?"

"The big guy, My Lord?"

He sighed. "Yes, the big guy."

"Bottom floor. It's —"

"I know the way, thank you." He held out his hand.

"My Liege?"

"The key, my dear fellow. The key."

The Jailor fumbled at his belt, eventually handing the ring over. Seto took it and opened the first door. Immediately beyond, he turned down a set of steps and then a second, and after unlocking another door, a third. He wrinkled his nose at the bottom. Prisons. All the same. Dead sweat, bad hay and human waste.

Seto strode toward a pair of figures at an open cell near the end of a row. He ignored the rather unimaginative calls from the inhabitants, and stopped before two guards. One gaped and the other combined a bow with frantic brushing at his silver and blue uniform. Comical.

"That will be all, gentlemen."

"Yes, Your Majesty," they chimed as they left.

Luik stood within the open cell, his nasty-looking mace belted over a dark tunic. "Glad you're here, Seto. Fancy robe you've got there."

"Never mind that. And why am I here exactly, Luik? This lump?" He gestured to the occupant, who lay in a heap on the floor. "You know I've had to leave off preparing for a meeting to come here."

"You seem heartbroken."

Seto grinned. "Well?"

"You won't believe me, so I'll let you look. Just remember, doesn't make sense. I figured that much out already."

Seto bent by the body. A familiar face, covered in grime and twisted into a mask of death, stared up at him.

Vinezi.

He sucked in a breath. "Impossible."

"I thought so too."

Seto prodded the body with his toe. Soft. And the smell another clue – enough to know the prisoner had been dead for some time. Weeks. There was no way the corpse before him could have set off the explosion at the Iron Pig, let alone attacked the palace.

"See his neck?"

Seto's brows drew together. Vinezi still wore the blindfold from the interrogation, it had fallen down around his throat. "By all the Ocean Gods."

"There's more."

"I couldn't be more surprised, Luik."

He pulled up Vinezi's pant cuff. "Someone cut his foot off." Only a festering stub remained.

Seto raised an eyebrow. "I retract my earlier claim. Who cut him?"

Luik sighed. "I'll be back."

Seto bent down to address the corpse. "Dead all along it seems. Then who was your friend? A brother?" He rose, meeting Luik and one of the jailors outside.

Luik gestured. "This is Adilo, Your Majesty."

"Who visited the prisoner, Adilo?"

He swallowed. "It was weeks ago now, Sire, but one of the masks, ah, Mascare-is, well, he came in and said he wanted 'the big prisoner' that was just put in." He spread his hands. "We took the mask, but when we got to the cell, the prisoner wasn't in good shape."

"Continue."

"He was dead, Sire. I'd say whoever dropped him off had worked him over, broken something inside. Anyway, the mask screamed at us, as if it were our fault, then demanded an axe. Took a bit, but we found one." Adilo scratched at his cheek. "Well, I don't really understand the point of what happened next. But I won't never forget it-is. He took the axe and chopped the fellow's foot right off. Snatched it up and told us to move the body down here-is, and not to disturb it until he returned. We've been waiting since. Only sent word because of the smell."

What madness was afoot? Seto almost smiled at his own joke. Instead, he saved it for the guard. "You did the right thing, Adilo. Know that I am pleased. Return to your post now."

He bowed and scurried off.

"What's happening, Seto?" Luik's voice was a little unsteady.

"This man died some weeks ago."

"Right after Flir and I dumped him here by the looks of things."

"And then, he did not escape as we assumed – as we witnessed – but instead, has lain in this corner of the prison ever since?"

"Doesn't seem real." Luik shook his head. "And then some mask comes and hacks off a foot? Imposter?"

"Baffling but it would appear so. Arrange to have the body taken to the palace."

"Seto?"

"I will investigate this further. I've no idea what it could mean. But we have to accept that there may be two of Vinezi out there."

"Twins? Or brothers?"

Seto shrugged. "Possibly." It wasn't something that could be solved right away. The pit of dark stone and human refuse was not the venue either. "It's more likely that this body, whoever he was, was no more than a ploy."

"Doesn't explain why he's missing a foot."

"Nothing does." He pointed toward the entrance. "Have anyone who has been on guard duty since his arrival report to the palace. Then go find Flir."

"Yes, Seto."

A Note from Ashley

Hi! I hope you enjoyed *City of Masks* and thanks for reading.

I'd like to ask if you could help me out by leaving an honest review of the book at your place of purchase? Long or short, bad or good, it all helps!

AND if you'd like to sign up to my newsletter you'll receive *The Amber Isle* for free, the first title in my second epic fantasy series.

Further, you'll also be the first to know when *Greatmask* (Book 3 of The Bone Mask Trilogy) is released. You'll also have first access to preview chapters and pre-release editions of the book, in addition to being automatically added into the draw for giveaways.

Ashley

ACKNOWLEDGMENTS

First, thank you to my wife Brooke, who has supported me tirelessly for years. Not only with this book, but with all my writing and all my doubts. I love you.

To Mum and Dad for encouraging me from the day I wrote my first story in primary school (heavily influenced by *The Goonies*) and also to my extended family for their support too.

Thanks also to those awesome folk who were kind enough to beta all or parts of the *City of Masks* and offer their feedback: Chris, Belinda, Jordan, Rafael, Allison and especially Kerry, and Aderyn.

A huge thank you must go to the members of my writing group 'Alchemy' – for your insight and your patience with my endless questions and drafts. You've each made a difference to this story and my writing – so thank you again, Cheryl, Rebekah and Tess!

And thank you too, to Jennifer Fallon for her guidance, support and belief over many years as a patient and insightful mentor and all around awesome writer, someone I have long looked up to and who taught me bucket-loads!

Thanks also to team at Snapping Turtle Books, especially Tracey and David, both for believing in my stories and for being so fantastic to work with. Your faith in me means a lot and I will always value the hard work you put into the first edition of this book.

And I cannot forget Rebkah at Vivid Covers for the stunning new cover art, wow!

Thank you to anyone else I may have missed – I appreciate your support too!

Ashley Capes

ABOUT ASHLEY

Ashley Capes is an Australian novelist, poet and teacher. *City of Masks* is his first novel and the follow up is *The Lost Mask*. The trilogy will be complete with *Greatmask* in 2016. Ashley is also the author of five poetry collections and various other novels. He loves Studio Ghibli films and strongly believes Nausicaa is one of the greatest heroines out there.

Visit his blogs at *www.cityofmasks.com* & *www.ashleycapes.com* or follow him on twitter @Ash_Capes.

Other titles by Ashley:

The Bone Mask Trilogy
1. *City of Masks*
2. *The Lost Mask*
3. *Greatmask (forthcoming)*

Book of Never
1. *The Amber Isle*
2. *A Forest of Eyes*
3. *River God*
4. *The Peaks of Autumn (forthcoming)*
5. *Imperial Towers (forthcoming)*
0. *Never (Prequel to The Amber Isle)*